JAR OF HEARTS

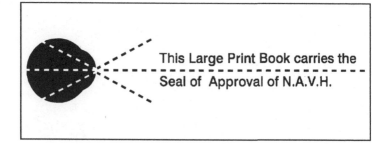

This Large Print Book carries the Seal of Approval of N.A.V.H.

JAR OF HEARTS

JENNIFER HILLIER

WHEELER PUBLISHING
A part of Gale, a Cengage Company

Farmington Hills, Mich • San Francisco • New York • Waterville, Maine
Meriden, Conn • Mason, Ohio • Chicago

LIBRARY OF CONGRESS CIP DATA ON FILE.
CATALOGUING IN PUBLICATION FOR THIS BOOK
IS AVAILABLE FROM THE LIBRARY OF CONGRESS

ISBN-13: 978-1-4328-5599-4 (hardcover)

Published in 2018 by arrangement with Macmillan Publishing Group, LLC/St. Martin's Press

Printed in Mexico
1 2 3 4 5 6 7 22 21 20 19 18

For Mox

For Max

■ ■ ■ ■

PART ONE:
DENIAL

■ ■ ■ ■

"I don't even know what I was running for
— I guess I just felt like it."
~ *J. D. Salinger,*
The Catcher in the Rye

Part One
Denial

1

The trial has barely made a dent in the national news. Which is good, because it means less publicity, fewer reporters. But it's also bad, because just how depraved do crimes have to be nowadays to garner national headlines?

Pretty fucking bad, it seems.

There's only a brief mention of Calvin James, a.k.a. the Sweetbay Strangler, in the *New York Times* and on CNN, and his crimes aren't quite sensational enough to be featured in *People* magazine or be talked about on *The View*. But for Pacific Northwesters — people in Washington state, Idaho, and Oregon — the trial of the Sweetbay Strangler is a big deal. The disappearance of Angela Wong fourteen years ago caused a noticeable ripple throughout the Seattle area, as Angela's father is a bigwig at Microsoft and a friend of Bill Gates. There were search parties, interviews, a monetary reward that increased with each passing day she didn't come home. The discovery of the sixteen-year-old's remains all these years later — only a half mile away from her house — sent shockwaves through the community. The locals remember. #JusticeFor Angela was trending on Twitter this morning. It was the ninth or tenth most popular hashtag for only about three hours, but still.

Angela's parents are present in court. They divorced a year after their daughter was reported missing, her disappearance the last thread in a marriage that had been unraveling for a decade. They sit side by side now, a few rows back from the prosecutor's table, with their current spouses, united in their grief and desire to see justice served.

Georgina Shaw can't bring herself to make eye contact with them. Seeing their faces, etched with equal parts heartache and fury, is the worst part of this whole thing. She could have spared them fourteen years of sleepless nights. She could have told them what happened the night it actually happened.

Geo could have done a lot of things.

Angela's mother was a shallow, materialistic woman fourteen years ago, more concerned with her country-club status than checking up on her teenage daughter. Her father wasn't much better, a workaholic who preferred to play golf and poker on the weekends rather than spend time with his family. Until Angela went missing. Then they banded together, only to fall apart. They reacted to her disappearance the way any normal, loving parents would. They became vulnerable. Emotional. Geo almost doesn't recognize Candace Wong, now Candace Platten. She's gained twenty pounds on a frame that used to be impossibly thin, but the extra weight makes her look healthier. Victor Wong looks more or less the same, with a slightly larger paunch and a lot less hair.

Geo spent a good chunk of her childhood at Angela's house, eating take-out pizza in their kitchen, sleeping over countless times when her father worked nights in the ER at the hospital. She embraced the Wongs during the days when their only child didn't come home, offering them reassurances that their daughter would be found, giving them answers that made them feel better, but were far from truthful. The Wongs were invited to the St. Martin's High School graduation, where they received a special award on behalf of Angela, who'd been captain of the cheerleading squad, a star volleyball player, and an honor student. And every year after high school, wherever she was in the world, Candace Wong Platten mailed Geo a Christmas card. A dozen cards, all signed the same way. *Love, Angie's mom.*

They hate her now. Angela's parents haven't taken their eyes off Geo since she entered the courtroom. Neither has the jury, now that she's seated in the witness box.

Geo is prepared for the questions, and she answers them as she's practiced, keeping her eyes fixed on a random spot at the back of the courtroom as she testifies. The assistant district attorney has prepped her well for this day, and in a lot of ways it seems like she's just here to shed light on the events of that night, to add drama and color to the trial. Otherwise, the ADA's case seems like a slam dunk. They have more than enough evidence to convict Calvin James on three other murders that happened long after Angela's, but Geo is only here to talk about the night her best friend died. It's the only murder she's been involved in, and once her testimony is given, she'll be shipped to Hazelwood Correctional Institute to begin serving her five-year sentence.

Five years. It's both a nightmare and a

gift, the result of a savvy plea deal by her fancy high-priced lawyer and the pressure on the district attorney to get the Sweetbay Strangler put away. The public is screaming for the death penalty for the serial killer, but it won't happen. Not in a city as defiantly liberal as Seattle. The ADA has a good shot at consecutive life sentences for Calvin James, so in contrast, Geo's five-year sentence isn't nearly long enough, according to some of the #JusticeForAngela comments on social media. Geo will still be young when she's released, with plenty of time to start over. She can still get married, have children, have a life.

In theory, anyway.

She chances a glance over at Andrew, seated stoically beside her father in the third row from the back. He's the reason she looks nice today; he had her favorite Dior dress and Louboutin pumps brought to her that morning. Their eyes meet. Andrew offers her a small smile of encouragement, and it warms her a little, but she knows it won't last.

Her fiancé doesn't know what she's done. He'll soon find out. Geo looks down at her hands, folded neatly in her lap. Her diamond engagement ring, a three-carat oval with an additional carat of smaller diamonds encircling the center stone, is still on her finger. For now. Andrew Shipp has impeccable taste. Of course he does; it comes from good breeding, an important family name, and a big bank account. After he ends it — which of course he will, because the only thing that matters more to him than Geo is his family's company — she'll give the ring back.

Of course she will. It's the right thing to do.

A poster-size photo of Angela is mounted on an easel facing the jury. Geo remembers the day that photo was taken, a few weeks after their junior year started at St. Martin's High School. Geo has the full version of the photo somewhere at home, where the two best friends are standing side by side at the Puyallup Fair (now renamed the Washington State Fair) — Geo with a cloud of blue cotton candy in her hand, and Angela with a rapidly melting ice cream cone. The photo, now enlarged with Geo cropped out of it, is a close-up of Angela laughing, the sun beaming down on her hair, her brown eyes sparkling. A beautiful girl on a beautiful day, with the world at her feet.

Beside that photo, on a separate easel, is another poster-size enlargement. It shows Angela's remains, which were found in the woods behind Geo's childhood home. Just a pile of bones in the dirt, and anyone would agree that you could see a lot worse on TV. The only difference is, the bones in this photo are real, belonging to a girl who died much too young and much too violently for anyone to comprehend.

The prosecutor continues to ask questions, painting a picture for the jury of Angela Wong through Geo's eyes. She continues to answer them, not adding any more detail than is necessary. Her voice carries through the small courtroom speakers, and she sounds calmer than she feels. Her profound sadness — which she's carried with her every day of her life since Angela's murder — seems diluted in her quest to speak clearly and articulately.

Calvin watches her closely from the defendant's table as she speaks, his gaze penetrating right through her. It's like being violated all over again. Geo tells the court about their relationship back then, when they were boyfriend and girlfriend, when he was still Calvin and not yet the Sweetbay Strangler, when she was just sixteen and thought they were in love. She recounts the abuse, both verbal and physical, telling the enthralled courtroom spectators about Calvin's obsessive and controlling nature. She describes her fear and confusion, things she's never discussed with anyone before, not even Angela, and certainly not her father. Things that for years were packed away in a mental lockbox, stored in a corner of her mind that she never allowed herself to visit.

If they gave degrees for compartmentalizing, Geo would have a Ph.D.

"Years later, when you saw the news reports, did you put it together that Calvin James was the Sweetbay Strangler?" the ADA asks her.

Geo shakes her head. "I never watched the news. I'd heard a little something about it from my father, since he still lives in Sweetbay, but I never made the connection. I suppose I wasn't paying attention."

This part is true, and when she glances over at Calvin, the corners of his mouth are raised just a millimeter. A tiny smile. Her old boyfriend was handsome at twenty-one, nobody would disagree with that. But today, at thirty-five, he looks like a movie star. His face is fuller and more chiseled, his hair tousled in perfect McDreamy waves, the speck of gray in his sideburns and the lines around his eyes only adding to his appeal. He sits easily in his seat, dressed in a simple suit and tie, scribbling notes on a yellow pad of paper. The tiny smile hasn't left his face since Geo entered the courtroom. She suspects she's the only one who can see it. She suspects it's meant for her.

When their eyes meet, a tingle goes through her. That goddamned tingle, even now, even after everything. From the first day they met to the last day she saw him, that tingle has never gone away. She's never felt anything like it before, or since. Not even with Andrew. Especially not with Andrew. Her fiancé — assuming he could still be called that, since the wedding planned for next summer isn't going to happen — never inspired that feeling.

Her hands remain in her lap, and she twists her ring around, feeling the weight of it, the security of it. It was symbolic when Andrew gave it to her, not just of her promise to marry him, but also of the life she'd built. Undergraduate degree at Puget Sound State University. MBA from the University of Washington. At thirty, the youngest vice president at Shipp Pharmaceuticals. So what if some of her career success is because she got engaged to Andrew Shipp, the CEO and heir to the throne? The rest of it is because she's worked her goddamned ass off.

No matter. That life is gone now.

On the one hand, she knows she's gotten

off easy. Her fancy lawyer was worth every penny Andrew paid him. But on the other hand, *five fucking years.* In prison, nobody will care that she was educated or successful on the outside, that up till her arrest she was earning a mid-six-figure salary (including bonus), and that she was about to become part of one of Seattle's oldest and most elite families. When she gets out — assuming she survives prison and doesn't get shanked in the shower — she'll have a criminal record. A felony. She'll never be able to get a regular job. Anytime anyone googles her name, the Sweetbay Strangler case will come up, because nothing on the internet ever dies. She'll have to start her life completely over again. But not from the bottom, lower than the bottom, clawing her way out of the hole she dug herself into.

She continues to speak clearly and succinctly, recounting the events of that terrible night. The jury and spectators listen with rapt attention. Keeping her gaze focused on that random spot at the back of the courtroom, she describes it all. The football after party at Chad Fenton's house. The barrel of fruit punch, so spiked with vodka that *spiked* didn't seem like the right word for it. She and Angela leaving the party early, the two of them giggling and stumbling over to Calvin's place in their skimpy dresses, completely drunk. The pulsing music from Calvin's stereo. Angela dancing. Angela flirting. Drinking some more, the world spinning, turning into a kaleidoscope of dizzying shapes and colors until Geo finally passed out.

Then, sometime later, the car ride back to Geo's house, Calvin driving, Angela folded into the trunk of the car. The long trek into the woods, guided only by a dim miniflashlight attached to Calvin's keychain. The cool night air. The smell of the trees. The thickness of the soil. The sound of crying. Geo's dress, dirty, covered in earth and grass and blood.

"You didn't actually see Calvin James cut up her body?" the prosecutor presses. Geo winces. He's trying to put the spotlight on Angela's dismemberment, trying to make it sound as horrific as possible, even though her best friend was already dead by then, which was horrific enough.

"I didn't watch him do it, no," she answers. She doesn't look at Calvin when she says this. She can't.

"What did he use?"

"A saw. From the shed in the backyard."

"Your father's saw?"

"Yes." She closes her eyes. She can still

see the flash of steel when Calvin holds it up in the moonlight. The wood handle, the jagged teeth. Later, it would be covered in blood, skin, and hair. "The ground was too . . . there were too many rocks. We couldn't dig a large enough hole for . . . for . . . all of her."

There's a movement in the courtroom. A rustling, and then a low murmur. Andrew Shipp has stood up. He looks at Geo; their eyes meet. He nods to her, an apologetic tilt of his head, and then her fiancé makes his way out of the courtroom, disappearing behind the heavy doors at the back.

It's possible she'll never see him again. It hurts more than she thought it would. On her lap, she twists the ring furiously for a few seconds, then mentally tucks the pain away for another time.

Walter Shaw, now with an empty place beside him, doesn't move. Geo's father isn't known for being an emotionally expressive man, and the only evidence of his true feelings is the lone tear running down his face. He's never heard this story before, either, and she won't blame him if he follows Andrew out the door. But her father doesn't leave. Thank god.

"How long did it take? To cut her up?" the prosecutor is asking.

"A while," Geo says softly. A sob emanates from the center of the room. Candace Wong Platten's shoulders shake, and her ex-husband puts an arm around her, though it's clear he's about to lose it, too. Their current spouses sit in silent horror, unsure how to react, not knowing what to do. It's not their daughter, not their loss, but they feel it all the same. "It felt like it took a long time."

Everyone's eyes are on her. Calvin's eyes are on her. Slowly, Geo shifts her gaze until their eyes finally meet. For the first time since she's arrived at the courtroom, she holds eye contact. Almost imperceptibly, in a tiny movement only she can pick up on because she's watching for it, he nods. She averts her gaze and refocuses her attention on the prosecutor, who pauses to take a sip of water.

"So you left her there," the assistant district attorney says, walking back toward the witness box. "And then you went on with your life like it never happened. You lied to the cops. You lied to her parents. You let them suffer for fourteen years, not knowing what happened to their only child."

He stops. Makes a show of looking right at Geo, and then at Calvin, and then at the jurors. When he speaks again, his voice is a few decibels above a whisper, so that everyone in the courtroom has to strain to hear him. "You left your best friend buried in the woods, a mere hundred yards from the house you lived in, after your boyfriend cut her up into pieces."

"Yes," she says, closing her eyes again. She knows how terrible it sounds, because she knows how terrible it was. But the tears won't come. She doesn't have any left.

Someone in the courtroom is crying softly. More like a whimper, really. Angela's mother's chest is heaving, her face in her hands, her bright red nail polish visibly chipped even from where Geo is seated. Beside her, Victor Wong is not crying. But as he reaches into the breast pocket of his suit to pull out a handkerchief to give to his ex-wife, his hands tremble violently.

The prosecutor has no further questions. The judge calls a recess for lunch. The jurors file out, and the spectators in the courtroom stand up and stretch. Phone calls are made. Reporters type furiously into laptops. The bailiff helps Geo out of the witness box, and she walks slowly past the defense table where Calvin is seated. He rises and grabs her hand as she passes, stopping her momentarily.

"It's good to see you," he says. "Even

under the circumstances."

Their faces are inches away. His eyes are exactly as she remembers, vivid green, with the same touch of gold encircling the pupils. She sees those eyes in her dreams sometimes, hears his voice, feels his hands on her body, and she's woken up more than a few times covered in her own sweat. But now here he is, real as ever.

She says nothing, because there's nothing to say, not with everyone around watching them, listening. She extracts her hand. The bailiff nudges her forward.

She feels the piece of paper Calvin slipped into her palm and curls her hand over it as she slides it into the pocket of her dress. She stops to say good-bye to her father, twisting off her engagement ring to give to him, the only jewelry she's wearing. Walter Shaw embraces her roughly. Then he lets her go, turning away so she won't see his face crumple.

The trial isn't over, but Geo's part in it is. The next time she sees her father, it will be when he visits her in prison. The bailiff leads her back to the holding cell. She takes a seat on the bench in the back corner, and when the bailiff's footsteps recede, she reaches into her pocket.

It's a torn piece of yellow notepad paper.

On it, Calvin has scrawled a note in his small, neat handwriting.

You're welcome.

Beside the two words, he's drawn a small heart.

She crumples it up into a tiny bead and swallows it. Because the only way to get rid of it is to consume it.

Geo sits alone in the cell, immersed in her thoughts. The past, present, and future all mingle together, the inner voices chattering alongside the actual voices of the police officers down the hallway. She can hear them discussing last night's episode of *Grey's Anatomy,* and wonders randomly if they'll show *Grey's Anatomy* in prison. She has no idea how much time has passed until a shadow appears on the other side of the cell bars.

She looks up to see Detective Kaiser Brody standing there. He's holding a paper bag from a local burger joint, and a milkshake. Strawberry. The bag is covered in grease spots, and immediately her mouth waters. She hasn't had anything to eat since breakfast, just a small bowl of cold oatmeal served on a dirty metal tray here in the holding cell.

"If that's not for me, then you're just cruel," she says.

Kaiser holds up the bag. "It is for you. And you can have it . . . so long as you tell me what Calvin James slipped you in court."

Geo stares at the bag. "I don't know what you're talking about."

"He took your hand, and he gave you something."

She shakes her head. She can smell grilled beef. Fried onions. French fries. Her stomach growls audibly. "He didn't give me anything, Kai, I swear. He grabbed my hand, said it was good to see me, and I yanked my hand away and didn't say anything back. That's it."

The detective doesn't believe her. He signals the guard, who unlocks the metal door. He checks her hands, then checks the floor. He motions for her to stand up, and she complies. He pats her down, checking her pockets. Resignedly, he hands her the bag. She tears it open.

"Easy." He takes a seat beside her on the cold steel bench. "There's two burgers in there. One's for me."

Geo already has hers unwrapped. She takes a giant bite, the grease from the ground beef dribbling onto the front of her designer dress. She doesn't care. "Is this allowed?"

"What? The burger?" Kaiser removes the

top of his burger bun and places fries on top of the patty. He replaces the bun and takes a large bite of his own. "You signed your plea agreement, nobody cares if I talk to you."

"I can't believe you still do that." She looks at his burger in mock distaste. "Fries inside your burger. That's so high school."

"In some ways, I've changed," he says. "In some ways, I haven't. Bet you can say the same."

"So what are you doing here?" she asks a few minutes later, when she's eaten half her burger and her stomach has stopped hurting.

"I don't know. I guess I just wanted you to know that I don't hate you."

"You'd have every reason to."

"Not anymore," Kaiser says, then sighs. "I finally have closure. I can now let it go. I'd advise you to do to the same. You kept that secret a long time. Fourteen years . . . I can't imagine what that did to you. It's a punishment all its own."

"I don't think Angela's parents would agree with you." But she's glad he said it. It makes her feel like less of a monster. But only a little.

"But that's why you're going to prison. So you can do your time and then get out and start over, fresh. You'll survive this. You always were strong." Kaiser puts his burger down. "You know, it's funny. When I found out what you'd done, I wanted to kill you. For what you did to Angela. For what you put everyone through. For what you put *me* through. But when I saw you again . . ."

"What?"

"I remembered how it used to be. We were all best friends, for fuck's sake. That shit doesn't go away."

"I know." Geo looks at him. Underneath the tough cop exterior, she sees kindness. There's always been kindness at Kaiser's core. "I wanted to tell you back then what happened, what I did, so many times. You would have known what to do. You were always my . . ."

"What?"

"Moral compass," she says. "I've done a lot of shitty things, Kai. Pushing you away was one of them."

"You were sixteen." Kaiser heaves another long sigh. "Just a kid. Like I was. Like Angela was."

"But old enough to know better."

"Looking back, a lot of things make sense now. The way you were after that night. The way you pulled back from me. Dropping out of school for the rest of the year. Calvin really did a number on you. I didn't realize how bad it was." Kaiser touches her face. "But today you told the truth. It's done now. Finally."

"Finally," she repeats, taking a big bite of her burger even though she's no longer hungry.

It's easier to lie when your mouth is full.

2

There are three types of currency in prison: drugs, sex, and information. While the last of the three tends to be the most valuable, crank and blow jobs are always the most reliable. And since Geo doesn't do drugs, cash will have to do. There are things she needs to survive prison, which she'll procure as soon as she's able, once she's assigned a unit and a job.

Every new or returning inmate at Hazelwood Correctional Institute — or Hellwood, as it's sometimes called — spends their first two weeks in receiving while their assessment is being completed. A battery of psychological tests, along with a couple of interviews and a thorough background check, are performed in order to determine where the inmate will sleep and work. Geo's hoping for medium security and a job in the hair salon. But what she can realistically expect, according to her first meeting with the prison counselor, is maximum security for the first three years and a job in janitorial services.

"It's not a bad thing," the counselor says, in an attempt to reassure her. The name plate on the desk says P. MARTIN. "There are more guards in maximum. Minimum comes with privileges, but maximum comes with protection."

It sounds like bullshit to Geo, but as she's never been to prison before, she's in no position to argue. It's been three hours since she arrived at Hazelwood, and the counselor is the first person she's spoken to who isn't wearing a uniform. P. Martin — Pamela? Patricia? there's no indication of the woman's first name anywhere in the room — seems to genuinely care about the inmates' well-being. Geo wonders what brought her here. It can't be the money. The counselor's pantsuit is cheap; the fabric of her jacket pulls around the armpits and there are loose threads along the seams.

"Who's your support system?" the counselor asks. When Geo doesn't answer, she rephrases. "Who'll be visiting you in here? Who are you looking forward to seeing when you get out? Because that day will come, and you should be thinking about those people every day that you're in here.

It'll keep you focused."

"My dad," Geo says. She never had many friends, and after the trial, it was safe to say she had none. "I was supposed to get married, but . . . that's not happening now."

"What about your mother?"

"She died. When I was five."

"One last question," Martin says. "Which race do you identify with? You look white, but your intake form says 'other.' "

"Other is correct," Geo says. "My mother was half Filipino, and my dad is a quarter Jamaican. I'm mixed."

Clicking her pen, the counselor nods and jots something down in her file. "It's sixty-five percent white in here, and since you look white, you'll blend in. But if you're part black, you can make black friends. That's good."

"I'm also a quarter Asian."

"Less than one percent of the inmate population is Pacific Islander. It won't help you." The counselor looks at her intently. "So, how are you feeling? Depressed? Anxious? Any suicidal thoughts?"

"If I say yes, does that mean I can go home?"

The counselor chuckled. "Good. A sense of humor. Hold on to that." She slaps the file folder shut. "All right, kiddo. We're done

31

for now. I'll talk to you in a week. You need me before that, tell a guard."

The first two weeks pass without incident, although all new inmates are on suicide watch because prison is a fucking depressing place. Geo keeps her head down and speaks only when spoken to, spending the majority of her time alone. On the morning of the day she's to be integrated into the general population, she's awake well before the morning bell.

It's hard to believe that just over six months ago, she was interviewed for an article in *Pacific Northwest* magazine profiling Shipp Pharmaceuticals in their annual "Top 100 Companies to Work For" feature. At thirty, Geo was the youngest female executive at Shipp by a decade, and the article was titled, "Steering the Shipp in a New Direction: The Young Face of One of America's Oldest Companies." The photo they used showed Geo sitting on the edge of the long table inside the thirty-fourth-floor glass-enclosed boardroom, legs crossed, skirt hem well above the knee, red soles of her high heels visible, smiling into the camera. The theme of the write-up was diversity in the workplace, though, ironically, not one mention was made of Geo's mixed-race heritage. The article focused solely on her youth and her gender — both of which were enough to make her a stand-out in the old white-boys' club of Big Pharma — and her plans to expand the lifestyle-and-beauty division of the company.

She suspected the majority of the executive team at Shipp hated that photo, that she was the one chosen to represent them, though nobody ever said so to her face.

The day of her arrest, Geo was speaking in that boardroom. The doors swung open and a tall man in dark jeans and a battered leather jacket strode in, accompanied by three uniformed Seattle PD officers. A flustered administrative assistant followed, her hands gesturing apologetically as she tried to keep up with them. The twelve heads sitting at the giant table turned at the sound of the commotion.

"I'm sorry, they wouldn't wait for me to knock," said the breathless administrative assistant, a young woman named Penny who'd only been with the company for a month.

The man in the leather jacket stared at Geo. He looked extremely familiar, and her mind raced frantically to place him. There was a detective's shield clipped to his breast pocket, and she could see the slight bulge of his holstered gun near the hem of his jacket. He was tall and quite fit, a far cry from how he looked in high school, when he was forty pounds skinnier and half a foot shorter. . . .

Kaiser Brody. Holy hell.

It hit Geo then, and her heart stopped. Her knees felt weak and the room spun a little, forcing her to lean against the table for support. The boardroom, cool and airy only seconds before, was suddenly hot. The detective caught her reaction and smirked.

"Georgina Shaw?" he said, but he knew damn well it was her. He headed toward her, making his way around the long oval table with the uniformed officers in tow, past the shocked faces of the executives. "You're under arrest."

Geo didn't protest, didn't say a word, didn't make a sound. She simply closed her laptop, her presentation disappearing from the large projection screen behind her. The detective took out his handcuffs. The sight of them made her wince.

"It's protocol," he said. "I'd apologize, but you know I'm not sorry."

The members of the executive team seemed not to know what do with themselves, and they watched in stunned silence as the detective pulled her arms behind her back, snapped on the cuffs, and began marching her out of the room. Their confusion was understandable. The Georgina Shaw they knew wasn't the kind of woman who got arrested for anything. She was the new face of Shipp, after all. She was a VP of the company. She was Andrew Shipp's goddamned fiancée, and everything about this looked completely wrong.

The CEO's voice rang out loud and clear, and everyone turned. Andrew Shipp hadn't been part of the meeting, but his office was just down the hall, and clearly someone had told him what was going on. He was standing at the boardroom doors, barring their way.

"What the hell do you think you're doing?" Andrew tried to reach for her, but a young police officer blocked him. The CEO's face reddened, no doubt because nobody had ever dared to block him from anything before. "This is *ludicrous*. What are the charges? Get her out of those handcuffs immediately. This is *ridiculous.*"

Geo tried to smile at him, tried to reassure him that she was okay, but Andrew wasn't looking at her at all. He was glaring at the police officers, every inch of his body radiating that special blend of outrage and self-entitlement one can only have if one grew up with serious money.

But the police officers didn't care. They didn't care that the woman in handcuffs had a corner office two floors down, or that her wedding reception was going to take place at the pretentious golf club her fiancé's family belonged to, or that she thought it was insane they were charging four hundred dollars a plate for dinner for what basically amounted to steak and French fries. They didn't care that she'd picked pink peonies for her bouquet or that her wedding dress was being flown in from New York. They didn't give one righteous shit. As they shouldn't. Because none of it mattered anymore. And it probably never did.

The detective walked her out of the boardroom. His hand was on the small of her back, not pushing, but guiding firmly. Kaiser Brody didn't smell anything like she remembered. The boy she'd known back in the day never wore cologne, but she could detect a sweet, musky scent on him now, which she recognized immediately as Yves Saint Laurent. She always did have a great nose. She bought the same cologne for Andrew once, but he never wore it, complaining it gave him a headache. A lot of things gave Andrew a headache.

The cuffs jangled around her wrists. They

were loose enough that with some maneuvering, she could probably have wriggled out of them. Kaiser had put them on just for show, to make a point. To cause a scene. To humiliate her.

Andrew was walking backward in an attempt to impede their path, and Kaiser waved an arrest warrant in his face.

"Detective Kaiser Brody, Seattle PD. The charge is murder, sir."

Andrew snatched the warrant from him and read through it with bulging eyes. Even in his two-thousand-dollar suit, he was just short of handsome, with his soft frame, his round face, his thinning hair. Andrew's strength came from a different place. But while being rich and well-connected could accomplish a lot, he couldn't fix this.

"Say nothing," he said to her. "Not a word. I'll call Fred. We'll take care of this."

Fred Argent was head of Shipp's in-house counsel. He handled corporate strategy, contracts, litigation issues. He wasn't a criminal-defense attorney by any stretch, and that's what Geo needed. But there was no time to have that discussion. The detective was hustling her out of the boardroom as the rest of the executive team stood frozen, mouths gaping open.

Andrew kept up with them all the way to

the elevator, which was down the hallway and around the corner. Word of Geo's arrest seemed to spread faster than they were walking. She passed her assistant Carrie Ann's desk and said, "Call my father. I don't want him to see it on the news." The younger woman nodded, her eyes wide, the small spot of spilled coffee still noticeable on her skirt even after her vigorous attempt to remove it earlier that morning. Less than an hour ago, they'd had a discussion about how best to get that stain out, searching the office for one of those Tide pens as Geo talked about the new restaurant she and Andrew had gone to the evening before.

That life was over now. Everything she'd worked for, everything she'd created, the life she'd built on top of the secret she tried to keep hidden . . . it was all evaporating right before her eyes.

"It's going to be okay," Andrew said to her at the elevator. "Say nothing, do you hear me? *Nothing.* Fred will meet you at the police station. We'll get you the best attorney. Don't worry about anything." He glared at Kaiser, his face full of fury. The detective returned the look with a mild one of his own. "This charge is utter bullshit, Detective. You've made a gigantic mistake. Chief Heron, your boss, is a member of my golf club, and I'm going to call him personally. Prepare yourselves for a lawsuit."

The detective said nothing, but once again the corners of his mouth lifted up slightly. Another smirk. Did he have that smirk in high school? Geo couldn't remember.

The elevator doors closed on Andrew yelling for his assistant to bring him his cell phone. For the next minute, she and the detective stood motionless in front of the mirrored doors. The music from the hidden speakers played softly. Geo could hear one of the uniformed officers breathing behind her. A soft wheeze, with a slight whistling sound behind it. Deviated septum, probably. Kaiser's hand was still resting on the small of her back. She didn't mind. The pressure was reassuring.

No Muzak instrumental background tunes for Shipp; the elevators were fancy, wired into Pandora, which was set to play a selection of easy-listening tracks by the artists of yesterday and today. Mostly yesterday. The numbers on the screen counted down silently to the soft strains of Oasis, a band Geo liked back in high school. One of the other officers, a younger woman whose septum sounded fine, sang along quietly. Geo did not sing along to "Wonderwall," even though she knew all the words.

The numbers continued to change as they passed each floor, hurtling toward the bottom. Maybe she'd get lucky. Maybe the elevator would hit the ground and explode. Sixteen, fifteen, fourteen . . .

"You don't seem surprised I'm here," Kaiser said, watching her in the mirror.

Geo said nothing, because there was nothing to say. She had played this scenario out a million times in her head, but never had any of her fantasies cast her old friend in the role of arresting police officer. She didn't even know Kaiser had become a cop, but she had to admit he wore the badge well. There was only a hint of the boy she used to know. Scruff covered the jawline where there used to be acne. The angles of his face were sharper. But the eyes were the same. Haunted. Disappointed.

He was right. She wasn't surprised. She'd been waiting for this day for a long time, knowing on some level it would come eventually. And now that it was here, there was no more hiding. No more carrying the secret around like the unbearably heavy two-ton block of cement it had come to be. Slowly exhaling the long breath she'd been

40

holding for fourteen years, she allowed her shoulders to relax. The tight muscles in her back and neck loosened. She gave her old friend a small smile, and he raised an eyebrow. No, she wasn't surprised at all.

She was *relieved.*

"Shaw," a sharp voice says, shaking Geo out of her reverie. The morning bell has rung. She looks up to see a corrections officer standing at the door of her cell, dressed in a dark-blue uniform, hair pulled back in a tight bun. The CO is short, but stocky and muscular, and Geo has no doubt she could wrestle someone twice her size to the ground. "Your assessment's done. We're transferring you. Let's go."

"Where are they putting me?"

"Maximum," the guard says, and Geo's heart sinks. "You're in the big room, though, because your unit is under construction."

The "big room" is temporary housing. She overheard an inmate complaining about how crowded it is to a guard the other day, and she balks. "The big room? Then can't I just say here in receiving until —"

The CO's bark of a laugh cuts her off. "You think this is a hotel? That if you don't like your accommodations you can complain and get an upgrade? Move your ass, Shaw, before I make you move it."

41

Geo grabs what few belongings she has. Right now they consist of a small plastic bin full of cheap toiletries and a sweatshirt with DOC printed on the back in large letters.

"You're working in the hair salon, though," the guard tells her. "You should be happy about that. Most newbies start in the kitchen, but they need someone who can cut and color hair. Did you work in the beauty industry on the outside?"

"Sort of," Geo says.

"Hey." The CO peers at her closely as they walk down the hallway. "I know you. Aren't you the chick who sliced up her best friend? Like, a long time ago?"

Geo doesn't answer.

"That's some sick shit," the CO says, and it's hard to tell if she's disgusted or impressed. Maybe both. "I'm surprised they're letting you work with scissors."

Me, too, Geo thinks. *Me, too.*

3

In the beginning, Geo never expected to get away with it. Angela Wong was too popular, too in love with her life, for anyone to believe she was missing of her own accord. But when the first few days passed with no knock on the door, she started to wonder if it was possible that nobody would find out what she had done. Days turned into weeks. Weeks turned into months. And then the next thing Geo knew, years had passed, and it seemed like maybe the past would stay buried. A bad pun, but fitting nonetheless.

When it all finally caught up to her, Geo might not have been surprised, but she was wholly unprepared. Because really, what can prepare you for prison? Not the movies or television, which are designed to entertain and titillate. The reality of prison — the bleakness of it, the sameness of it, the unrelenting fear of getting attacked — is horrific. Her first two weeks in receiving, with her private cell that had its own sink and toilet, now seem like a cakewalk compared to the nightmare she's currently facing, also known as "gen pop."

Welcome to Hellwood.

Her counselor, P. Martin, was right in that the maximum-security units have more guards. But more guards don't make it safer, especially when you're sleeping in a crowded space where everyone's in a shitty mood, *especially* the guards. Though Hazelwood is far from crowded, the two units undergoing construction have caused the other three to fill to capacity, and the overflow has been funneled into a large recreation room that's been converted into communal housing. It's the worst-case scenario as far as life in prison goes.

Gone are any expectations of privacy. Fights break out daily. Personal items are frequently stolen. The threat of violence hangs in the air like a storm cloud. Fifty grown women sleeping in such close proximity to each other isn't normal. The big room contains twenty-five double bunks, lined up in rows of five. The constant noise makes the room feel smaller than it is, and the persistent aroma of sweat and farts makes it feel claustrophobic.

The corrections officer escorts Geo to a

double bunk in the back corner, all the way across the room. The women eye her as she passes, and she works to keep a neutral expression on her face so no one will think she's weak or hostile — in here, one is just as bad as the other. Geo is aware that she looks a little different than the rest of them. Her dark hair is expensively highlighted. She has perfect teeth. She doesn't have face tattoos — or any tattoos, for that matter. She's not part of a gang on the outside, nor was she involved in drugs. And unlike the majority of her fellow inmates, this is her first time incarcerated anywhere. She might be dressed in the exact same gray prison scrubs as everyone else, but she's nothing like them, and it shows.

She's a prison virgin. And they can smell it on her.

"This is you," the guard says flatly, stopping at the double bunk.

There's a sweatshirt on the top mattress, and two tattered magazines draped on the bottom bed. Geo isn't sure which bunk is unoccupied. "Am I the top or bottom?" Geo asks.

The guard shrugs and turns to leave. "Don't know. Ask your bunkmate."

A large white woman of indiscernible age — somewhere between thirty and fifty is

Geo's best guess — waddles over. The inmate has to weigh well over three hundred pounds, and Geo catches a whiff of her sour body odor as she approaches. A messy bun of dry, bleached-blond hair is piled atop her head, showcasing three inches of dark-brown roots. She has no visible neck; what used to be there is now covered by a mass of double chin. Her eyebrows are painted on in matching thin black lines, and they furrow when she sees Geo. There are letters tattooed on each one of her sausage fingers. Her right hand spells out FUNS. Her left hand spells out OVER.

Fun's over. Indeed.

The woman takes a seat on the bottom mattress. There's a short metal footlocker in between each double bunk, and half a dozen photographs are taped to the door, showing the woman when she was slightly younger, and slightly thinner. In one of them, a lean black man stands next to her, and beside him is a young boy. The boy is skinny like his father, but his round face is a good blend of the two of them, with large brown eyes, soft mocha skin, and a grin full of oversized teeth. All three look happy in the photo.

Her bunkmate, intimidating as she might seem, is a mother. Okay, then. It can't be so bad.

"I'm Bernadette," the inmate says. Her voice is deep, with a slight accent. Something eastern European. Polish, perhaps. Or Czech. Sliding a hand under the mattress, she pulls out a bag of licorice whips. She doesn't offer Geo any, but she does offer something resembling a smile. "Everyone calls me Bernie."

"Georgina," she says, returning the smile. "Everyone calls me Geo."

"Welcome." Bernie looks up at her, and Geo can see rings of dirt around her neck that were previously hidden in the folds of her skin. "Since we're going to be bunkmates, you should know I have three rules."

"Okay." Geo's still standing, holding her stuff, mainly because she's not sure where she should put it. Since the woman is sitting on the bottom bunk, she's assuming the top bunk is for her, but the woman's sweatshirt is still on the mattress. She doesn't dare move it.

"One. Don't eat my food. Ever." The large inmate takes another bite of her licorice whip, chewing with her mouth partially open. "You see any food lying on my bed, that's not an invitation to have some. Don't even ask me for any."

"Got it."

"Two. I snore. Loud. You complain to the

guard about me, like the last girl did, and I'll beat your ass, like I did her. My snoring bothers you, get earplugs from commissary."

"No problem." Geo can't help but think that it will be the woman's smell that will bother her more than anything else.

"Three. I like the top bunk. You sleep on the bottom."

"Really?" Geo is surprised. She thought bottom bunks were prized, and besides, she can't imagine the woman and all her weight climbing up to the top bunk every time she needs to lie down.

"Yeah, the air feels fresher up there. These fuckers in here are always farting and burping, and by midnight it smells like a fucking toilet. I got a sensitive nose," Bernie says, and her small, mean eyes challenge Geo to disagree with her. "You got a problem with the bottom bunk?"

"Not at all," Geo says, wondering if anyone's ever died from a top bunk collapsing. Getting her chest crushed in while she's sleeping would be a hell of a way to go.

As if reading her mind, Bernie says, "Don't worry. The bed won't break. If that's what you were thinking."

Geo shakes her head quickly. "I wasn't worried."

"First time in Hellwood?" Her new bunkmate extracts another licorice whip and stuffs half of it into her mouth. Her teeth are red from the food coloring. It looks a little like blood.

"Yes," Geo says, figuring that it's better to be honest. "Any tips for me?"

The woman shrugs. "It's not as bad as people think it is. You get used to it. This arrangement is a shit show" — she waved an enormous arm in the general direction of the room — "but it gets better once we get our cells back. I've stayed all over. This place isn't the best, but it's not the worst, either."

Geo nods. She doesn't ask what the woman did to get here. She heard it's not polite. Neither would it be polite to ask the woman to move so she could sit down on the bed they already agreed was hers. Instead, she points to the photos on the locker door. "Your family?"

"Yup," Bernie says, and finally grins. "I keep those pictures there to remind me of what I have to go home to." She finally stands up, leaving behind an indent on the mattress in the shape of her ass and thighs.

The sheets already reek of the woman's odor, but Geo forces herself to return the smile as she finally sets her things down on the bed. The metal frame groans as Bernie climbs slowly up to the top bunk and lies down. "You got a man waiting for you on the outside?"

"I'm not actually sure." It's the most truthful answer she can give. "Hey, are we allowed to use the phones?"

"Yup, anytime up till thirty minutes before lights-out," Bernie says. "Down the hall, near the bathrooms. Check in with the guard before you try to leave, though. They have to buzz you out."

The women whisper among themselves as Geo makes her way to the guard's booth, but nobody speaks to her. She wonders if they're curious because they've seen her on TV, or because she's new. Probably both.

There's a long line for the phones, and the CO on duty informs her that she can talk for only fifteen minutes at a time before she has to hang up and get back in line. Geo stands for what feels like an hour until a phone frees up, then takes a deep breath and dials Andrew's cell number. The call rings five times and then goes to voicemail.

Thinking he might not want to pick up because he doesn't recognize the number, she tries calling him at work. His assistant answers, which means she had to press 1 to accept the charges.

"Hi, Bonnie," Geo says. "Is Andrew in?"

"Miss Shaw," the assistant says, sounding flustered. Instantly, Geo knows that everything has changed. She's always been friendly with Bonnie, and not once since she began dating Andrew has the woman ever addressed her by anything other than her first name. "I'm sorry, but Mr. Shipp doesn't wish to speak to you."

Geo closes her eyes. *Miss Shaw. Mr. Shipp.* She opens her eyes again. "He told you to say that?"

"Yes, ma'am, he did. I'm only authorized to speak to you this one time."

Geo lets out a breath, slowly, trying to gather her thoughts. When she speaks again, her voice is tight. "What would he like me to do with the ring?" Her engagement ring is now in a box at her father's house along with all her other personal belongings, as her house is currently for sale. "Does he want me to have it sent to him, or would he like to pick it up?"

"He says you should send it here to the office." There's a catch in the assistant's voice, and Geo recognizes the conversation must be equally awkward for her.

"Bonnie —"

"Geo, I can't speak to you." Bonnie's voice is hushed. "I'm sorry. I really am. The

51

company's going crazy. We've been getting so many calls; everyone wants to know if Andrew has anything to say about his former fiancée and a VP of the company being a convicted murderer and the girl-friend of a serial killer."

"But I wasn't convicted for —"

"It's what everyone *thinks* that matters," Bonnie said. Her voice is barely above a whisper. "And you know how it is here, Geo. Everybody's concerned about the company's reputation. We've had to issue a press statement."

"What did it say?" When the woman doesn't answer right away, Geo says, "Bonnie. Please. Tell me."

"It says we do not condone or support you in any way, and that we're sympathetic to the victim's family. Andrew . . ." Bonnie pauses. "Andrew wrote it himself. I'm sorry."

"He paid my legal fees." Geo's voice, even to her own ears, sounds hollow.

"I know. He took some heat for that from his father, but you were his fiancée at the time. Geo, I'm sorry, but I have to hang up now." Bonnie sounds genuinely upset. "Please . . . please don't call here again."

The line goes dead.

So that's it, then. No good-bye, no chance

to explain or apologize. Andrew had ended it, taking the coward's way out by allowing his assistant to deliver the blow. A two-year relationship over, just like that. She hangs the receiver in its cradle, moving aside for the next inmate. Not quick enough, though. Their shoulders graze.

The woman's eyes narrow. She's smaller than Geo, but there's no fear in her face. "Watch it, bitch."

"Sorry," Geo replies, managing to sound somewhat sincere, even though it was the other inmate who bumped into her. The last thing she needs is a fight, but if the woman starts one, she'll have no choice but to try and finish it. Otherwise she risks being seen as weak. She's watched enough TV to know that if she gets her ass kicked and a CO later asks her who did it, she can never, ever say. Tattling to the guards about anything is a giant no-no. In prison, the only thing lower than a pedophile (which is pretty fucking low) is a rat. And if you're a rat once, you're a rat forever. The other inmates will never trust you, and they'll make your life a living hell.

Bernie is in a good mood when Geo returns. She's still stretched out on the top mattress, a mountain of woman. The package of licorice whips is empty, the plastic bag dangling off the edge of the bed. She rolls over on her side, and with Geo standing, they're pretty much eye-to-eye.

"Good phone call?" Bernie asks.

"You asked me earlier if I had a man. I can now officially say I don't."

The woman reaches forward and moves a lock of hair out of Geo's face. "That's okay. In here, we don't need them. There's lots we can do without them."

Geo moves away, uneasy. She resists the urge to outwardly shudder, but inside, she feels sick. The inmate in the next bunk glances over, and a look of what appears to be pity crosses her face before she looks away again. Or maybe Geo's imagining it. Maybe she's being paranoid.

Nothing bad happens that night, or the night after, even though Geo lies in bed for hours, fists and jaw clenched, anticipating the worst. Every night, before she falls asleep, she can't believe this is her life. Every morning when she wakes up, she can't believe this is her life. It's finally hit her, that depression P. Martin warned her about. The overwhelming feeling that she doesn't truly belong here — that somewhere along the way a giant mistake has been made — is impossible to shake.

And the cloak of denial isn't protective at

all. It doesn't help. It suffocates her. It makes her vulnerable. It feels like someone took her life, shattered it into small pieces, and then put it back together, all messed up. The pieces are recognizable, but they're all in the wrong places.

On her third day in the big room, she notices her bunkmate is in an extra-good mood. They go to dinner together that evening, sitting across from each other at a table with four other women. Bernie is chatty with Geo and the other inmates, talking up a storm about the good visit she had with her son earlier that morning. Every time she laughs, she places a hand on Geo's arm. It seems harmless enough.

A woman with deep chocolate skin and a close-cropped Afro stares at Geo from a nearby table. There's no hostility in her expression, just open curiosity. The other women at her table appear to defer to her, and occasionally they look over, too, murmuring to each other. Geo wonders what they see when they look at her. She knows she looks white, but she's also aware that her ethnicity is evident if people are really looking for it. It's in the caramel undertone to her skin, the slight almond shape of her eyes. Her hair, however, is straight. Her mother's hair.

When Geo finishes eating, the black woman meets her at the tray return. The other women from her table stand behind her, a few feet away, not close enough to hear their conversation, but close enough to react if anything happens. Her security detail, clearly.

"Are you black?" the woman asks. There's almost a nobility in the way she speaks. Her voice is rich, the pronunciation exact. Up close, her face is beautiful, unlined and smooth, with high cheekbones. Her eyes are almost black.

"One-eighth," Geo says, feeling the need to be specific, though she doesn't bother to explain the rest of it.

"I see you've made friends with Bernadette." The woman glances over at Bernie, who's still eating at their table. Then her gaze returns to Geo, her eyes roving over her skin, her eyes, her hair. "They call her the Mammoth." No explanation is required.

"We're not friends. She's my bunkmate."

The woman nods. "Let me know how that arrangement works out for you. If it doesn't, perhaps we can get you reassigned."

Bernie's good mood continues after dinner, and Geo is beginning to understand that her cellmate's moods are tied directly to how recently she ate. She's talkative up until lights-out, telling Geo about the various prisons she's done time in, including Oregon and California. Drugs and theft, mainly — typical charges for most of the women here. A career criminal. You'd think after a third conviction she'd find another profession, but that's not how a criminal's mind works.

The doors to the big room always remain open during the day unless there's a lockdown, but at lights-out the women are shut inside. If you need to pee, you have to ask one of the guards inside the booth, who are likely to be sleeping or watching a movie. Geo lies in bed and fatigue overcomes her instantly. She hasn't slept well since she's been here, and it's catching up with her. Finally, blissfully, she falls asleep.

It isn't until her bunkmate's sausage fingers are deep inside her vagina that she wakes up. Bernie is on top of her, her exorbitant flesh spilling over Geo's smaller body like a giant water balloon, the skin warm and moist and salty, breath reeking like spoiled milk. Her beady eyes resemble raisins in a mound of dough, and they stare right through her. Bernie smiles and licks Geo's face from her chin to her cheekbone. In the dark of the big room, her tongue looks purple.

Bottom bunk. This is why. Easier to rape someone. It's difficult to see their bunk from where the guard's booth is located at the other end of the room. And to make matters worse, Bernie has tucked the edges of her bedsheet under the upper mattress so that it falls around Geo's bunk like a curtain. If a CO glances over, all they'll see is the sheet. It gives Bernie enough time to get off her and to insist that what they're doing is mutual if the guard rips the sheet away. Punishment for consensual sex between inmates is a stay in maximum security.

They're already in maximum security.

Geo opens her mouth to scream, but Bernie is ready for that, and the large woman stuffs a sock into her mouth. It isn't necessary, though, because her lungs are already compressed. The Mammoth, well over twice her weight and three times her width, is suffocating her. Panicked, she begins to writhe and kick as best she can, but her bunkmate just presses down harder, her sour breath wafting into Geo's ears as she touches herself. "Do you like it? Does it feel good? Get wet for me, baby."

Barely able to move, Geo's hand swipes at the sheet, but she can't grasp it well enough to tear it down. She only manages to move it a little bit, enough to catch a glimpse of the inmate in the next bunk staring over. After a second or two, the inmate looks away.

Somehow, in a room full of women, Geo is alone with her attacker.

Unable to do anything, she has no choice but to lie still. Tears roll silently down the sides of her face. A minute later, Bernie grunts and rolls off, allowing Geo to take several gasping breaths.

"Nobody can see anything in this corner, bitch," her bunkmate whispers, straightening her clothes. "Our bunk doesn't show on camera. So all you gotta do is say nothing, and I won't have to kill you. But you liked it, didn't you? I know you did."

Geo lets out a loud sob, cut short when the Mammoth punches her in the face. Then she removes the sheet and climbs back up to her bed. Geo places her pillow over her mouth so she can cry into it without being heard.

She doesn't understand any of this. Bernie is a *mother.* Her son's picture is taped on to the goddamned locker less than two feet away. Geo lies in bed the rest of the night, stinking of the woman's vinegary sweat, her legs squeezed together, terrified that the Mammoth will come back into her bed again. She takes comfort in the loud snores coming from above; it means her bunkmate is sound asleep.

Geo, however, does not sleep. Just like she didn't sleep the last time she was raped, all those years ago. She knows from experience that it takes a while before your soul comes back to you.

And it takes even longer before your soul stops bleeding.

4

The next morning, Geo listlessly picks at her soggy oatmeal and burned toast as her bunkmate sits across from her at the table, in her usual spot. She starts her job in the hair salon today, which, relatively speaking, should have been something to look forward to, but all she wants is to find a quiet spot and hide. If Bernie was in a good mood yesterday, she's in an even better mood today. Geo's managed to avoid making eye contact up till now, but when their eyes finally meet, the Mammoth smiles.

Not taking her eyes off Geo, Bernie waggles her fingers, then makes a show of putting them to her nose and inhaling deeply. Then she inserts her first and middle fingers into her mouth, and sucks. The women at their table laugh at the obscene gesture, albeit nervously. Geo's stomach turns. Before she can stop herself, she vomits into her tray and all over the front of her own shirt, and learns that oatmeal looks exactly the same coming up as it does going down.

"Shit!" The inmate sitting beside her jumps out of her seat. "You disgusting bitch."

A corrections officer is at her side a few seconds later.

"Get up, Shaw," he says, his face a mask of revulsion as he surveys the regurgitated oatmeal all over Geo's shirt and pants. "Do you need to go to the infirmary? What happened to your face?"

Geo's cheekbone is purple from where Bernie slammed her fist into it a few hours before, but it only comprises a fraction of the pain she's feeling. She shakes her head, still feeling nauseated. The last thing she wants is to be checked over by a nurse. She absolutely does not want to be touched. Everyone's eyes are on her, including the Mammoth's. "Just . . . just a shower, I think. I'm fine."

"Go straight to the bathroom, clean yourself up." He speaks into his shoulder where his walkie-talkie sits. "Janitorial in chow hall, stat."

Geo leaves the cafeteria, humiliated, while the other inmates smirk. She doesn't have to look at Bernie to know that her bunkmate is laughing along with the others.

62

She showers by herself in a tiny stall with a ripped curtain, wearing her rubber flip-flops. The shower is cranked all the way up, but the temperature never gets hotter than lukewarm, and the water will shut off in eight minutes whether she's finished or not. Working fast, she uses her bar of soap on both her hair and her body, as someone's already stolen her shampoo. She scrubs her skin raw with her fingernails.

When the shower shuts off, she opens the curtain a little and feels around on the outer wall for her towel. It's not hanging where she left it. She pulls the curtain open wider and jumps when she sees someone standing there, leaning against the counter across from the stall. Geo's towel is draped over her arm.

It's the black woman from the day before. She has no entourage today. They're alone in the bathroom.

"I'm Ella Frank," she says. When Geo doesn't move, she holds out the towel. "You must be freezing."

Geo is cold, but there's no way to reach the towel without stepping out of the shower. She finally does, dripping wet, and the woman hands it to her. Geo wraps the towel around herself quickly, trembling. But it's not just from the cool air. She's aware of Ella Frank's reputation. Everyone in here is, though up till this point, Geo didn't know exactly which inmate she was until the woman said her name. And now here they are, standing in front of each other, and Geo is practically naked. She has no weapons to stab with, no boots on her feet to kick with. She doesn't know what this woman wants from her, but she does know she can't handle being raped again. She'd rather die.

"I'm not going to hurt you," Ella Frank says. "I'm not the Mammoth."

Geo's throat closes up. "You know?"

"I have eyes and ears all over."

"Why didn't you say anything to me yesterday?" The words are out before Geo can stop them, and she winces at their bluntness.

"It's not my job to protect you. Unless you want it to be." The woman fixes her gaze on Geo. It's intense. Unblinking. They're about the same size — if anything, the black woman is a bit thinner — but Geo has no doubt Ella Frank could kill her without breaking a sweat. "You know who I am?"

Geo nods, the full story coming back to her. In her media photos, as the wife of drug lord James Frank, Ella was always impeccably dressed, with long black hair and bright fuchsia lipstick. The prison version of Ella Frank is more subtle — the weave is gone, the hair is short, the lips are bare, the clothes are same prison scrubs everyone else wears — but she looks just as dangerous. It's in the way she stands, the way she speaks, the way she's looking at Geo now. Ella ran her husband's security team, killing his perceived enemies by shooting them in the head with the small-caliber weapon she wore strapped around her thigh. She's in for the murder of two rivals, though rumor has it she's killed at least a dozen.

And she's no less powerful in here than she was on the outside. Ella Frank is responsible for almost all the drugs that find their way into Hazelwood on a regular basis. Currently embroiled in a turf battle with another drug dealer, she's in a situation that's getting ugly. But unlike most of the women in Hazelwood who'll be released at some point in the future, Ella Frank is serving back-to-back life sentences. She'll never get out; she'll die in here. Which means she has nothing whatsoever to lose. This makes her extremely dangerous.

"You're Georgina Shaw," Ella says. "I read about you. Big-time executive on the outside. You made a lot of money, I bet."

"I spent a lot of money, too."

Ella laughs softly. "I feel you. Life's short. Might as well enjoy it while you have it, am I right?" Her eyes are fixed on Geo's face. The irises are so dark that Geo can't see her pupils. "So. Your bunkmate has taken a significant liking to you. How do you feel about that?"

"It's terrible," Geo says. It comes out a whisper.

Ella nods. "I know Bernadette from another prison. She must have creamed her double-XL underwear when you were assigned to her bunk. You're just her type. White. Pretty. Classy. You understand it will keep happening?"

"Yes." This time, the word comes out a whimper.

"I can make it stop," the black woman says, her eyes never leaving Geo's face. "I can make it so that nobody in here ever touches you again. Do you want my help?"

Geo closes her eyes, knowing that the next word she says will change everything. "Yes."

"My help isn't free."

She opens her eyes again. "I know."

"Okay," Ella says, and smiles. "I'll take care of it. You get dressed now. But before I go, allow me to offer some advice, woman to woman."

Geo eyes the fresh clothes folded on the counter beside Ella. She doesn't dare reach for them. It requires moving closer. "Of course," she says.

"Hold your head high," Ella says. "Carry yourself like you run the place. Don't back down from anybody. The way you look, with your pretty white-girl hair and your pretty white-girl face, you're never going to be invisible in here. Not after what you did on the outside. So own it. Someone gets in your face, you cut a bitch. You understand me? I can and will protect you, but I could get shanked tomorrow. And then where will you be?"

Geo nods. "I understand. Thank you."

Ella hands Geo her clothes. As she reaches for them, her towel slips, and suddenly she's naked again. The other woman's eyes flicker up and down her body. She chuckles. "Yeah, you're beautiful. But you're not my type. I like dick."

Geo dresses hastily.

"One of my girls will find you in the hair salon later," Ella says. "When she does, you give her what she asks for."

Two hours pass before someone approaches her in the hair salon. Geo recognizes her as one of the women on Ella's security detail. She gives the woman what she asks for, keeping one eye on the camera mounted on the ceiling.

"Don't worry about it," the woman says. "The guard who's supposed to be watching the monitor is . . . distracted."

Less than a half hour later, the woman is back. "I rinsed them, but get some bleach on it," she says. "And they were never out of your sight, you understand?"

Geo understands. An hour after that, while she's in the chow hall eating lunch, the prison goes on lockdown.

Bernadette Novotny, also known as the Mammoth, is dead.

News spreads like wildfire in prison. Bernie was found in the prison laundry behind the steam press. There's no question how it happened. Multiple stab wounds punctured her carotid artery; she would have bled out in seconds.

Geo lies on the floor with her hands beside her head, alongside the other inmates in the chow hall. The guards are searching for the murder weapon and pulling Bernie's known enemies — of which there are many — into the office for questioning. But they won't solve this. The shears that Geo gave to Ella's associate were bleached clean and locked back in the drawer before she left for lunch, by the same CO who signed them out to her earlier that morning.

Over the course of the day, with no other leads, the guards question women in the big room, one by one. They start with Geo, since it was her bunkmate who died. She says the same thing everyone else will say — she saw nothing, heard nothing, and has no idea who might have done it. She ignores the looks and whispers from the other inmates, and for a brief moment considers pointing the finger at the woman in the next bunk over, who knew Geo was being raped and did nothing. She decides against it. Had their positions been reversed, Geo might have done the same thing.

Later in the day, the body is finally moved. The lockdown is lifted, and life in prison returns to normal. But now it's a new normal. With the bunk above her empty, Geo sleeps. For the first time since she's been at Hellwood, she sleeps a full eight hours.

The next morning at breakfast, Ella Frank sits down at her table in the chow hall. She smiles at Geo. Geo smiles back. They sit across from each other like two old friends, eating their overcooked sausage and rubbery eggs.

"How's it going, Georgina?" Ella asks pleasantly. "You look rested."

"I slept well," she answers. "And my friends call me Geo."

Ella chuckles. "So we're friends now? And here I thought we had a simple business deal. I perform a service, you perform a service. Quid pro quo. That's how it works in here."

"What if this was more than just a business transaction?" Geo asks. She has no intention of sticking drugs up her ass or being part of the woman's security squad. "What if we become . . . business associates? You have a business to run, and I'm a businesswoman. If you recall, I was pretty good at my last job. One of my responsibilities — and perhaps the most important one — was maximizing profits. I think you and I could work well together. I think you already know that, actually. Otherwise you wouldn't have bothered helping me in the first place."

The other woman's smile makes her look younger. Softer. But her voice, as mellifluous as it is, is still laced with steel. "You learn fast, G. And it's an attractive offer. But you forgot one thing. I don't need you."

It's Geo's turn to smile. "You have kids, right?"

"Excuse me?" Ella's voice hardened.

"Have you ever thought about starting a college fund for them?" Geo speaks fast, before Ella goes ballistic. She's on dangerous ground; even mentioning another woman's children could get you killed in here. "I know they're little now, but I bet they're smart. What if they want to go to college one day? Student loans can be crippling. I can help with that." She pauses to let what she's said sink in. "There's no reason your family can't thrive financially, in a legitimate way. I can help you create a nest egg for them. Something they can build on when they're grown."

Ella's dark eyes appraise her, searching for any indication that Geo is trying to bullshit her. Finding none, she finally says, "Okay. I'm listening."

They talk for the remainder of breakfast.

When Geo gets back to her bunk after her work shift later that day, her hygiene bin, which she forgot to stow away after her shower that morning, is still on her bed where she left it. For once, nobody touched it. Shampoo, toothpaste, even a new bar of soap; it's all there. A guard finds her a few minutes later.

"Shaw, you're being transferred," she barks.

Geo frowns. "Where to?"

"Private cell. One just opened up."

"How? I thought the other units were full

due to the construction."

The CO raises an eyebrow. "You want it or not? Get your shit and meet me in the hallway."

Once again, Geo collects her things. As she makes her way out of the big room for the last time, her fellow inmates move out of her way. A few of the women even avert their eyes after making eye contact. It's a sign of deference. A sign of respect.

In the real world, you earned it through hard work, admiration, loyalty, and sometimes love. In prison, there was only one way: You earned respect through fear.

In her new private cell, Geo finds a cell phone tucked under her mattress, just where Ella Frank said it would be.

5

The letter looks innocent enough from the outside.

Plain blue envelope with her name, DOC number, and the address of Hazelwood Correctional Institute written in neat, even letters. The name and return address is one Geo doesn't recognize. She opens the envelope, which contains a single sheet of matching blue paper, folded carefully, and more of that neat handwriting. She begins to read.

Thirty seconds later, the letter is stuffed is back inside its envelope, and the envelope is shoved into the middle of a book that she's read twice already. The book is then placed on the shelf above her desk, never to be touched again.

She looks down at her hands; they're shaking. *He wrote to her.* Goddammit. The memories threaten to flood in, to break the barrier that Geo has spent years constructing around her head and her heart. She doesn't want to think about him; it's always been so much easier to pretend he's not out there somewhere. Her ability to compartmentalize the different pieces of her life is the only fucking reason she's sane.

No. No no no. Goddammit.

She feels something on her face and touches it, and is shocked to discover that she's crying.

Goddammit.

"Bad time?" The inmate from the cell next door is standing in her open doorway, watching her with a concerned expression. The older woman is in her late fifties, a sprite of a lady with bright burgundy curls and an expressive mouth that's always laughing, eating, or cussing. Sometimes all three at the same time. Ella Frank might be Geo's business associate, but Cat Bonaducci is Geo's friend. The first real girlfriend she's had in a long time.

The last one was Angela.

"Kind of," Geo says, but she waves her in. "What's up?"

"I want to take a new picture. For the pen pal thing I told you about. Can you do my hair?" She holds up a box of Nice'n Easy hair color, the only kind you can purchase from commissary.

"Write-A-Prisoner? You sure it's not really called Date-A-Prisoner?" Geo wipes her eyes. "Sure. I have a bit of time before my first appointment."

Cat follows Geo out of the cell. They buzz to be let out and head down to the education wing, where the prison hair salon is located. Cat also brings her small bag of cosmetics; she'll probably ask for help with her makeup, too. Inmates are technically allowed only six makeup items each, but it's a moronic rule that the prison never enforces. The better women look, the better they feel. The better they feel, the higher the overall morale. And when morale is high, incidents of violence are low.

The salon is really just a small, plain room with a wash sink, chair, small desk, and mirror. Inmates have to buy their own hair color from commissary, and Geo only has access to the shears after a CO unlocks the drawer and signs them out. She opens the box of Nice'n Easy and starts mixing Cat's color.

"What's going on with you?" Cat asks as Geo begins to apply the hair color to her friend's gray roots. "Were you crying?"

Geo doesn't answer. She doesn't want to talk about the letter. The past needs to stay in the past; it's the only way to keep moving forward. "Maybe. Now shut up and let me work my magic."

"You never did tell me how you got so good at doing hair and makeup," Cat says, closing her eyes as Geo works. The fumes are strong. "I thought you had a desk job on the outside."

"I went to beauty school for a year. In between college and my master's degree."

"You're shitting me."

Geo smiles. "That's the exact same thing my dad said. When I told him after graduation that I'd enrolled at the Emerald Beauty Academy, he thought I was joking. He thought it would be a waste of time."

Actually, the exact thing Walter Shaw had said to her was, "Beauty school is for people who can't get into college, Georgina. You have a degree, for Christ's sakes, and you're attending a school that takes high school dropouts?" But she doesn't want to say this to Cat, who never finished high school.

"It was fun," she says instead. "I spent five days a week learning everything there was to learn about makeup and hair. After that, I landed an internship at Shipp Pharmaceuticals, and the rest, as they say, is history. They have an MBA reimbursement program, so I took advantage of it and worked my way up."

76

Telling Cat the story makes her think of Andrew. It's been two months, and her ex-fiancé's name is still on her approved-visitors list. She never bothered to take it off. It means going down to the visitor's office and telling them to remove his name, and Andrew Shipp — bless his rich, white, entitled ass — doesn't deserve the ounce of energy that would take. Not that she wishes him ill. She just doesn't wish him anything at all. Her dad always said that you only get one real chance at love, and if that was true, Geo had wasted hers at the age of sixteen on a boyfriend who'd turned out to be a serial killer known as the Sweetbay Strangler.

She remembers thinking it was such as a silly name when Kaiser Brody first told her about it, the day he'd come to arrest her. They were sitting across from each other in the interrogation room at Seattle PD. Fred Argent, the head of Shipp's in-house counsel, was seated beside her, way out of his depth as Kaiser explained what her old boyfriend Calvin James had done.

It didn't sound so silly anymore.

"Wait," Fred had said, looking every inch the corporate attorney he was trained to be — late fifties, white, and completely outraged at the thought that one of Shipp's own was being treated like a common criminal. "I thought you were arresting Miss Shaw for the murder of someone named Angela Wong."

"We are, but that's not the only crime Calvin James has been charged with," Kaiser said. "He's murdered three other women that we know of over the past decade."

Geo drew in a sharp breath. Immediately, Fred leaned over to whisper in her ear. His breath was rank with stale whiskey; it was no big secret that the old lawyer kept a bottle of Jack Daniel's in his desk drawer. He'd probably taken a couple of shots before meeting her here. "I've called Daniel Attenbaum, the best criminal defense attorney in Seattle. He'll be here shortly. Andrew said not to worry about anything. He'll cover all the expenses out of his personal account. In the meantime, say nothing, okay?"

Geo nodded. Kaiser was watching the two of them with amusement. Then he opened the manila file folder on the table and pulled out the photos.

Two of them, both eight by tens, full color. Keeping them side by side, he pushed them across the table. "Angela Wong," he said.

Fred Argent looked at the photos and blanched, his eyes darting back and forth between the two pictures several times. Geo glanced down, drew in another breath, and then averted her gaze. It was exactly as horrific as she imagined it would be.

"My god." The lawyer put a hand over his mouth. "Is that . . ." He didn't finish the sentence. He couldn't. Fred spent most of his day in a cushy office, drafting contracts, reading fine print, and discussing the legal aspects of the pharmaceutical business. He looked positively traumatized.

Then again, a photograph of a pile of human bones and tattered clothing would traumatize anyone.

"Her purse was buried with her," Kaiser said, speaking to Geo. "It contained her driver's license and her high school ID card. Also her camera. There's no doubt it's her."

Geo said nothing.

"Remember that camera?" Kaiser smiled. "Some fancy thing her dad won in a golf tournament? Small, but not digital. They didn't really have a digital cameras for the consumer back then. It was a thirty-five millimeter. She was always buying film at the 7-Eleven. Always carrying it around, taking pictures of everything. Remember?"

Geo remembered.

"The film was preserved inside the camera from that night," Kaiser said. "We got the pictures developed. Want to see? You and I are in a whole bunch of them. It's a real blast from the past."

Internally, Geo shook her head rapidly. Externally, she didn't blink.

"Come again?" Fred Argent said. "I'm afraid I don't understand any of this. You're speaking to Miss Shaw like you have a previous relationship with her. Do you two know each other outside of this . . . situation?"

"Catch up, dude," Kaiser said nonchalantly, and Geo almost laughed. It was something he used to say in high school. "*Miss Shaw* and I go way back. We were — how do the kids put it now? — *BFFs* back in the day. Best friends, along with Angela Wong. Right, Geo?"

Again, Geo said nothing.

Kaiser reached into the folder again and pulled out a smaller envelope filled with photos. He removed them and placed them in a stack in front of Geo. "These are from Angela's camera. Have a look. You'll be tickled, I'm sure. We all look so young."

She didn't want to look, but she couldn't help it. The picture on top was of the three of them, taken a few days before the night Angela died. They were standing in the entryway of Angela's house and Kaiser had snapped a picture of their reflection in the full-length hallway mirror. Geo plucked the photo from the stack and examined it closer. Kaiser was right; they looked very young. He was skinnier then, and not quite as tall as he was now. Geo appeared shy and self-conscious standing beside him. Angela was on his other side, posing with a hand on her hip and her hair tossed to the side, hamming it up for the camera. Geo looked pretty. Angela looked beautiful.

She started thumbing through the rest of the photos. Angela had indeed taken pictures of everything in the days before she died — school, cheer practice, the football game, Chad Fenton's party . . . and then Calvin. He was in the very last photo with Geo. They were sitting side by side on his bed, in his apartment, after the party. Geo was wearing a short blue dress, and it had hiked up almost to her underwear. Her head was resting on Calvin's shoulder, and he had a hand on her thigh. He could never be near her and not touch her. He was always stroking her, playing with her hair, squeezing her hand. She shuddered. She hadn't thought about that in a long time.

She hadn't *allowed* herself to think about it in a long time.

She didn't remember this picture being taken. But then, why would she? The picture didn't show it, but she was so drunk that night she could barely stand.

"Who is that?" Fred Argent was leaning in toward Geo, frowning at the photo.

"That, sir, is the Sweetbay Strangler," Kaiser said. "Back when he used to date Georgina."

A sharp intake of breath. For once, not Geo's. She glanced over at Shipp's lawyer where beads of sweat were forming at his hairline. The man's blood pressure was probably up twenty points, no doubt because his CEO's fiancée was in major trouble here. And he was stuck with the task of protecting her, something he obviously wasn't cut out to do.

"What's so crazy is that discovering Angela's remains after all these years allowed us to solve three other murders, just like that." Kaiser snapped his fingers for emphasis. "We already had his DNA in the database for three other murders, but no ID. But then we developed the pictures in Angela's camera. Imagine my shock — my utter fucking shock — when I realized Calvin James was with Angela the night she died. As were you."

"But that doesn't mean she —" Fred began, but Kaiser raised a hand.

"Now we had an ID on a possible suspect," the detective continued. "We tracked Calvin down, arrested him at a diner in Blaine. You know where Blaine is, right? Right by the Canadian border? Fucker was about to cross into Canada. Had a passport and everything. Had he done that, we might never have caught him. Guess what he was eating when we caught him. Guess."

Geo said nothing.

"A salad," Kaiser said. "Isn't that funny? Because you never think about what serial killers eat, do you? I mean, other than Jeffrey Dahmer."

Fred Argent paled.

"Sorry, bad joke," Kaiser said with a smirk, not sorry at all. "But it turns out psychopaths are just like you and me in some ways. They watch their waistlines; they care about their blood pressure. Did you know that something like five percent of all CEOs can be classified as psychopaths? I read that somewhere."

It was 4 percent. Geo had read that book, too.

"And you were on the fast track to success at your company, weren't you? How many people did you step on to get there? I've been keeping tabs on you. Does your rich heir-to-the-throne fiancé know your secret?" Kaiser's voice was polite, but there was no mistaking the edge that lay right beneath the surface. "Had you gone to the police the night you killed Angela, you might have saved three more lives from being taken. Calvin James was twenty-one; you were only sixteen. You could have struck a deal, and you might never have seen the inside of a jail cell. You could have spared her parents fourteen years of agony, of not knowing where their daughter was or what happened to her. You have would spared her friends the pain of all those unanswered questions. Because all this time, you knew, Georgina. You knew. *You knew.*"

The last two words weren't shouted, but they might as well have been. Geo winced as if he'd slapped her.

"Want to know what he did to the other three women? The women he killed because you never said anything?" Kaiser was breathing fast now, his chest heaving. He pulls more photographs out of the file folder and shoves them across the table. The pictures are gory, the bodies discolored, bloated. Because death was ugly. "He raped them first, then he strangled them, and then he buried their bodies in the woods. He probably figured he got away with it once and it turned him on, so why not do it again? And again. And again. You murdered your best friend, and then you went on with your life *like it never fucking happened.*"

The words stung. Geo felt herself sag into her chair. "I loved her," she whispered again. "You know that."

"Georgina, stop speaking," Fred said to her. His phone beeped, and he checked the text message. "Goddamn it, Attenbaum is stuck in traffic. He'll be another twenty minutes at least. Not another word until he's inside this room, you understand?"

"Calvin says you secretly hated her," Kaiser said.

Geo's insides tightened. "Calvin's here?"

"He was, for a while, but he's been moved." Her old friend leaned forward, his eyes never leaving Geo's face. "You wouldn't recognize him right now. He's got long hair, a thick beard. I'm sure he'll clean himself up for the trial. He said that back then, you and Angela had a rivalry going. And it's funny, because as soon as he said that, I realized he was right. I was always playing the peacemaker with you guys, but I just thought all the bickering and competition was a girl thing."

"I never wanted anything bad to happen to her," Geo said.

"Jesus Christ, Georgina, *please*," Fred Argent said, glaring at the closed door, as if he thought he could summon Daniel Atten-baum through sheer willpower.

"The good news is, the DA doesn't want you," Kaiser said, saying the line that every cop used in the movies. "They want Calvin."

"How am I supposed to help?" she asked.

Fred Argent sighed deeply and placed his head in his hands.

"Testify," Kaiser said. "The district at-torney will agree to a plea deal in exchange for your testimony. But you need to make a decision quick, before the DA decides she doesn't need you."

"Georgina, Andrew said —" Fred began, but she shook her head.

"It doesn't matter what Andrew said." Geo took a deep breath. "You can go now, Fred. I'll wait for Attenbaum. If you see Andrew, tell him I love him, and that I'm grateful for his help and support, and that I'm sorry for any embarrassment I caused. Go ahead and put together my severance package; I'll sign off on it tonight."

"Severance package?" The lawyer looked completely caught off guard.

Geo turned to him and managed a rueful smile. "I have to disassociate myself from the company, of course. All of this will be terrible publicity for Shipp. But I'd like you to treat me fairly. I've been a valuable asset, and I want what I'm entitled to. I think one year's salary, plus the bonus I would have received, is reasonable."

"That's . . . premature," Fred said, his mouth slightly ajar. "Andrew will —"

"The trial will be public, I'm sure. However, if I a sign a nondisclosure agreement — which I'm happy to do if the settlement is fair — we can prevent my personal situation from affecting Shipp. Talk to Andrew. I'm sure he'll agree it's best for the company."

She caught Kaiser's look, knew what he must be thinking. It was a hell of a time to be making a business deal, but she would never have made it to the executive level of a major corporation by the age of thirty without the ability to negotiate under pressure.

Thankfully, it's a transferrable skill, one that will make all the difference between surviving prison and dying in here. It's also self-preservation. Her corporate career is over. The best she can hope for is to take the settlement and invest it, adding whatever she and Ella make to the pot. By the time she's released, she might have enough to start over. She could always renew her cosmetology license and open a salon.

She puts the finishing touches on Cat's

face, then hands her friend a small plastic mirror. "You're done. Take a look."

Cat checks her reflection and nods her approval. "Where did you go just now? You zoned out. Did you hear anything I said in the last ten minutes?"

"Sorry." Geo sighs. "It's been that kind of day."

"It's Hellwood. Every day is that kind of day." Cat stands up. "I'm off. Catch you in chow hall. Ta-ta."

Cat practically skips out, a small woman with a heart and spirit so big, Geo wishes they could know each other outside these prison walls. The older woman has made some giant mistakes in her life, but Cat's a good person.

Geo's next "client" is not a good person. She takes a seat in the chair and hands Geo a few pages ripped from old beauty magazines they keep in the recreation room. Geo listens politely, trying not to think about how the woman and her husband used to own a daycare where they would film the children naked and upload the footage to a child pornography site. The woman is serving out her sentence in protective custody for her own safety, and is allowed two haircuts per year. Her husband was beaten to death in the men's prison two years ago.

The pedophile tells her she wants bangs.

This is Geo's life now, surrounded by all manner of wicked human beings who do nothing to make the world a better place, who take and take and take, giving absolutely nothing back. And in a lot of ways, she's no better than they are. This is exactly what she deserves. She picks up her shears and starts snipping.

See, Dad? Told you beauty school would come in handy.

It's almost lunchtime before she gets a break, but she's stopped by a corrections officer as she's heading toward the chow hall. Shawna Lyle.

"Shaw," the CO snaps. The woman is only five-two, and the tight fit of her uniform showcases the rolls around her midsection and the expanse of her thighs. But her physical softness is deceiving; she's nobody to be trifled with. "You have a visitor."

"Who is it?" Geo's stomach is growling. She heard they were serving chili today, which is one of the things the kitchen staff cooks that actually tastes like it's supposed to.

"I'm not your fucking social secretary." If looks could kill, Geo would have been pushed through a meat grinder. "You want to see him or not?"

89

It's probably her father, but he usually visits on Sundays. Geo's in no mood to socialize, but she follows the guard down the hallway toward the visitor's lounge, an open area with a dozen tables and chairs and a row of vending machines across the side wall. There's even a play area for the kids and a nice view of the gardens behind the prison.

"Not in there," the CO says. "There." She points toward one of the private visitor's rooms. Much less comfortable, but inside there's complete privacy. No guards watching, no cameras, just a small table with four chairs and a door that closes. Usually these rooms are saved for lawyer visits, but fancy Daniel Attenbaum isn't needed anymore, now that Calvin's trial is over.

Confused, she pushes open the door. Kaiser Brody is leaning against the edge of the table, checking his phone.

"What are you doing here?" she asks, silently wondering if she somehow conjured him by losing herself in the past earlier.

Kaiser looks her over, at her hair, her clothes. She finds herself feeling self-conscious under his scrutiny. Prison scrubs are far from flattering, and she's not wearing makeup. She looked much better the last time they saw each other. But then again, so did he. The detective's eyes are bloodshot, and they're cradled in deep, dark circles. A patchy three-day beard covers the lower half of his face.

"You okay?" Kaiser asks.

"Yeah," Geo says. "Are *you*?"

"Shut the door." She does as he asks. He puts his phone away and straightens up. "I'm going to ask you straight out. Have you been in touch with Calvin James since you've been in here?"

"Of course I haven't," she says, her breath quickening. "He's in prison, too. Inmates aren't allowed to contact other inmates. Besides, he'd have no reason to. We're not connected by anything anymore."

"Are you sure?"

She thinks of the letter she received earlier that day, the blue paper in the blue envelope with an unfamiliar name and return address, then pushes it out of her mind. "Yes, I'm sure."

Kaiser's eyes search her face. "What did he give you that day in court? And don't say 'nothing,' because I know he gave you something. It was a piece of paper, yellow, small, torn from his notepad. What was written on it?"

"Nothing —"

"Stop," he says, raising a hand. "Just

fucking stop. Don't lie to me. I know he gave you something. I saw it. And I need to know what it was, so don't fucking play me, Georgina. Was it a phone number? Some way to contact him? *What did he give you?*"

The last five words come out a shout. Kaiser's spittle lands on her nose and cheeks. Shocked at his fury, she wipes it away, backing up all the way to the closed door.

"It was a note. I don't remember what it said. He drew a heart on it." It's half a lie. She remembers exactly what it said. *You're welcome.* But she can't tell Kaiser this, because then she'll have to explain what it means. And she can't do that. She'll never do that.

"It wasn't an address of some kind? Or a phone number?" Kaiser's jaw is tense. Both his hands are curled up into fists, so tightly that the knuckles are white. He's about to lose it, and suddenly she's afraid he might hit her. She looks up at the ceiling. No cameras in here.

"Nothing like that," she says again, hoping she sounds more convincing. "It was a silly note. What I remember is the heart. There was no contact information on it, I promise you. Why is this important?"

"Because he escaped from prison," Kaiser

92

says, and just like that, Geo's heart stops. "Three days ago. He had help on the inside. A prison guard and his counselor. Both female. Both are now dead."

Her mouth opens, but nothing comes out. She snaps it shut, then opens it again, then still can't think of what to say. She shuts it again.

"Okay, so you didn't know." Kaiser seems satisfied with her reaction. He lets out a long breath and leans back against the table again. "I believe you."

"Of course I didn't know," Geo says, finally finding her voice. "But why are you telling me? Look where I am. Obviously I can't help you find him."

"I thought you'd want to know," Kaiser says. "Because at some point you'll be out of here. And I don't want you to think I didn't warn you."

"Warn me about what?"

Kaiser reaches into his pocket and pulls out a folded piece of yellow-pad paper. It's the same piece of paper that Calvin had been doodling on the day she'd testified in court. A piece was torn off from the bottom.

The piece he'd handed to her. The piece she'd swallowed.

She takes it from Kaiser and unfolds it.

The outer edges are a mess of scribbles, doodles, pictures, and random words. But right in the center, Calvin drew a large heart. And inside the heart he'd written two initials in flowing cursive.

GS.

Her heart stops for a full second, then starts beating again triple time. She works hard to not let her reaction show.

"I feel strongly that he's going to try and contact you," Kaiser says, rubbing his face. He looks exhausted. "I don't know how, but when he does, I need you to tell me."

The blue letter flits through her mind again, then flits out.

Geo hands the paper back to him. "He won't," she says, so defiantly and authoritatively that she almost believes it herself. "He has no reason to. Now I have to go." If she doesn't leave now, he'll see right through her. She turns away and opens the door.

"Georgina," Kaiser says. "Take care of yourself in here."

She pauses, then turns to her old friend one last time. With the badge on his hip, the worn leather jacket, the scruffy face . . . he looks like a stranger. Maybe he loved her once, when they were kids, but that was a long time ago, when she was worthy of love.

Everything's different now. It hurts to look at him.

He reminds her of the person she used to be.

"I don't want to see you anymore, Kai," Geo says softly. "Please don't come here again."

■ ■ ■ ■

Part Two:
Anger

■ ■ ■ ■

"Whoever fights monsters should see to it
that in the process he does not become
a monster."
~ Friedrich Nietzsche

Part Two:
Anger

"Whoever fights monsters should see to it
that in the process he does not become
a monster."
— Friedrich Nietzsche

6

The soft ping of his email app wakes Kaiser Brody, and he reaches for his iPhone on the nightstand to check it. It's only 5:30 A.M. and not yet light outside. Beside him, Kim murmurs softly. She doesn't move. Her blond hair fans out in messy strands over the pillow, and he watches her sleep for a moment, feeling that strange mix of emotions he always does whenever they do this. He'll have to wake her up at six so she has enough time to get back home before her husband — scheduled for night shifts this week — realizes she's been gone all night.

Or maybe he won't wake her. See what happens, what excuses she'll make, both to her husband for being out all night, and to him, when she tells him later on that they'll need to lie low for a few days until things at home "settle back down."

He sighs and clicks on the new email.

It's from the prison guard at Hazelwood

Correctional Institute, the one he pays to send him a monthly report on inmate number 110214, also known as Georgina Maria Shaw. It only costs him a hundred bucks, sent anonymously via PayPal, which isn't much. But over five years, every month, that shit adds up. Their arrangement is over as of today though, as Georgina is scheduled for release next week.

Five fucking years. In some ways it feels like the time went by fast, and yet in other ways, it seems like nothing has changed at all.

The PDF report contains a lot of information that doesn't say much. There's a detailed log of her incoming and outgoing phone calls, her incoming and outgoing mail, and a list of everybody who's visited her over the past month. Other than her attorney and Kaiser himself, the only other person who's ever gone to see Georgina in prison is her father. Her ex-fiancé, that snooty CEO with the soft paunch and thinning hair, never went to see her once.

Her phone records tend to show a bit more depth. She had her usual phone call with a man named Raymond Yoo, who, according to his website, is an "independent financial planner specializing in unique and outside-the-box investment opportunities."

Kaiser can only assume this means the man's a pro in laundering money. And once a year, on the same day, Georgina makes a long distance phone call to a ninety-year-old woman named Lucilla Gallardo in Toronto. Her maternal grandmother.

There's also detailed information about medical visits (only one in the past six months, for a rash on her shoulder), her work assignment (in the prison hair salon), volunteer efforts (she tutors fellow inmates working toward their GED), and even what she purchased in commissary (tampons, moisturizer, chocolate). If she filed any complaints or received any disciplinary actions, those would appear in the report as well. In five years, she never has.

Which doesn't mean they haven't happened.

Kaiser peruses these reports every month, telling himself he's keeping an eye out for any contact between Georgina and her ex-boyfriend, Calvin James. But if he's being honest with himself (and why the fuck would he want to do that?), he knows it's simply because he wants to know how she's doing. The last time he saw her, she expressly told him not to visit her. So he hasn't. But that doesn't mean he doesn't care.

Not that he feels guilty for arresting her. He doesn't, not really. But he can't say he ever felt good about it, either.

Accompanying every report is a paragraph personally written by the corrections officer, giving him tidbits on Georgina's life over the past month. This is really what he pays the hundred bucks for — the things that *aren't* in the report. Who her friends are, who she's argued with, who she's fucking, what contraband the CO suspects she's hiding, her overall morale.

Georgina's been doing well. Her closest friends are a woman named Cat Bonaducci (a woman who killed someone while driving drunk and was sentenced to fifteen years) and Ella Frank.

The Ella Frank. Wife of James Frank, the drug kingpin, currently incarcerated for life in the Washington State Penitentiary. Georgina formed a friendship with her early in her stay, and the CO has noted several times that she might be involved somehow in Ella Frank's drug business. Kaiser doesn't give a shit. Far as he can tell, the Franks haven't had any contact with Calvin James, a.k.a. the Sweetbay Strangler, and that's the only thing that matters to him.

What Georgina does to survive in prison is her business.

"Everything okay?" Kim's face is mushed into the pillow, her voice muffled. The room is dark, illuminated only by the glow of Kaiser's phone.

"Go back to sleep," he says to her, and she does.

On the one hand, he likes that Kim's here, because it's nice lying bedside someone who understands him, understands his work, and who doesn't expect or want anything more than what he can give. But on the other hand, he hates that she's here, because she's married and he knows it's wrong.

They've never discussed where this would go. The affair — an ugly word, but he's always believed in calling a spade a spade — started more than a year ago. Kim's husband, Dave, is also a cop, working out of a different precinct, and his hours are crazy. Their schedules rarely mesh. They were supposed to start trying for a family, but first Kim put it off, and now Dave's putting it off. She's lonely, hungry for attention and validation, and she needs a warm body next to her just as much as Kaiser does.

But this can't go on indefinitely. It's already gone on way too long, and he's starting to get sick of the sneaking around, having to hide it from everybody at work. It isn't worth it, especially since he doesn't —

nor will he ever — love Kim. Kaiser's not sure he's capable of really loving anyone anymore.

It makes him the ideal cop. Nobody to apologize to for working long hours, no kids to worry about, no family plans to fuck up. Nobody to take care of, not even a plant or a goldfish. He can work the hours he wants, sleep when he wants, eat when he wants. He only really feels "single" — which is a dumbass word, a label designed to make people feel like losers, because people are just people — at Thanksgiving and Christmas, and sometimes, not even then.

He was married once, to a nurse he met in the ER while getting stitched up after breaking up a bar fight shortly after he graduated from the police academy. It lasted a tumultuous eighteen months, ending just as decisively as it began. He never blamed her; he'd become unbearable to live with, consumed with work, never putting her first. She left him for a guy she met on the internet, and when the ink was dry on the divorce papers, he swore he'd never get married again.

He leans back on the pillow and brushes a strand of Kim's hair away from her cheek. You'd think after a year of this her husband would catch on that his wife isn't sleeping at home when he's working. But so far, he hasn't, and maybe it's because he doesn't want to know. Kaiser met Dave once, a few months back, at the precinct's annual family barbecue. Had shaken the man's hand. If the other cop suspected anything, he didn't show it. The smile had been warm to match the handshake, and they'd spent a few minutes talking about sports, which is what men do when they're new to each other and have nothing else to talk about.

Kim stirs again, opens one eye, peers up at him. "What time is it?"

"Don't worry," he says. He knows the drill. "I'll wake you at six."

She smiles at him, pulls the covers up to her chin, and falls back asleep.

He checks through the report again, hungry for details that aren't there. Is Georgina happy? Is she lonely? Is she excited to get out, or is she dreading rejoining civilized society after what she did? The discovery of Angela Wong's remains fourteen long years after the teenager went missing rocked Seattle because everybody remembered that case. There was wild speculation about what could have happened to her. Mike Bennett, the quarterback of the St. Martin's High School football team and her on-and-off-again boyfriend, was questioned extensively in her disappearance, leading some to believe he might have killed her. It could have ruined Mike's life, and yet Georgina had said nothing.

The one thing he never asked her, the day he arrested her, was why. Why had she done it? And why had she kept it a secret? Deep down, though, Kaiser knew the answer. He didn't ask because he didn't want her to lie to him again. He remembers how she was with Calvin James. The profound effect Calvin had on her. She acted differently around him. Spoke differently around him. *Moved* differently around him. It was like Calvin tapped into a part of her control panel that nobody else could reach, turning on a switch that nobody else realized was even there. Not even Georgina herself.

Calvin James changed her life. He had changed all their lives . . . for the worse. He'd pulled off the prison escape of the decade, killing a prison guard and a counselor in the process. The three men who'd escaped with him had all been found dead in the months to follow. Not Calvin James, though. He's still out there somewhere.

Kaiser still remembers the conversation he had with the serial killer at the precinct shortly after his arrest. The Sweetbay Strangler sat easily in the interrogation room, hands resting on the table, his wrists cuffed together, relaxed. Jeans, T-shirt, no jewelry except for a watch with a leather band on his right wrist, which Kaiser always thought was strange, as Calvin was right-handed. He looked completely unconcerned, as if he just assumed the world would fall into line with whatever it was he wanted.

Which it always did in the end, didn't it? The arrogant sonofabitch.

"You know why you're here, don't you?" Kaiser asked.

Calvin nodded. "You think I killed someone."

His lawyer leaned over. "I strongly suggest that you don't say anything, Mr. James. Let me speak for you."

Calvin shrugged. Again, unconcerned.

He'd been assigned a public defender, a thin, scraggly man named Aaron Rooney, whom Kaiser had met only once before. Rooney graduated from law school eight months earlier and was scratching out a living working for the state, which was about the worst job a lawyer starting out could have, with the worst clients. There was zero glory in being a public defender. Some trial experience, maybe, but the majority of cases were pled out and never saw the inside of a courtroom. Rooney was dressed in a baggy brown suit, his beard five days old, his hair flattened down with too much gel.

"We've been looking for you for a long time," Kaiser said. "Three victims over the past nine years, buried in shallow graves. I'm sure there are more, but we just haven't found them yet. Took us a while to ID you. Since we didn't know your name, we've been calling you the Sweetbay Strangler."

"I like it," Calvin said.

"Want to know how we finally found you?"

"Why don't you just tell us?" the lawyer said.

"The first girl you killed all those years ago finally turned up, which now brings your murder count to four." Kaiser watched Calvin's face. The man's expression was neutral, with only a slight etching of polite interest. Bright eyes. Handsome motherfucker. Might have been a movie star had he gone a different way with his life, but men like Calvin James — men who raped and murdered women — never went another way. Their urges always got the better of them. "You remember your first one, right? You buried her body in the woods, after you chopped her up. She was a high school junior, a cheerleader."

Calvin said nothing, continuing to listen politely.

"In case you forgot, her name was Angela Wong. Sixteen-year-old, reported missing some fourteen years ago." Kaiser slid a manila folder across the table and opened it. Inside was a high school photo of Angela, full color. "She'd be thirty now, same age as me. And she was a good friend of mine, which makes me a little more than pissed off to be sitting across the table from her killer."

"Detective, if you have a personal grudge against my client —" Rooney began.

"Fuck off," Kaiser said to him, his eyes never leaving Calvin's face. "Angela was a beautiful girl, wasn't she? Now there's nothing left of her but a pile of bones and her purse. Oh, and her camera, which had pictures of you in it." He leaned in. "Tell me. Did you know from the day you met her that you were going to kill her? Was it Angela you really wanted all along? I don't know if it was planned or not, and I don't give a fuck. But killing her gave you a taste for it, didn't it? Except you didn't dismember the others. Only Angela. Only the first one."

Calvin James's lips twitched, but he said nothing.

"You sick motherfucker," Kaiser said. "Is that why you got close to Georgina back then, so you could get to her best friend?"

At the mention of Georgina's name, Calvin's mouth opened slightly. Then he smiled, the connection finally dawning on him.

"I know you," he said softly. "Holy shit-balls. You were their little high school friend, the skinny dude who was always following them around like a puppy, always so grateful whenever they paid any attention to you. You were persistent, I'll give you that." His grin widened, revealing even, white teeth. "I see your man meat finally came in. You're looking well, buddy. All grown up, all macho. Now you're a guy with a gun and a badge. Just look at you."

Kaiser returned the smile.

"So tell me, how is our lovely Georgina?" Calvin asked. "How long did she keep you in the friend zone? Did you two ever get drunk and just make out one night? How far up her skirt did you get before she slapped your hand away? She never slapped mine."

"This is all very fascinating, but who's Georgina?" Calvin's lawyer interrupted, looking pained.

The criminal and the cop both ignored him.

"How involved was she?" Kaiser spoke

directly to Calvin. "Did she help you?"

"You haven't talked to her?" Calvin sat back in his chair and rubbed his chin. The handcuffs clanged together. He looked as relaxed as could be. "You should talk to her. I can't speak for her. She wouldn't like that."

"At the very most, she was your accomplice." Kaiser glanced at Aaron Rooney. The public defender seemed completely out of his depth. "At the very least, she'll turn state's evidence against you. We're going to pick her up later today."

Calvin snorted. "So I guess that means you two aren't friends anymore."

"We have you cold, Calvin," Kaiser said with an icy smile. "You don't have to talk to me. I'm sure Georgina will. And even if she doesn't, I'll find out what happened that night. Like you said, I've always been persistent. I'm like a dog with a bone with this kind of thing. I'll dig and dig until I figure it out. See you at the trial." He stood, pushing his chair out.

"She still beautiful?" Calvin asked. "Not that she was quite as beautiful as Angela, but Georgina had something back then, didn't she? Something . . . special. I think you and I were the only ones who ever saw it. We have that in common, at least."

"Fuck you," Kaiser said, bristling at the

thought that he and this murderer were anything alike.

Calvin James laughed.

Kaiser's phone vibrates on the nightstand beside him, bringing him back to the present. It's five minutes before six A.M., and nobody calls him this early unless somebody's dead. He checks the number and answers it, because he's a cop and that's his damn job.

"Morning, Lieutenant," he says softly, so he doesn't wake Kim.

"Good morning." The voice on the other end is gravelly and female, the voice of a lifelong chain-smoker who's only recently quit. It's his boss, Luca Miller. "You sound awake."

"Been up for a bit. Got something for me?"

"Two bodies near Green Lake." She coughed into his ear. "Supposed to be Canning's case but thought you might want it."

"Why's that?"

"One of them is a dismembered woman. Buried in a series of shallow graves."

Kaiser sits up straighter. "What did you say the address was?"

"I didn't," she says, and recites it for him.

"You're shitting me," he says, stunned, when the GPS in his head pinpoints the location. "I'll take a shower, be there in thirty minutes."

"No rush, they're already dead." Luca Miller says this without a trace of sarcasm. She's been on the job a long time, and she's just stating facts. "CSI's just starting. An hour's fine. When you get there, do what you can at the scene, and I'll have Peebles ready for you."

She's referring to Greg Peebles, the head medical examiner for King County. He's the best of the best, but he's usually unavailable at short notice because he's always in high demand.

"Peebles? Really?" Kaiser says. "How are you going to make that happen? Rub a genie and make a wish?"

"I said there were two bodies," Luca says. "One's a child."

That'll do it. They always prioritize children. And if the child was found with a dismembered woman, chances are the kid didn't die by accident.

He disconnects the call. Kim sits up beside him, rubbing her eyes, her tangled hair spilling over her bare shoulders. She's not a classically beautiful woman, but she's undeniably attractive, and there's a warmth in her smile that people are drawn to. She's often compared to Jennifer Aniston. "What's going on?"

He tells her, and when he finishes speaking, she looks more awake.

"You think this is Calvin James?" she asks.

"It could be coincidence, but you know how I feel about coincidences. Anyway, it's after six. You should probably get going." Kaiser eases out of bed and heads for the bathroom. He doesn't have to walk far. His apartment is small. He likes it that way — less to clean. And besides, he's rarely ever home for long. "I gotta take a shower."

"Want some company?"

He pauses, then sighs. Really, it has to stop. This can't continue. It's wrong and it's messy and the longer it goes, the more complicated it feels. They work together, for fuck's sake. She's his goddamned partner.

He doesn't answer her, pretends he didn't hear the question. He enters the bathroom.

But he leaves the door open.

7

A drop of water lands on Kaiser's forehead, falling from a leaf or a branch somewhere above him. It drizzled earlier, and the scent of the soil and trees would have been refreshing if not for the circumstances. Kaiser hasn't been in these woods in over five years. And yet the crime scene now looks eerily similar to the one from back then. Only this time around, there are two victims: a woman and a child.

The woman was found first. Or, to put it more accurately, the woman's *body parts* were found first. Her torso is in one large piece, buried two and a half feet deep in the ground between two trees. Scattered around it, in a series of shallow minigraves, are her feet, lower legs, upper legs, hands, forearms, upper arms, and head. Her eyes are missing. Two jagged holes remain where her eyeballs once were, now scraped out of their sockets. Crime-scene investigators are still looking for them, but they won't be found. Whoever took her eyes did so for a reason.

It's anyone's guess what she looked like when she was alive. The face is cold and gray, the skin waxy, the lips pulled back from the teeth in the classic death grimace. There's too much dirt and soil matted into the hair to determine whether it's black or brown. Based on the tearing of the skin, she was taken apart with a tool that had teeth. Maybe a saw. Dismemberments are always horrific, but this one feels especially gruesome.

She's buried in almost the exact same place as Angela Wong.

He turns his attention to the child, whose body, thankfully, has been left intact. Found less than five feet away from the woman, the grave is a foot and a half deep, three feet long, one foot wide. A tiny grave for a tiny body.

He looks to be about two years old, based on his size and the number of teeth he has. He's dressed in Spider-Man pajama pants and a blue hoodie, no T-shirt, little legs tucked into shiny red rubber rain boots. While cause of death is always determined by the medical examiner, it's clear the boy has been strangled. The dark-red marks around the throat and the self-inflicted bite marks on the boy's tongue are both consistent with asphyxiation, along with the telltale pinpoint blood clots in the sclera, also known as petechial hemorrhaging. Other than a few faded bruises on his shins — consistent with being an active toddler — he looks normal. The cheeks are still chubby, the belly comfortably round. The top of his diaper is sticking out of his pajama pants.

Just a baby, really.

The hoodie is open to reveal markings on the boy's small chest. At first glance, Kaiser thought it was blood. But it's not, because dried blood smears in the rain, and this has not budged. The killer drew on him, using dark-red lipstick to draw a perfect heart. And in the center of the heart are two short words.

SEE ME.

"I see you," Kaiser says quietly to the dead child. "I see you."

The crime-scene photographer bends over and takes several more pictures of the boy, the bright flash from the camera illuminating everything around her in brief sparks. "This is terrible, huh? Seen anything like this before, Kai?" she asks.

He resists the urge to zip up the boy's hoodie. "Yes," he says, his tone curt.

She waits for him to elaborate, but he doesn't. Correctly sensing that he's not in a chatty mood, she steps back, leaving him alone with his thoughts. He nods to the paramedics, waiting patiently nearby with a stretcher, indicating that the bodies are ready for transport to the morgue. The crime-scene techs are handling the female victim's remains, which all have to be photographed and catalogued individually.

Are they mother and son? Is this the work of Calvin James? The heart on the boy's chest reminds Kaiser of the doodle on his notepad from the trial. Everything about this reeks of the Sweetbay Strangler.

Except for the gouged-out eyes. That's new. As is killing a child. But monsters, like everyone else, can evolve.

The scene is secure, cordoned off with yellow crime-scene tape. The entrance to this section of the woods is located at the edge of a cul-de-sac, right between two houses on Briar Crescent. Kaiser leaves the woods and heads back to the street, unsurprised to find that a sizable crowd has gathered behind the road barricades. Curious neighbors, of course, along with a couple of news vans and a few reporters.

Less than two hundred yards away is the house with the blue door. Georgina's old house. He hasn't set foot inside it since he was sixteen, but he can still remember the smell of the Crock-Pot, always bubbling with something. Neither Georgina nor her busy doctor father were ever great cooks, but they could make a mean beef stew in the slow cooker.

How many times did Kaiser ring that doorbell to pick her up to go the movies, or the food court at the mall? How many times did he sit in her living room watching *Melrose Place,* a show he pretended to hate but secretly enjoyed because it meant he could spend time with her? How many times did they sit on her floor in her bedroom, drinking Slurpees from the 7-Eleven and listening to Soundgarden and Pearl Jam, on the nights her father worked late? Right here, on this street, nineteen years ago, when they were juniors at St. Martin's high . . . and also best friends.

Back when Angela was still here. Back before she was declared a missing person, before her face was on posters all over the city, before her bones were found in these same woods years later. Before Calvin James was arrested. Before Georgina went to prison.

Before.

Before.

Before.

Kaiser wonders who lives there now, wonders if they know the baggage that house comes with, the secrets it hides. It was photographed extensively after Angela's remains were found. Reporters were titillated by the fact that her body was buried less than a football field's length away from where the woman charged with her murder slept every night.

Kim Kellogg approaches, dressed in tight jeans and a fitted jacket, her blond hair swept up into a sleek ponytail. The only indication that his partner is a police detective and not a college student is the gold shield clipped to her jacket. Kim is method where he's madness, and they're a good fit on the job. And in bed, too, if he's being honest.

Everybody has a weakness. Kaiser's has always been unavailable women.

"How'd it go?" He keeps his voice clipped and professional. There are too many other cops around for him to speak to her casually.

"I checked the missing-persons reports in Seattle," she says. A stray strand of blond hair blows across her face, and Kaiser moves to brush it away. He catches himself just in time. "Nobody matches the description of

120

the boy. I've sent a request out to the surrounding cities, so I'm sure we'll get a hit soon."

"He was healthy, with newer clothes," Kaiser says. "Somebody loved that kid. What about the woman?"

"Nothing yet. I have two officers down at the precinct working on it, but there are too many missing females in that age range."

"Where's the guy who found them?"

Kim points to an older couple standing on the sidewalk, talking with a few of the other neighbors. "Mr. and Mrs. Heller. He found them; she called 911. I'll bring them over."

Cliff Heller is a sixtysomething-year-old retiree with snow-white hair and a beard to match, and he looks completely traumatized to have discovered the bodies. Roberta Heller is a full foot shorter than her husband, dressed in a fluffy white bathrobe with exactly one pink hair curler secured above her forehead. In contrast, she looks elated to be involved in the most exciting thing that's happened in her neighborhood in a while. Her enthusiasm would be dampened considerably if she had actually seen the two dead bodies.

"I have a '69 'Vette that I've been trying to fix up for the past few years," Cliff Heller tells Kaiser. "Body's in good shape; she'd be sweet if I could get her going again. I popped into the garage after breakfast, thinking I'd get a bit of work done on it before we had to leave for church —"

"He doesn't care about the stupid Corvette," his wife interrupts.

"Right. So the dog starts yapping and I thought I'd take her into the woods for a go." Heller sighs. "Usually I walk her, but it was raining —"

"He doesn't care about the rain," his wife snaps again.

"And that's when you found the bodies," Kaiser prompts.

"Maggie found them," Heller says, his shoulders sagging. He points to their house, where Kaiser could make out a furry golden face in the window, watching the street commotion. "She started barking, and then she was digging at something, and I saw an arm sticking out of the dirt. At first I thought it was a doll, but when I got closer, I realized it wasn't attached to anything. It was . . . it was quite a shock. I fell back, and that's when I found the boy."

Heller's chin begins to waver, and then his voice chokes. "I know I wasn't supposed to touch him, but when I saw his face and his arm peeking out from the hole, I didn't think, I just reacted. I . . . I pulled him out of the dirt. He's so small. We got grandkids that age." He takes a deep breath and closes his eyes. When he opens them again a moment later, he's calmer. "I didn't mess up the crime scene, did I?"

"You reacted how any normal person would."

"Thank god." The confirmation that he didn't screw anything up seems to make Heller feel better. His wife rubs his back with one hand. With the other hand, she takes a sip of her coffee, her gaze flitting around, watching the officers work.

Kaiser asks a few more questions. Neither Heller remembers seeing anything strange the evening before, no unfamiliar cars parked in the cul-de-sac, no flashlights, and no noises or voices.

"We do go to bed pretty early," Cliff Heller says. "Eight-thirty, nine at the latest. So we wouldn't have seen anything after then, anyway."

"Say, does this have anything to do with Angela Wong?" Roberta Heller asks brightly, looking up at Kaiser. The lone pink curler above her forehead bobs. "You know, the girl who went missing all those years ago? Her remains were found in these woods, I'm not sure if you're aware of that. It could be related. Walter must be going out of his mind wondering what the heck is going on."

Kaiser's head snaps up. "Walter?"

"Walter Shaw," Mrs. Heller says. She points to the house with the blue door. "His daughter was the one who —"

"I know who she is." Kaiser stares at the blue door. "He still lives there?" He could have sworn Walter sold the house a few years back.

"Yes, and his daughter will be moving in with him in a few days." Roberta Heller sniffs. "Back here, to this neighborhood! She's been in prison, you know. I like Walter, but let me tell you, his daughter is a piece of work. Uppity little thing with her big important job, always clicking around in her high heels whenever she came back to visit. And all along, her best friend is buried in these very woods. I always knew something was off about her —"

"Enough, Roberta," her husband says, placing a hand on her arm. "Enough."

It's all Kaiser can do not to rip the ridiculous curler out of the woman's hair. Instead, he hands Cliff Heller his card. "You think of anything more, call me, day or night."

The bodies are being moved. Kim has done a good job pushing the crowd farther away from the cul-de-sac, and only a hand-

124

ful of neighbors standing nearby can see the covered remains — one of them extremely small — being loaded into the backs of the emergency vehicles. Cliff Heller looks as if he might cry again, and even Roberta Heller softens a little at the sight of that tiny shape.

Kaiser takes a moment to scan the handful of people who are still milling around. All appear to be residents of the neighborhood, coffee cups or dog leashes in hand; more than a few are still in their pajamas. Civilians are always drawn to the excitement of a crime scene.

A second later, his eyes fix on a face. Not a face in the crowd. A face behind glass. Someone is home in the house with the blue door. Kaiser walks toward it, and a few seconds later his finger is poised above the doorbell. The door opens before he can press it.

Walter Shaw stands there, an inch shorter than Kaiser's own six feet two inch height. His short hair is grayer, and there are more lines around his eyes and mouth than were there the last time Kaiser saw him, five years ago. Other than that, Georgina's father looks more or less the same.

"You really still live here?" Kaiser asks, more a statement than a question. "I thought you would have sold the house.

After the . . . after the trial."

"Hello to you, too." Walter doesn't appear happy to see him at all. "Market was way down, and I wasn't going to sell it for pennies on the dollar. Besides that, nobody wanted it. Too much bad press, thanks to you."

"Is Georgina coming back here when she gets out?"

"This is my home, which makes it her home." The older man crosses his arms. "And where the hell else would she go?"

Kaiser stares at Walter Shaw, the father of his best friend from high school, the father of the woman he arrested. He'd sat at Walt's table, had eaten Walt's beef stew, had drunk Walt's beer when he wasn't home, had been in love with Walt's daughter.

Georgina's father stares back. It feels like a face-off of sorts, neither man wanting to back down, but neither knowing what to say next, either.

Kaiser speaks first. "Walt, I care about your daughter. I've always cared. I hope you know I was just doing my job." It's not exactly an apology, but it's the best he can do.

After a moment, Walter nods. It's not exactly an acceptance, but it's the best *he* can do. He jerks his head toward the activity in the cul-de-sac. "So what the hell's going on over there, anyway?"

"We're still figuring it out," Kaiser says. "By the way, has Georgina ever said anything to you about where Calvin James might be?"

The older man frowns. He doesn't like the question. Before Kaiser can rephrase it, the door slams shut in his face.

8

The dead child has been identified as Henry Bowen, age twenty-two months. His parents, Amelia and Tyson Bowen of Redmond, filed a report first thing that morning, and as far as they know, their young son is still missing. Kaiser will do the official death notification when they arrive.

At the very least, it's two mysteries solved. They know the child's name, and they've confirmed that their Jane Doe isn't the child's mother. Though it might have been easier, from an investigative standpoint, if she had been.

Thanks to the wonders of modern technology — also known as the smartphone — the photo Amelia Bowen used in her child's missing-person report was taken at bedtime the night before. Kaiser has no doubt it's their boy. He has the same hair, the same front teeth, the same Spider-Man pajamas. Whatever happened to Henry occurred sometime between 11:30 P.M., when his mother checked the video monitor before falling asleep, and 8:30 A.M., when she woke up and checked it again.

"What do we know about the parents?" he asks Kim. They're in the small break room of the morgue, where Kim tracked him down.

She pulls out her little black notebook. Though she's a whiz at technology, Kaiser's partner is old school when it comes to note taking, preferring to jot notes by hand rather than type into her phone, as most cops did nowadays. She even uses pencil, so she can erase mistakes if necessary. She says the act of handwriting helps her concentrate.

"They both work for Microsoft; he's a software engineer, she's in marketing. They live in a nice house; Zillow values it at just under a million. She drives a Lexus, he drives a BMW. Henry was in daycare at a place called Rainbow Jungle not far from the Microsoft campus."

"Rich," Kaiser says.

Kim makes a face. "That's not rich. That's slightly upper middle class — for Redmond, anyway."

He doesn't argue. He grew up in an apartment in Seattle with a single mother and ate Kraft macaroni and cheese three nights out of every week. His grandparents scraped together the money to pay for his Catholic education. Kim grew up near Bill Gates's neighborhood on the Eastside and went to private school. Their definition of "rich" differed, to say the least.

"What else? How did they sound on the phone?"

"I didn't speak to them, I spoke to the officer who's bringing them here." Kim is fixing herself a coffee. It's common knowledge within Seattle PD that the morgue has the best coffee, for reasons nobody can explain. "The mother said he normally wakes up around seven and hollers, but neither of them heard anything this morning so they stayed in bed. She went to check on him around eight-thirty. Found the window wide open and the little boy gone. She woke her husband and called 911 immediately because he's not yet able to climb out of the crib on his own."

"Do they have a nanny or a babysitter?" Kaiser asks, thinking about the dismembered woman.

"His only caregivers are the ones at the daycare, and the teenage girl who lives next door, who babysits for date nights. The teenage girl is fine, I checked her Instagram

130

and she's already posted three selfies this morning." Kim tugs at her ponytail. "None of the four caregivers at the daycare fit our Jane Doe. Two are too old, and the younger ones are both Jamaican. Our best bet is to ask the Bowens if they recognize her."

Kaiser looks up at her. "And how are we supposed to do that? Take a picture of just the nose and mouth?"

"Shit, that's right, the eyes are missing. I forgot."

Kaiser suppresses a sigh. Kim's a smart woman when it comes to certain things. Organized, meticulous with her notes and reports, very thorough. But every once in a while, her mind slips on an obvious detail, for no fucking reason. It drives Kaiser batshit, but he bites his tongue.

"When are the parents getting here?" he asks.

"There's traffic. Seahawks game. Might be an hour, maybe more."

"I'm going to go talk to Peebles." Kaiser stands up and stretches. The vertebrae in his spine crack in gratitude. "Call me when they get here."

He knocks before entering the room, though he doubts Greg Peebles hears anything when he's in the zone, working. The bodies have been placed on examining tables a few feet apart, and the ME is leaning over the boy. The child is covered with a sheet from the waist down, the heart drawn on his chest stark and unfaded.

SEE ME.

What the fuck does that mean? Donning a pair of latex-free gloves, Kaiser touches the heart gently with a gloved hand. It doesn't smudge.

The woman has been — for lack of a better expression — pieced back together, and from a distance it might appear that she's intact. But she's not. Under the harsh lights of the overhead lamp, the half-inch gap separating her head, legs, feet, arms, and hands from her torso is glaringly evident.

"I hate that you brought me a kid," Greg Peebles says to Kaiser in his slow drawl. No matter what's going on, the medical examiner never sounds like he's in a hurry, never sounds rushed or stressed. It's a great quality to never be unnerved, but it can be a pain in the ass for Kaiser when he's under pressure to find answers. Like right now. "This is my least favorite part of the job."

"But a dismembered woman is okay?"

Peebles shrugs. "I wasn't trying to be political, Kai. But an adult dead body shows up, part of you can't help but think, even just for a split second, 'What could that person have done to deserve that? What situation did they put themselves in?' But a dead kid shows up, and *nobody* thinks that, ever. Children are innocent. They're small. They can't defend themselves against predators. They've done nothing to warrant any violence against them. Bad things aren't supposed to happen to kids. It goes against everything we as a civilized society think is acceptable. Your protective instincts kick in." He pauses, then looks up, the light from his head lamp hitting Kaiser square in the eyes. "Okay, perhaps that was a bit political."

"Can you turn that off?" Kaiser asks, putting a hand up over his face to shield himself.

"Sorry." Peebles reaches up and switches the head lamp off. "So. The bodies are clean."

"Come on, Greg." Kaiser stares at the child in front of him. He doesn't disagree with Peebles; there is something incredibly wrong with seeing a person that small on an autopsy table. He's a homicide cop and trained to be objective, but a dead child goes straight to the heart of what makes him human. But so does a dismembered woman, and he hopes he never loses that empathy. "Don't fucking tell me that. Give me something. Start with the child."

"He's almost two years old, based on his teeth. But you already know that." Peebles switches his head lamp back on, his voice morphing back into that professional-but-mellow tone he always uses when describing his findings. "Well nourished, no signs of sexual trauma or physical abuse. No traces of bodily fluids on his clothing other than a copious amount of dried saliva on his hoodie. Probably his own; he had molars coming in."

"Nothing under the fingernails?"

"Bits of dirt and sand, but that's consistent with being a kid. He's been bathed recently. You can still smell the shampoo if you lean in close." Peebles leans over the body and inhales. If it were anyone else, it would be creepy. "Burt's Bees, same stuff my kids used when they were little. Supposed to be all-natural. He wasn't neglected. His parents loved him." His head snaps up, blinding Kaiser again with his head lamp. "Wait. The parents aren't the doers, are they?"

"Doesn't look like it," Kaiser says, squinting. "Cause of death?"

"All signs point to asphyxiation. Pressure marks on the neck indicate someone used his or her hands. I'm guessing it was a male because the marks looks like larger fingers, but don't take that to the bank. After my divorce, I dated this woman who had extremely large hands. It was rather disturbing. They made everything she touched seem small."

Despite the gravity of the situation, Kaiser snickers. Peebles blinks, not sure what he said that was so funny. They move over to the next table.

"Now for our Jane Doe. Rohypnol and alcohol in her system, small traces of THC. She smoked marijuana sometime in the past two days," Peebles says. "She also engaged in sexual activity — traces of condom lube and spermicide are present — and while there are some indications the sex was rough, I can't confirm she was raped. Traces of skin under the fingernails. At least some of it's her own, but I'll test it. She was dismembered with a saw, definitely postmortem."

"How postmortem?"

"Immediately after. It would have been messy. The unevenness of the cutting patterns suggests that the killer did it by hand. So, not a chainsaw. No tattoos, a small birthmark on her upper right thigh. Hair brown, but dyed an even darker brown. Nice manicure. She was probably around five-five, one-twenty. I'd put her age around twenty-one, maybe twenty-two years old. But don't take that to the bank."

"And her eyes?" Kaiser asks.

"Removed with something dull. My first thought was spoon, but now I'm thinking butter knife because there's minute tearing consistent with that." Peebles straightens up and removes his head lamp. It leaves an indent in his graying hair. "Fairly certain she was strangled with a foreign object, something stiffer that was placed around her neck."

"Bungee cord?"

"Belt would be my guess. There are scratches on the side of her jaw where she would have clawed at it to get it off. There's bruising on her back, as if someone held her down with a knee and choked her from behind. Want me to demonstrate?"

"No need," Kaiser says. He can picture it.

"Remind you of anything?" Peebles asks. His raised eyebrow tells Kaiser he's thinking the same thing. "Or anyone?"

"Calvin James." He lets out a long breath, thinking of the three women the Sweetbay Strangler murdered after Angela Wong. All three were killed in a similar manner, right down to the knee in the back, but he doesn't say anything further, and Peebles doesn't push. Greg's the medical examiner, Kaiser's the detective. They don't do each other's jobs.

"I thought I read something about him being spotted in Brazil," Peebles says. "Passing for a local, looking tanned and healthy. Or was it Argentina? This might have been a couple years ago now."

Kaiser doesn't answer. He'd read the same thing, but no police in any country had ever gotten a strong enough whiff of Calvin James to track him down. And that included the U.S.

"I'll give you some time with them." The ME peels off his gloves. They've been working together a long time, and if anyone knows what the detective's process is during this stage of a homicide investigation, it's Greg Peebles.

The door closes, and Kaiser pulls up a stool between the two tables. He focuses on the child. Only the night before, this little boy had been alive. Laughing, splashing in the tub, playing with his toys. One or both of his parents shampooed his hair with the Burt's Bees stuff lovingly, believing — as was absolutely their right — that there would be ten thousand more baths, ten thousand more laughs, ten thousand more bedtimes.

They're about to receive the worst news

of their lives. There'll be crying, shouting, and hysteria, interspersed with denial and disbelief. They'll weep over the child, then turn on each other, one accusing the other of leaving the window unlocked, one blaming the other for not checking on Henry first thing in the morning. Whether they can get through it, only time will tell, but the divorce rate for parents who've lost a child to kidnapping or foul play is exorbitantly high. They're each other's best reminder of the worst thing that's ever happened to them.

And the woman. She was somebody's daughter, granddaughter, friend. People are missing her, too. She wasn't a transient. Her teeth are white. She colored her hair. Her fingernails are covered in gel overlay, something you had a pay a manicurist to do. Homeless women did not spend money on manicures. And yet somebody had desecrated her, cutting her into pieces like she was a cardboard box ready for disposal.

It was something only a monster could do. Kaiser had met a monster like that once, had been introduced to him through his old friend Georgina.

And what does she know about this? She might be in prison, but has she been in touch somehow with Calvin James, in a way that doesn't show up on those monthly reports? Is she aware that two dead bodies have been found in the woods behind her house just days before she's due to come home, killed in a similar manner to her old boyfriend's signature style?

Kaiser reins himself in. It's extremely dangerous to assume this is the work of the Sweetbay Strangler. He has to stay objective or he'll miss something. Besides, it would be incredibly reckless, and stupid, for Calvin James to come back here. Not that psychopaths operate using the same logic as regular people.

Kaiser touches the heart on the boy's chest again. The dark-red lipstick really does resemble blood. With any luck, they might be able to find out what brand it is, and if it turns out to be something exotic or hard to get, it might provide a lead. A long shot, but they had nothing else to go on.

"I don't know how you can sit in here by yourself," Kim's voice behind him says, and he jumps. She's back, a sheet of paper in her hand. "I know this is how you work, but it's strange."

Kaiser stifles his annoyance, both at her comment and at being interrupted. "What's up?"

"The parents are here."

"That was fast." Alarmed, Kaiser stands up. "The body isn't ready. The boy needs to be washed before they can see him."

"I thought it would be longer, but traffic opened up. You have to go talk to them, at least. They're going out of their minds."

"Fuck." Kaiser thinks fast. "Okay. Call Counseling Services. Get a grief counselor here, pronto. And then go find me a mask."

Kim blinks, confused. "What kind of mask?"

"Some kind of mask," Kaiser says, impatient. He hates having to explain things to anyone. As much as he likes Kim, he's irritated that after a year of working and sleeping together, she still can't read his damn mind. "Not a costume mask. Something plain, like a sleeping mask, so I can cover the woman's empty eye sockets and take a picture. Hopefully they can tell us who she is."

"No need for a mask. There's an app for that."

"Huh?"

Kim reaches over and plucks his iPhone out of his jacket pocket. She taps at the screen for a few seconds, then hands the phone back.

"It's called a censor-bar app," she says. "You take the picture, then add a black bar anywhere you want." Seeing the look on his face — Kaiser is the first to admit he's not great when it comes to new technology — she takes the phone from him again. "Allow me."

She positions herself above the table where Jane Doe is and snaps a photo. She then taps the phone again a few times before handing it back to Kaiser. The whole thing takes less than a minute. "Done. Saved in your camera roll. I even filtered it a little to make her skin look like it has some color. Just be sure not to accidentally show them the original."

He checks the photo and has to admit he's impressed. From the neck up, with the black bar across the eyes, the woman in the photo still looks dead, but not *as* dead. Thanks to the filter Kim used, the grayish skin appears pinker. "This actually works. Thanks."

She puts a hand on his arm. "This is bugging you more than usual, isn't it, Kai? You think this is Calvin James?"

Clearly everyone else seems to think so or they wouldn't keep asking. Kim wasn't his partner back when Angela's remains were found, and Kaiser didn't even work the first two Sweetbay Strangler murders; they were another detective's cases. But yes, it's hitting him hard. It all feels too familiar, too close to home, as if this is all happening specifically to remind him of the past.

Again, it's a narrow-minded line of thinking, and very dangerous. His job isn't to find evidence to fit the theory. It's to come up with a theory based on the evidence. He has to stay objective, but it's getting harder.

In the elevator, Kim touches his hand, speaking in a low, soft voice. "Dave's working tonight, graveyard shift. I can come over after ten-thirty, stay all night. If you want."

"Maybe," Kaiser says.

But he already knows he wants her to, and he hates himself for it.

9

Henry Bowen's parents react exactly as Kaiser knew they would. They scream, cry, blame the police, blame each other, and then eventually fall silent as they try to individually process the new reality they now face.

Amelia Bowen's eyes are slightly glazed. She sits silently on a small blue sofa in the police station's conference room, subdued on the outside, raging fire on the inside. Tyson Bowen paces the room like a caged lion, eyes bright and intense, hands curled into claws, ready to destroy someone. Based on Henry's age, Kaiser expected to meet younger parents, but the Bowens are older, mid-forties.

"We adopted him." Amelia Bowen's voice is soft and distant. "Tyson and I met in college, but we were so busy, we thought we'd wait to have kids until we were at least thirty, and just enjoy our time together."

Tyson Bowen stops pacing. "Amelia, don't —"

Kaiser raises a hand. It's better to let her speak; she'll be more responsive and apt to remember something if she's allowed to think things through in her own way. The first question he'll ask, of course, is about Henry's biological mother, now that he knows Amelia didn't give birth to him. He has the phone in his hand, the censor-bar photo of the female victim just a tap away.

But not yet.

"All our friends seemed to be waiting to have kids, too," Amelia continues, "and it was nice to go out for dinner and drinks, to be twenty-six, and then twenty-eight, and then twenty-nine, and not have to worry about sleepless nights and babysitters and the expense of having a child. Then we turned thirty, and it still wasn't the right time, because we decided we wanted to be further along in our careers before slowing down to become parents. We worked hard, both got promoted, and then we realized we needed the right house, in the right neighborhood, in a good school district. And then suddenly we were thirty-five, and we started trying to get pregnant, only to find out we'd waited too long and now we couldn't. Four rounds of IVF, two miscarriages. We put ourselves on the adoption list, waited two years to get picked. And when we got word that Henry's biological mother selected us, it was the greatest day of our lives."

The disconnect in her voice fades. She pauses. The loose bun at the top of her head is askew, and she reaches up and plays with an errant lock of brown hair dangling down one side.

"We were in the delivery room. The first time I held him, a minute after he was born, he instantly felt like mine. It didn't matter that he had just come out of another woman's body. He was mine, and I felt it, and I know Henry felt it, because he looked up at me and we both just knew. And I thought, why the hell did we wait so long? Why did we think everything had to be perfect? Because children are perfect, and everything falls into place when you hold your child in your arms. All the things you think you're going to worry about don't matter." She meets her husband's gaze. Tyson Bowen is standing in the corner, watching her with tears in his eyes. "And now he's gone. I don't understand. I don't understand. I don't understand."

She leans forward, her chest racked with sobs. Her husband sits down beside her and holds her tightly.

"I'll give you a few minutes," Kaiser says, but neither of them acknowledge him. Right now, it's just them, wrapped around each other, their grief wrapped around them.

He slips out of the room, indicating to the grief counselor that she can go on in. The Bowens' child is dead, and while there is a sense of urgency to find out what happened to him, he can allow them ten minutes to cry. He heads to his desk down the hall and logs into his computer.

"Report came back on the lipstick used to write on the kid's chest," Kim says. She's seated at her desk, directly across from him. "I saw you were busy with the parents and didn't want to interrupt you."

"I see that," he says, clicking on the report. "Shit, that was fast."

"It's because I had them narrow it down," Kim says, and he looks up. "I asked them to check if it was a brand made by Shipp Pharmaceuticals."

"Why would —" he begins, and then stops as he makes the connection. "Oh. Right."

Shipp Pharmaceuticals, Georgina's old company. And that, right there, is why he appreciates Kim. For every obvious detail she misses, there's one she finds that nobody else would possibly have thought of.

"My hunch was right. It *is* a Shipp-made

product." There's a note of triumph in his partner's voice. "They're about to launch a new line of cosmetics, and this particular lipstick only comes in ten shades. The heart on the kid's chest was drawn in one of them."

"About to launch?"

"They're not widely available yet. You can only buy the lipstick at Nordstrom, and only at the flagship store here in Seattle. It's only been on sale for one week."

"One week? That's it?"

She smiles, pleased that he's pleased. "That's it."

"Call the store and —"

"Done. They'll send over the security footage shortly."

He sits back in his chair and gives her a smile. "Great work."

"It all ties back to Georgina Shaw, Kai." Kim is bouncing in her chair, her ponytail bobbing behind her. "Clearly someone's trying to get her attention. I called down to Hazelwood, requested copies of her visitor's log, phone calls, mail. Maybe she's been in contact with Calvin James."

Even if she has, the reports won't show that, as Kaiser well knows. But he can't tell Kim he's been paying a prison guard for information on Georgina, so he simply says,

"Good thinking."

"You could always talk to her, too. She gets out in a couple of days."

Kaiser turns away. He doesn't want his partner to see his face. His feelings for Georgina are complicated, and they always have been.

"I know you two were close once, but that was a long time ago," Kim says. "Don't let your bias get in the way of doing everything you can to solve these murders. The female victim was killed in the exact same way as Angela Wong. She was buried in the same woods, right by Georgina's house. The lipstick is from a company she worked for. You know how many brands of lipstick there are in the United States, Kai? I looked it up. Thousands. Big names, small names, brands that are now discontinued but that you can still find on eBay. This wasn't some old lipstick the killer had lying around. It was chosen deliberately."

Kim's mind is in full analytic mode. He can tell by the way she's speaking but not looking at him, her speech rapid but extra clear. "It has to be Calvin James. He's still out there. Maybe he's back. And maybe your old friend Georgina knows all about it."

"You didn't see her at the trial five years

ago, Kim," he says. "She wouldn't even look at him. She never made eye contact with him while she was testifying, not until the very end, and that's only because he spoke to her."

"She was terrified?"

"No, it wasn't fear. Something else. Resentment, maybe. Like he was a reminder of the person she used to be, and she hated him for it."

Calvin James might have been charged with the murders of four women, but it was Georgina Shaw's arrest that kicked the case into the media spotlight. A Big Pharma executive involved in the cold-case murder of her teenage best friend? It was more entertaining than a Lifetime movie, more titillating than an episode of *20/20*.

Nothing is more satisfying to humans than watching another person fail. Especially when it's someone who has everything you don't: beauty, brains, an education, a high-paying job, a rich fiancé.

There are three versions of Georgina Shaw that Kaiser knows. The first is the girl he knew in high school — the sweet cheerleader who had friends in every social circle, and who got straight As. The second was the girl she'd become after she'd met Calvin — distracted, consumed, unavailable, selfish. The third was the woman he'd arrested in the Shipp boardroom fourteen years later — successful, mature, exhausted . . . and remorseful.

Which version is she now?

Kim is on the phone, talking to someone who can only be her husband, judging by the gentle tone of her voice. Kaiser makes his way back to the Bowens, his mind sifting through all the questions he still needs answers to.

Is it possible that Georgina is still in love with Calvin, and that her avoidance of him during the trial five years ago was all just an act? He slipped her something that day in the courtroom, something that still eats at Kaiser whenever he thinks of it. She denied it was anything important, but he doesn't believe her. Of course he doesn't. Remorseful or not, nobody's a better liar than Georgina Shaw.

He opens the door to the conference room. The Bowens are huddled together on the couch. The grief counselor is speaking softly. Three heads look up at Kaiser when he enters.

"I'm so sorry," he says again. There's no point in asking them how they're doing.

"We want to find out who did this," Tyson Bowen says. He's a bit calmer than he was earlier, but not much. His voice is shaking. Beside him, his wife nods.

"Absolutely." Kaiser pulls out his phone, and taps it to pull up the picture of the dead woman with the censor bar. "I need you to look at this picture and tell me if you recognize the woman."

Amelia Bowen leans forward, takes a good look at his phone, and gasps. "That's Claire Toliver," she says. "Oh my god." She looks to her husband for confirmation, and though it takes him a few seconds longer, he confirms her statement with a brisk nod.

"Who's Claire Toliver?" Kaiser asks them.

"Henry's birth mother," Amelia Bowen says. "Is she dead? What's wrong with her eyes?"

Kaiser answers the first question, but not the second. They don't need to know.

10

The report Kim requested from the warden at Hazelwood is in Kaiser's email the following morning. Encompassing all five years of Georgina's prison stay, it's too large to download to his phone, so he sits at Kim's desk with his coffee and logs into her computer. His partner won't be in for another hour — she left his apartment early this morning to shower and change — and whenever she's not in, he prefers to sit at her desk. She's neater. The top of Kim's desk is always clear, the pens arranged like a bouquet in their ceramic holder. In contrast, Kaiser's desk looks like a junkie tossed it searching for drugs.

He scrolls through the report quickly. There's less detail in it than the reports he receives from the corrections officer he pays every month, and of course there are no personal notes. But it is interesting to see the past five years of Georgina Shaw's life summed up in one long spreadsheet. It gives Kaiser a different perspective on the information he's had all along.

Her mail, for instance. Like any inmate of notoriety, Georgina gets fan mail, and in the span of five years she's received over a thousand letters. But ten of those letters were sent from the same address. Somehow, this didn't register when Kaiser received his monthly reports from his inside source, and he can only assume he missed it because those reports only listed sender *names,* which are all different.

Whoever wrote to Georgina from an address in Spokane, Washington, used a different moniker each time. Tony Stark. Clark Kent. Bruce Banner. Charles Xavier. And so on. The "real-life" identities of fictional superheroes.

"Fuck," Kaiser mutters. It's a hell of an oversight, and he has nobody to blame but himself.

He runs the Spokane address through the Seattle PD database and comes up with a hit for Ursula Archer. In her mid-sixties, she's a retired librarian whose husband passed away the year before. Kaiser picks up the phone and dials the number.

Thirty seconds later he's speaking to the woman. It takes another fifteen seconds to explain who he is and why he's calling, but she's not suspicious. If anything, the woman sounds happy to have someone to talk to.

"You must be calling about Dominic," Ursula Archer says. Her voice is both soft and sharp, every syllable pronounced crisply, although her tone isn't harsh. She reminds Kaiser of a teacher he had in high school. "He stayed with us a few years ago. We were his foster parents for three years. He wrote letters to a woman, you said?"

Kaiser stifles his disappointment. Clearly the letters aren't from Calvin James. "Yes, to an inmate at Hazelwood Correctional Institute named Georgina Shaw."

The woman sighs, and he can almost picture her shaking her head on the other line. Her driver's license photo, which he's pulled up on his computer screen, depicts a woman with dark-blond hair in the early stages of gray, cut in a short bob that's slightly longer at the front.

"The name doesn't ring a bell," she says. "But then, Dominic wrote to quite a few people in prison. It started as school project. He was doing some kind of research on life in prison after Scared Straight came to his school to do a talk. You've heard of that program?"

Kaiser was only vaguely familiar with it,

154

but knew the gist — it involved former inmates convincing kids to stay in school and away from drugs and gangs. He glances toward the wall clock at the precinct, wondering how he can get her off the phone. "Yes, ma'am. Well, I'm sorry to have bothered —"

"Anyway, Dominic decided to do his social studies project on life behind bars, and he came across a website where you can write to inmates. Next thing we know, we've got mail coming from prisons all over the country. Graham, my late husband, was pretty upset. After all, these were convicted criminals who were sending letters to our home address. He didn't want Dominic writing to them anymore, but I convinced him to let it go, that it didn't seem to be doing any harm. We ended up getting him a post office box so he could have mail sent there instead. We told him to never give out personal information, and to never send anyone money."

Despite none of this being useful to his investigation, Kaiser finds himself curious. "What was he writing to them about?"

"Initially he was fascinated with how they ended up there, but after a while he was only writing to the female inmates. Some of them sent love letters. I think he liked the attention."

Kaiser stifles a chuckle. "Well, I appreciate your time —"

"I think about him often, you know. He had a rough start, was in foster care since he was very young." Ursula sighs into his ear. "But he has exceptional survival skills. That, I believe."

"He did use superhero names on all his correspondence," Kaiser says.

"That's something he'd do," Ursula says with a laugh. "He always wished he was someone else."

It takes Kaiser another minute before he can wrangle himself off the phone politely, but he's not too annoyed; the woman sounded lonely.

"Seriously?" a voice behind Kaiser says, and he turns to find Kim standing there, coffee in hand. "You realize you have your own desk three feet away, right? I hate it when you sit at my desk. You make everything . . . messy." She waves her free hand in a gesture of distaste.

"I like your desk," he says, but he picks himself up out of the chair and moves over. "It's so clean. Even the air around it smells fresher. Thought you weren't going to be in for another half hour."

"I decided to come in earlier after all,"

she says, and very subtly, her body language changes in a way that would only be noticeable to someone who knows her intimately. And Kaiser knows her intimately. Her voice drops. "Dave was waiting for me when I got home. He didn't ask me questions," she adds quickly, seeing the look on Kaiser's face, "but he did say he thinks we need to get away for the weekend and spend some time together. So we're going to Scottsdale on Friday, back to the resort where we got married. He already booked it." She holds Kaiser's gaze for a full ten seconds before looking away.

"Ah." He keeps his tone light. "Sounds nice. I'm sure you'll have a great time."

It's all he can say. The heaviness in his heart surprises him, even though he knows the affair should have ended ages ago.

Fuck that. It should have never started in the first place.

He busies himself with tidying up his desk so they don't have to talk. Their relationship plays out in his mind in a series of snapshots: Kim propped up in bed beside him as he catches up on some computer work, her bare breasts glowing from the light of the laptop screen, nipples like fresh mosquito bites. Kim snaking her hand into his boxer briefs as she makes a phone call to her husband to tell him that she'll be working all night. Kim in the shower only that morning, the water sliding down her back as she bends forward so he can take her from behind. He swallows the memories down with a long sip of hot coffee, burning his throat in the process.

His desk phone rings, and he's grateful for the distraction. It's Julia Chan, returning his call. She's the roommate of Henry Bowen's biological mother, and he tried calling her last night, after Claire's parents met him at the morgue to confirm their daughter's identity. It had been a long night, especially since Kim had come over afterward.

"I just got your message. I'm heading into work, Detective," the young woman says, sounding distracted and put out. "I have an early meeting and I'm already late. What's this about?"

"I have some questions about Claire Toliver," he says. "Can I stop by your office and speak to you today?"

"Sure. Do me a favor and flash your badge. It's the only way they'll let me out of the meeting early."

He leaves the precinct without saying good-bye to Kim. But at the elevator, he takes one last look at the back of his partner's head, blond hair pulled back neatly into her signature ponytail. She seems to feel his eyes on her and looks up. He avoids eye contact and steps into the elevator.

It's over.

Thank fucking god.

11

Strathroy, Oakwood & Strauss looks like every other big law firm Kaiser's ever been in, and at eight A.M., it's already bustling. A giant engraved logo behind the reception desk greets him, where two young women, probably fresh out of college, are wearing headsets and answering the phones with bored efficiency. The badge gets their attention, and he's assured that the person he's asking for will be located as soon as possible. In the meantime, would he like a cup of coffee while he waits?

Yes. Yes, he would.

The coffee is hot and frothy and covered with cinnamon sprinkles. It's also damned good, and he sips it slowly. Claire Toliver's parents took the news of their daughter's death terribly the night before, as there's no other way to take it. Her father demanded questions Kaiser had no answers for. Her mother's sobs could be heard from one end of the long morgue hallway to the other. And now here he is at the law firm, waiting to speak to Claire's roommate in order to learn more about the young woman's life.

He uses the downtime to investigate his dead victim's social media accounts. There's only one that he can find, a LinkedIn profile, and this surprises him, considering Claire came of age at the height of social media. She has no Facebook, no Instagram, no Twitter. Her LinkedIn profile tells him she graduated from Puget Sound State University with a bachelor's degree in political science and a French minor. She was in her second year of law school at the same university and doing a three-month internship at Strathroy, Oakwood & Strauss, "because they have a special focus on women's rights, which are human rights." She was clearly a fan of Hillary Clinton.

The professional photo Claire uploaded to her LinkedIn account looks nothing like the corpse on the table at the morgue. And yet there's no mistaking it's her. Same long, dark hair, same face shape. The only detail the photo adds are her eyes. Blue. A beautiful young woman who had a bright future ahead of her.

"Detective?" a voice says, and Kaiser looks up to see an attractive woman in her early twenties standing there. "I'm Julia Chan. Sorry to keep you waiting. I was in a meeting and my phone was on silent. Someone had to track me down."

"Not a problem," Kaiser says, shaking the outstretched hand. The hand is small but the grip is firm.

"We can talk in one of the conference rooms," she says. "Interns are only assigned cubicles, and we wouldn't get any privacy there."

He follows her down the hall and around the corner. Despite the early hour, everyone is dressed in business attire and moving with an air of harried importance. They look at Kaiser curiously as they pass, but Julia Chan doesn't break stride, her taupe-colored pumps tapping soundlessly on the carpet in machinelike precision. She's dressed in a pleated, black knee-length skirt and crisp white blouse, her hair pulled back into a bun at the nape of her neck. They enter the first conference room, and she closes the door.

Only when they're alone does he see the stress on her pretty face.

"I've been covering for her here since last Thursday," Julia says, sitting down at the table and gesturing for him to do the same. "This isn't the first time she's done this. I swear to god, if she's not dead, I'm going to kill her. I knew it was a bad idea for us to take the same internship."

"Done what?" Kaiser asks.

"Disappeared. It happened once before. She met a guy, spent the entire weekend at his house, forgot to tell people. Smartest but flakiest girl you'll ever meet. She came back three days later, but I was furious. Now her phone is going straight to voice-mail. Which means the battery is dead, or she's turned it off."

Julia obviously hasn't spoken to Claire's parents yet. She puts her hand to her mouth and chews on a fingernail. Kaiser checks out her other hand, which rests on the table. The nails are ragged, worn down to little stumps. She notices him noticing and puts her hands in her lap.

"Strathroy, Oakwood and Strauss has a one-hundred percent attendance policy here for interns," Julia says. "You have to be gravely ill to call in sick, and you'd better have a doctor's note to back it up. When she didn't show up for work last Thursday, I told our boss that a member of her family died and that she asked me to relay the news. They weren't happy about it, but I couldn't let her get fired. I hope they don't ask her for a death certificate when she gets back. So? Is she dead?"

The next word he says will change this young woman's life forever, and as gently as possible, he says, "Yes."

Julia blinks. She searches Kaiser's face for any sign that he's joking, and when none appears, she freezes. A full thirty seconds pass before she slumps into her chair. "Fuck." Her eyes well up with tears, but she blinks them away. The fingers are back in her mouth. "Fuck," she says again. "How?"

"She was killed. We're still figuring the rest out."

"She was murdered?" Her gaze flickers to his badge. "This is a homicide?"

"Yes."

How? Julia asks again, more forcefully this time, and a tear slips down her cheek. She swipes at it, almost angrily, as if it's a nuisance, as if there's no place in this conversation for crying.

"It's not important for you to know —"

"You can either tell me or I'll be googling the shit out of it later." Julia's dark eyes are full of sorrow. But behind it, there's determination. She's a strong young woman, and she wants answers. "And I'm sure it will be less traumatic hearing about it from you. Please tell me. She's my friend. I need to know."

So Kaiser lays out what he knows. As gently as possible, he tells the young woman how her friend was strangled, dismembered, and then buried in the woods.

He doesn't tell her about Henry. He doesn't know if she's aware that Claire gave up a baby for adoption, and it's not his place to reveal it.

Julia Chan listens without interrupting. When he finishes, she stands up, smooths her skirt, and says, "Excuse me a moment," and leaves him alone in the conference room.

He half expected it. Death notifications are always hard, and though he's tried not to think about Kim this morning, he finds himself wishing she were here. She's better at this kind of thing than he is. He uses the time to check his messages, and he's just putting his phone back in his pocket when Julia comes back into the conference room. She was gone a full ten minutes.

She sits beside him once again, rolling her chair a bit farther away this time, but she's composed, ready to talk. The shakiness is gone. The only noticeable difference is her eyes. They're red and puffy from the tears she's cried. When she speaks, her voice is hoarse and there's a slight disconnect to it. Kaiser recognizes what she's doing, because it's something he does himself, every day. Julia Chan is compartmentalizing. She'll make a hell of a lawyer someday.

"I hope the next thing you tell me is that you're going to find the sonofabitch who did it," she says. "And I hope you rip him to pieces the way he did her."

"I'm going to find the sonofabitch who did it," Kaiser says, and he means it. That much he feels comfortable promising. "Claire's parents said you were her roommate."

"Since freshman year of undergrad. We were more than roommates; we were really good friends. We're both only children, so we were probably the closest thing to having a sister —" Julia's face crumples, but she fights it.

"I'm trying to trace her whereabouts in the days before she was killed," Kaiser says. "Her parents hadn't seen her for a couple of weeks."

"Well, she's busy. *Was* busy," Julia corrected, and then her face falls again. "She works — worked, *shit* — part-time at a coffee shop in the U-District. The Green Bean. Last I saw her, which I think was Wednesday of last week, that's where she was. I'm taking a night course on top of this internship and usually pop in to study if she's working because she gives me free lattes. Anyway, she didn't come back to the apartment that night."

"And that's typical?"

"Yeah. *Yes.* But usually she'll text and she didn't, so I figured she was hooking up with the guy I saw her talking to."

Kaiser straightens up. "Which guy?"

"Some guy. I didn't get a good look. He was sitting in the corner."

"Age? Height? Hair color?"

"White guy for sure, baseball cap pulled low. Jeans and a T-shirt. Not overly built, but not skinny. Clean shaven, I think. He had long legs, and so my impression is that he was tall." Her head snaps up. "Oh shit. Is he . . . you think he killed her?"

"I don't know," Kaiser says, and it's the most honest answer he can give. "I'm looking at everything. What else can you tell me?"

"That's all," Julia says, and her face crumples all the way this time, a lone tear seeping out of the corner of her eye. "I don't know for a fact that she got together with him. But it's something she's done. She's a beautiful girl; guys are constantly hitting on her. She has no interest in a relationship, so she, you know, keeps it casual." She stops, closes her eyes, takes a breath. *"Was,"* she says, when she opens them again. "She *was* a beautiful girl."

"I've seen her picture on LinkedIn."

Julia manages a snort. "That's her professional pic. She's not buttoned up like that when she's not in the office." She reaches into the pocket of her skirt and pulls out her phone. Scrolls through it, then hands it to him.

The picture on it was of the two of them, dressed up for a night out at the club. Julia Chan was a pretty young woman, but Claire Toliver was, to put it mildly, stunning. Dressed in a low-cut, slinky black minidress and high heels, she could have passed for a model or an actress, easily. Long, almost-black hair, small waist, generous breasts and hips, legs for days. The word that came to mind as Kaiser examined the photo was *lush.*

"That was in Vegas last spring, after we graduated." A small smile crossed Julia's face. "That was a fun weekend. We're doing a trip to Miami this May once we — *shit* . . ."

Kaiser allows her to cry, sitting patiently until she's able to get herself under control once again. The conference room door opens and a middle-aged woman looks in, concern etched all over her face at the sight

168

of the younger woman in tears. "Everything okay here? Julia? You all right?"

"I'm fine, Heather, thank you." Julia wipes her face quickly with her hands. "We're finishing up. I'll be right out."

The woman closes the door, but not before giving Kaiser a dirty look, as if to say, *Damn you for making her cry.*

"Have you told her parents?" Julia asks.

"Spoke to them yesterday," Kaiser says, fumbling in his pocket for a tissue. He finds one, wrinkled but clean, and offers it to her. "That's how I found you."

"I'll have to call them." She blows her nose. "And the Bowens, too. Oh god. How do I tell them . . ." Her voice trails off.

Kaiser is surprised. "The Bowens? You know about Henry?"

She gives him a look like he's said the stupidest thing ever. "That she had a son she gave up for adoption? Of course, yeah. *Yes.* We were living together, Detective. I sat with her watching all those adoption videos when she was trying to pick a family. Kinda hard to hide your pregnancy from your roommate."

"I didn't want to assume it was common knowledge. . . ."

"Well, it wasn't, but it wasn't really a secret, either." Julia rubs her eyes. "She got pregnant midway through her senior year at PSSU. It wasn't like she announced she was knocked up on Facebook or anything. She carried small, wore baggy clothes, and was off for the summer, so nobody really knew what was going on. Not that she would have denied it if anyone asked. It's just, people tend to get excited over pregnant women, and it was weird for her to tell people that she was giving the baby up."

"Understandable."

"How did *you* know about the Bowens?" Julia is staring at him. "Her parents *never* talk about Henry — it's a sore subject — so it's hard to imagine them bringing it up."

Kaiser is silent for a moment. If Claire and Julia were so close, then the young woman might remember additional information that could be helpful, and he needs her to stay focused and talking. Her anxiety is already so high, though, that the news of Henry's death might send her over the edge. He's not sure he wants to tell her this part.

"They didn't," he finally says. "We know about the Bowens because we found Henry when we found Claire."

"I don't understand," she says, and it's clear she doesn't. "She never saw Henry. It was an open adoption, but she only kept up with him via emails the Bowens sent. They didn't have a relationship. They agreed to let him decide on that when he got older. Is he okay?"

"I'm afraid not."

He allows this information to sink in. Julia stares at him, as if waiting for the punch line. When it doesn't come, she sits back in her chair, her fingers at her mouth again. She chews furiously. There isn't much fingernail there; she'll hit skin if she doesn't stop.

"Can I show you a picture?" Kaiser asks. He pulls out his phone.

"Of *Claire*?" Julia stops chewing, her face a mask of horror.

"No, of the guy she might have been talking to at The Green Bean the last time you saw her."

She relaxes a little, nods, and he taps on his phone, bringing up a picture of Calvin James. It's the most recent one he can find, from five years ago, and it's Calvin's mug shot from the day Kaiser arrested him. The name board is cropped out. He hands her the phone, wondering if she pays attention to the news, wondering if she'll recognize him as the Sweetbay Strangler.

Julia's brow furrows as she zooms in on the picture. She stares at it, then looks up at Kaiser, confused. "I don't understand."

"He's not the man from the coffee shop?"

"Of course he isn't," Julia says. She's still looking at him funny. "That's Calvin."

So she does recognize him. But her use of only his first name strikes Kaiser as odd. "So you know who he is, then?" he says.

"Of course I do," the young woman says, and the line between her eyebrows deepens. "But he's not the guy Claire was with the other night. That would be ridiculous, I wouldn't have let her hook up with him again."

"Again?"

"Remember I told you she disappeared for a few days once before? He was the guy she was with. They had a hot and heavy fling, pretty much all sex, no talking, she never even got his last name. But I guess he must have rocked her world because when she finally came home, she was like the human equivalent of that heart-eyed emoji face in your iPhone." Julia shakes her head. "She really liked him. He was older, nothing like the guys she usually hooks up with, and she thought maybe it would turn into something real. But when she texted him the next day, he never responded. Douchebag. And when she found out she was pregnant six weeks later, she tried calling him, figured he deserved to know. But by

172

then his number was disconnected."

"Wait," Kaiser says, holding up a hand, not sure if he heard her correctly. *"What?"*

"Are we not on the same page here?" Julia is looking at him like he's an idiot. "Detective, the picture you just showed me is of Henry's biological father."

Kaiser opens his mouth to speak, but he's so caught off guard, no words come out.

"That asshole is long gone," Julia says flatly, making a face. "And good riddance. Hey, was he arrested? Was that a mug shot you showed me?"

Still processing it all, Kaiser says, his voice faint, "Yes, it was. I guess you don't watch the news. That's okay, I don't either. It's all terrible, anyway."

"So? What was he arrested for?"

He looks at her; she wants to know. He might as well tell her. Like she said earlier, she'll just google the shit out of it, anyway.

"Murder. Calvin James is the Sweetbay Strangler."

"Wait . . . *what*?"

"Exactly," Kaiser says, watching as Julia's fingers fly back into her mouth. A spot of blood appears on one of them as she gnaws. "Exactly."

■ ■ ■ ■

PART THREE:
BARGAINING

■ ■ ■ ■

"You save yourself or you remain
unsaved."
~ *Alice Sebold,* Lucky

12

Five years is a long time to wear uncomfortable panties.

Prison underwear is scratchy. So are prison bedsheets. So are prison clothes. Prison isn't designed for comfort. It's designed to keep the criminal away from the outside world, or the outside world away from the criminal. Which aren't the same thing, and the distinction is important.

Geo, flat on her back inside the prison library, spreads her legs a little wider. Her panties are in a puddle beside her head, and the cheap industrial carpet feels like sandpaper against her bare ass. She can't remember the last time she had sex on an actual bed. The carpet smells vaguely of mildew, and maybe it's the fibers or maybe it's the mold, but ever since she started having sex here, she's had a chronic rash on the back of her shoulder that won't go away.

She thinks about this rash now while

absently staring at the mop of dark hair bobbing between her legs. Her shoulder is so itchy, and her tube of hydrocortisone ointment is in her pants pocket. Her pants are somewhere behind her head. Can she reach it?

Corrections officer Chris Bukowski looks up and licks his lips. "What's the matter? Not into it?"

"Keep going. I'm getting close."

Bukowski's head goes back down and Geo makes a swipe for her pants, but can't quite reach them. She makes a few grunting noises and moves her hips a little, timing it to his rhythm. They only ever do oral because Bukowski, only twenty-five years old and one of the newer COs at Hazelwood, is terrified of getting her pregnant. There's no access to birth control here, which makes sense, since the inmates aren't allowed to have sex, and especially not with the guards. Bukowski is risking his job and a prison sentence if they're ever caught, but that's not Geo's problem. As far as she's concerned, being friends with a CO has made life a bit easier.

She and Bukowski have been "friends" for about six months now. During that time, Geo's received special privileges, like extra fresh fruit at mealtimes and a personal TV for her cell. He also brings her books, cosmetics, and toothpaste that isn't available in the commissary. It's funny how something as fucking insignificant as Sensodyne can suddenly feel so important. Everything is magnified is prison. On the outside, you bump into someone, you apologize and go on your way. The worst that might happen is they give you a dirty look, tell you to watch where you're going. In here, bumping into the wrong bitch can land you in the infirmary for a couple of days.

Bukowski isn't married, but he's had the same girlfriend since high school and the relationship has gone stale. Lori — or is it Traci? — certainly wouldn't be pleased to know what her boyfriend does at work all day. He isn't the first guard Geo's slept with, but thankfully, he'll be the last. Bukowski is in love with her — which again, is his problem — but it's getting annoying. At least he's nicer than the others. Helpful. Eager. Sweet, even. Right now it feels like a puppy is licking Geo's palm. Except it's not her palm.

Thirty seconds later she pretends to orgasm, and then she and Bukowski switch positions. Geo has no preference over giving or receiving. Her mind is elsewhere anyway, and she thinks about a hundred other things as her tongue and lips work efficiently. Fortunately, Bukowski's been handling himself the entire time so he's most of the way there. They're in their usual spot, in a little-used area in the nonfiction section, somewhere between auto mechanics and home repair. The library is closed for another ten minutes while the other guard is on lunch break, and that right there is the only good thing about getting it on with someone you're not attracted to in prison — you have no choice but to make it quick.

Three minutes later, Bukowski is smiling and pulling up his polyester-blend pants. Hazelwood changed the COs' uniforms from gray to navy blue a few months ago, and the dark color looks good on him. She supposes he's handsome, not that it matters. He hands her a bottle of water, and she takes a long sip. Bukowski watches as she smooths her hair and attempts to make it look like she hasn't just had sex.

"You're out tomorrow," he says. "What's the first thing you're going to do?"

Everybody's been asking her this. It's a stupid question. Geo's answered it a number of different ways so far, depending on what she thinks the other person expects to hear. "A bath," she says. "A long, hot, bubble bath and a glass of red wine."

"Can't wait to join you."

Only a lovesick prison guard could say something like that to an inmate and think it was somehow romantic. Geo's been at Hazelwood for five fucking years. The absolute last thing she wants to do is hang out with a CO once she's free. She forces a smile and sips more water, swishing it around it her mouth before swallowing. Bukowski's taste is strong, and it's lingering. "Don't think your girlfriend would appreciate that, Chris."

"I'm thinking of ending it with her."

Geo pauses. "Why?"

"You know why." He tucks in his shirt and buckles his belt. "You're a free woman tomorrow. We can start seeing each other openly. We can have actual sex. Have you thought about going on the pill? We —"

"You're ten years younger than me," Geo says. "And I'm going to be an ex-con. Not exactly a winning combination."

"So? I know what we have is special."

I know what we have is sexual assault, Geo thinks, but doesn't say. By law, inmates can't consent to having sex with a corrections officer. It's legally the same thing as rape. He seems anxious, so she smiles at him. "We'll figure it out. Give me a few days to get settled. You know I'm staying with my dad until I get a place of my own."

It's the right thing to say, and he relaxes. Keeping Bukowski happy for the twenty-four hours until her release is important. Geo never intended for things to get so serious between them (on his end, anyway), and now she has to be careful she doesn't hurt him. She's seen firsthand what can happen if an inmate crosses a guard. Two years ago, a young inmate tried to end her intimate relationship with a CO five days before her two-year sentence was up. The CO, an older, married man with five kids, didn't take the rejection well. The next day, a bag of heroin and a shank were found in the inmate's cell. She got an additional five years on her sentence. It was that simple.

Before they exit the library, Bukowski sneaks in a quick kiss. It's all Geo can do not to flinch. Sex is one thing; kissing is another. They say good-bye, and with any luck, it will be the last time Geo ever has sex in prison.

She heads down the hallway and is soon approached by a tall, extremely skinny woman named Yolanda Carter. Geo doesn't break stride, but eventually she has to, since the woman is in her way. She stops, already aware that the conversation won't be a good one. They've spoken before. It's never gone particularly well.

"What do you want, Boney?" she asks.

The woman's short Afro is shaved at the sides, and both of her long, veiny arms are covered in tattoos. Sharply defined collarbones match equally sharp elbows, which jut out from the sleeves of her prison scrubs. It's easy to see where she got her nickname, but there's no dieting involved — Geo's seen in her in chow hall, and the woman *eats.* She speaks almost as fast as her metabolism digests food, and she gets right in Geo's face.

"Where's your black bitch?" Boney says with only a trace of an accent. Her voice is almost as deep as a man's. Rumor has it she used to be a princess in Nigeria, but Boney probably started that rumor herself.

"She's not my bitch, and I'm not her keeper."

Boney puts a hand on Geo's arm. "You tell her —"

"Don't touch me," Geo says softly, staring right into the woman's eyes.

The woman removes her hand and takes a half step back. "You tell your friend that if she sells to another one of my customers, I will come for her. And not just in here. I

183

got friends on the outside. I'll come for her kids."

"They're her customers, and I'm not telling her shit." Geo turns and walks away.

"Oh, so you're only the banker, huh?" Boney calls, her baritone carrying down the hallway. "You think you're not involved in this? You're involved, bitch. You got involved the first day you met her, bitch."

Geo continues down the hallway without glancing back. When she turns the corner, she stops for a second to catch her breath and allow her heart rate to slow down. There's no room for weakness in here. It's all good and fine to be a nice person, to be pleasant and cooperative and do whatever you're told with no attitude, but the moment someone gets in your face — the moment someone gets in your *space* — you can't back down or show fear. Ever. You'll get eaten alive.

And if someone hurts you, you have to retaliate. Every time. Because if you don't, they'll keep coming.

Right, Bernie?

She buzzes into the medium-security wing and sees Cat being escorted down the hallway toward their cells, which are next to each other. They both got transferred out of maximum three years ago — Geo for good behavior, and Cat because she got sick. Geo is dismayed to notice that Cat's prison scrubs look even bigger on her rapidly shrinking frame than they seemed a week ago. It's hard to get her friend to eat, and when she does, it's even harder to get the food to stay down.

Kellerman, the corrections officer assigned to drive Cat to and from the hospital, looks put out. Cat needs help walking, but he isn't helping her. His hand is barely touching her elbow, as if he's disgusted to be near her.

As if stage four cancer is contagious.

"How'd it go?" Geo asks when she catches up to them.

"Fine," Cat says pleasantly enough, but she's not smiling. Her face is paler than usual, the circles under her eyes the color of eggplant. Her auburn hair, coiffed to perfection on a good day, is limp, and her gray roots are showing. "Same shit, different day."

"What are you doing out of work, Shaw?" Built like a power lifter, CO Kellerman is actually nicer than he looks, but very strict, with zero sense of humor. Meaty arms flank a barrel chest. "You're supposed to stay at your work assignment until three-thirty."

Geo has her explanation ready. "Bukowski

said I could close the salon early to help with Cat. She's going to vomit in about two minutes."

Kellerman hesitates. He's assigned to bring Cat back, but a sick, vomiting inmate is wholly unappealing.

"I guess that's fine," he says, managing to sound as if he's doing them a favor. He lets go of Cat's arm and it drops to her side. "But you take Bonaducci straight back to her cell, you understand? No detours, except the bathroom."

"Oh, pity, I was hoping to go on a walking tour," Cat says.

The CO glares at her, but despite her snark, the woman is obviously feeling poorly. The light sheen of sweat across her forehead highlights how pale she is, and her glazed eyes are a tad unfocused.

"Straight to your cells," Kellerman says again, before walking away.

Geo puts an arm around her friend, supporting her as they walk slowly down the hallway. Cat has lost so much weight, she feels like a bird whose hollow bones might snap under too much pressure. It's a far cry from the woman Geo met five years ago, so robust and full of life. They reach Cat's cell and Geo helps her friend sit on the bed, then grabs the bottle of water on the desk.

It's already filled in preparation for Cat's return from the hospital; after two rounds of this, they both know the drill.

"Easy," Geo says when the water dribbles down Cat's chin. "Take your time."

Cat finishes the water and leans back on her mattress. Her brow is furrowed, an expression of exhaustion and pain. "Fuck, I hate this."

"I know." Geo strokes what's left of Cat's hair. She still has it, thank god, but it's thin and has lost all of its former luster. She always looks pale after chemo, but today her skin is the color of tissue paper. "Hang in there. That was your last session."

"Yeah, for this round," Cat says. "But how many more rounds? The fucking chemo feels worse than the cancer. If the cancer doesn't kill me, the goddamned chemo will."

Geo adjusts Cat's pillow and removes her running shoes. She covers her with the blanket, then moves the bucket on the floor closer to the bed, within easy reach. At some point, Cat will need to throw up, and because there's no toilet inside the cell, the bucket will have to do. They have wet cells — cells with their own sink and toilet — only in maximum, and Cat refuses to go back to the maximum-security ward. The inmates are worse, and, besides, she doesn't have friends there.

Every week after chemotherapy, Geo takes care of Cat's bucket of vomit, bringing it to the bathroom to empty out and clean. She helps her use the toilet, helps her shower, helps her brush her teeth. Geo doesn't mind. Caring for Cat reminds her that she's still a good person, that she can still do good things. It's easy to forget that in here.

"Look at the bright side," Geo says with a smile. "You're done with the chemo for now. Tomorrow you'll get some energy back, and you'll feel like yourself again. Lenny's coming on Saturday —"

"He's not coming," Cat says.

"What do you mean?"

"He wants a divorce." Cat's voice cracks, and her eyes moisten. "Lenny's leaving me. He met a woman at one of the casinos, says he's in love. She owns a nail salon. She probably has great nails." Cat holds up a gnarled hand. Her fingernails are brutally short and yellowed from the cancer-killing toxins being pumped into her body each week. "Not like mine."

"Why didn't you tell me?" Geo is shocked. "When did you find out?"

"He told me last week."

"And you kept it to yourself the whole

time?" Geo feels her anger welling up and does her best to contain it. Anger won't help Cat now. But the whole thing is so god-damned unfair. "That sonofabitch."

Cat and Lenny met through the Write-A-Prisoner program. They exchanged letters for six months before he finally came to see her in person. A truck driver who's on the road three weeks out of every month, their relationship worked quite well; Lenny finally got himself a wife who couldn't nag him for always being away. They spoke on the phone throughout the week, and he came to see her every weekend when he was home. And every few months they were granted a twenty-four-hour conjugal visit. Hazelwood has half a dozen trailers at the back of the prison equipped with full kitchens, queen-size beds, and TVs, and they would spend that time together eating, watching movies, and having sex. Cat would glow for a whole week when she got back to her cell, recounting every tiny detail to Geo with relish.

When she got sick eight months ago, Lenny vowed to stay with her. Cat's in her sixties now, but before the cancer, she looked fifteen years younger than that. The look on Lenny's face when Cat said "I do" to him in the prison chapel remains imprinted in Geo's brain. And she can still remember the look on her friend's face that day. The fucking sun had shone out of the woman's eyes.

Now, her friend's brown eyes are glassy. The cancer has dried up her once-luminous skin, hollowing out her cheeks, the sagging skin creating jowls around a neck that used to be smooth and firm. Her once-vibrant auburn hair is a brassy rust color, despite Geo's best efforts in the hair salon. She's lost so much weight, the skin on her arms and legs hangs like an extra layer of clothing that's a size too big.

Cat has stage four colon cancer, for fuck's sake, and her husband can't *wait*? She could fucking kill Lenny. Without him, Cat will go downhill even faster.

"Don't be angry at him." Her friend's voice breaks into her thoughts. "I know what you're thinking. You're going to get out tomorrow and track him down and yell at him, force him to come see me. But don't, okay?"

It's exactly what Geo is planning to do. "Give me one good reason why not."

"Because I'm asking you not to." Cat squeezes her hand. "It's more than the cancer that's killing me, hon. It's more than Lenny. It's this goddamned *place*. The grayness of it, the monotony, the fact that every fucking day is the same. It's the daily bickering and drama between women that are too old to live in a sorority house, which is exactly what it feels like here, doesn't it? Minus the cute clothes and the boyfriends?"

Geo opens her mouth to respond, but Cat isn't done.

"I can't blame Lenny for not loving me anymore. Everything he loved about me is gone. My looks. My laugh. My sex drive. Last time we had a conjugal visit, I spent half the time sleeping. Best I could manage was a hand job." The older woman attempts a smile, but it's weak. "This isn't what he signed up for. We had plans for when I got out. Mount Rushmore, Mount St. Helens, the Grand Canyon — we were going to sleep in motel rooms, fuck like rabbits, collect those souvenir shot glasses from every place we visited. I got sick and changed all that."

"He's a goddamned cheating bastard," Geo spits. She can't help it. "It's not right. It's not fair."

"Yes, and yes," Cat says patiently. "But we already know that about life. Tomorrow, you'll be a free woman, and I want you to go home and never look back. Rebuild your life. Find a man. Get married. Have kids. Put all this shit behind you. And don't ever come back here, ever. Not even to see me. Not even when I'm dying."

"Stop it." Hot tears sting Geo's eyes, but she blinks them away before they can fall. "You're not going to die in here. They're going to grant you compassionate parole. We're supposed to hear back from the parole board any day now. And when you get out, I'll take you to all those places —"

"I won't make it," Cat says gently, stroking Geo's arm. "Accept it."

"No —"

"Accept it," Cat says again, more firmly.

Never, Geo thinks, but she nods. It's not her place to argue with a sick woman.

Her friend's gaze flickers to the TV sitting on the desk. "What's that doing there?"

"That's your brand-new TV," Geo says. "Otherwise known as my old TV, which you can now have. Eight inches of non-high-definition color, for your viewing pleasure."

"I wish it was eight inches of something else for my pleasure."

Geo snorts. "Like you could handle that."

"You'd be surprised. I'm small, but I'm mighty."

The women share a hearty laugh.

"It's yours now." Geo turns it on and fiddles with it for a moment. "Look, *The Young and the Restless* is on."

She sits on the chair next to the bed. Technically, Cat needs to be approved to have a TV in her cell, but Geo can't imagine anyone will deny her sick friend something that Geo doesn't need anymore, anyway. *The Young and the Restless* is Cat's favorite soap opera. It brings her comfort to watch the two lead characters scream at each other yet again.

"When will she realize that he's no good for her?" Cat says with a dramatic sigh.

"Never," Geo says, her feet propped up on the desk. She munches on one of Cat's crackers and files her nails with the small emery board she bought in commissary. "Their angst will go on forever until one of them dies. It's a soap opera."

The irony of fussing with her nails while watching *The Young and the Restless* isn't lost on her. Five years ago, Geo had regular appointments at the nail salon down the street from her house. It was owned by a small Vietnamese woman named May, who was learning English through American soap operas. The salon had a TV mounted in the corner and *The Young and the Restless* was always playing at full volume. Geo would relax in a puffy faux-leather chair, her feet soaking in a tub full of swirly water, as May worked on her manicure. Every so often the woman would look up and ask, "What mean *scandal?*" or, "What mean *adulterer?*" and Geo would explain.

Those mani-pedi appointments seem like an absurd luxury now. Along with her Range Rover, her twelve-hundred-thread-count Egyptian cotton sheets, her countless pairs of Stuart Weitzman high heels. Everything has been stored at her dad's place since her house was sold, and while she's looking forward to getting out of Hellwood, she's dreading going back to her childhood home. But there's nowhere else to go.

The Young and the Restless ends, and Geo turns to find Cat asleep, her breathing deep and even. Geo watches her for a moment, her heart swelling and breaking at exactly the same time. The papery skin, the blue-veined eyelids, the dry, deflated lips. How can she leave her friend in here to die?

Fucking Lenny. It isn't fucking fair.

"You're being creepy." Cat's eyes are still closed, but there's a hint of a smile on her face. "I love you, too. Stop staring and let an old woman rest."

The news comes on. Geo watches absently as a pretty blonde reporter highlights the day's top stories. And then suddenly her father's house appears on the TV screen.

She sits up straight, pulling the TV a few

inches closer. There's no mistaking her childhood home. Same taupe-gray siding, same bright blue door, same dark-red Japanese maple tree to the left of the garage that's always been there. Geo strains to listen, not wanting to turn the volume up because she doesn't want to wake Cat.

"Police haven't yet confirmed the identities of the victims, but we can confirm that one is an adult female and the other is a minor," the reporter says, her diction clear and even. "To recap, both bodies were discovered in the woods just behind Briar Crescent in the Sweetbay neighborhood, reminding local residents of a similar discovery more than five years ago. More to come after the break."

The news cuts to commercial, and Geo sinks back into the chair. Terror seizes her heart in a vice grip, wrapping it in steel fingers that won't let up. Beside her, Cat snores.

Calvin's back.

Just in time to welcome her home.

13

The first time Geo laid eyes on Calvin James, she was sixteen.

It was a day like any other. She was with Angela and Kaiser, the three of them leaving the 7-Eleven down the street from St. Martin's, refreshments in hand. Grape Slurpee for Angela, blue raspberry Slurpee for Geo, and a Big Gulp Mountain Dew for Kai, who didn't like Slurpees at all. The red Trans Am was parked two spots over from Angela's cute little Dodge Neon, a gift from Angela's parents the day she turned sixteen. Her father was a VP at Microsoft, and her mother came from money, so Angela was rich. It was something Geo's friend neither bragged about nor tried to hide. It was what it was.

The Trans Am was surrounded by four guys, and they all looked about the same age, early twenties. All of them were smoking cigarettes and drinking beer out of cans hidden in paper lunch bags. It was two-thirty on a Thursday afternoon. That right there should have been the first red flag.

The older boys — guys? men? — looked over as the trio approached the Neon, taking note of their matching white button-down shirts with the St. Martin's High School crest on the breast pockets. Angela and Geo wore identical maroon-and-gray plaid kilts, knee socks, and black loafers. Kaiser was wearing gray dress slacks and a maroon tie. Geo sensed her friends' postures changing as they got closer. Kaiser, tall but skinny, seemed to shrink a little as the older guys stared him down. Angela, on the other hand, blossomed with the attention, adding a slight swing to her hips that hadn't been there a few seconds ago.

"St. Martin's girls," one of the guys said, loudly enough for them to hear. His friends laughed. "One of them your girlfriend, bro?"

Kaiser didn't answer. He simply waited by the back door of the Neon on the driver's side, his designated spot when they were in Angela's car, looking as if he wished he could disappear.

Angela placed her Slurpee on the roof as she unlocked the car, her cool gaze belying her excitement at having been noticed by older guys. The three of them got in. Geo rolled her eyes as she shut the door and buckled her seatbelt.

"They're too old," she said to Angela. "And they're drinking. In the middle of the day, which means they're at least twenty-one. Why aren't they at work?"

"They probably don't have jobs," Kaiser piped up from the backseat, comfortable speaking now that they were safely inside the vehicle. "They don't look like they're in college, either."

"Don't be judgmental, Kai," Angela snapped, flipping down her visor so she could check her face. She had checked it five minutes before they'd gone into the 7-Eleven, and she'd checked it five minutes before that, when they'd gotten into the car to drive over here from school. Satisfied that she hadn't suddenly gotten a pimple in the last three hundred seconds and that her face was still perfect — which it was, there was no denying that — she flipped the visor back up. Her dark eyes cut past Geo toward the group, still looking over at them. "Maybe they work nights. You don't know anything." To Geo, she said, "And what, you prefer the boys at school? Look, that one there is cute."

"Which one?" Geo said, sipping her Slurpee. She didn't dare look.

"The tall one. Good lord," Angela said,

her voice slightly breathless. "Seriously, he's beautiful. Jared Leto face, Kurt Cobain vibe."

Geo chanced a glance in their direction. The tall one was pretty good-looking, she supposed, if you liked the whole bad-boy thing, which Angela did. Ripped jeans, black T-shirt, hair a tad long and brushed back off his chiseled face. He saw her watching him, and she turned her face away from the window. "Ang, come on, let's go. I have to finish my English essay before *Melrose Place.*"

"Yeah, can we go already?" Kaiser said, sounding moody.

"He's coming over," Angela said.

"What?"

"He's walking toward the car," Angela hissed. "Roll down your window, see what he wants. God, I hope the Trans Am's his."

"I'm not rolling —"

The tap on the glass made them both jump. Geo couldn't help but laugh. Stuff like this always happened whenever Angela went anywhere. Her best friend met guys just by walking down the street; in fact, that very thing had happened the day before. A car turned around in the middle of the shopping center parking lot, nearly hitting someone, just so the driver could ask for

Angela's number. She said no, unimpressed by his car, an old Jetta covered in rust spots.

Geo cranked the window down. His smell was the first thing she noticed, and it wafted into the car, an intoxicating blend of Budweiser, Calvin Klein Eternity cologne, and Marlboros. If *Your Parents Would Hate Him* were the name of a cologne, this was exactly what it would smell like.

"Can we help you?" she said. Her voice was sharper than she intended, and she knew it sounded prissy.

Angela smacked her arm, then leaned across Geo to smile at the guy through the window, her hair tickling Geo's legs. She was doing damage control. God forbid the hot guy didn't like her because of something awkward Geo said. The guy smiled back, first at Angela, then at Geo. He held her gaze, and she felt a flutter in her stomach. Angela was right. He was beautiful.

"Bro," he said finally, nodding to Kaiser in the backseat without breaking eye contact.

"Hey," Kaiser replied, but it came out a squeak.

"You left your Slurpee on the roof." He was speaking to Angela, but he hadn't taken his eyes off Geo. "Didn't want you to drive away and have it fall."

"Oh shit. Thanks for telling me." Angela opened her door and got halfway out, reaching for her drink on top of the car.

"Blue raspberry, right?" he said to Geo, nodding at her oversized cup.

"How'd you know?"

"Your tongue is blue."

"Oh." She blushed. "I guess that's a dead giveaway. Although I'm not sure why you're looking at my tongue. That's kinda pervy."

He laughed, and she was pleased with herself. That was a good quip.

"Oh my god," Kaiser muttered from the backseat, but if the older guy heard him, he didn't react.

His stare was disconcerting. And there was nowhere else to look except directly back. He had green eyes, bright gold in the center. Feline eyes. They contrasted intensely with his dark hair. One arm rested comfortably on the ledge of the open window. "Haven't I seen you here before?"

"Wow, such an original line," Angela said, slamming the car door shut again. Geo glanced over at her friend, only to find her expression sullen, full lips pressed into a thin line. She was angry because the hot guy wasn't paying attention to her. He wasn't even *looking* at her, and Angela was masking her feelings of rejection and disappointment by pretending to be totally bored with the conversation. "You think up that line all by yourself or did you steal it from your dad?"

The guy grinned, then winked at Geo, as if to say, *I know why she's mad, and you do, too. And who gives a shit.*

"So what's your name?" he said to Geo, ignoring Angela.

"Her name is Jailbait," Angela snapped before Geo could respond. "Now, it was nice talking to you, but we have homework to do. I'm sure you remember what homework is, right?"

Now he's too old? Geo thought, incredulous. To the guy, she said, "I'm Georgina. My friends call me Geo."

"Then I'll call you Georgina," he said. "Because I think we should be more than friends."

She laughed. Beside her, Angela let out an impatient sigh and started the car.

Geo knew exactly why her friend was being rude, and it was because the hot older guy with the cool older friends wasn't interested in her. Well, you know what? Tough shit. How many times had Geo sat back and played wingwoman while guys hit on her best friend? There was even a term for it in this situation: *grenade.* In every girl group, there was the hot one, and there was the grenade. Angela was always the hot one, the one the guys wanted, the one they competed for. Geo was the grenade, the one the guys had to be nice to and treat with kid gloves, because if it blew up — if the grenade didn't like you — then the entire group of girls would leave, and there went your chances with the hot one.

For reasons Geo couldn't begin to understand, they had switched roles today, and neither girl was prepared for it. Not that Geo wasn't pretty. She was, and most days, she felt it. But Angela Wong was beautiful. Everybody said so. Waist-length black hair, dark almond-shaped eyes, porcelain skin. She was also confident — one of the most popular girls in their junior year. When she spoke to you, she could make you feel like you were the only person in the room, or she could shred you with one dirty look.

Geo had none of these qualities. Yet somehow, the hot guy wanted *her*. Predictably, Angela was pissed. The hot guy wasn't playing the game right by not showing her best friend any interest. The grenade was about to blow.

Luckily, he figured it out.

"Listen, the reason I came over is that my friend over there thinks you're gorgeous."

He directed his attention to Angela now, and pointed to where his friends were standing. One of them raised a hand to wave. "That's Jonas. He plays in a band. They got a gig at the G-Spot tomorrow night, and we can get you in for free. Bartender's a buddy of mine, so free drinks all night. You guys have ID, right?"

He meant fake ID, and of course they did, though Geo got nervous any time she used hers, which wasn't often. Still miffed, Angela craned her neck to get a better look at Jonas, who in Geo's opinion looked to be about twenty-five years old. But he was cute enough, and the fact that he was in a band would appeal to Angela.

"Maybe," her friend finally said, but she allowed a small smile. Geo let out a breath. The pin was staying in the grenade. For now.

"You're in the band, too?" Geo asked him.

"Nah, not me," he said with a lazy grin. "Can't carry a tune to save my life. But I support my buddies, you know? Whatever they want, I want for them. That's what a good friend does."

It was a jab at Angela, but her friend was too busy checking her face again in the visor mirror to notice. He smiled knowingly, and Geo smiled back, and already it felt like they shared a secret.

Already, it felt intimate.

"I'll give you my number and you can page me," he said. "Got a pen?"

Geo found one in the armrest and handed it to him. He reached into the car and took her hand, taking his time writing on the back of it. The sensation tickled, and she wanted to laugh, but there was something about him that made her feel all warm inside and a little bit dizzy. Geo looked down at the number he'd given her, and the name right under it. *Calvin.*

"Hope to see you guys." He held her hand for a second longer than was necessary. "You're welcome to come, too, bro," he said to Kaiser, as an afterthought.

"Pretty sure I have homework," Kaiser said, sipping his Big Gulp.

"See you soon, Georgina," Calvin said, kissing her hand before letting it go.

Angela started the engine and pulled out of the parking lot, driving slowly past the three other friends leaning against the red Trans Am.

"Jonas is cute," Geo offered, twisting around to look at Kaiser in the backseat. "Don't you think, Kai?"

"You don't want to know what I think," he said, sounding glum.

"He is, right?" Angela said, but her voice was doubtful. They drove in silence for a bit. Geo was basking in the glow of Calvin's interest in her and dying to talk about it, but she knew if she opened her mouth too quickly, it could ruin the rest of the afternoon. She had to wait for Angela to bring it up, and for her friend to decide she was okay with what happened. Instead, Geo smiled down at her hands. She'd already memorized Calvin's number, in case the ink rubbed off before she had a chance to call.

"I can't believe you took the guy's digits." Kaiser didn't sound happy. "Your dad will kill you. He's like, so old."

"Shut up, Kai," Geo said, cross. She didn't expect him to be happy about it, for different reasons than Angela, but the least the both of them could do was not shit all over it. Things like this didn't happen to her every day, and she wanted to enjoy it a little. "I'm not telling my dad."

Angela sighed. "Fine, whatever. He's hot, you lucky bitch. We'd better figure out what we're going to wear tomorrow night. You're coming with us, right, Kai?"

"Bite me," he said.

As it turned out, her outfit hadn't mattered. Geo had spent the following night in the back room of the G-Spot, making out

206

with Calvin on an old green sofa that smelled of beer and pizza. It was the first time she'd ever French-kissed a guy, the first time she'd ever sucked someone's tongue. They hadn't gone all the way because Geo was still a virgin and nowhere near ready for that, but she'd let his hands go wherever they wanted. Down her shirt and into her bra. Up her skirt and inside her panties. He'd given her the first orgasm she'd ever had with another person, and she came hard, looking directly into his eyes. She didn't know it could feel like that.

Afterward, he'd laced his fingers through hers, and whispered, "This is crazy. I'm so into you, it hurts."

That first night with Calvin was the first and last time the relationship felt beautiful. The first and last time it didn't feel complicated. The first and last time that Geo's heart and mind were pure. If she could somehow isolate that one night and remember it all by itself, it might actually be a happy memory. After all, Calvin James was her first love.

But it doesn't work that way. The past is always with you, whether you choose to think about it or not, whether you take responsibility for it or not. You carry the past with you because it transforms you.

You can try to bury it and pretend it never happened, but that doesn't work. Geo knows that from experience.

Because buried things can, and do, come back.

14

1,826 days. That's how long Geo has been inside Hazelwood. And she would have been free hours ago, except for one small glitch.

The prison is currently on lockdown.

Yolanda Carter, the skinny black inmate also known as Boney, was stabbed in the shower this morning. She was found by a guard during count, and had probably been in the shower for at least an hour already, with inmates coming and going as they got ready for the day. But of course nobody said anything. That's how things work in prison. Nobody wants to be the "bitch who snitched."

Geo didn't see what happened, but according to the rumors — which move faster than lightning in prison — Boney's death was a scene from a horror movie. The shower, timed to shut off after eight minutes, hadn't rinsed much away, and the inmate-slash-drug dealer had been found crumpled on the tiled floor dressed in nothing but her shower shoes, covered in her own blood. When Geo heard the news, she wasn't surprised, especially considering her conversation with the woman the day before. Boney had been moving in on Ella Frank's turf for a while now, and not only here in Hellwood, but on the outside, too. That's why Boney had to go. You didn't threaten a woman's family. And you sure as shit *never* threatened a woman's children. Maybe if Boney had given birth to a child, she would have understood that. But she didn't, and now she's dead. Everybody knows it was Ella, even the guards, who've been questioning her all morning. Whether they can prove it, however, is a different story.

An alarm bell sounds, signifying the end of the lockdown. Geo swings her legs over the edge of the bed, a sudden sense of urgency flooding over her. It doesn't take long to organize her things. She doesn't have much to take with her other than a small notebook filled with numbers, a thin stack of birthday and Christmas cards, and a packet of unopened letters written on blue stationery and tied with string. The cards are from her father, and she stuffs them into the cheap duffel bag they've given her. Her dad isn't much of a writer, signing almost all of them with a simple *Chin up, kiddo! Love, Dad,* but it doesn't feel right to throw them away.

The letters give her pause. They're not from her father, and she's only read the first one. For the hundredth time, she debates throwing them into the trash, but even now, she can't bring herself to do it. She stuffs them into the bag with the cards and the notebook. She's already given her cell phone to Ella, the third one she's owned since she's been here. Ella will resell it, probably for three times what it retails for on the outside. And she'll have no shortage of potential buyers.

Everything else, Geo will leave with Cat. This includes her TV, books, cosmetics, and two blankets she'll no longer be needing. There's still no word on whether her friend's application for compassionate parole has been approved, which is frustrating and makes Geo think she'll have to try to attack it a different way once she's on the outside.

She was only five when her mother died of cancer, and there was nothing she could do for her then. Not this time. Not again.

"Thought once the bell sounded, you'd Speedy Gonzales right outta here," a dry voice says, and she turns.

It's Cat, smiling at her from the doorway. Geo frowns, even though the other woman looks a lot better today. The color has returned to her face and her eyes are brighter, though it's clear from the way she's leaning against the door frame that the older woman is exhausted.

"What are you still doing here?" Geo asks, cross. "You're supposed to be at your appointment."

"You think you were gonna leave without saying good-bye?"

"We said our good-byes last night. Cat, these appointments are important."

"So maybe I want to say good-bye again." Cat moves past Geo and sits down on the bed. She pats the spot beside her. "It's just a follow-up. It can wait till tomorrow."

Geo stifles a sigh and takes a seat on the mattress beside her friend. Cat takes her hand, squeezing her palm.

"In case my parole doesn't go through, I want to make sure you know how much I appreciate everything you've done for me," Cat says.

"Your parole will go through." Geo knows where this conversation is going, and she doesn't want to have it. She's not ready. She will never be ready.

Cat sighs. She technically has three years

left to go on her sentence, and Geo understands that optimism can be a dangerous thing in here. Optimism can make the minutes feel like days, and three years feel like thirty. But her friend is getting out, come hell or high water. Cat Bonaducci will not die in this shithole, if it's the last thing Geo does.

"You need to stay positive —" she says, but Cat cuts her off.

"Shush. Don't interrupt an old woman when she's speaking. That's rude."

Geo can't help but laugh. "Okay. Continue."

"I've been in here a long time. Nine years. The first four were shitty. There were days when I didn't know how I was going to get through it. And then you came along." Cat's eyes grow moist. "And it got better. You're the best thing that ever happened to me."

Geo bites her lip. She will not cry. She stares at a spot on the wall until she gets herself under control, and then pats Cat on the leg. "You know I feel the same way. That won't change, no matter where you are."

Cat reaches into her pocket. "I got a box of stuff from Lenny yesterday. He moved most of my things into storage, but he sent me a box of my old photos, figuring I'd want to see them before I . . ." She doesn't finish the sentence. "Anyway, I thought you'd get a kick out of seeing this one."

Geo looks down at the photo her friend is holding. Four by six inches, it's a faded color photo of a young woman wearing a tight black satin corset, sheer black pantyhose, and bunny ears. Wavy auburn hair spills over small porcelain shoulders, and large brown eyes are accented with thick, precisely applied wing-tipped eyeliner. The corset has cinched her waist to nothing, and her breasts are soft and full. Around her neck is a thin leather strap, and attached to it is an open box of cigars.

"I used to be a cigar girl at the Playboy Club," Cat says with a smile. "I was nineteen."

"This is you?" Stunned, Geo turns over the photograph. On the back in fading blue ink, someone has scrawled *Catherine "Cat" Bonaducci, Chicago, 1973.* She turns it over again, admiring the image. "Holy shit, look at you."

"Always a Cat, never a Cathy." Her friend taps the photo. "I want you to have this. This is how I want you to remember me."

The sudden lump in Geo's throat is painful. There's no denying that Cat no longer resembles the young woman in the photo, not by a long shot. Her breasts aren't perky, her skin is loose, her lips chapped, her hair devoid of any shine. But her eyes are unchanged. Still large, still warm, a perfect shade of coffee brown. Catherine Bonaducci is still beautiful, if you take the time to look.

"Well, it isn't how I want to remember you," Geo says. "I didn't know you then. But I'll keep the photo for you. I'll put it in my room, in a frame, and when you get out, you can have it back."

"In case we don't see each other —"

"Stop it."

"— I want you know how special you are. You might never get a job working for a big company again. I know that's hard. But you have brains, and you have money. I know you'll figure it out." Cat kisses her on the cheek. "I love you, Georgina. Like you're my own blood."

Geo is desperate to find something positive to say, something uplifting, but they know each other too well. Cat can't tolerate bullshit, and Geo can't dish it, anyway. Cat is sick. She's going to die, maybe not tomorrow, maybe not in three months, but soon. The question is, will she die inside Hellwood or in some hospital, surrounded by strangers? Or will she die with Geo by her side, holding her hand?

Dying from cancer isn't pretty. Cancer

takes its time, and it kills from the inside out. If Geo had to choose, she'd rather go the way Boney did — short, fast, furious. Geo's father kept her away from her mother in her last days, terrified that his young daughter would be haunted by the memories of her mother wasting away.

But what haunts Geo now is the memory of waking up early one morning only to be told that her mother had passed away in the night. She never got a chance to say one last good-bye, to give one last kiss while her mother's cheeks were still warm. She's never quite forgiven her dad for that.

There's someone at the doorway, and both women look up. It's Chris Bukowski. Geo's not overly surprised to see the CO today, though he's not technically assigned to her ward. She should have known he'd want to say good-bye and escort her out; she just hopes he doesn't suggest a quick trip to the library first.

"Ready?" he asks.

Geo stands, taking one last look around. She won't miss this place, with its gray walls, gray floors, and no windows. There's literally nothing here she wants to remember, except for the small, thin woman still sitting on the bed. She helps Cat up, taking both of her friend's hands in her own.

"I'll see you soon, okay? Go to all of your appointments, and try to eat and drink as much as you can. Keep up your strength because there's so much I want us to do together when you get out."

"Georgina —"

"I'll be waiting for you." Embracing her friend, so tiny and frail and nothing like the picture that's now in her duffel bag, Geo desperately wants to say *I love you.* But Bukowski's watching, and the words won't come.

She takes her bag and leaves her cell for the last time, following Bukowski down the hallway and out of the ward. On the way to processing, he's stopped by another CO, and while the two are discussing some incident or other, she hears her name whispered softly. Ella Frank is standing just around the corner of the corridor, and she beckons Geo over.

Glancing at Bukowski, still deep in conversation with the other guard, Geo walks over. She's surprised to see Ella, who she assumed was still being questioned in Boney's murder.

"I wanted to say good-bye," Ella says, slipping something into Geo's hand. It's a piece of paper with an address written on it. "I made a call; he's expecting you. Go today, okay? Before the kids get out of school."

"I will. Thank you. For . . . everything."

"Back atcha," Ella says softly.

Geo turns to check on Bukowski, who's finishing up his conversation. When she turns back, Ella is gone.

The exit process takes thirty minutes. Papers have to be signed, old belongings have to be found and returned, information has to be entered into the system. Bukowski hangs around, although there are surely more important things he could be doing. After all, an inmate was murdered earlier that day.

For Geo's five years of work — most of it in the hair salon earning less than four dollars a day, minus what she spent in commissary every month for "extras" — she will pocket a grand total of $223.48. The processing clerk informs her of this amount with some relish, as if Geo should be proud, somehow.

"Is that good?" she asks.

"Most inmates leave with only the hundred you're supposed to get on discharge day." The clerk, a balding middle-aged man, peers at up at her from his desk through Coke-bottle glasses. "The fact that you're getting more means you must have saved."

Geo never saved. She never had to. Her financial planner had been instructed to transfer money from her personal account to her prison account every month, so money for extras like better shampoo and ramen noodles was never an issue. "Can I transfer the funds to another inmate?"

"Nobody's ever asked that before." The clerk frowns. "Do you have her DOC number?" Geo gives him Cat's number. He taps his keyboard for a minute. "Done. You need a bus schedule?"

She shakes her head. "I have a ride."

"You're officially free." The clerk pushes some paperwork toward her, along with a plastic bin containing the clothing she was wearing the day she entered Hazelwood. "Sign here and here, then you can get changed in the bathroom down the hall. Leave your scrubs in the bin. Or you can take them with you. Like a souvenir." He laughs at his little joke, revealing uneven coffee-stained teeth.

Fuck, no.

In the bathroom, Geo peels off her prison sweats and puts on her old clothes. She's dismayed to discover that the Dior dress she wore at Calvin's trial is now tight on her, pulling at the hips and stomach, confirming that she's gained weight from all

219

the rehydrated, processed food she's been eating for the past five years. Nevertheless, as she checks out her reflection, she has to admit that it's nice to see herself looking like a person again, and not an inmate. The high heels feel strange on her feet. After five years in running shoes, they feel stiff and slippery. It's weird to think that she used to wear these all the time, and actually thought they were comfortable.

She exits the bathroom to find Bukowski waiting for her. His jaw drops when he sees her. "Wow," he says, his face flushing. "Holy shit. You look . . . wow."

"I'll take that as a compliment. Thank you."

They walk down the hallway together toward double doors marked with an EXIT sign. Bukowski reaches for the buzzer on the wall, then stops and turns to her. "You got my number, right?" he says in a low voice. He glances up at the camera above her head. Normally Geo hated all the cameras in Hazelwood, but she's grateful for them now. It means the guard won't try to kiss her, or even touch her.

"I do." It's a lie. Geo doesn't have it. Bukowski scrawled it on a napkin the other day, and she slipped it into her pocket. Far as she knew, it was still there, in the pants that were now crumpled in a plastic bin in the bathroom down the hall. "I'll call you once I get settled."

The doors beckon. Beyond them is her father . . . and her freedom.

"I'll miss you." Bukowski's eyes are wet.

Open the fucking door, you asshole. She pulls her duffel bag over her shoulder. "Me, too, Chris."

The CO hits the red button, and the double doors buzz open. Drops of rain and crisp morning air hit Geo's face. Her father is standing beside his old Lexus, same one he had when Geo was arrested five years ago. He waves to her. She waves back, and without giving Bukowski another glance, she pulls off her high heels and runs forward to meet him in her bare feet.

"Good to see you, Dad." Her voice breaks as Walter Shaw's arms engulf her. They were allowed brief hugs in prison on visitor's days, but Geo never allowed her father to visit her more than once a month. It was too hard.

"You, too, sweetheart. Let's blow this pop stand."

She laughs a little too hard at the silly phrase. Classic Walt. In the past she would have rolled her eyes, but not today. She climbs into the car, holding her breath for another minute as they drive past the final guard check, and then past the gate. Only when they're on the open road does she allow herself to exhale.

"Hungry?" her father asks. "There's a diner I passed on the way here, about thirty minutes out. You can get a burger and fries."

Geo shakes her head. "Actually, Dad, what I really want is a green tea latte from Starbucks. And I need to stop and see someone on the way home. Any chance we can make both of those happen?"

"Sure. Who are we seeing?"

"He's the brother of a friend from Hazelwood," she says carefully, not wanting to lie to him, but unable to tell him the whole truth. "He's expecting me. You don't need to get out of the car; I'll only be a few minutes." She tells him the address. It's in south Seattle.

Walt raises an eyebrow. "Georgina, you're not involved in anything shady, are you?"

She rolls down the window a few inches. There's nothing much to see on this particular stretch of highway except miles of road, endless gray skies, and drops of rain on the windshield. But the air smells like freedom, and she breathes it in. She thinks about the notebook in her duffel bag, the small one she carried around in her pocket whenever it wasn't stashed away in an overhead air vent at the hair salon. It contains account numbers, logins, passwords, and the name of the financial planner Geo used to launder Ella Frank's money while at Hazelwood. In a couple of hours, it will all be turned over to Ella's brother, Samuel, the woman's only surviving adult relative and the caregiver to her children. Samuel will receive the keys to the kingdom, and in return, he's going to give her a gun. To protect herself and her father from the monster that's still out there.

"No, Dad," she says. "Not anymore."

15

It looks like blood from a distance, but as they pull into the driveway, it's clear that it's red spray paint.

MURDERER. Written across their white double garage doors in a series of angry slashes large enough to be read from a block away. It's out of place, the word screaming into the pleasant suburb as loudly as if someone were actually shouting it.

Walt cuts the engine. Geo stares at the garage, then chances a glance in her father's direction. Both his large hands are still on the steering wheel, but his knuckles are pale, his jaw set in stone. Walter Shaw has lived here for over forty years. It's the only house he's ever owned, the mortgage paid off long before Geo went to Hazelwood. Walter Shaw is a good man, a successful doctor, and an upstanding citizen of the community. He doesn't deserve this. Someone has desecrated his house because of her, and the guilt stabs her like a prison shank, quickly and painfully and in multiple places.

"Dad —"

"This wasn't here when I left," he says. He yanks the keys out of the ignition and tosses them into her lap. "Let yourself in the house. I'll take care of this. *Now,* Georgina."

She does as she's told, bringing with her the empty Starbucks cups and her duffel bag, now containing the gun she picked up from Samuel on the way here. She plans to stick it under her pillow. Though the neighborhood is quiet — it's midafternoon on a Monday and most people are still at work — she can't help but feel like she's being observed, as if the neighbors are peering out their windows to witness Walt's infamous daughter's not-so-triumphant return home.

MURDERER. It's not the welcome home she expected, but that doesn't mean it's not the welcome home she deserves.

The house looks exactly the same as she remembers. It's both comforting and surreal. Taking a moment to pause in the front entryway, she breathes in the smell that hasn't changed since she was a little girl. Walt's signature beef stew is simmering in the slow cooker in the kitchen. It's not a large house, but it's always been enough for the two of them.

The portrait of her parents on their wedding day still rests in the center of the fireplace mantel in the living room, full color, but with that seventies retro green-gold tint. Walter and Grace Gallardo Shaw were a beautiful couple. Her father, one-quarter Jamaican, looking sharp in a gray tuxedo complete with satin stripe and oversize lapels. Her mother, half Filipino, dressed in a simple lace gown with bell sleeves, her black hair swept up into a chignon. They were an elegant mixed-race couple during a time when it wasn't as widely accepted as it is now, and Geo got the best of both of them.

Unless her dad moved it, her mother's wedding dress should still be hanging in the upstairs closet. Geo always thought she'd wear it on her wedding day. But after she and Andrew got engaged and the wedding preparations began, the dress suddenly seemed inappropriate for what they were planning — it was too modest, too old-fashioned. The thought shames her now. Sometimes she wonders if this is why she truly ended up in prison — to save her from herself.

She looks at the rest of the pictures on the

mantel, photos she hasn't seen in five years. Grace Shaw is in most of them, but the only real memories Geo has of her mother are from when she was sick. They discovered a lump in her breast when Geo was only two, and she died a few months after Geo turned five. She picks up the photo of herself sitting on her mother's lap on her fifth birthday, surrounded by balloons, a giant chocolate cake in the center of the table. Her mother's head is wrapped in a colorful scarf to hide the hair loss.

Her father only had two girlfriends after his wife died, the first while Geo was in grade school and the second while she was in high school. Both women were very nice, but neither relationship lasted long. A few months each, if that.

"You only get one heart," Walt said to his daughter after the second one ended. He seemed sad, but not regretful. "I gave mine to your mother the day I met her. And she still has it."

For a long time Geo believed that was true. One heart, one chance at love. It had certainly felt that way with Calvin. At sixteen, she couldn't imagine loving anyone the way she loved Calvin James — and the truth was, she never did. It had been different with Andrew, after all. Less passionate but more secure. More mature but less spontaneous. Less exciting but completely fucking safe. As a healthy relationship probably should be.

According to her father, Andrew was married now, to a sales rep who used to work at Shipp. They had twin girls the year before. Geo didn't blame him for moving on with his life. She'd have done the same.

She hears the pressure washer turn on outside. Washing the garage doors is the last thing her dad needs today. Sighing, she heads upstairs.

The last time she lived in this house, she had just turned eighteen. She had packed what she could for college, first staying in the dorms at Puget Sound State, and then renting a house a few minutes off campus with four other girls for her remaining three years. She could have lived at home and commuted to PSSU, but she knew she needed to get away. Once she did, she never moved back.

And it wasn't because her dad was difficult to live with. Quite the opposite. Growing up, she never had a curfew. There were never set rules to follow. She never even had a list of chores, because it was never necessary. Between the two of them, they managed to fill the holes her mother left when she died. Geo did the dishes because her dad did the cooking. She cleaned the inside of the house because he took care of the yard and maintenance. She rarely stayed out late, because Walt could never fall asleep until she was home and she didn't want him to go to work tired. Because she was offered so much freedom, she hardly ever felt the need to take it. Funny how that worked.

She debates going into her old bedroom first, but the idea of a bubble bath is just too tempting. Her bathroom looks exactly the same, and Geo smiles in anticipation of her first hot soak in years. She plugs the bathtub drain and turns on the faucet. She painted the walls a light purple when she was fifteen, and after five years of prison gray, the color is a welcome sight. Or had she been sixteen? She thinks for a moment. It was before she met Calvin, so that meant she'd just turned sixteen.

Funny how she still does that. All the memories of her life are neatly divided into sections. Before Calvin. After Calvin. Before prison. And now, after prison.

As the bathtub fills, she peels off her clothes and takes a look at herself in the mirror. She's aged. It's jarring. Not that she looks older than her thirty-five years — she doesn't. If anything, she can pass for thirty.

But she's much older compared to the last time she saw her face in this particular bathroom, in this particular mirror, in this particular light. There are faint lines around her eyes that weren't there when she was eighteen. There's a new groove etched between her eyebrows, and her skin, once luminous, looks dull and tired after five years of mediocre jailhouse cuisine, sleepless nights, and minimal fresh air.

But she's home. Finally. She's home.

She sinks into the bathtub, the hot, soapy water engulfing her body. It feels so good, she groans. She closes her eyes and allows herself to relax.

Twenty minutes later, she steps out, only because her finger pads have pruned and the water has begun to cool. She wraps herself in an old towel, her mood about fifty pounds lighter than it was the day before. It's almost hard to believe that only that morning she was still in prison, eating runny oatmeal and overcooked eggs, a criminal among criminals.

The good mood doesn't last long. As soon as she steps into the bedroom — her *childhood* bedroom — it all comes back. Her father hasn't touched her room, and it looks exactly as she left it. Just like that, it's nineteen years ago.

The floral bedspread. *Calvin.*

The window he used to climb through late at night. *Calvin.*

The empty jar on the dresser, which used to be filled with candy. *Calvin.*

The memories surround her, crushing her, and panic takes over, sinking its claws in. Dizzy, she puts a hand on the wall to steady herself and takes several deep breaths. Closing her eyes, she forces herself to count down from ten, focusing on her chest rising and falling, her lungs expanding and contracting, listening to her breath as it moves in and out of her body. A simple relaxation technique, something she'd learned in yoga class years ago. By the fifth breath, she's out of danger. By the eighth, she's calm. Her heart slows back to its normal rate, and she opens her eyes again, more prepared.

Calvin may not be gone, but he's not here. And that's good enough for now.

A beam of afternoon sunlight is streaming in from the window, filtered by the pink lace curtains she's had since she was a baby. The room is cast in a soft pink glow. The poster of Mariah Carey hangs in the same spot beside her closet door. Vanilla-scented candles in various stages of melt top the bookshelf. The second shelf is filled with Stephen King paperbacks, a stack of high school yearbooks, ribbons she'd won in dance and cheerleading competitions, and the stuffed gorilla her dad bought her at the Woodland Park Zoo when she was twelve. "Look, Ma, they caught a monkey!" a small child had exclaimed delightedly when they'd come out of the gift shop, Geo swinging the stuffed ape by one of its legs. Everyone around had laughed.

The framed photograph of herself and Angela is still on her bedside table, unmoved after all these years. It was taken a month before her best friend died, when they were both sixteen and laughing on a sunny day at the fair. A frozen moment in time. It was the photo that Geo could never bear to look at afterward. It was also the photo she could never bear to put away.

They had used that photo on Angela's missing-person flyer, the one that had been pasted on lampposts throughout Seattle, the same one that had been in all the newspapers and on TV. They'd also used it in the courtroom years later, and Geo didn't blame them. No one had been more in love with life than Angela Wong.

She picks up the empty Mason jar, the one Calvin filled with cinnamon hearts to give to her. It had been a present, his way of apologizing after the first time he hit her.

Geo never particularly liked the candy, which was the kind that was sweet on your tongue at first, only to turn hot the longer you kept it there. Cinnamon hearts were his favorite candy, not hers. But she'd accepted the gift anyway, because she thought the bright red hearts inside the glass looked pretty. Calvin ended up eating them all, the candy disappearing slowly, until only the empty jar was left.

Geo takes the jar into her hands. She should have done this years ago, right when Calvin gave it to her. She hurls it at her bedroom wall as hard as she can, anticipating the satisfying sound of shattering glass. It smacks the wall, hard, indenting the Sheetrock and scraping the paint.

But it doesn't break.

16

In the beginning, he was all Geo could see.
It was magical, at first. It was heady,
trippy, whatever word best describes being
young and intoxicatingly in love for the very
first time. She loved the way he smelled and
how his cologne stayed on her clothes long
after he'd left. She knew the shape of his
hand, and how it felt when hers was in it,
the exact places his fingers squeezed. And it
stayed magical even when it turned violent.
That's the part nobody explains to you.

The first time Calvin hit her, it was after
the Soundgarden concert. She wore, at his
request, "something sexy" — in this case a
low-cut black top and short skirt she bor-
rowed from Angela. Some guy stared at her
all night, and because she'd eventually
smiled back at him, Calvin had been forced
to punch the guy in the face. When they got
back to his place later that night, they
argued. Calvin yelled and accused and

smashed things. She yelled back, defensive at first, certain she'd done nothing wrong, which only enraged him more.

It was confusing; he seemed to want other guys to notice her, but god forbid they looked too long, or smiled, or spoke to her. He wanted her to look sexy, but god help her if she acted slutty. It was all about lines with Calvin, very fine lines, and she never knew exactly where they were until he told her. And he didn't tell her with words. He told her with punches, slaps, and shoves, all designed to make her feel small and unimportant and humiliated.

Being in an abusive relationship was nothing like Geo expected. She knew hitting was wrong, of course. She wasn't stupid. They had discussed the issue of domestic violence back in sixth grade health class. It was also part of the social studies curriculum in seventh grade. And then in her freshman year of high school, a police officer had come to St. Martin's to give a talk about how to get out of an abusive relationship. On any given day, there were posters tacked up in the hallways, encouraging girls in bad relationships to seek help. *Your guidance counselors are your friends. Talk to us.* Everybody knew that violence in a relationship was wrong. Just like smoking, drugs, alcohol, unprotected sex, sex without consent, and so on. Nobody was clueless about this stuff. There was no lack of education; ignorance was not the problem.

The problem was that none of those public service announcements addressed any of the real issues behind abusive relationships. A relationship isn't supposed to make you feel out of control; it's not supposed to consume you; it's not supposed to change you into someone you don't want to be. But how do you teach that? How do you explain to someone who's never been in a romantic relationship what a healthy relationship feels like?

How do you explain to a sixteen-year-old girl who's never been in love what *love* is supposed to feel like?

And another thing these "lessons" didn't address? Just how quickly the abuse would start to feel normal. Geo's father had never hit her, not once, ever. This was no pattern from her past that was repeating itself. She loved Calvin so much that she began to accept that this was part of the package, part of the price she had to pay to be with him. Because the alternative — not being with him — was unfathomable. And, of course, he didn't always hit. Ninety-nine percent of the time, he was affectionate, kind, generous. It wasn't like Geo was covered in bruises from head to toe. And it wasn't like he was breaking her arm. So, okay, every once in a while he got mad. Usually because of something stupid Geo did. They would argue. If she pushed him too far — if she said something snarky or sarcastic or she hurt his feelings — he'd hit her. End of argument. No big deal. All couples fought. Most of the time, he didn't hurt her. When things were good, they were great.

But when they were bad, they were terrible.

Deep down, though, there was a small part of Geo that liked it. Liked how worked up he could get, enjoyed how jealous he could feel. It was so easy to mistake control for love, to believe he was upset because he cared, that he was protective because he loved her so goddamn much. Sometimes she liked pushing those boundaries, seeing how far she could go before he snapped, seeing how crazy she could make him. It was her way of controlling him, too, because yes, it went both ways.

And yes, she was fooling herself. None of it was okay. But she loved him. Every part of her loved every part of him.

Calvin waited for her most days after school in his bright red Trans Am, and Geo would feel a surge of pride every time she bounced down those school steps. He would be leaning against the car, waiting for her. It was like a scene out of a movie. It was like *Sixteen Candles,* and she was the regular girl, and he was the ungettable guy. The other girls gawked, and while Calvin might smile at them, it was Geo he kissed, Geo he opened the car door for, Geo who drove off with him into the metaphorical sunset.

He had a day job as a house painter, but he didn't work all the time, and so he sold drugs — weed, speed, and painkillers, mainly — on the side to pay the bills, and to pay for the car. Geo was alarmed at first, but then she realized it wasn't as shady as the movies made it out to be. His customers were mostly college students, suburban housewives, and overachieving high school kids. They would come to the apartment, money would change hands, everyone was polite. After a while, that began to feel normal, too.

He never pushed her into having sex. He knew she was a virgin, and that she wasn't ready. So they did other things, things with his hands and his tongue that made her cry out his name as her eyes rolled back in her head. But full-on sex, never.

"I want your first time to be special," he

said. "I can wait."

It only made her love him more.

Calvin took up an enormous amount of space in her life. The more time she spent with him, the less she saw Angela and Kaiser. Cheer practice, something that was scheduled three days a week after school, was becoming more and more of an annoyance for both of them.

"I can't see you tonight," Geo said to him one afternoon. They were sitting in his car at the far end of the parking lot behind the school, near the wooded area. Classes had let out for the day, and she had practice in fifteen minutes. "My dad's expecting me home for dinner, and I have so much homework."

She didn't tell him her grades were slipping. She didn't want him to think of her as a child. He was twenty-one, his high school days long behind him.

"So quit cheer," Calvin said.

"I can't quit." She was appalled at the suggestion. "I'm a cheerleader. Nobody's ever quit cheer before. Do you know how hard it is to make the team?"

"But it's so stupid." Calvin traced a finger up her bare thigh. The hem of her school kilt was short when she stood; it was practically nonexistent when she sat. Reflexively, she spread her legs a little, closing her eyes as his fingers brushed the outer edge of her panties. She wanted them inside her, but she was still shy about asking. Thankfully, she didn't have to. He leaned over and kissed her again, his tongue intertwining with hers, tasting faintly of beer, cigarettes, and cinnamon hearts. It was a taste she would forever equate with feeling like a child and an adult at the same time, which is really what a teenager is. His fingers slipped inside her panties and stroked her, and it felt like she was melting and firming up at exactly the same time.

"Quit," he said again. His middle finger entered her a little deeper, but not much; she was a virgin, after all. His thumb kept pressure on exactly the right spot. It felt good, so good that it couldn't possibly be the same thing as what they'd learned about in sex ed. She spread her legs even wider, feeling an orgasm approaching as he kissed his way down her neck. "If you quit, we'll have more time together. Then I won't have to stop."

Abruptly, he pulled his hand away. She gasped at the sudden absence of pleasure. It almost hurt.

"It's time for practice," he said. "Better get going. You don't want to be late."

She stared at him in disbelief, but the clock on the dashboard didn't lie. She had two minutes to get to the gym, but she could have finished in ten seconds if he hadn't stopped. "You're mean," she said.

"Then don't go."

She couldn't not go. She'd already been late the last three practices. Trying to put herself back together, she flipped down the visor and quickly checked her face. "I hate this as much as you do."

"Doubt that."

"I can't quit," she said. "Angela would kill me."

He snorted. "You care way too much about what she thinks."

"She's my best friend." She gave him a look. "I've known her since the fourth grade."

"Then she'll understand that cheer is stupid and that you now have better things to do."

"She won't see it that way." Geo pushed the visor back up. "She's not exactly understanding."

"She's a bitch, if you ask me."

"Stop it!" Geo smacked his thigh lightly. "Don't say that. This has been hard for her. We used to do everything together, and since I met you, I hardly see her anymore. I think that's why she's so grumpy —"

"Bitchy."

"— *irritated* all the time. I need to spend some time with her." Geo grabbed her knapsack. "It's Kaiser's birthday tomorrow. We're taking him out for pizza and a movie."

"I thought we were going out tomorrow." Calvin's eyes darkened.

Geo braced herself. She knew what that look could lead to. Which is why she'd told him here, at the parking lot at school, a minute before she had to leave. Their fights never escalated when there was a chance someone could see them, and by the time they talked about it again the next day, he'd be calm about it.

And truth be told, Geo didn't like it much when they went out. She was underage, so if they went to a bar, there was always a buddy he'd have to talk to in order to sneak her in without scrutinizing her fake ID. She didn't like the taste of alcohol so she rarely drank. The bars were always dark, shoddy, and filled with smoke. Some guy would always look at her wrong and then Calvin would be "forced" to have words with him. It was exciting at the beginning, but after a couple of months, it had lost its appeal. She missed sleepovers with the girls, poring over old yearbooks and gossiping about who looked better and who looked fat. She missed pizza and Diet Coke, hanging out at the mall, going to the movies. She missed the Friday night parties after the football game.

She missed being sixteen. She even missed Kaiser, who sometimes got on her nerves with his puppylike adoration, but who made her laugh like no one else. She couldn't tell her boyfriend any of this, though, because that world didn't include him. And Calvin didn't like anything he wasn't included in.

"You could come," she said, but they both knew it wouldn't happen. She didn't want him there, and he sure as shit had no desire to hang out with a bunch of teenagers. He didn't respond, and when she went to kiss him, he turned his face so she only got his cheek.

She was three minutes late to cheer practice. The girls were stretching as she ran into the gym, out of breath and slightly disheveled. Tess DeMarco, a fellow cheerleader and a girl who desperately wanted to be Angela's best friend, gave her the once-over.

"You're late," Tess said. "Again. What is it now, the fourth time?"

"Shut up, Tess," Geo said.

Angela, who was on the floor stretching

her hamstrings, looked up. "Don't tell her to shut up. You *are* late. And this is the fourth time."

The gym went quiet. Bodies stopped moving. The rest of the squad always listened with rapt attention whenever Angela, their cheer captain, spoke.

"Ang, come on, it's three minutes." Geo glanced up at the clock on the gym wall. "I'm here. I'm ready to work."

"You're not even dressed," Angela said. Geo was still wearing her school uniform. "You might as well have stayed with Calvin. He's all you give a shit about now, anyway."

Geo felt her face redden, painfully aware that the other girls were hanging on every word. Tess in particular wore a vicious smile, enjoying every second of it.

"Ang, stop it. It'll take me two minutes to change."

"If this is so inconvenient for you, then why do you even want to do this? You clearly think you're too good for it. For the team. And for me and Kaiser, who, by the way, says you haven't returned any of his calls in, like, two weeks."

"Of course I don't," Geo said. This was getting way out of hand, and she was desperate to end the conversation. "You know how much you —"

"You don't want to quit? Fine, I'll do it for you," Angela snapped, cutting her off. She made a point of addressing the other girls. "Who here wants Georgina off the squad?"

Tess's arm shot up, but the other girls looked at each other with wide eyes, completely unsure if this was real or not.

"Stop it," Geo said, alarmed. "You can't —"

"You're always late for practice," Angela said. "And when you're here, you're distracted. Our pyramid almost collapsed last week because you didn't know where your arms were supposed to be. You're lazy, unreliable, and we all know you don't want to be here. And, I hate to say it, but you've gained weight."

Gasps all around.

"I have *not* gained weight," Geo said hotly, and that's when her best friend smiled. Angela knew she hadn't gained any weight, but she also knew it would get a rise out of Geo if she said it. She'd done it to be nasty, and to embarrass her in front of the other girls. "You know what? Calvin's right." Geo could be nasty, too. "You are a bitch."

More gasps. One girl's hand even flew up to cover her gaping mouth. Nobody at St. Martin's had ever called Angela Wong a bitch. At least not publicly, and most certainly not to her face. Several of the girls took a step back, away from Geo, as if to distance themselves from the social pariah she had just become.

"Get out." Angela's own face was a deep shade of maroon. She took several breaths but remained calm. "We'll need your uniform back first thing tomorrow, and your locker cleaned out by lunchtime."

Cheerleaders had extra-wide lockers, same as the football players. It was a privilege to have one. Like it was a privilege to be a cheerleader.

"You heard her," Tess said, her face filled with triumph. It made her look ugly. "The gym is reserved for cheer practice right now. And you're not a cheerleader anymore. So get out."

Fighting back tears, Geo turned and left the gym, running smack into Kaiser outside the lockers. He was dressed for soccer practice. She pulled back, looked up at him, and then burst into tears.

"Whoa," he said, his face filled with alarm, grabbing her shoulders. "Are you okay? What's the matter? Talk to me."

"Leave me alone." She shook him off and continued down the hallway.

She was still crying when she paged

Calvin from the pay phone outside the cafeteria a moment later.

"Come get me," she said, sobbing, when he called back a minute later.

He was out front within ten minutes. She had calmed down by then, her despair turning into anger. She told him what happened, and he listened quietly, nodding, murmuring soothing things, his hand on her thigh, squeezing every so often to comfort her.

Finally, he said, "Cheer means this much to you, huh?"

Geo nodded. She did love cheer. She loved being part of a team, wearing the uniform to school on game days, cheering in front of thousands of fans under the Friday night lights. She might have lost some of her focus lately, but that didn't mean she wanted out. Hell, it was the very thing she and Calvin had almost argued about earlier.

"Okay, then," he said. "We'll fix it."

"How?"

"We'll fix it," he said again. "I've known girls like that my whole life — self-entitled girls, girls who think the whole world revolves around them because they were born beautiful, something they had no control over, anyway. Give it a few days, then apologize. And when things are a bit better, set something up for the three of us to get together. She resents me because she doesn't know me. I should let her get to know me. I'll charm her, and she'll give you your spot back. Trust me."

It was a sensible idea; smart, even. He leaned over and kissed her, gently at first, then passionately, and slowly she felt herself begin to relax. Because she did trust him.

God help her, she did.

17

The room is too dark, the bed too soft, the blankets too warm, the house too quiet. Geo had a routine in prison, specific times of the day when she ate, showered, used the toilet, socialized, cut hair, watched TV, and slept. Rinse, repeat. It will take some time to get used to her new life, which is really her old life, which feels strange and foreign to her now. Things on the outside look the same as they used to, but they don't *feel* at all like they used to. It's strange to not have a routine, to not be told when she can or can't do something. She feels untethered, and it isn't as liberating as she'd imagined.

Sleep won't come, and she stares up at the ceiling at the glow-in-the-dark stars that have been there since she was five. Her father came home from work one day with several packs of them, in various shapes and sizes, and they spent an hour sticking them on. Her mother had died a month earlier, and she was having awful nightmares. Her father promised her that as long as the stars were shining down on her, nothing bad would ever happen.

He was wrong, of course.

A little after ten P.M., she finally gives up on sleep, padding downstairs to the kitchen to make herself some tea. Her father is scheduled to work at the hospital till midnight, and she probably won't be able to fall asleep until he's home. It's weird being in the house alone. After all, she hasn't been alone in five years.

On her way to the kitchen, she glances out the front window, and stops. A black car with tinted windows is parked at the curb, its headlights off. But its interior light is on, and she can detect the shape of someone sitting inside. She freezes.

Then the car door opens and Kaiser Brody steps out. Exhaling, she heads to the front door. She has it open before he even gets to the porch.

"What are you doing here?" she asks him, her breath trailing her words in a mist of white in the cold night air. The chill doesn't bother her. She never got to see her breath in prison; the inmates weren't allowed in the recreation yard at night, when temperatures were the lowest.

"Hello to you, too," Kaiser says. "I was about to leave, and I saw the light come on. Can I come in?"

"How long were you out there?"

He pauses. "A while."

"Why?" she asks.

"You know why." Kaiser looks exhausted, the lines around his eyes and mouth a little deeper than the last time she saw him. He looks older. But then again, she does, too.

"I haven't heard from him," Geo offers. She doesn't have to say who "him" is. They both know.

"Okay." He turns to leave.

"Wait," she says, and her voice sounds more desperate than she intends. She doesn't want him to go. She doesn't want to be alone. "I was going to make some tea. You're welcome to join me."

He turns back, gives her a tired smile. "Sure. Thanks."

He steps inside the house, and she closes the door behind him, locking it with both the dead bolt and the chain. They stand awkwardly for a moment. Like the last time she saw him, she notices how much taller he is now, how different he looks, how different he *smells*. This version of Kaiser doesn't jibe with the boy she always pictures in her head.

This version of Kaiser is a man.

He follows her to the kitchen, and Geo frowns as she scans the counter. "We used to have a teakettle," she says, opening cupboard doors one after the other.

"Use that." Kaiser points to a machine she hasn't seen before. It's sitting beside the fridge, and it looks like a miniature shiny red version of a coffee shop espresso maker. "I'd prefer coffee anyway, if you have decaf."

"I don't even know what that is."

"It's a Nespresso," he says. Seeing the blank look on her face, he points to the table. "Sit. Allow me. We have one of these at the precinct. It's pretty good, though the coffee in the morgue is better."

"The morgue?"

He chuckles, pulling open the tray underneath the Nespresso machine, which also doubles as a stand. He selects a pod, then opens the fridge and takes out the milk. There's a foamer sitting beside the coffee-maker, and he appears to know exactly what he's doing as he makes her a decaf latte. He hands it to her, waits for her to take a sip.

"Well, shit," Geo says. "It's good. I can see why my dad bought one of these."

He fixes a cup for himself and takes a seat across from her at the kitchen table. It's sur-real to be in the kitchen with him, the same place they'd spent a lot of time in as teen-agers, eating pizza and hot dogs, working on a chemistry project, making Jell-O shots for a party they weren't supposed to go to using vodka that her father forgot he had. Now it's only when he smiles that she sees glimmers of the old Kaiser underneath the leather jacket and three-day scruff.

She wonders what she looks like to him.

As if reading her mind, he says, "You look good."

She looks down at her coffee. "Liar."

"No, you do," he says. "You really look okay. The woman I arrested that day five years ago, I didn't recognize her. But you, right now? This is a person I remember."

"It must be the sweatpants and no makeup," she says, but he doesn't laugh. And if she's being honest with herself, she knows what he means.

"Are you mad at me?" he asks. Just like that, they're sixteen again.

She shakes her head, allowing a small smile. "For what? Doing your job?"

"Walter hates me."

"My dad doesn't hate anyone. He's pro-tective. And he blames himself."

"For what?" Kaiser looks surprised.

"For working too much. For not being home a lot." Geo sighs. "For not knowing I was dating a guy so much older. Mind you, Calvin was only twenty-one. But that was a big age difference back then."

"Huge," he says with a nod. "I never liked him. Calvin, not your dad."

"I know. You were a really good friend to me back then, Kai. I'm sorry I wasn't a better friend to you."

"At least I know why now," he says. "And for what it's worth, I forgive you."

"Thank you," she says. It comes out a whisper. His forgiveness means more to her than she realized.

Now, if only she could forgive herself. She sighs inwardly. She knows she never will.

"Did your dad tell you what we found out there the other day?" Kaiser asks, gesturing to the kitchen window. It's too dark to see anything other than their reflections in the glass, but she knows he's referring to the woods beyond. His gaze is fixed on her, searching and intense.

"He didn't have to. I saw it on the news. I had a TV in my cell." She sips her coffee. "They said it was a woman and a minor."

"The woman was dismembered," he says. "And the minor was a child. Strangled. A two-year-old boy."

Geo's sharp, sudden intake of breath sounds like a hiss.

"I need you to look at something," Kaiser says, pulling out his iPhone. It's gigantic, like a small tablet, and it looks even bigger in person than it did in the television commercials. Geo hasn't seen one in real life before. "A picture of the boy."

"No."

"Please," he says, tapping on the phone. "It's important. Just look."

He slides his phone across the table toward her, and despite everything inside her that's screaming *don't look,* she looks. He was, indeed, a child. Cheeks and hands still chubby, eyes closed, belly protruding. If not for the mild grayish cast to his skin, he might have been sleeping.

The heart drawn on his chest looks like blood. Two words are written inside in neat block letters. SEE ME.

"Jesus Christ," she says softly, because she doesn't know what else to say.

"They were found right there," Kaiser says, making no move to take back the phone. "Almost in the exact same spot Angela was buried."

"Maybe it's a coincidence."

"I don't believe in those," he says. "The woman was killed the same way Angela was, and dismembered the same way she was. With a saw. Head cut off, arms at the shoulders and elbows, legs at the hips and knees, hands, feet. She was buried in a series of shallow graves, her torso in one of them, the rest of her scattered around it. The boy was in a tiny grave about five feet away."

He reaches forward, swipes at the phone, changing the picture. Geo closes her eyes.

"Look," he says. "For god's sake, *look.*"

She looks down again. It's a photo of a woman on an autopsy table, same grayish cast to her skin as the boy, hair matted with dirt. Except this image is even more horrific. The woman's arms and legs aren't attached to her torso, and her head isn't attached to her neck. There's a small gap between each, because she's in pieces.

"This is Calvin's work," Kaiser says. "You know it, and I know it."

Geo's stomach turns and she's out of her chair in a flash. She makes it to the powder room just in time, dropping her knees onto the cold tile as the bile comes up her throat. She retches into the toilet until every last trace of her father's beef stew is gone. When her stomach is empty, she stands up shakily and flushes, dizzy from the exertion.

She turns to the sink and splashes her face with cold water. As she rinses out her mouth, she tries not to think about the woman in the picture, and how much it all reminds her of Angela. It's becoming painfully clear that it doesn't matter how long ago it was, it doesn't matter how much guilt and remorse she feels, it doesn't matter how much time and energy she's spent trying to forget it, or how many years she's served in prison. What happened to Angela that night will never leave her.

Something that changes you so profoundly never could. And not only because of how the world sees you, but because of the way you see yourself. It wasn't just Angela who died that night. Part of Geo did, too, and she's long suspected it was the best part of her.

She heads back to the kitchen and takes a seat once again. Kaiser knows exactly what happened in the bathroom, but he looks neither satisfied nor concerned.

"What do you want from me, Kai?" Geo looks at him through bleary eyes. The sour taste of vomit is still faintly in her mouth, and she takes a long sip of her coffee despite her still-queasy stomach. "I don't know what I can say or what I can do. I haven't had any contact with Calvin since that day in the courtroom. I hope I never do."

Kaiser looks at his phone again, and Geo is scared he's going to make her look at another photo. She's relieved when he tucks it back into his pocket.

"Tell me what you know about Shipp Pharmaceuticals's new cosmetic line," he says.

She almost chokes on her coffee. That's about the last thing she expected him to say. "What?"

"You worked for Shipp up until five years ago. Now they have a lipstick line. What do you know about it?" He sees the look on her face. "Indulge me, please."

"I don't know anything about it," Geo says, confused. "At the time I went away we'd just launched a line of health and hygiene products. Shampoo, conditioner, body lotion, body wash, et cetera. There were no cosmetics then, but they were part of my long-term plan. I was VP of lifestyle and beauty."

"Well, they're doing lipsticks now."

She waits for him to elaborate, and when he doesn't, she says, "Okay. So what? That's not surprising. That was always the plan I —" She stops herself again. "That was always the direction the brand was going to go. It makes sense to start with lipstick. They can start out with a few shades, see how they're received, and begin expanding."

"There are ten shades so far," he says. "But the thing is, they've only been on sale for a week. And they're only available in one store in the entire country — Nordstrom's flagship store in downtown Seattle."

"Okay," Geo says again. She has no idea where he's going with this. "That's not uncommon. Both Shipp and Nordstrom are Seattle-based companies, and it's a good test market. If it sells well at the flagship store, Nordstrom will place it in all their stores."

"Do you know how many lipsticks there are in the U.S.? Taking into account all the brands, old and new, and all the shades, current and discontinued?"

"Millions," Geo says without hesitation.

"Want to take a guess on how many Shipp lipsticks were sold at Nordstrom this past week?"

"I have no idea. I don't know how they well they marketed it."

"Less than fifty," Kaiser says. "Which, I'm told, is unspectacular, and goes to show how hard it is to launch a new lipstick when there are already so many to choose from."

"It's competitive, yes. But Shipp knows that."

"Almost all of those new Shipp lipsticks were sold to women —"

"Makes sense."

"— except for one," Kaiser says. "The day

before the woman and child were murdered, a guy bought one of them, a few minutes before the store closed. We requested their security footage."

He takes out his phone again, finds a picture, and slides it to Geo.

For the second time that night, she freezes. The photo is black and white and bit grainy, taken from an odd angle at a distance, but Geo is looking at a close-up. The man standing at the Shipp lipstick kiosk is undeniably tall, dressed in a T-shirt, jeans, and boots. He's wearing a ball cap pulled low, and while the camera can't see the top of his head, the curve of his jaw is instantly familiar. He's even wearing an oversized watch on the right wrist, something he always did, even though he was right-handed.

"Calvin," she says, her voice choked.

"Are you sure?" Kaiser asks.

"It looks exactly like him." She stares at the photo, trying to make sense of it. "I . . . I don't understand. I saw a snippet on the news while I was in prison. They said he was spotted somewhere in Europe — Poland, or Czech Republic. . . ." Her voice dies.

Kaiser swipes the phone, returning it to the picture of the little boy with the heart on his chest. Then he reaches into his breast pocket, pulling out a sheet of torn yellow notepad paper. She's seen it before. It's the same paper he showed her the first and only time he visited her in prison. It's the paper Calvin was doodling on during the trial, the one with the heart on it, the one with her name inside it.

He places the photo and the piece of paper side by side. The hearts and handwriting look almost identical.

One says GS. The other says SEE ME.

"What does he want you to see?" Kaiser asks. His face is neutral, but his neck is flushed.

"I don't know."

"What does he want you to see?" It's practically a roar, and she jumps in her chair.

"I don't know," she says. Her voice is loud, too, but it's not filled with anger and frustration like his is. It's filled with confusion, desperation . . . and fear. "Kai, I swear, I don't know."

"He's sending you a message."

"I don't —"

"He's going to come for you," Kaiser says flatly. The chair scrapes the kitchen tile as he pushes it away from the table and stands up. She sees then that his coffee mug is empty — she doesn't remember him drinking it. Hers is half-full. And cold. "This is all about you, I feel it. If that concerns you at all."

"Of course it does," Geo says, looking up at him. "But I can't run anymore, Kai. I did that already, remember? I'm tired. This is where I am. If he's going to come for me, then let him come. If you're so concerned, you'll catch him this time and put him in prison, like you did me."

"I did catch him —"

"Yeah, and he got away," she says bitterly. "I'm terrified, okay? Is that what you want to hear? Maybe this is about me, and maybe it isn't, but he had fourteen years to come back and kill me after Angela. He didn't. He killed other women instead, and who knows how many more, because you guys didn't do your fucking job and keep him in prison with the rest of the criminals. I was sixteen when I did the worst, most terrible thing I have ever done, or will do. You were thirty when he escaped from that prison, and now it's five years later and more victims are turning up and you still haven't caught him. We can sit here and discuss who's the bigger failure, but I'll save you the trouble: We both are."

Kaiser's jaw works. He doesn't respond.

Geo pushes her chair back and stands up. "I can see you're ready to leave. Let me walk you to the door so you can leave faster."

Geo escorts him down the hallway, resisting the urge to place her hands on his back so she can get him out of her sight quicker. He unlocks the front door, then stops. He looks down at her, his face etched in weariness, mirroring hers.

"One last thing," he says, reaching into his pants pocket. He hands her a slender plastic tube, black matte finish, gold lettering. It's the new Shipp lipstick. "The name of the shade of lipstick used on the boy? It's called Cinnamon Heart. If that means anything to you."

He turns and leaves, slamming the door shut behind him. He doesn't get to see the look on Geo's face, the blood fading from her cheeks as she pales, the new wave of nausea that hits her so fast she might have thrown up again had her stomach not already been emptied. She leans against the wall for support, looking down at the lipstick he'd given her.

Cinnamon Heart. If that means anything to you.

Yes. It does.

18

Toothpicks in her eyes. That's what it feels like to Geo after a short, terrible sleep. Her internal clock woke her at 5:45 A.M., which is when the bell always goes off at Hazelwood, signaling the start of another bleak day. She's still on prison time. Her dad, surprised to see her in the kitchen so early that morning as he was leaving for work, reminded her that it would take a while to readjust to "normal" life.

Whatever the fuck that is now.

Geo's on her second Starbucks Grande of the morning as she meets the gaze of one of the mortgage specialists at her local bank, a rude woman who seemed to dislike Geo the minute her name popped up on the screen. Geo had asked to see someone else, but as she didn't have an appointment, this was who she got.

"I can't approve you for a mortgage," the woman says, folding her hands in her lap.

"I'm sorry. You could try another bank, but they'll likely tell you the same thing."

There's no desk plaque, but the woman has her diploma from Puget Sound State University framed behind her on the wall. Mona Sharp. Undergraduate degree in finance with a minor in communications, graduated three years after Geo did. *Well, Mona Sharp, your communications skills suck.*

"I don't need a lot," Geo says. "As you can see, I have enough to put sixty-five percent down on a house price of —"

"I'm sorry."

"I've maintained excellent credit," Geo says, keeping her breathing regular and even. "I've owned two properties before. And I've had a checking account at this bank since I was twelve. If that means anything to you."

"We certainly appreciate your loyalty —"

"I really want to speak to your manager."

The woman sighs, then leaves the office. She returns a few minutes later with the middle-aged man Geo had hoped to see when she first walked in. Harry Rudnick has been the bank manager at this branch for over twenty years. He's also a friend of her father's.

"Georgina, come on into my office," Harry says. "We'll talk there."

She follows him, giving Mona Sharp an unfiltered stare as she passes. The woman steps back a foot, clearly uncertain as to whether Geo has a prison shank stuffed inside her bra. Geo rolls her eyes.

Harry Rudnick's office is a bit larger, with a view of the parking lot beneath. He shuts the door. "Have a seat," he says, tapping the chair in front of his desk before sitting down on the other side. "How's Walt? Happy to have you home, I bet."

"He's good," Geo says. "And I'm sure he is, but I need a place of my own, Harry."

"I wish you'd brought him with you," the manager says, drumming his fingers on the table. "We can't give you a mortgage, Georgina."

Her back stiffens. "And why not?"

"You don't have a job, for one."

"I'll get one," Geo says. "And I don't see why that's the deal breaker if I'm putting down two-thirds of the money. If I don't pay every month, you take the house. Pretty simple. I know you've approved mortgages before based on assets over income. As you can see, I have assets."

"Yes, I see that." Harry taps on his keyboard, his eyes fixed on the computer screen for a few seconds. "But we can't verify where this money came from."

"Investments."

"Legitimate investments?" Harry asks, then sighs. "Sorry. Look, ask Walt to come in with you. His house is paid. He makes great money at the hospital. He can cosign."

"No."

"Why not?"

"Because he's done enough," Geo says, frustrated that she has to explain it. This is a far cry from the conversation she had with Harry ten years ago, when he approved her to buy her first condo. And three years after that, when she sold the condo and upgraded to a house. "And I don't need him. I can handle this on my own."

"You do need him. In this instance, you do. Perhaps you could rent for a while."

Harry speaks gently, but all she can hear is his condescension. Like the guy at Verizon earlier that morning, when she went to get a cell phone. She was approved, but once he looked up her old account, he clearly recognized her name, because he smirked. It was all Geo could do not to reach across the counter and claw the look off his face. The fancy rose-gold iPhone now sitting in the pocket of her jacket was a small consolation prize, at least.

"Come back tomorrow with Walt," Harry says. "He's your dad. Let him help you."

There's no point in arguing, and there's no point in checking with another bank. Geo shakes his outstretched hand and leaves, heading back to the parking lot where her white Range Rover is parked. Her dad stored it for her in his garage the entire time Geo was incarcerated. She presses the fob and the doors unlock with a soft beep. The luxury SUV feels ridiculous now. It's a vehicle meant for a young, flashy executive, and Geo feels neither young nor flashy. And she sure as shit isn't an executive anymore.

Before she can get in, a shriek comes from her left, and she freezes. She exhales when she sees it's just a child and her mother, a few parking spots away. The toddler is crying, protesting having to get inside the car, a large Mercedes-Benz SUV. Another child is already inside the car, strapped securely, but crying because her sister is crying. The father is about to climb into the driver's side, not making any attempt to assist with either kid, when he looks over at Geo. Their eyes lock.

Andrew.

The shock that registers on his face is almost comical — his mouth forms an O, his eyes bulge — but he's forced to snap out of it a few seconds later when his wife screeches at him to help her. Geo gets inside her car, continuing to observe the family through her dark tinted windows.

Andrew looks . . . different. Geo's former fiancé had just turned forty-two when she was arrested, and now he's firmly rooted in middle age. There's a defined bald spot at the top of his pate, and he's heavier than when she last saw him. Softer. His wife is at least fifteen years younger, dressed in yoga attire. When they finally succeed in getting the squirming toddler into the car, the wife straps on her seatbelt and yells at him. Geo can't hear what she's saying, but there's no mistaking the fury on her face, and the look of resignation on his.

Geo starts her car and heads for home. She was only months away from marrying Andrew Shipp five years ago — the venue was booked, the dress on special order, the wedding invitations set to go out. If she hadn't gone to prison, she would have been his wife. She shudders.

Living a life that isn't meant for you is its own version of hell.

A new message on the garage door greets her when she gets home, as red and angry as the one her father washed off the day before. She parks at the curb and gets out, once again feeling like everybody in the neighborhood is watching her. The graffiti wasn't there when she left this morning; it's clear that whoever's doing it knows when the house is unoccupied. It's also clear that the vandal gives no fucks whatsoever about desecrating the house during daylight hours.

Today's lovely sentiment? BURN IN HELL.

Geo enters a four-digit code to open the garage door — her mother's birthday — and is relieved when the door rolls up into the ceiling, taking the words with it. She needs to figure out how to use the pressure washer. She can't let her father see this. Not again. Goddammit, she needs to get out of this neighborhood.

"They hate you, huh?"

She turns, surprised, and finds a boy just shy of being a teenager sitting on his bike at the end of the driveway.

"Who's 'they'?" she asks, walking back toward him.

He shrugs. He's wearing a thin T-shirt, no jacket or hoodie, and jeans. His hair is too long and his sneakers are dirty. But his face is open, nonjudgmental, and observant.

"Whoever did it," he says.

"Do you know who 'they' are?" Geo asks. "Because this is my dad's house, and this kind of thing is upsetting to him."

The boy shrugs again and rolls a bit closer to her. "Probably some kids at St. Martin's.

270

I dunno. You're famous, though."

"You mean infamous."

A third shrug. It seems to be the kid's primary form of communication. "Whatever. Did you do it?"

"Do what?"

"Kill your friend, way back when."

He seems to genuinely want to know. He's pedaling in circles now, but not going too far. Geo watches him, not answering. Finally, she says, "What do you think?"

Before he can respond, the front door of the house across the street opens, and a woman marches out. She makes a beeline for them. The boy sees her.

"Shit," he says. "That's Mrs. Heller. She's gonna rat me out for cutting class. I gotta go." He stands up on his bike, pumps the pedals, and is almost out of sight before the neighbor steps off the sidewalk and onto the street.

"You're going to get a new message every day until you move out, you know," Mrs. Heller says when she reaches Geo. A retired elementary school secretary, Mrs. Heller has been living across the street with her husband for as long as Geo can remember. Her face, devoid of makeup, is more wrinkled, but the eyes are no less sharp than when Geo was a kid. "Nobody wants you here,

Georgina."

The Hellers are courteous neighbors. Cliff Heller has a leaf blower and is happy to tidy Walt's yard without asking. They pick up the mail when Walt's out of town, and whenever Geo got sick as a kid, Mrs. Heller would bring over a pot of homemade chicken soup. Were they *nice* people, though? Cliff, yes. Roberta, not so much.

"Good morning, Mrs. Heller." Geo doesn't smile, but she keeps her tone pleasant. With the pressure washer out, she presses the button to close the garage door so she can clean it. "I don't suppose you saw who did it. It happened in the last couple of hours."

Every neighborhood has that one busybody who knows everybody's business and seems more invested than everyone else in keeping the "riffraff" out. Roberta Heller is that neighbor, on steroids. Blessed — or cursed? — with an overdeveloped sense of justice, Mrs. Heller is the first to condemn you for anything you've done wrong. Geo used to fear her bad side.

It doesn't scare her anymore.

"I obviously don't approve of this," Mrs. Heller said, jerking her coffee mug in the direction of the garage and almost spilling its contents. "But people are upset with you,

Georgina. Surely you understand that. I can't imagine why Walt would have you come back here. All your presence does is remind people of something they don't want to remember."

"I won't be here long," Geo says.

"Glad to hear it. I've always liked your father, you know," Mrs. Heller says. "Cliff, too. Walt is a good man, and he did his best trying to raise you, but in my opinion, he wasn't home enough. Damn shame you lost your mother as young as you did. You might have made some different choices."

"Don't talk about my mother." The words are out before Geo can stop herself. "How dare you."

If it were anyone else, they might have backed off. But not Roberta Heller. The old woman's eyes gleam, and she steps forward, getting right in Geo's face.

"I used to think you were a good kid." The woman is so close Geo can smell the stale coffee on her breath. "But you surprised us all, didn't you? Turned out you were a wild one, and nobody knew. You had everybody fooled."

Her neighbor is wrong. Geo had been a good kid. She never did drugs, not even pot. She only tried smoking cigarettes once, taking exactly one puff of a Marlboro Light after school in seventh grade, and only because Angela insisted. She felt so sick afterward that she never tried it again. She was drunk twice in high school — the first time was at Angela's house, just the two of them, when her parents were away for the weekend. The second time was the night her best friend died.

No, she wasn't a "wild one." The only wild thing Geo ever did was . . . Calvin.

In fairness to Mrs. Heller, though, that was probably more than enough. She shakes her head at Geo, her face an expression of dramatic disappointment. "Your mother would be so dismayed to see you now."

Geo's fists clench, and she forces herself to take a deep breath, counting to five. It feels like eternity. She relaxes her hands. "You've been good to my dad, Mrs. Heller," she says quietly. "So I'll let that slide. Now please get out of our driveway."

"Your old boyfriend went on to rape and murder how many more women?" The woman isn't done yet. If anything, she's getting herself worked up even more. Her mug is shaking, but not from old-age palsy. She's angry. "Three, wasn't it? Which wouldn't have happened if you'd told the truth all those years ago. And now another woman and little boy — a *baby* — are dead, because he escaped from prison. How do you sleep at night?"

"Mrs. Heller —"

"You should be ashamed of yourself. We don't want you here. Nobody in the neighborhood wants you here. So move out, as quick as you can. Your father doesn't deserve to go through any more than he already has. He loves you, Georgina, which blinds him to who you really are."

"And who am I?"

"The devil. With a pretty face and a showy car."

Geo opens her mouth to retort, but then closes it again. What's the point? Geo served her time. She lost her job. She lost her fiancé. Wherever she goes, for the rest of her life, she's a google hit away from everybody knowing the terrible thing she did.

So fuck this woman. She didn't even know Angela Wong. Fuck Roberta Heller and her self-righteousness and her bad breath.

"Get off my father's property," Geo says. "Before I remove you myself. You are trespass—"

She never gets a chance to finish her sentence because the woman throws what's left of her coffee right into Geo's face. Fortunately, the liquid's not too hot, but it does hit Geo in the eyes while they're open, which stings like hell. Some of it lands in her mouth, too, and she can taste it. No cream or sugar, just bitter. Like Roberta Heller.

If this had happened the day before, she'd have the woman on the ground in a choke-hold. But this isn't prison.

"Roberta!" Cliff Heller is running across the street toward them, and by the look on his face, he saw the whole thing. He's aghast when he reaches his wife, taking her by the arm and shaking her a little. "What are you doing? You stop this. What's the matter with you?"

"I don't want her here, Cliff," Mrs. Heller spits, shaking her husband's arm off while still glaring at Geo. "She's a menace. We're not safe. I don't know what her connection is to the dead bodies in the woods —"

"Stop that now. There's no connection." Cliff Heller looks at Geo, sees her face and shirt covered in coffee, and digs into his pocket. He hands her a wrinkled handker-chief, and Geo takes it without comment, wiping her face as best she can. "She's been in prison. She can't have contact with anyone while she's in there. She's not involved in what happened to those people."

"You don't know that." Mrs. Heller, emboldened by her outrage, takes another step toward Geo. Her husband holds her back. "Nobody knows anything about who she really is. You ought to be ashamed of yourself," she says again.

"I am ashamed," Geo says.

"How dare you come back here?" Roberta Heller's voice is a few decibels shy of a shriek. "Haven't you done enough?"

"Please," Cliff Heller says, but he's speaking to Geo now. "Please, go inside the house. Leave the pressure washer out. I'll clean your garage door; I would have offered, anyway. Please, Georgina."

She nods and leaves the man to deal with his obnoxious wife. They continue to argue in the driveway for another moment, and then finally Mrs. Heller stomps back across the street, bathed in her own indignation. Mr. Heller, glancing around furtively in embarrassment, turns on the pressure washer.

Her father is home for lunch an hour later, armed with tacos and French fries. Geo, dressed in a clean shirt, accepts the food gratefully. When Walt asks her how her morning's been, she shows him her new cell phone, almost identical to the one he owns. She doesn't mention the bank, or the graffiti, or Roberta Heller. If he noticed the wet driveway when he pulled in, he doesn't say anything.

When they're finished eating, she cleans up.

"I have to get back to the hospital," he says with some regret. "What will you do for the rest of today?"

"I thought I'd take a walk," she answers. "To Rose Hill."

It's the cemetery where her mother is buried, and that coaxes a smile out of the normally stoic Walt. Grace Gallardo Shaw is buried under a tree, her headstone made of polished white marble. It's the prettiest spot on the hill.

"Stop at the corner market and bring her some daisies," he says, squeezing her arm. "You remember how much she loved daisies."

Geo nods and returns the smile. She doesn't remember, she was too little, but she knows it comforts her dad to believe that she does.

At the market on the way to the cemetery, she picks out two different bouquets of flowers from the bins out front, paying in cash because her old debit card is expired and she forgot to get a new one at the bank. The daisies, of course, are for her mother.

The wildflowers, colorful and fiery with their pinks and oranges and yellows, are for

Angela. She, too, is buried at Rose Hill, but on the other side.

19

Things were testy with Angela ever since their argument at practice the week before, but Geo took Calvin's advice and kept her distance. Angela lived for drama, some of it real and most of it imagined, and it was best to let her cool off.

On the third day, unable to stand it any longer, Geo worked up the courage to ring Angela's doorbell after school, two Slurpees from the 7-Eleven in hand. Grape for Angela, of course. Blue raspberry for Geo.

She wasn't entirely surprised when Kaiser opened the door. The poor guy had been trying to get them to speak to each other since their fight, without success.

"Thank fucking god," he said when he saw her. "I can't take it anymore."

"Where's Ang?"

"In the kitchen, looking in the fridge at food she won't allow herself to eat. She's doing her whole 'I'm so fat' thing right now.

Come on in." He stood aside to let Geo in, nodding his approval at the oversize containers filled with artificially flavored slush. "She might drink that, though. Where's my Big Gulp?"

"Didn't know you'd be here." She stepped in and stood in the entryway awkwardly, unsure what to do. Angela came around the corner, stopping in her tracks when she saw Geo.

"Peace offering?" Geo said, holding out the grape Slurpee. She must have been squeezing too hard, because the lid popped off and grape slush seeped out the top and onto her hand.

"Oh, nice. Come on in and make a mess, why don't you." Angela had her high-horse voice going, as if nobody had ever spilled anything before.

Kaiser looked back and forth between the two of them. "I'll get some paper towels," he said, backing away. "When I get back in thirty seconds, I fully expect that the two of you will have made up, because you're both killing me right now."

Angela rolled her eyes, and Kaiser disappeared down the hallway.

"I came by to bring you this." Geo offered her the Slurpee. It was dripping onto the floor, but Angela didn't take it. "And to say that I'm sorry. Everything you said was right. I haven't been myself lately, and that needs to change. I've been a shitty friend."

"Yes, you've been a bitch," Angela stated bluntly. Then her demeanor softened. "But I guess I was, too. I shouldn't have yelled at you in front of the other girls. That wasn't cool."

"Thank god," Kaiser said, coming back with a towel. "Is the Great Fight of St. Martin's finally over?" He took Angela's drink and wiped it, then handed Geo the towel so she could clean the floor.

"Shut up, Kai," Angela said absently. The two girls stared at each other. Finally, Angela shrugged and took the Slurpee, taking a long sip. "Yeah. Okay. It's over."

"Hug it out," Kaiser said. When they didn't move, he engulfed them both in a bear hug. Skinny arms wrapped around them, squeezing them tight, and the three of them stood like that for a moment. Nobody said anything.

Then, Kaiser being Kaiser, he ruined it. "Every man's fantasy, right here," he quipped. "Ang, where's your camera? Let's take a picture."

They broke apart, and Angela smacked him on the arm. But she was smiling, and so was Geo. She'd forgotten how much she'd missed this, the weird and comforting dynamic of the three of them. Angela's camera was in the kitchen, and Kaiser grabbed it, taking a picture of them together in the hallway mirror.

"I'm ordering pizza," he announced, traipsing back down the hallway. There was a phone in the living room. The two girls exchanged a look and followed.

They spent the next few hours eating Domino's and fooling around with Angela's new camera. It was a brand-new Nikon, something her father had won in a golf tournament but had no use for, and which he'd bestowed upon his daughter as if he'd picked out the gift on purpose. They snapped a bunch of silly pictures, wasting film, until Kaiser had to go.

"He likes you," Angela said when he was gone. They were up in her bedroom now, listening to one of her mix tapes. Pearl Jam, Alanis Morissette, No Doubt. "And not just as a friend."

"I know," Geo said, feeling a little bad.

"He hates Calvin."

"I know," she said again, and this made her feel worse.

Geo had met Kaiser on the first day of freshman year at St. Martin's. He sat behind her in science, and wouldn't stop kicking the back of her chair, even though she'd turned around and glared at him twice. After class, he followed her down the hallway, a little too closely. She was about to accuse him of bothering her, until she realized his locker was right beside hers. He spent the rest of the year annoying the hell out of her, but along the way, she learned to accept his friendship. He gave it so damned freely, with no expectation of anything in return except kindness.

Angela didn't know what to do with Kaiser at first. His social status was only barely acceptable thanks to his prowess on the soccer field and basketball court, and he'd have been reasonably cute if he didn't have acne on his jaw. And braces. But over time, he grew on her, too. He was mild-mannered and unassuming, and he laughed at her jokes.

"He's thinking of dating someone now," Angela said. She was lying upside down on the bed, her legs resting against the headboard. Geo was sitting on the carpet, legs crossed, near the stereo. "Now that you're with Calvin and there's officially no hope." Angela paused for dramatic effect, then said, "Barb Polanco."

"Backseat Barbie?" Geo was horrified. "No. You tell him no way."

"I'm not telling him shit," her friend said with a laugh. "*Au contraire.* I told him to go for it. The guy deserves to get laid."

Geo knew Barb a little bit from gym class, and the truth was, she didn't think the girl was a slut at all. It was a nasty rumor started by Barb's ex-boyfriend after she dumped him, and Geo felt slightly ashamed for saying the unfortunate nickname out loud. Deep down, she knew why she did.

She was a tiny little bit jealous. She'd never had to share Kaiser with anyone but Angela, and even so, not really.

Out loud, she said, "You're right. It's great. Good for him."

Angela rolled over to look at her. "So you don't care? I thought you liked that he pines for you. If he has a girlfriend, he won't be around as much." She frowned. "You know what? Now that I think about it, you both suck. I would never ignore either of you for a guy."

Geo couldn't argue. Because it was true. God knows Angela had her flaws — she was moody, critical, and bossy as hell — but not once had she ever allowed a boy to come between them. And that was saying a lot, considering how many boys she had chasing her at any one time. What Geo had been doing with Calvin was a direct violation of girl code, a big offense. She had a lot of making up to do.

"You were right about my head being up my ass." She joined Angela on the bed, propping her legs up on the headboard as well. "Our fight . . . that was a wake-up call. I don't want to throw my whole life away for a guy. My grades are slipping, my dad doesn't know anything about Calvin, and I've been lying to him about where I go . . . and now I'm off cheer. It's got to stop. It's just, I've never felt this way about a guy before. You know me, Ang. I don't go crazy. I don't get stupid. But with Calvin, I can't control it. I want to be with him all the time, and I know it's not healthy."

"You guys had sex yet?" Angela asked, her voice casual.

"No!"

"Seriously?" She seemed genuinely surprised. "I figured all the orgasms were messing with your brain."

"I didn't say I wasn't having orgasms," Geo said, her face reddening instantly. She had never been completely comfortable discussing sex, even with Angela, who had lost her virginity the year before and was completely open to talking about it. It felt even weirder because it was Calvin. She loved him, and she believed that certain things should stay private. However, she sensed that holding back about her relationship with him was not the way to go, considering the problems it had already caused. Geo was the one who had changed, who had shut Angela out. She had to let her best friend be part of what was happening with her boyfriend. "We do . . . other stuff."

"Does he go down on you?" Angela's grin was knowing and wicked.

"Ang," Geo said, pained, but a few seconds later, she pulled a pillow over her face. "Yes." Her voice was muffled. "All the time. He . . . he likes it."

Angela cackled. "No wonder you disappeared. But I get it. Has he tried talking you into going all the way?"

Geo moved the pillow. "No, actually. He says it should only happen when I'm ready. And I think I'm getting there."

"You only get one first time," Angela said, her voice matter-of-fact. "Don't do what I did and waste it on the wrong person."

A comfortable silence fell between them, and Geo couldn't help but smile. It was starting to feel like it used to, and she was grateful for the second chance. It only proved she was happier when she had her shit together. Her grades, for instance, needed to be the focus from now on. She had midterms coming up, and she couldn't afford to blow it.

"Bring Calvin to the party at Chad's this Friday," Angela said. "If he wants to be with a sixteen-year-old, then he needs to see what your life is like. No more bullshit compartmentalizing."

"I already asked him," Geo said with a sigh. "He won't go to any high school parties. He said he'd feel stupid because he'll be three years older than the oldest guy. So I told him I didn't want to go bars with him anymore because I hate being five years younger than the youngest girl." She looked up at the celling. "It's, uh, something we argue about a lot."

"He doesn't hit you, does he?" Angela said. Her tone was nonchalant, but Geo could detect the concern behind it.

"What? No." Geo continued to stare at the ceiling. "Of course not."

"Tess said she noticed bruises on your arm during practice a couple weeks ago. She said they looked like fingers, like someone gripped you too hard."

"Tess is making shit up because she wants to be your new bestie." Geo spoke fiercely, glaring at her friend. The bruises were high up on her arm, close to her shoulder, and she hoped that Angela wouldn't insist on checking. "Anyone with two eyes can see that."

Her friend raised an eyebrow. Geo was being too defensive.

"If he was hitting me, I would tell you," she said, softening her tone. To her own ears she sounded completely sincere. "I know that shit's not okay."

The sad part was, she did, too.

Angela was quiet another moment. "Okay," she said. "Well, if he's going to be in your life, that means he's going to be in my life, so I guess I should at least try get to know him. Plan something this weekend so we can all hang out. But not Friday. Friday's the football game and Chad's party, and you're doing both, because we're fucking sixteen, and that's the shit we do. Now get up. I'll help you with your split jump. We have to work off that pizza."

"I'm back on the squad?" Geo held her breath.

"Yes, bitch," Angela said with a smile. "Now, up. I love you, but your thighs are getting fat, and who else would have the balls to tell you that but me?"

20

They both got drunk at Chad's party. It was unintended — Geo didn't even like alcohol, but Friday was a long day, and she hadn't eaten since lunch. Chad Fenton, not a football player or athlete of any kind, was popular at St. Martin's for exactly two reasons: his epic parties (because his parents were never home) and his fruit punch (because his college dropout brother was happy to buy all his booze).

It was the fruit that did Geo in. Chad made his infamous punch in a giant plastic paint barrel, adding watermelon, cantaloupe, strawberries, orange slices, and pineapple to water, club soda, and vodka. Lots of vodka. He made it in the morning, so that by the time people started coming over, the fruit was saturated with alcohol. Geo, starving, passed on the beer, but munched on the fruit. By eleven P.M., she was hammered.

The music was loud and pulsing, Montell Jordan and R. Kelly blasting through speakers set up all around the house. For the first time in months, Geo felt like herself. She was surrounded by people her own age, listening to music she liked, not feeling like she had to apologize for being too young or too busy with school. It was funny how when she was around Calvin, she felt like a totally different person. And while she liked who she was around him — sexy, slightly out of control — she liked being this person, too.

Still, she missed him.

She had no idea where Angela ended up, and she wandered around the large house for a few minutes trying not to look as drunk as she felt. She eventually found her best friend in the den at the back of the house. She was nestled in the lap of Mike Bennett, St. Martin's starting quarterback, her short dress hiked up to expose her long, lean thighs. Geo was wearing a similar dress, but everything always looked better on Angela.

Geo watched them kiss for a few seconds, more amused than surprised. The two had an on-again, off-again relationship, and the on times seemed to be more out of obligation to their respective statuses as the football star and cheer captain — people assumed they should date, so they did.

However, Angela was pretty damn sure Mike was gay. He sometimes lost his erection with her — something she swore never happened with any other guy — and a few months ago, in his bedroom, she'd found a gay porn magazine tucked in his gym bag under the bed. When she'd confronted him, he'd laughed it off, saying that one of the guys on the team must have stuck it there as a joke. She'd broken it off shortly after.

"I'm nobody's beard," she'd told Geo. "But he is the quarterback. If I don't have anyone to go to prom with, it'll be him."

You would never guess he was gay now, the way his tongue was rammed down her friend's throat. Geo headed over to the two of them, the room spinning a bit, and almost tripped on the way there. She tapped Angela on the shoulder.

"Ang, I'm gonna go."

Her friend looked up, lips shiny with Mike's saliva. "Why? It's only eleven."

The room spun again, and Geo placed a hand on the wall to support herself. "I don't feel so great."

"Holy shit, you're wasted. I told you not to eat the fruit." Angela looked back at Mike, then up at Geo. "How are you getting home?"

"I'll walk," Geo said. "I need the air."

"If you need to go with her, that's cool," Mike said, not sounding particularly disappointed. It made Geo think Angela was right about him. You didn't get a girl to sit on your lap and make out with you — let alone the most beautiful girl in school — and then let her go home early without a hint of protest.

"I'm really okay," Geo said. "Stay where you are. I'll call you tomorrow."

She found her coat underneath a stack of other coats in the front living room and slipped it on as Kaiser was coming through the front door. He was with Barb Polanco, and they were holding hands. Geo felt a slight sting, but it passed. She had a boyfriend, after all. Why couldn't Kaiser have a girlfriend?

Because, her brain said stubbornly. *Because he's supposed to be in love with you forever and ever; that's the way this is supposed to work.* A completely selfish thought, but it's how she felt, nonetheless.

"Heading out already?" Kaiser said to her, helping Barb out of her coat.

Barb smiled shyly at Geo. She looked even blonder this week than she had the week before. Since when did Kaiser like blondes?

Geo forced herself to smile back.

"Yeah, I'm wiped."

Looking at her closely, he frowned. "You drunk?"

"Only a little," she said.

"Did you eat the fruit?"

"I'm fine," Geo said, annoyed. "I'll see you guys Monday."

"How are you getting home?"

"She'll be okay," Barb said to him. "She's got it handled. Let's go get a drink."

"One minute," he said to her, handing her back her coat. "Geo. Let's go talk."

Geo rolled her eyes. "I'm fine, Kai," she said again, but he took her by the elbow and led her to the laundry room down the hall, leaving Barb standing by herself in the front hallway, holding her coat.

He shut the door, muting the music pulsing throughout the rest of the house. Geo leaned against the dryer and looked up at him. The room smelled fresh, like laundry detergent and fabric softener and the lavender sachets that Chad's mom kept in a wicker bowl on one of the shelves. "Shouldn't you be with your girlfriend?"

"She's not my girlfriend," he said, looking down at her with concern.

"I'm a little drunk, so what?" The room was spinning. "I just need to lie down."

"I'll take you home."

Geo shook her head. "Not necessary. Besides, I don't think Barb would appreciate it."

"Are you okay with that?" he said. "About me and Barb?"

"Why would you even ask me that?" She frowned. The lights in the laundry room were bright, and she had to squint to look up at him. "I didn't ask you what you thought about me and Calvin."

"I know you didn't. But I'll tell you what I think if you want me to."

"Kai, come on —" Geo took a step toward the door, but he barred her way.

"Why can't it be me and you?" he said, moving close to her. Their hips were almost touching. He placed a hand on her back, sliding it up underneath her hair until it was cupping the back of her neck. "You have to know how I feel about you."

"Because we're best friends," she said. Had he always been this cute, or was it because he had a girlfriend now? His blue eyes were locked on hers. He had long eyelashes.

"That should be the reason why, not the reason why not," he said.

"What about Barb? And Calvin?"

"Well, I like Barb . . . ," he said, but didn't

continue.

"Well, I love Calvin," she said.

He dropped his hand. That hurt him. She could see it in his face. But what was she supposed to do? Lie?

Suddenly, he moved in, and his lips were on hers. They were surprisingly soft, filled with urgency. Geo didn't respond at first, but then she did, opening her mouth. His hands were on the sides of her face, and he kissed her like she was the only person who existed to him. He tasted so different from Calvin. Sweeter. Younger. Gentler. Which was exactly how he was. She felt herself responding, leaning into him, and it was a whole different feeling. With Calvin, there was never anything physical that wasn't accompanied by some degree of guilt. Guilt that he was too old, guilt that he was taking over her life, guilt that she was hiding him from her father. With Kaiser, there was none of that. She was fully herself, and she felt safe. Kaiser would never hurt her, never push her to be anything other than who she was . . . but she had the capacity to shred him to pieces.

No.

She pushed him away. "Kai, I can't."

"Geo —" His breath was coming fast, his face flushed.

"Barb's waiting for you."

"Let's talk about this."

She moved past him and opened the laundry room door. The music flooded back in, surrounding them, taking away the intimacy. At the end of the hallway, Barb was talking to another girl, looking over her shoulder periodically at the laundry room. When she saw Kaiser, she looked relieved.

"She's a nice girl, Kai," Geo said. "Go, have fun."

"And what about you?" Kaiser was staring at her, his expression a blend of frustration and longing. "This thing with Calvin . . . it's real?"

"I love him," she said again. "And if you love me, you'll be happy for me. Like I'm happy for you."

She left the laundry room, walking quickly down the hallway and back to the front door. She gave Barb's arm a quick squeeze before she left.

"He's all yours," Geo said.

The cold night air blasted her in the face when she left the house. Chad Fenton's parties usually went on long past midnight, but she was fading fast. Her father was working at the hospital tonight, and Calvin was expecting her to stop by his place for a bit, but she was too tired to go over there now.

Oh, well. They could fight about it tomorrow.

There was a presence behind her on the sidewalk, and she turned around. Angela was a few steps back and hustling to catch up, the wind whipping her unbuttoned coat back. Neither one of them, in their short dresses, was dressed appropriately for this weather, which was colder than usual.

"What are you doing?" Geo said in surprise. "I thought you were staying."

"Fuck him," Angela said breathlessly, finally catching up. She was carrying her oversize purse and she switched it from her left shoulder to the right. Her camera must be inside it; Geo had seen her snapping pictures of everyone earlier that night. "He is so gay. His tongue was doing all the right things, but his dick? Like an overcooked spaghetti noodle."

Geo had to laugh.

"We're still going to prom, though. Assuming nobody better comes along. For me, not him. I'm as good as it gets, as far as he's concerned." Angela said this matter-of-factly, without a trace of arrogance. When it came to her social status, she was practical. If Mike Bennett was gay and in the closet, then he needed her to keep up appearances. Which was fine, as long as there was something in it for her.

"What about your car?" Geo said, the wind biting her bare legs.

"Still at Chad's. I've had three beers." Puffs of white breath accompanied Angela's words. "I can't drive home like this. My dad will be in the kitchen playing poker with his golf buddies and he'll smell me. I'll come back for the car in the morning. My parents think I'm sleeping at your place, anyway, so they won't even know."

"I told my dad I was sleeping at your place so I could stay out late." Geo shivered under her thin coat. "Do you have an extra sweater in your bag?"

"No, all I have is my camera. It weighs a ton." Angela thought for moment. "Let's go to Calvin's."

Geo gave her a side glance. "Seriously?"

Her best friend shrugged. "I told you I was willing to get to know him, and I meant it. Besides, maybe he can call Jonas to come over and we can all hang out. It would be nice to make out with a guy I can actually turn on."

Geo considered it. She was tired, but she did promise Calvin she'd go over there. "Let's go this way, then. It'll take us twenty minutes to walk there. I should call him."

"Nah, let's surprise him," Angela said.

"Besides, I don't want to go back to Chad's. When I left, Kai was in the corner with Backseat Barbie. Swear to god, her hands were down his pants."

"Shut up," Geo said. "I don't want to know that."

"Knew it bothered you." Her friend's voice was triumphant.

Geo considered telling her about the kiss in the laundry room, then decided against it. That was between her and Kaiser. Some things were private, after all.

Calvin lived in a house on Trelawney Street, in a two-story Craftsman that had been converted into three apartments. The main floor housed an unmarried couple with a baby, and the apartment on the second floor was shared by two sisters in their thirties, both single, both of whom had hit on Calvin numerous times. He lived in the small studio above the garage. It used to be where the owner practiced his drums, and it was fully soundproofed. The studio had a separate entrance at the back, and Geo and Angela giggled as they made their way up the steep steps.

The lights were off inside the apartment, but Geo could see the flickering of the TV behind the window blinds. She rapped on the door and waited. No answer.

"Sure he's home?" Angela asked.

"His car's parked on the street." Geo rapped again, and a few seconds later the light above the door flicked on. Calvin opened the door, hair slightly disheveled, wearing an old pair of low-slung jeans and nothing else. He had a beer in one hand. The light reflected off his lean stomach, highlighting every ab muscle. He looked like a god.

Angela's eyes trailed up and down his body. "Well, fuck me," she said.

Calvin raised an eyebrow.

"So this is what you've been busy with," Angela said, more to herself than to Geo. "I get it now. You gonna let us in, cowboy? Because it's freezing out. You're hot, but you're not that hot."

"That's a matter of opinion," Calvin said, standing to the side so they could enter. "Watch your step. Part of the doormat is sticking up."

Angela went first, giving Calvin a knowing look as she passed him. Geo hesitated, her mind flashing back to Kaiser in the laundry room, the smell of those lavender sachets as he kissed her, the way he felt against her, loving and urgent and gentle.

Then she forced her best friend out of her mind, stepping carefully but purposefully over the threshold and into Calvin's domain.

21

Geo's new iPhone rings loudly, waking her from the first real sleep she's had since Hazelwood. She reaches for it blindly and checks the number. It's nothing she recognizes, but she answers it, anyway. An automated voice speaks robotically in her ear, the words pausing as the computer generates the sentence.

"You have a collect call . . . from . . . *Cat*" — Cat's voice here, and Geo's heart leaps — "at . . . Hazelwood Correctional Institution. This call will cost you . . . one dollar and seventy-five cents . . . and will appear on your next billing statement. To accept, press one. To decline, please press two or hang up."

She presses one, and a moment later, Cat's voice is in her ear.

"Georgina? You there, hon?"

"I'm here," Geo says, and despite her grogginess, her eyes well up with tears. It's only been a week, but it's the longest she's gone without hearing her friend's voice since they met five years ago. "Goddammit, it's so good to hear from you. Why haven't you called sooner?"

"I wanted to give you a chance to get settled. Last thing I figured you needed was to be reminded of this hellhole."

Geo can hear the low hum of Hazelwood through the phone. Voices bantering in different accents and cadences — Mexican, Polish, the melodic lilt of a woman who sounds a lot like Ella Frank, the bark of a CO telling someone to get back in line. She can picture Cat, dressed in shapeless prison sweats two sizes too large, standing at the bank of pay phones. There are exactly six, mounted to the wall, no dividers between them, no privacy. Not that privacy mattered, anyway. All calls are monitored in prison. The legal ones, anyway.

"How are you?" Geo asks. "And don't bullshit me."

"I'm shitty," Cat says, and Geo stifles a sigh. But she wants to hear it, so she doesn't say anything yet. "Oncologist said the cancer is spreading. I've got two new tumors in my femur — wait, is that the thigh bone or shin bone?"

"Thigh bone."

"So yeah, femur. Doc still thinks another round of chemo is the way to go, but I gotta tell you, hon, I'm not sure I'm up for it. He wants to start next week. I already feel half-dead."

"That's because I'm not there," Geo says, feeling about as helpless as she'd ever felt. She picks at a loose stitch on her floral comforter, wishing in that moment she could be there to have this conversation in person. But ex-cons, especially ones who just got out of prison, don't normally make it onto the approved-visitors list.

"I do have good news, though. My parole was approved. I should be out Monday."

"No fucking way!" Geo sits straight up on the bed, feeling like she's about to cry. "And you waited a whole minute to tell me that?"

"I wanted to build the suspense."

Ella Frank's brother, Samuel, had come through. And even quicker than Geo had hoped. She made a mental note to call him later and thank him again, both for the gun and for his help "convincing" someone on the parole board to vote for Cat's release. It had cost Geo a lot, but it was worth every penny.

"I have just enough time to get your room ready," Geo said. "You'll like it. It used to be my mother's sewing room —"

"Hon, about that." Cat sounds hesitant. "I don't know if you really want an old woman living with you. I haven't even met your father. Usually this kind of imposition is reserved for family —"

"You are family. And don't insult me by insinuating you aren't," Geo says firmly. "I talked it over with my dad. We have the room, and I have the time. Besides, we won't be here long, anyway. I'm working on getting a place of my own, and you're coming with me when I do. Now, what time can I pick you up?"

There's a silence on the other end of the line. From her old friend, anyway; the background is still filled with the din of prison life.

"Don't pick me up," Cat says, but Geo can hear the smile in her voice even from two hundred miles away. "I'm not going to make you drive back to this hellhole, and don't bother arguing, because it's not negotiable. I'll take the bus, and maybe you can pick me up at the bus depot in Seattle." Her voice chokes up. "Georgina, I can't tell you how much I appreciate this."

They chat a few minutes more. Geo tells Cat a heavily edited version about how things have been at home so far, making no mention of the spray-painted messages on the garage doors, or her failed trip to the bank, or her conversation with Kaiser about the most recent dead bodies. Cat tells her one of the newbies just got her work assignment as the new hairstylist at the salon.

"Apparently she went to beauty school for a year." Cat sounds dubious. "But I don't know, she has blue-and-green hair. I wouldn't go to a hairdresser with blue-and-green hair."

"Of course you wouldn't. You're sixty-two."

They say their good-byes. Geo hangs up the phone, feeling much better than she has the past couple of days. Cat's release is now something she can look forward to. There hasn't been another woman in the house since . . . well, since her mother died. Walt isn't crazy about the idea of another ex-con in the house, especially one he's never met before. But as an ER doctor, it's not in his nature to not help someone if he has the ability. Geo doesn't doubt they'll get along famously.

She showers and gets ready for the day, blow-drying her hair, putting on a little makeup, even though she has nowhere to be. She still feels discombobulated. In prison she had a routine, things that needed to get done every day. Here, there's almost too much freedom, too much choice, and it's overwhelming.

She has too much time to think.

The doorbell rings as she's making breakfast, and she pads down the hallway to see who it is. She opens the door to find Kaiser standing in her driveway, snapping pictures of her Range Rover with his phone. He didn't take the unmarked today; a silver Acura is parked at the curb. He's wearing a hoodie over a T-shirt, jeans, and Nikes, and he looks nothing like the police detective he is.

He looks goddamned adorable.

"Why are you taking pictures of my car?" she calls out, and he turns and glances her way.

"See for yourself," he replies.

She slips into a pair of flip-flops and steps out. She sees it as soon as she steps off the porch, and stops.

"Fuck," she says, deflating.

Across the side of her white Range Rover, in the same angry red paint, is the word BITCH.

"You have got to be fucking kidding me." She throws her hands up, staring at her SUV in frustration. "It's like they knew I was going to sell it. Fuck. *Fuck*."

Kaiser snaps another picture. "Let's talk

inside," he says. He gives her the once-over. "Unless you have somewhere to be."

She shakes her head, and he follows her back into the house. She catches a whiff of his cologne as he stands beside her unzipping his hoodie, which she takes and hangs in the closet. He smells great, and she's annoyed at herself for even noticing. It's been a long time since she's been around a man who isn't her father, her lawyer, or a corrections officer. And the last man she had sex with — actual sex, with penetration — was Andrew.

She mentally slaps herself. *It's Kaiser. Stop it.*

"What brings you by? Something new with the case?" she asks, heading into the kitchen where her bagel has already popped out of the toaster. "Coffee? I know how to use the Nespresso now."

"Coffee would be good, thanks." He leans against the counter. "I guess I'm here because I didn't like how we ended things the other day."

"And how was that?"

"You know . . . awkwardly." Running a hand through his hair, Kaiser sighs. "With you getting angry. With me feeling bad about it. I don't know . . . it reminded me of being in high school. It felt shitty then, and it feels shitty now. I don't enjoy upsetting you."

"I wasn't upset," Geo says, although in hindsight, she supposes she was. They did argue about Calvin James, which ironically is the only thing they've ever argued about, even going all the way back to high school. "Anyway, why do you care?"

"Because I care about you," he says, taking the cup of coffee she offers him. He sips it black. "I've always cared about you. You're the girl who —" He stops abruptly, his cheeks flushing slightly, and looks away.

She looks up at him. "The girl who got away?"

"I was going to say that, but no, you're not." Kaiser meets her gaze. "Because that implies I once had you. We both know I never did."

They stand in silence for a moment, Kaiser sipping his coffee, Geo ignoring the bagel that's now cooling in the toaster. She notices he's not wearing a wedding ring. "Did you ever get married, Kai?" she asks, her voice soft.

He seems surprised by the question. Nods. "Briefly. It wasn't a good relationship. She's married to someone else now, and they have a kid."

"Andrew got married. They have twins. I

310

saw him the other day, by accident. He was with his family."

"How'd he look?"

"Terrible," she says, and they both chuckle. "But it made me realize that he wasn't for me. That I was chasing the wrong thing. I've always chased the wrong thing."

She lets her words hang in the air for moment. Kaiser doesn't respond, but his eyes are flicking over her clothes, her face, her hair. Not in an intrusive way, in an observant way, and she begins to feel a bit self-conscious. Which is ridiculous, because it's Kaiser. His opinion of her appearance isn't supposed to matter. But she finds herself feeling glad she washed her hair that morning, that she took a minute to swipe on a coat of mascara and a bit of tinted lip balm.

The Shipp lipstick he left with her, Cinnamon Heart, she stuck in a bottom drawer. She didn't try it on. It's now beside the Mason jar that wouldn't break. Where it belongs.

"You look good," he says. "Rested."

"I'm sleeping better," she says. "It's amazing the things you take for granted. I can take showers longer than eight minutes, with water as hot as I like, and without having to wear shower shoes or worry that someone is going to open the curtain before

I'm finished. My dad made steaks last night for dinner. And this morning I got a call from a friend in Hazelwood, who's getting out soon. She's coming to stay here. She has cancer. She . . . she doesn't have much time."

Kaiser nods, a small smile crossing his face. He understands. He knew about her mother.

"Was it terrible?" he asks. "Prison?"

"In some ways, it was horrible," she says. "And in some ways, it was fine. You adapt, you know?"

She's aware that he's now standing too close, smelling too good, looking too clean. She takes a step back.

"I took a few pictures of your car," he says. "I'll file a report when I get back to the precinct. I don't think anything'll come of it, though. It's not like we can get a search warrant for every house in the neighborhood to see who has a can of red spray paint in their garage. Any ideas who did it?"

"Well, it's not the first time," Geo says, and she explains about the two other messages left on the garage door. "I'd love to blame it on that old bat across the street, but she wouldn't do something like this. A neighbor like me reflects poorly on her, and she wouldn't draw attention to it."

"Mrs. Heller? She didn't recognize me when I talked to her last week," Kaiser says with a smile. "She didn't remember that I was the one who broke her window with a baseball."

Geo laughs, delighted. "I forgot about that."

"And remember she came out yelling with that curler in her hair —"

"Which fell out, and you stepped on it and it broke in half —"

"And she picked it up and she looks at me and says —"

"You're a tornado of destruction, young man," they say in unison, dissolving into laughter. They laugh deeply, and fully, and for a long time. It hurts Geo's stomach, and it feels great.

"What was I, sixteen?" Kaiser can barely get the words out.

"Fifteen," Geo says, wiping a tear. "It was at the end of freshman year. I remember because that was the last time my hair was short."

"Your birthday weekend," he says. "I forgot, you're older than me."

"By three months." She punches his arm. "And it's really rude to keep reminding me of that."

"You could pass for twenty-five."

"I feel forty-five."

"Same." He smiles down at her, and just like that, everything feels . . . better. "So why are you selling the Range Rover?"

"I don't want it anymore. It's too expensive and too pretentious, the kind of thing an affluent young executive drives when she wants everyone to know she's an affluent young executive." She gives him a small smile. "I'm not that person anymore. Mind you, I'm not the person I was when I was sixteen, either."

"So who are you, then?" His tone is gentle.

"An unemployed ex-con who has no idea what the fuck to do with the rest of her life." It's the most honest answer Geo can give. "And I'm learning that it doesn't matter how sorry I am — and *I am so fucking sorry* — or how much time I spend in prison, or how many college degrees I have, or how much money I made . . . I will always be judged on the one terrible, horrific thing I did when I was sixteen. I'm not complaining about that, because I know I deserve it, but I don't know how to make up for it. Because if I could, I would."

"So reinvent yourself," Kaiser says, and it's only when he touches her cheek that she realizes she's crying.

"I thought I did that already. How many

times can one person press the reset button?"

"As many times as it takes. But you have to move past it. You have to forgive yourself. Even if nobody else does."

Why they're even having this conversation, Geo doesn't know, but she feels an overwhelming need to explain herself to him. And he seems to want to know.

"It's not that I don't think I can move past it," she says. "It's that I *did* move past it. I think everyone might have forgiven me back then had I told the truth right away, and had I turned Calvin in right after it happened. I was sixteen, only a kid, and kids make mistakes. But what upsets people isn't just what I did that night. It's that I had the *audacity* to go on with my life. I went to college, climbed the corporate ladder, bought a nice car, got myself a rich fiancé. I built a successful life *on top of* the shitty, horrific thing I did. Without owning up to it. Without paying for it first. That's what people can't forgive. And I understand it, I really do. Because it's almost as terrible as the thing I actually did."

"Wow." Kaiser lets out a long breath. "That's pretty fucking self-aware."

"I've had a lot of time to think about it," she says. "It's my fault more women are dead. It's my fault that little boy is dead."

"You couldn't have known he would go on to do those things," Kaiser says. "You didn't know who Calvin was. Back then, *he* might not even have known who he was."

Geo searches Kaiser's face for any hint of sarcasm or condescension and finds none. If anything, she sees kindness. Compassion. "Why are you being nice to me?"

"Because we're friends," Kaiser says. "We have history. That means something to me."

"You're going to catch him, right?"

He nods. "I did it once. I can do it again." He hesitates. "There's actually something I need to tell you about the victim. About the little boy."

"What about him?"

"He was adop—"

His cell phone rings loudly and they both jump, making Geo realize exactly how close they'd been standing to each other. He pulls it out, checks the display, and frowns. Holding up a finger, he steps into the living room, and she can hear him speaking in low tones. He's back a moment later.

"I have to go," he says to her, slipping his phone into his jeans pocket.

"You were going to tell me about the little boy."

"Next time," he says. "It was more of an

FYI anyway, but there's no time to get into it now. There's a lead on Calvin."

She freezes, a sour taste at the back of her throat. "What kind of lead?"

"Nothing that concerns you right now. It may not pan out." Kaiser heads for the door. He grabs his hoodie from the closet, slips it on, then stops. "You sure there's nothing you can tell me? Nothing at all?"

Geo thinks of the letters she received in prison, ten of them, only one of them read. The rest are in a box upstairs, under the bed. Where secrets hide.

"There's nothing," she says, touching his arm briefly. "But I understand why you keep asking me. I do. And if anything changes, I'll let you know."

She closes the door behind him, locks it, and lets out a long breath. There are things that came out at the trial, ugly things, horrific things. She told the court — and by extension, the public — what they needed to know.

The rest, she keeps to herself. And always will. She wasn't perfect, but neither was Angela. In every story, there's a hero and villain.

Sometimes one person can be both.

22

Geo watched in a haze as her best friend stared at her boyfriend. Angela's lips were parted slightly, her tongue skimming lightly over her top lip. Her signature move, something she did when there was something — or someone — she liked. Geo used to think she wasn't aware she was doing it, but of course she was. She saw that now. Calvin took in the sight of them, in their short dresses, the way they were leaning into each other even though they were technically standing still. He turned the TV off.

"You girls want something to drink?" he said, grabbing a T-shirt off the bed and pulling it over his head. If he noticed Angela watching him, he wasn't acting like it. "I've got beer, orange juice, vodka, rum, Coke. . . ."

"Rum and Coke for me," Angela said.

"Orange juice," Geo said. She walked toward the bed, shrugging out of her coat, then sat down on the edge of the mattress, wondering where Angela would choose to sit. The apartment was tiny — five hundred square feet, if that. Other than Calvin's bed, there was only a love seat and a small dining table with two wooden chairs.

But Angela didn't sit. She fiddled with the stereo instead, leaning over it with her back to the room, the hem of her dress hiked up to reveal an eighth of an inch of ass cheeks.

As if Geo weren't here. As if Angela were visiting her own boyfriend.

Calvin was back with the drinks, and Geo took a long gulp of hers, gagging a little as the strong liquid went down. There was vodka in it, which she hadn't asked for, but she sensed she might need it. He handed Angela her drink and came back to sit beside Geo, kissing her, his lips lingering on hers for a few seconds. She felt herself relax.

"You taste sweet," he said. "And drunk. I kind of like it, even though I don't like you drinking without me."

"I wasn't really drinking. I just had some fruit."

He frowned, not understanding what she meant by that, but he didn't ask for clarification. "It's late. Where does your dad think you are?"

"Her house," Geo said, looking at Angela.

Her best friend was watching them with a small smile on her face, but behind it there was something else.

Jealousy. And Geo liked it. Because, just like the day they met Calvin, it was role reversal. She was never the girl who made other girls jealous, and she was enjoying being that girl, for once.

"And where do her parents think she is?" Calvin asked. He was looking at Angela, too, but his expression was hard to read.

"My house," Geo said.

It was warm in the apartment, and the alcohol was making her warmer. She reached down to pull her ankle boots off. Angela already had her shoes and jacket off and was wandering around, taking it all in, not that there was much to see. Small kitchen with a fridge, stove, and a few cabinets. The bathroom was only large enough for a shower stall, tiny sink, and toilet. Calvin's bed was in the living room-slash-bedroom, covered in a red plaid comforter, and the wall unit with the stereo and TV was across from it. The love seat was against the side wall. This little apartment was nothing special, but Geo loved it.

Angela reached into her bag and pulled out her camera. "Come on, kiss again. I want a picture of you two. You're both so fucking hot." She pointed the camera at them and it flashed. "Come on, you guys. Kiss."

Calvin kissed her, and the camera flashed again. "Creep" by Radiohead was playing and Angela turned the volume up. The studio was soundproofed, so there was no risk of disturbing the other tenants or the neighbors next door. Geo finished her drink, and Calvin made her another. The room was beginning to spin again. She'd only been drunk once before, sophomore year, at Angela's when her parents were away and her dad's liquor cabinet was left unlocked. She finished her drink, then climbed up on the bed to lie down. No more, she was cutting herself off. She was one sip away from puking.

The camera flashed a few more times, and then it was in Calvin's hands. In the center of the small apartment, Angela twirled. The short skirt of her tiny dress billowed up around her as she spun, showing more of her thighs, her skin the perfect shade of golden thanks to her last tanning-bed session. Geo caught a glimpse of Angela's white lace bikini panties, but before she could get upset, Calvin pointed the camera at her, and she forced herself to smile.

She coughed into the back of her hand,

tasting something sour. Calvin noticed and came over to the bed, rubbing her bare leg. "You feeling okay?"

"I'm fine," Geo said, but in truth, she was beginning to feel queasy. Grabbing his T-shirt, she pulled him closer to her and said into his ear, "Stop fucking staring at her."

"She wants to be stared at." Calvin shrugged her off. "It's no big deal."

"You don't like it when other guys stare at me."

"Because you're not asking for the attention. Therefore, it's my duty to defend you." The music was loud, and he leaned over to speak into her ear, his breath hot on her neck. "But girls like your friend here, they wither and die if guys don't validate them. I knew that from the minute we met. She's the girl guys fuck. You're the girl guys marry. You're the one I want, Georgina. Only you."

Sure, they were only words, but they did make her feel better. Geo kissed him. He kissed her back, hungrily, his hands running up her thighs and under her dress as he pushed her back onto the bed.

"Oh my god, you guys," Angela said. "Get a room."

"We have one already," Calvin said.

Angela finished her drink in one gulp, her

322

second one since they'd been here. Or maybe it was her third. Some of it dribbled down her chin, and she wiped it away sloppily, almost losing her balance in the process.

"Sorry, we'll stop," Geo said with a giggle, her queasiness under control for the moment. But they didn't stop. Calvin's erection pressed against her hip, and she subtly rubbed against it as he continued to kiss her neck. The vodka was making her uncharacteristically uninhibited. Or maybe it was because *she* was the one with the hot guy who couldn't keep his hands off her, and Angela was the third wheel. For once.

Radiohead ended, and the song changed to Nine Inch Nails' "Closer," a sexy song if there ever was one.

"Dance for us," Calvin said, lifting his head long enough to smile at Angela. "Come on. You know you want to."

Angela laughed, swaying a bit. The heavy beat was easy to dance to and the perfect tempo, not too fast, not too slow. She set her glass on top of the stereo, turned up the volume another notch, and began to move. A trained dancer after years of jazz and ballet classes — same as Geo — she raised her arms up over her head, her long hair trailing down her back all the way to her waist.

As she moved, she mouthed the lyrics.

YOU LET ME VIOLATE YOU
YOU LET ME DESECRATE YOU

She slowly moved her hips, then lowered an arm and cocked a finger toward Geo. "Come dance with me."

Geo laughed and shook her head, but Calvin seemed to like the idea. He cupped her breast, then kissed her again, a lopsided grin on his handsome face. "I know I'd enjoy that." Leaning closer, he spoke into her ear again. "You're hotter than she is any day of the week."

HELP ME
I'VE GOT NO SOUL TO SELL

Bolstered by the booze and Calvin's words, Geo got up off the bed and joined her friend in the middle of the room. Angela grabbed her around the waist and turned her so that Geo's ass was pressing into her crotch. She ran her hands down Geo's shoulders, stopping at her breasts, which she massaged for a few seconds. Shocked but too drunk to protest — she and Angela had never touched each other like that before — she looked over at Calvin. There was no doubt he was loving every bit of it.

Lying back on the bed, propped up on a pillow with arms behind his head, his grin said everything. Geo continued to dance with her best friend, the music wrapping around them like a blanket.

I WANT TO FUCK YOU LIKE AN ANIMAL
I WANT TO FEEL YOU FROM THE INSIDE

Aware of Calvin's eyes on them, Geo turned and faced her friend. Angela's eyes were glazed, her face lit up with drunk amusement. Because she sensed Calvin wanted her to, Geo leaned in and kissed her. She felt the other girl jolt in surprise. They'd never done that before, either, but there was something about knowing Calvin was watching that was a total turn-on. Angela must have felt the same, because her lips parted and they started making out. Hard.

Angela's lips were soft. She was smaller than any guy, and gentler. It all felt more . . . polite somehow. Wetter. Sweeter. She tasted of Coke and rum and lip gloss. It wasn't exactly good, but it wasn't really bad, either. It was . . . different. And not as weird as Geo might have thought it would be, if she'd thought about it before at all.

Calvin was behind her now, his hands

snaking up her dress, his lips on the side of her neck. Angela was still in front of her, and they were still kissing, but her friend's eyes were open. Watching everything. Missing nothing.

But then the room began to spin again, the queasiness back with a vengeance. Geo hated throwing up. She would not throw up, no matter what. It would be the ultimate buzzkill, and they were all having a good time.

Weren't they?

"Need a break," she said, gasping a little. She extricated herself from the group. "You guys keep dancing."

She fell back onto the bed, almost sighing with pleasure as her back hit the mattress. It felt so good to lie down, to close her eyes, to let the pulsing music wash over her. She could hear Calvin saying something and Angela laughing, and after a few moments she forced her eyes open to peer at them. They were still dancing, Angela grinding up against Calvin. Her boyfriend was shaking his head, but he was grinning, too. He pulled Angela closer, wrapping his arms around her, his hips pressed into hers as they moved to the beat.

It bothered Geo. Of course it did. But it was all in good fun, right? Angela was her best friend. Calvin was her boyfriend. They loved her. They weren't going to do anything inappropriate. It would be all right. Geo could take a little snooze and wake up refreshed, ready to keep partying.

She closed her eyes, and it was blissful. The music faded. The world went black.

Geo didn't know how long she was out, but her ears woke up before her eyes did. The music had stopped. She heard a grunt, followed by heavy breathing, and then another grunt.

When she finally opened her eyes, she was met with darkness, and it took her a moment to focus. All the lights in Calvin's apartment were off now except for the night-light in the kitchen, casting a dim glow. Still lying down — her head felt like it weighed a million pounds and there was an intense throbbing behind both eyes — she forced herself to pinpoint the sound of the breathing. She spotted Calvin on the love seat against the side wall. He was on top of someone. Geo could make out an arm dangling over the edge, a flash of dress, and bare legs spread wide open. Her boyfriend was in between them, moving at a rhythmic pace.

Angela.

White lace panties were crumpled on the floor. Calvin's jeans were piled beside them, along with his boxer briefs. Geo could see the mounds of his bare ass cheeks flexing as he thrusted, grunting as he did it, making a sound she had never heard him make before.

Her boyfriend and her best friend were having sex.

Geo opened her mouth to say something, but no words came out. Her throat was tight, and her stomach felt like it was churning butter. She tried to sit up, but her muscles were Jell-O, jiggly and soft and without substance, utterly useless.

She tried to speak again, but the words still wouldn't come. Her eyes were adjusting to the dimness, and it was then that she caught sight of Angela's face.

Her best friend's eyes were open but glazed, her lips parted. The two girls locked eyes, and Angela's mouth formed a word that Geo couldn't hear.

But there was no mistaking what the word was, and Geo wasn't even a lip-reader.

No.

Calvin grunted and made one final thrust, his body shaking as he finished. He pulled out, and Geo could see his penis, still erect, glistening in the dim light. He hadn't worn a condom. He stood up, reaching for his underwear and his jeans. Angela remained on the couch in the same position she'd been in, legs still splayed, dress hiked up to her waist, vagina exposed. Her eyes were dull, her face ashy, and when she moved her head, a tear ran down her temple, disappearing into her ear. She moaned a little, finally bringing her legs together.

The fog in Geo's head was heavy. It seemed impossible to process what just happened.

What had they done? Had Angela even wanted it? Did she even *know*?

Geo's throat opened up, and the words finally came. "What did you do?" she said to Calvin, her voice hoarse.

Her boyfriend turned and saw Geo staring. He grimaced.

"She wanted it," he said. "She was all over me. She wouldn't stop. It wasn't my fault. So if you're going to get mad at anybody, get mad at her." He bent down and picked up the ball of panties on the floor, tossing them into Angela's lap. "Cover yourself up."

There was no mistaking the disgust in his voice.

On the love seat, bottom half still naked and exposed, Angela began whimpering. It was the worst sound Geo had ever heard.

Her best friend sounded like a baby, the sobs small and shallow and weak.

"What did you do?" Geo's gaze focused on Calvin once again. "This is . . . this is not okay."

She struggled to sit up. Her skull was pounding, like someone was taking a basketball and throwing it at her head, over and over again.

"He wouldn't stop," Angela finally said, looking at Geo, her eyes wide and her voice full of shock. "I said no, I asked him to stop, he wouldn't stop —"

"Shut up, bitch," Calvin said to her. "She wanted it," he said again to Geo. On the love seat, her friend's sobs grew louder, deeper. "Your friend is a whore. It shouldn't have happened, but she got me so worked up there was no way I could —"

"You raped me!" Angela's scream was like a bolt of lightning, cutting through the air powerfully and without warning. "You fucking raped me, you sick sonofabitch!"

Geo rubbed the spot on her temple where her headache was getting worse. Calvin was staring at Angela, his lips curled up, his eyes narrow, his hands clenched. Geo recognized that look. She had seen it before and she knew exactly what it meant. Angela had to stop screaming. The screaming would make it worse. She needed to warn her friend, but her brain was working in slow motion, and the words wouldn't come together.

"Shut up," Calvin said to Angela. "You're a fucking whore, and you asked for it —"

"I didn't ask for it! You raped me, you animal!" Angela's screams were feral. She yanked her dress down over her thighs, trying to sit up on the couch. Her hair was stringy, falling over her face in a tangled mess. Her makeup was smudged, her eyeliner and mascara blending together in circles under her eyes. "You're a sick fuck! You raped me, you hurt me, you're a disgusting sonofabitch and I'm going to call the police and you're going to rot in jail, you fucking sick fuck —"

She didn't get a chance to finish her sentence because Calvin punched her in the face. She fell back into the sofa, dazed, but seemed to come to a couple of seconds later. She leapt off the couch with surprising force and made a run for the door. Before she could get there, Calvin was on top of her once again. Only this time his hands were around her throat from behind, squeezing. She managed to wriggle away, but he grabbed her again, pulling her back by the hair, snapping her head back. He yanked his belt out of his jeans, then wrapped it around her neck and pulled, one knee on Angela's back as he held her down. Her friend's nails scratched furiously at Calvin's arms, her belly pressed into the carpet, her legs kicking and flailing in the air like she was swimming.

It was all happening so fast, it didn't seem real.

"Calvin, stop," Geo said, getting up off the bed. She managed to plant both feet on the floor, but when she took a step forward she stumbled. "Calvin, please. *Stop.*"

He didn't hear her, or he didn't care, but either way, he didn't stop. Angela's eyes bulged, her legs still jerking, but the fight was going out of her.

Geo took another step forward, but the room spun mercilessly and she fell. She looked up from the floor as her friend stopped struggling. Still, Calvin held on for a moment longer, until finally letting go, his arms dropping at his sides, the belt still clenched in one fist.

Angela didn't move. Her head was turned unnaturally to one side, her cheek resting on the carpet, her lips parted. A line of drool oozed out onto her chin. Her eyes were wide open and utterly blank. She looked like a life-sized rag doll someone had tossed onto the floor with abandon.

Geo turned her head to the side and vomited.

"Help me with her," Calvin said to Geo, stepping over Angela. He pulled the comforter off the bed and spread it onto the floor. "Come on, help me."

"What are you doing?" Geo's stomach was heaving. Beside her, the mound of vomit was filling up the small apartment with a disgusting reek. Calvin didn't seem to notice. The smell of it made her want to retch again, and she forced herself to stand up. "You hurt her. We have to call 911. We have to call an ambulance."

"She's dead."

"She's not dead!" Geo shrieked.

The idea was absolutely absurd. Of course her best friend wasn't dead. That wasn't possible. Angela Wong was a cheerleader, a good student, universally admired by everyone at St. Martin's High School. She'd been alive and sitting on Mike Bennett's lap a few hours ago, dancing with Geo, laughing, being Angela, being *alive.* There was no fucking way she could be dead.

No. *No.*

But yet there Angela was, sprawled out on the floor, not moving.

Yes. Oh god. Yes. Angela was dead. Because Calvin had killed her. After he raped her.

Geo vomited again, emptying what was left in her stomach.

She needed to get out of here. She needed to get help. She needed to tell someone.

"You're in this too," Calvin said, as if he'd read her mind. He picked Angela up with a grunt, moving her limp body onto one side of the blanket, and began to roll her up. Nonsensically, Geo was reminded of the home economics class she and Angela had taken in seventh grade, when they'd learned to make spring rolls.

"We have to call the police," Geo said, and for the first time that night, her voice sounded coherent. "Where's your phone?"

"If you call the police we'll both go to jail." Sweat was beading around Calvin's hairline as he grunted with exertion. "You did this, too. You brought her here."

"This isn't my fault!"

"It's *all* your fault," he said, pointing at her. On reflex, she cringed. "You brought her here, the both of you hardly wearing anything, and she's dancing all over me, rubbing herself all over me like the fucking slut she is —"

"Shut up! This isn't her fault!"

"Help me with her," Calvin said again.

334

"Let's get her out of here, and we'll figure it out later."

"I can't," Geo said, beginning to cry. "I loved her."

"And I love you," Calvin said, and she blinked. It was the first time he had ever said it. "And if you love me — if you ever loved me — you'll help me get her out of here. You don't, and we'll both go to jail. Don't let her destroy your whole life. We can make this go away. For fuck's sake, help me. *Now.*"

When she didn't move, he dropped his voice, and the next words he spoke were soft, gentle, and completely menacing. "Georgina, please. Don't make me hurt you, too."

Angela Wong, queen of St. Martin's and Geo's best friend, was now a rolled-up lump in the middle of the floor.

Calvin was putting his shoes on. He threw a sweatshirt over his T-shirt. Then he bent over, picking up the body with effort, heaving it over his shoulder.

"Get the door for me," he said.

They buried her in the woods behind Geo's house, the only place she could think of where there would be no traffic at that time of night. She helped her boyfriend carry her best friend's body into the woods, and it felt like they had walked ten miles to find a spot, even though it had been only a few hundred feet.

Everyone has a single defining moment in life, something that thrusts them irrevocably into a new direction, something that affects them at their core, something that changes them forever. Her last image of Angela — with dirt all over her face as Calvin shoveled soil onto her — would stay with Geo for the rest of her life. She had seen that face every night for fourteen years, until the police showed up at her workplace to arrest her. Only then did the dreams stop.

But the guilt? It never leaves. It hangs around like a bad smell that no amount of bleach can eliminate. You can get yourself a new life, get yourself a new love, go to jail for the terrible thing you helped do . . . but the guilt is still there, stinking like an invisible piece of rotting garbage underneath your bed that won't go away no matter how many attempts you make to clean it.

Because that smell — of rotting flesh, of rotting soul — is you.

23

The letters Geo received in prison are opened and read, spread out on the bed around her. One by one, she refolds them, tucking the blue paper back into the envelopes they were sent in. She places the letters in a box. She puts the box in her nightstand drawer, the one on the very bottom, beside the empty jar.

She feels everything, and nothing, all at the same time.

It's easy to get lost in the past, to get buried under the weight and the complexity of the memories she carries with her. The only way to survive it, to have any kind of life despite it, is to compartmentalize it. That chapter in her life all those years ago in high school is best put away in a locked box and shoved into a drawer, to be taken out and dissected only when she's forced to. The rest of the time, it's best not to think about it.

There is no other way to move forward.

It's taking longer than she expected for her life after Hazelwood to feel normal again. Everything seems like a luxury that she doesn't really deserve. Long, hot showers. Staying up late. Sleeping in. Netflix. Ordering pizza. Credit cards. Even the selection of tampons at her local Walgreens is mind-blowing. In prison, there'd been one kind; you bought them in packs of two, and they were terrible.

She doesn't enjoy leaving the house. Except for Mrs. Heller, who makes a point of staring at her, the neighbors avoid Geo at all costs. A woman who lives down the block was pushing a stroller on the way to the park that morning, and at the sight of Geo dragging a recycling bin to the curb, she crossed the street. As if she thought Geo would hurt her. Or the baby. Christ, did people actually think she was capable of that? But stories get twisted, and the more time that passes, the more they grow.

Later that afternoon, someone at the grocery store snapped a picture of her buying a can of baked beans. *Beans,* for Christ's sake. He wasn't even trying to be discreet about it; he whipped out his phone and took her picture. His Facebook post for the day, no doubt.

Geo's back at home now, wrapped in her mom's old sofa blanket, which is stained and worn in several places, but which her dad can't bear to throw away. The TV is on and she has the volume turned up loud in an attempt to distract herself from her own thoughts. She knows she's lonely, and the irony isn't lost on her. In prison, she had friends. Her appointment book at the hair salon was always full. People were happy to see her, to talk to her, and there was laughter and conversation. She felt useful. Now, her fancy smartphone never rings, and the only emails she receives are from Domino's, about the day's pizza specials. She has all the freedom in the world and can't enjoy it.

It's the ultimate punishment. But Cat would be out soon, and things would get better. They had to.

She contacted six hair salons that morning, all of which had advertised on the Emerald Beauty Academy's website that they were hiring new stylists. Geo had renewed her cosmetology license while at Hazelwood. Upon giving her name and asking politely to speak to the manager, two salons had hung up on her. Another two said the positions were filled and they were no longer hiring. The last two invited her in for an interview, presumably because they didn't know who she was.

But they did once she arrived. The first manager, blanching at the sight of Geo's face, asked her to leave. At the second place, the owner of the salon stared at her incredulously.

"You're kidding, right? I don't care how good you are with hair. I don't want my clients around you with sharp objects."

"I could answer phones, sweep up hair, prove myself —"

"I'm sorry, but no." The woman, about Geo's age, shook her head. "I'm a small business owner, and I can't afford the bad publicity."

Geo thanked her for her time and turned to leave.

"You don't remember me, do you?" the woman said when Geo's hand was on the door. "I went to high school with you and Angela."

Geo turned around slowly. Nearby, the receptionist messed around on the computer, pretending not to listen, even though she so obviously was.

"I'm Tess DeMarco," the owner said. "I was on the cheer team at St. Martin's."

Geo blinked, surprised. In high school, Tess had been brunette and very slender. Now she was blond and heavyset. But her eyes, full of accusation and judgment, were the same.

"It's funny," Tess said, walking closer to her. "When Angela went missing, I thought that maybe you did something to her. Because your fight at cheer practice the week before she disappeared was so ugly. I remember your face as she screamed at you in front of everyone; you were furious, and so embarrassed. But then you guys made up, and everything went back to normal, and I thought, nah, you could never have hurt her. I actually felt bad for thinking it. But I was right in the end, wasn't I?"

Geo said nothing.

"I believe in karma," Tess whispered. "And the fact that you're still here and Angela isn't means that yours is still coming. Now get out of my salon, Georgina. And never, ever come back here." She held the door open and continued watching through the glass as Geo made her way to her car.

It's not surprising Tess remembers Angela as this perfect person. Angela Wong could be as bright as the sun, and when she shined her light on you, nothing could make you feel more special, more important, more valued. But when she withheld it, which she often did over petty things, it could cast you into darkness. There was no in-between.

Angela felt everything fully, and if you were close to her, you felt everything she felt.

The only other person who could possibly understand this was Kaiser. He's the only person who loved Angela the same way she did, who felt the loss of her the same way she did. But unlike Geo, he didn't find out until years later what happened to her. He was almost driven mad by the not knowing.

Geo was driven mad by the knowing.

She must have fallen asleep on the sofa, because when the doorbell rings and wakes her up, a full hour has passed. She answers the door, still wrapped in the blanket. It's Kaiser, and he looks about as exhausted as she feels. He's wearing his badge, which means he's on duty.

"Come in," she says, moving aside so he can enter.

"I should have called first," he says, closing the door behind him. "I was in the area, doing some follow-up work in the woods. Saw your car."

"Anything new?"

He shakes his head, frustration etched on his face. "No. Nothing. The lead we had on Calvin didn't pan out. I feel like I'm missing something obvious, and it's driving me crazy. Something I can't see, that's right in front of me."

Geo is standing in front of him. She looks up, and their eyes meet. He's wearing the same cologne, the one that's mildly spicy-sweet, and again, it makes her hyperaware of how long it's been since she's made love to someone. Prison sex doesn't count.

"I'm glad to see you," she says, and she is. "I wish . . ."

"What?"

"Nothing." She takes a seat on the sofa, lets the blanket slide off her shoulders. She's wearing a T-shirt and sweatpants, her go-to outfit now that she has nowhere special to be. He takes a seat on the other end, watching her.

"There's something I was going to tell you the other day," Kaiser says. "About the double homicide I'm working. About the little boy."

"I remember. What is it?"

"The boy is — was — the female victim's son."

Geo frowns. "I don't understand. I saw his parents on the news. They were giving a press conference about it. His mother was grieving, but she's alive."

"She's his adoptive mother. The woman the boy was found with, she was his biological mother."

A long silence falls between them as Geo

processes this, and she becomes acutely aware of the different compartments inside her, each reacting differently to this revelation. The compartments bang against each other like metal on metal, screeching and clanking and noisy, although outwardly, she shows no sign of the turmoil she's feeling inside.

"That's not all," Kaiser says. "The biological father is Calvin James."

The clanking inside her stops. Inwardly and outwardly, Geo is still.

"I didn't tell you earlier because we're not releasing any of this to the press, not until we know for sure what it means," Kaiser says. "I haven't even told the Bowens, the little boy's parents. And I won't, until we have proof Calvin killed them."

"Why are you telling me?" she asks.

"Because I don't know who else to tell," he says. "You're the only person I know who knew Calvin intimately, and is still alive."

She closes her eyes, lets out a long breath, then opens them again. "So what is it you want to know? Whether or not I think Calvin is capable of killing his own child?"

"You don't think that's possible?" Kaiser's eyes never leave her face. "You knew him better than anyone. You've seen firsthand what he's capable of. Nineteen years is plenty of time to grow into a monster."

Geo lets out a laugh, but there's not a speck of humor in it. "Oh, Kai. Calvin didn't grow into a monster. Calvin was *always* a monster. I just didn't see it back then."

She's never felt so small, so alone. She doesn't remember feeling this way in prison, surrounded by the chatter, the voices of women, the presence of other people who were stuck in that box with her. She understood that it was her place to be there, and for five years, she made it work because she had to. There was comfort in always knowing where the walls were. She felt safe — not at first, maybe, but eventually. Here, untethered, unanchored, she is terrified.

She says none of this to Kaiser, but he seems to sense her thoughts. He reaches for her hand, his palm warm and pressing gently, his face full of compassion. It's taken her a while, but she can once again see the boy she used to know, the one who had loved her with his whole heart just the way she was, and who expected nothing in return but her friendship, although he'd made it clear once that he wished for more.

Before she can stop herself, she leans over and kisses him.

Startled, he tries to back away, but the

arm of the sofa is blocking him and there's nowhere for him to go unless he stands up. But he doesn't stand up. Instead, he kisses her back, forcefully and urgently, one hand in her hair, the other cupping her face, and it feels like it did the night of Chad Fenton's party, when they were alone in the laundry room. Had Geo made a different choice that night — had she said yes to Kaiser instead of pushing him away — none of what happened afterward would have transpired. She might not have gone to Calvin's, and Angela might still be alive.

Kaiser kisses her mouth, her neck, the soft spot behind her ears, and then her lips again. She responds, pressing against him, unable to get close enough. Her hand slips under his shirt, undoing his belt. His hand is fumbling with her bra, and then her shirt is off, the bra along with it, and his mouth finds her nipples. She's so aroused that it almost hurts. Every inch of her wants every part of him.

His kisses are a hair shy of rough. His hands move everywhere, and then, impatient, he stands her up, yanking her sweatpants down to the floor. The living room window is right there, but she doesn't care. Fuck the neighbors, let them see. He buries his face in the crotch of her panties, and a guttural groan escapes her lips. Then he slips a hand inside. It feels so good, she almost orgasms right then.

After a moment, she forces herself to pull back. She has to be sure that he's sure. She doesn't want to trick him. She's tired of deceiving people, of trying to pretend she's someone she isn't. Of trying to pretend she's good.

"You know I'm not a good person, right?" she says. "I need to make sure you know that, before we do anything, before it goes any further. I've hurt people, Kai. I've done terrible things."

"I know," Kaiser says. "I know. But you're all I can see, Georgina. You're all I could ever see."

They're upstairs, in her childhood bedroom, and the door is closed, even though they're alone in the house. The afternoon sun is bright, spilling into the bedroom in pink beams through the sheer lace curtains. There are no window blinds to close. Everything is lit up, everything is exposed.

She lies on the bed as he tugs her panties off, taking his time sliding them over her hips and then over her thighs and ankles, making her wait. The rest of her is already undressed. He pauses, his eyes feasting on her nakedness. She allows her legs to fall open slightly, letting him see everything he wants to see, baring it all. For once.

His face is flushed with arousal, and then he smiles. It's not a love smile. It's a smile of genuine amusement, and the sight of it alarms her.

"What's the matter?" she asks, propping herself up on her elbows, suddenly anxious. "Do I not look how you thought?"

Kaiser's grin widens. "No. That's the thing. You look better. But it occured to me that if this had happened at sixteen — and you have no idea how much I wished it would — I'd have come in my pants already."

Relieved, she laughs. "It's okay if you do."

"Fuck that," he says. "I'm a grown-up now, Georgina. Let me show you."

He pulls off his shirt, then his jeans, then his boxer briefs. He doesn't look anything like how she thought, but then, she had never really thought about it back then. He had no expectations to meet. Nevertheless, he is beautiful. He's hard, and he's ready.

Kaiser enters her, slowly but not gently, and she is transported.

24

An hour after he leaves, his smell is still on the sheets, and Geo sinks into them. The first prickles of self-doubt are beginning to creep in. She's an ex-con; Kaiser's a cop. How can this be anything more than what it was? An afternoon sex romp. He probably doesn't even see her as anyone other than the girl he could never have in high school. Now that it's out of his system, she'll probably never hear from him again. Cops have a hero complex, don't they? They need someone to save. Or, in Geo's case, redeem.

Except . . . it doesn't feel that way for her. Being with Kaiser makes her feel like she's exactly where she's supposed to be. And she hasn't felt that way since Angela died.

Rolling over, she reaches into the bottom drawer of her nightstand and pulls out the empty Mason jar. She sets it on the table, staring at the flecks of sunlight that hit it at different angles. Remembering.

The night of the murder, she didn't get back to her house until four o'clock in the morning. Her dad was working an overnight, and nobody was home. Every single house in the neighborhood was dark, and there were no streetlights. She hadn't been able to look at Calvin, the both of them covered in dirt and blood, his hands raw from all the shoveling. His Trans Am's interior light flicked on when he opened his car door, a soft repetitive beep emanating from the dashboard because the keys were in the ignition.

"Georgina —" he said, but she turned away before he could finish.

She let herself in the house and dragged herself up the stairs, every muscle in her body feeling like it had been run over by a truck. Her stomach still felt queasy from the alcohol, and now that the panic-induced adrenaline was fading, she couldn't stop shaking. She was so cold. Her little dress, which seemed like the right choice for Chad's party, seemed utterly silly now. It was covered with dirt, grass, bits of bark and leaves . . . and blood. So much blood. She peeled it off in the bathroom, letting it drop onto the bathmat. With the faucet cranked as hot as it would go, she stepped into the near-scalding spray, as if the water could somehow wash away the horrible thing she and Calvin had done.

Because yes, this was her fault as much as Calvin's. He was right. She had brought Angela to him.

The dirt and dried blood from her hands rinsed onto the bathtub floor in dark-brown streaks. The dirt they'd thrown over Angela's body. Over Angela's *face.*

How could she have let this happen? She knew Calvin was violent. He'd been violent with her, and she'd seen him threaten other guys in bars. She'd seen the way he was looking at Angela all night, simultaneously disgusted and turned-on by her lascivious behavior.

Her boyfriend had raped her best friend. Maybe Angela had gone too far with the dancing and the flirting, and maybe she'd even kissed him — Geo didn't know, she was passed out drunk, she had no way of knowing how it started. But she sure as shit knew how it ended. At some point, Angela wanted it to stop. She said no. Geo had seen her mouth form the word from across the room. There was no way Calvin didn't hear it. And Geo had done nothing to help her.

She stayed in the shower until the water began to cool. Back in her room, she changed into sweats and buried herself under the covers.

Somehow, she fell asleep, waking the next morning to the sound of the phone ringing. She opened a bleary eye to where the cordless phone sat on her night table, and saw Angela's home number on the call display. Automatically, she reached for the phone, and then her hand froze. Because it couldn't be Angela calling.

Angela is dead.

She sat up, watching the phone ring, and then ring some more. The call display flashed. Outside, her dad was home, mowing the lawn, and in an hour he would come upstairs, have a shower, and try and sleep for a few hours. That's what he did after an overnight on Friday.

The entire world was continuing on like normal, except for one thing.

Angela is dead.

She picked up the receiver slowly. "Hello?"

"Georgina? It's Candace Wong." Angela's mother's voice was brisk. "Sorry if I woke you, honey. Can I speak to Angie?"

"She's . . ." Geo swallowed. "She's not here, Mrs. Wong."

"Oh?" The woman paused. "I assumed she was with still with you, since she stayed over last night."

Geo took a breath. She had to tell her.

She had to tell Mrs. Wong what happened, that Angela was dead. How she could not tell her?

Mrs. Wong misread her hesitation. "You can tell me, dear. She should have called us last night, once she got to your place. Victor was up playing poker until two A.M. You think he would have noticed his only daughter didn't come home." She sounded cross, but not at Angela.

Candace Wong would never be cross with her daughter again.

Geo's heart was pounding, and so was her head. Her stomach felt like she swallowed something horribly acidic. It was churning, sending a rippling, burning pain throughout her abdomen.

"I . . . actually, she didn't stay over last night. I last saw her at Chad's."

She closed her eyes. She had just told the first — and most significant — lie that she would ever tell.

"Chad Fenton?" Mrs. Wong said. "Oh right, she did say something about a party last night. You girls didn't leave together? You weren't with Kaiser?"

Tell her. Tell her now. *We did leave together, but neither of us went home. . . .*

"No, she . . . we . . ." Geo took a breath, her thoughts spinning. "I left early, I wasn't feeling well. I walked home. Angela and Kai were still at the party when I left." The words were falling out of her mouth, and she couldn't stop them.

"Her car must still be at Chad's, then." Mrs. Wong sounded pissed off. "Honestly, Georgina, I wasn't too happy when her father bought her that car. She's spoiled enough as it is. Were you girls drinking last night?"

We were drinking. I ate the fruit. I got drunk. I passed out.

"A little."

A sigh on the other end of the line. "Well, there's no point in lecturing you on under-age drinking, that's your father's job. At least you girls had the good sense not to get behind the wheel of a car, but Angie is *so* grounded when she gets home. She's in big trouble now."

Yes, she is, Mrs. Wong. The worst kind. She's never coming home. Ever.

"I play tennis with Chad's mother," Mrs. Wong said, her voice dropping conspiratori-ally. "Rosemarie's a bit of a flake, and I know her husband's an alcoholic. They keep their damn liquor cabinet unlocked, and I know the older son — the dropout — drinks, too. I'll give her a call." Another sigh, impatient this time. "In the meantime,

Georgina, can you call around a bit? You'd know better than me where she's likely to have ended up. If you talk to her, tell her to get her butt home. I'm going to call Kaiser's house next, but if she spent the night at a boy's house, she's in big trouble."

She's in the woods, Mrs. Wong, buried in the dirt. . . .

Geo squeezed her eyes shut. She had to tell the truth. It was the very least she could do, and this was her opportunity to come clean, before she told any more lies, before they found out the horrible thing that happened.

It was now or never.

Fucking tell her!

But the words wouldn't come. Instead, Geo heard herself say, "I can call around. If I catch up with her, I'll tell her to call home."

Whoever said lying was hard was so, so wrong. Lying was easy. Lying was like a hot knife slicing through room-temperature butter. Lying was a bunch of words strung together in a pretty sentence designed to make the other person feel like everything was fine.

Telling the truth, however, was impossible.

They said their good-byes and hung up. Geo's leather Day-Timer, containing the phone numbers of all her friends, was sitting on her nightstand. She would have to call them all, ask if they'd seen or heard from Angela, ask if they knew where she might be.

Because that's what liars did. They lied. And then they lied some more to protect those lies.

She got up off the bed, looking down when she felt something small and pebble-like underneath her foot. It was a cinnamon heart candy, an escapee from the near-empty jar on her bedside table. The gift from Calvin. Looking down, it resembled a little splotch of blood on the cream-colored carpet.

Her stomach turned. She was not going to make it to the bathroom. She reached for her small trash can and threw up into it, heaving painfully, as there wasn't much left in her stomach after vomiting the night before. Clutching the can, she made her way down the hall to the bathroom. She was horrified to find her dress on the bathmat, lying in a crumpled heap where she'd left it. She snatched it up. Through the bathroom window, she could hear the lawn mower still going strong. Her dad was doing the back-yard now. He'd be out there for another twenty minutes.

She stuffed the dress and bathmat into the trash can, on top of the vomit, and headed downstairs to the kitchen, making a beeline for the door to the garage. The cement floor was cold and dusty under her bare feet as she stuffed the trash can into the larger blue bin, piling other garbage bags on top of it. Then she headed back to her room to call her friends, exactly as she'd promised Candace Wong she would do.

It wasn't like she had made one monstrous decision to lie. It was a series of small decisions and a series of small lies, but together, they were growing into a mountain.

The police rang the doorbell shortly after dinner. Geo's knees went weak at the sight of the two uniformed officers. She led them into the living room to where her father was finishing up the pizza they'd ordered. Walter knew Angela's mother had called earlier and was concerned, but he also knew his daughter's best friend had a reputation for being a bit of a party girl. His theory was that Angela had met a boy she hadn't told her parents about, and Geo hadn't said anything to the contrary.

As she spoke to the officers, Geo kept calm. But on the inside, she was screaming. If the cops suspected *anything,* she would tell the truth. She would.

"I got drunk last night," she said to them. She didn't have to look at her father to know that his face would be a mask of shock and disapproval. He'd never known her to drink, because she hardly ever had. "I didn't mean to, but I hadn't had anything to eat since lunch, and there was fruit at the bottom of the punch barrel —"

"You never eat the fruit," one of the cops said, the younger of the two. He wore a rueful smile, and his name tag read VAUGHN. "I've learned that the hard way."

The other cop, only slightly older, glared at him. His name tag read TORRANCE. If there was ever a good cop/bad cop situation, this was it, and these two were perfectly cast. Torrance was the ass, Vaughn was the one who was nice to you and got you talking.

"Keep going," Officer Torrance said to her.

"I didn't feel well. I wanted to go home, so I went to find Ang. We'd gone to Chad's together after the game. She was with Mike Bennett, and they were . . . close. She'd had a bit to drink, too. She seemed comfortable where she was, so I said good-bye and headed out."

"You're only sixteen," Torrance said, his face like stone. "You girls drink often?"

"Not at all," Geo said, feeling a bit defen-

358

sive, despite the fact that she had no right to be. Her father's lips were pressed into a thin line; he wasn't impressed. "I don't even like alcohol, and Ang only drinks if absolutely everybody else is. She's not the kind of girl who needs to drink to have a good time."

"Keep going," Torrance said.

"That's it. I ran into my friend Kaiser on the way out and we talked for a few minutes. Then I walked home by myself, was home before midnight. I was feeling pretty terrible. I got sick before I went to bed."

She couldn't help but think about her dress, currently covered in last night's evidence, stuffed into a vomit-filled trash can inside the garbage bin in the garage. Maybe the cops would sense something fishy about her story, demand to see what she was wearing last night. Maybe they'd find the dress in the garage.

If they did, she would tell the truth.

But they didn't ask. They didn't seem suspicious at all. They questioned her father instead, who confirmed — somewhat guiltily — that he'd worked all night at the hospital and wasn't aware that his daughter had come home drunk.

"And you said the last time you saw Angela she was with Mike Bennett at Chad

Fenton's house?" the younger officer asked.

"Yes." She wondered if he was repeating the question to try and trap her in a lie. She had left Chad's alone — Kaiser, if asked, could vouch for that, along with a dozen other people — but surely someone had seen Angela leave a few minutes later and catch up to Geo on the street.

If someone did, and they asked her about it, she would tell the truth.

But again, they didn't ask. Instead, the older officer said, "Angela have a boyfriend her parents don't know about? She ever say anything to you about running away?"

Is that what they thought? That was the direction they were going in? Geo glanced at her father, who seemed mildly triumphant that they were echoing his own theory.

"If she has a boyfriend other than Mike, she didn't say anything to me," she said, and it was the first completely truthful thing she'd offered all day. "As for the running away, I don't know how many friends of hers you've talked to already, but Ang has a lot going for her. I think running away is for people who don't like their lives. Ang loved hers."

"Well, I think that's all we need," Torrance said, standing up. Officer Vaughn followed.

"If you think of anything else, give me a call."

He left his card on the coffee table, shook hands with her father, and left.

Geo locked the door behind them, knowing she was about to get a lecture about the drinking. Which was fine, and she wasn't planning to argue. She had no desire to be anywhere but home, anyway.

"So? How long am I grounded for?" she asked her father before he could say anything.

"Is that what I'm supposed to do?" Walt said wearily, dropping onto the sofa. "Have I ever grounded you before?"

"No."

He rubbed his face with his hands. "You shouldn't be drinking. And even more than that, you shouldn't be walking home late at night. There are a lot of creeps out there."

I know. I'm one of them. "The neighborhood is safe, Dad."

"That's not the point," he said. "Ever since your mom died, it's just been you and me. And I work a lot, which means you're alone a lot."

"It's fine —"

"It's not fine, goddammit," he said. "You're sixteen. You're still supposed to need me for things, to be able to count on me, to be able to call me when you need a ride home. It's not okay that you left a party drunk and felt you had no way to get home other than to walk ten blocks at close to midnight. Yes, we live in a safe neighborhood, but there's still a lot of sickos out there. You should have called me. More important, you should feel like you can."

"But you were working." Geo could see that he was upset. God, if he only knew.

"The most important job I have is here, at home," Walt said, standing up. "I have enough seniority at the hospital that I don't have to do those overnights anymore. I agree to those shifts because they pay better. But it takes time away from you. It means I'm eating dinner in a cafeteria by myself and you're eating at home by yourself, and that's stupid. You're the most important person in my life, and I ought to start acting like it. This is a wake-up call for both of us, do you understand?"

Her father misinterpreted the look on her face and offered her a smile. "Don't worry, I don't plan to smother you. We both need our space. But I should be able to pick you up from somewhere until we can get you a car of your own. I should be home for dinner most nights." His body sagged. "What if it were you who was missing? What if one night you didn't come home? You're all I have, Georgina. Angela's parents, I know how they don't spend any time with her. And now look, nobody knows where she is. I can't even imagine."

"I'm sure she'll be back." The lie stuck in Geo's throat. She almost choked on it.

The cops questioned everyone who was at the party, but Mike Bennett got the worst of it. The St. Martin's High School quarterback was hauled down to the precinct and held for twenty-four hours. His parents had to hire a lawyer. Everybody who was at the party — at least a hundred kids over the course of the night — corroborated Geo's statement that Angela had spent most of her time with Mike. He admitted that Angela left him at Chad's at some point during the night, and that he had caught a ride home with his buddy Troy Sherman, the St. Martin's Bulldogs wide receiver. Troy had crashed at Mike's house after they'd had a couple more beers, both of them falling asleep after watching a video of their last football game. He hotly denied that they had a homosexual relationship, refusing to admit it even when the cops strongly suggested that he could avoid arrest if he were honest. Mike's parents threatened to sue if the cops didn't quit with that line of questioning, as their son was currently being scouted by several college teams. With no other proof, the police let him go.

Mike Bennett, so deep in the closet he was practically in Narnia, was overheard telling a couple of the guys in the locker room on Monday morning that he wouldn't be surprised if Angela had run off to become a porn star. "Never knew a girl who loved sex as much as she did. That cheerleader thing? It's all an act," he said. "She was into some kinky stuff."

Of course he'd refused to elaborate on what kind of kinky stuff, but of all the rumors that would sprout in the coming weeks, this was the one that upset Geo the most. Sure, Angela had done some stuff with Mike, but not that much, because, *hello,* Mike was gay. He was lying to cover his own ass. On more than one occasion, Geo had been tempted to confront him.

But she couldn't. And the hypocrisy of calling Mike Bennett a liar wasn't lost on her.

Angela Wong's disappearance was both big news and big gossip. People who didn't know anything about what happened were suddenly sure they had seen her places she'd never been, with people she didn't even know. The conversation was ongoing, happening in every classroom, every period, across St. Martin's High School, whether the kids knew her or not. And the more the kids talked, the more the stories grew, growing so ridiculous that Geo would have laughed had she not known the truth.

"I heard she was last seen near the 7-Eleven," Tess DeMarco said to Geo during their fourth-period calculus class. "And that she boarded a bus to San Francisco and is staying with some older guy. I bet she's back within a week. She just wants to freak her parents out and cause drama."

"Oh, so you're talking to me now?" Geo snapped, recalling the other girl's eagerness to get her kicked off the squad. Had that only been last week?

"What? We've always been friends." Tess blinked, feigning ignorance. For a girl who'd wanted to be Angela's best friend, she hadn't wasted any time cozying up to Mike Bennett in the cafeteria during lunch. And he was only too happy to have another girl on his arm to play the role Angela used to.

Lauren Benedict, also on the cheer team, piped up. "Seriously, guys, what if something bad happened to her? What if she found out Mike was gay, and he killed her? She could be buried in a ditch somewhere."

"Mike Bennett is *not* gay," Tess said, her cheeks flushing. "Don't talk about shit you don't know, Lauren."

Geo shook her head and buried herself in her calculus textbook. She only wanted to go home. It had taken every ounce of energy she had to get herself to school that morning. "Shut up, both of you. For real."

It had only been three days, but the weight of the lies was taking its toll. Geo couldn't sleep, couldn't eat. Angela's mother had called half a dozen times, wanting to know if Geo had heard anything new from her friends at school. The phone calls were torture, and after every one, she felt even worse. After the last call, she ran to the bathroom and threw up the chicken pot pie her father nuked for dinner. Walt chalked it up to anxiety over her missing best friend. And of course it was, but not in the way he or anyone else thought.

Geo kept expecting the cops to barge in and arrest her. She couldn't imagine how she'd get through another day at school pretending to be just as confused and concerned as everybody else. Exhaustion overtook her on the fourth night, and she finally fell asleep, only to wake up from a nightmare, her hair plastered to her sweaty face.

"You," the older cop had shouted in her dream. She was in the cafeteria and everybody was staring at her as the two police officers entered, pointing their guns and waving their badges. "You're the reason she's covered in dirt, rotting. You. *You.*"

She cried into her pillow, a full body sob that racked her from head to toe. She had to say something. She couldn't live like this, and it sure as hell wasn't fair to Angela's family. At the very least, Geo knew she had to tell her father. He would know what to do, but the thought tied her stomach in knots. She hated to disappoint her dad, and yet she knew his disappointment would be the least of what he felt once he found out what she'd helped do.

The clock read one A.M. Walt was long asleep, his bedroom door shut, the volume on his white-noise machine turned all the way up. First thing in the morning, she would confess all to her father, and they would go down to the police station together. Yes, it would ruin her life, but at least she had a life to ruin. Angela didn't. Her best friend never had a choice.

Tomorrow. She would come clean tomorrow.

The decision made, Geo managed to fall back asleep, only to be woken up again an hour later by a knock on her bedroom window.

The sound startled her, and she turned over in bed. At the sight of Calvin's face through the glass, her insides froze. They hadn't spoken to each other since it happened, and she was starting to let herself believe that the next time they faced each other, one or both of them would be in handcuffs.

She got out of bed. She was wearing an old pair of sweatpants and a T-shirt with a hole in the armpit. Her face was shiny, her hair twisted into a messy knot at the top of her head. She had three zits on her chin from stress. Calvin had never seen her looking anything less than put together, but she didn't care now. They'd already seen each other doing the worst thing they'd ever done; greasy hair and a few pimples would have no impact on that.

She opened the window and he climbed in, dragging with him a duffel bag that looked stuffed to the gills.

"Where's your car?" she asked, concerned that his bright red Trans Am was parked out front for all the neighbors to see.

"Sold it."

She didn't ask why. She didn't care. He took a seat on the edge of her bed, dropped his bag on the floor, and reached for the jar of cinnamon hearts on her nightstand. There were only a handful left, and he shook out what remained, started popping them into his mouth.

The jar was finally empty.

"How've you been?" He gave her the once-over, raising an eyebrow at her baggy sweats, the messy hair. "You look like shit."

"I feel even worse than that."

"Well, don't," he said. "There's nothing you can do about it now."

"I'm telling my father tomorrow," Geo said. "It's only a matter of time before the cops figure it out, anyway."

"No, they won't." Calvin reached for her hand, and squeezed. She tried to jerk it away, but he wouldn't let go. "If they knew anything, if they suspected, they would have arrested us by now. Nobody will find out, so long as we keep quiet."

"I'm sick inside," she said, staring at him. "Aren't you? How do you sleep? How do you eat? I'm barely functioning."

He let her hand go, ran his fingers through his hair. "Then don't think about it."

"How can I not?" Geo's voice was small. "You killed her."

"You killed her, too," he said.

Her head snapped up. "No, I didn't. How

369

can you even say that?"

"By law, it's the same thing. You helped me move her body. You helped me cover it up. You lied to the cops." Calvin's tone was soft, matter-of-fact, all-knowing. "If this ever gets out, you'll be just as guilty as me."

"So you're taking off?" she said, gesturing to his duffel bag. "That's what you've come to tell me? They're still investigating, they're still asking questions. I can't . . . I can't keep lying to everyone. I can't keep lying to her mom."

"You don't have to lie. Just don't say anything."

He met her gaze with a steady one of his own. On the surface, he looked the same as he always did — handsome, relaxed, confident. But there was something new beneath the surface. Something she'd caught glimpses of whenever they'd argue, something that would peek out for a brief moment, and then scoot back into its hiding place. Whatever it was, it wasn't hiding now. She sensed it. She could feel it staring at her, watching her from someplace inside him.

"I love you," Calvin said. "That hasn't changed. You could come with me."

The words made her stomach churn. Whatever he felt for her, it couldn't be how love was supposed to feel. What they had was something fucked up, something poisonous, something that would kill her if she didn't get as far away from it as possible.

"I can't," she said. "I have to finish school. And I can't leave my dad."

He nodded. "I know. But I thought I'd ask anyway."

He leaned in and kissed her. Her stomach turned, and she tried to move her face away, but he grabbed it in both hands and kissed her more deeply. He had a cinnamon heart in his mouth; she could feel its hard knobbiness rolling around on his tongue. Sweet and hot and spicy, all at the same time. A familiar taste, and it now made her sick.

"Stop," she said, but he didn't.

He pushed her back on the bed and rolled on top of her, one hundred eighty pounds of lean muscle pinning her down. It wasn't much different from when he'd kiss her after a bad fight, when he'd try to win her back after slapping or pinching or punching her. So she lay still while he kissed her passionately, knowing from past experience that squirming and protesting would only make him feel angry and rejected. If she lay still and let him touch her, he'd eventually see that she wasn't into it, and stop.

His hot breath was sickly spicy-sweet as

he kissed her neck, her ears, and her shoulders, working his way down, pulling her T-shirt up. When he flicked her nipple with his tongue, she whimpered. It was so wrong, so incredibly, terribly wrong . . . but it did feel a little bit good, too. As horrible as it all was, she couldn't deny her attraction to him. It was Calvin, after all, and this was their pattern. Plus, he was the only person in the world right now she didn't have to lie to.

And she still loved him, god help her. Feelings like that did not evaporate in a matter of days, much as she wished they would, much as she knew they should.

She didn't protest when he pulled her sweatpants down, or when he moved her panties to the side so he could find her wet spots and make them even wetter, the cool spice of the cinnamon on his tongue adding a layer of deliciousness that made her gasp. She was disgusted with herself but unable to help it. He had touched her like this so many times before, and he knew exactly what to do, exactly where to apply pressure, and for how long.

When she heard the sound of his belt unbuckling, her eyes opened. They had never had sex before — not real sex, as she thought of it, not intercourse. She was a virgin, and she pushed his hand away, trying to sit up on the bed.

"We can't," she said. "Calvin, please. You have to go."

He grinned, his teeth shining in the dim light of her bedroom. "Remember how I always told you we would wait until the right time?" he said, unzipping his jeans. His erection was obvious through his briefs, and he massaged himself through the thin material, never taking his eyes off her. "This is the right time, Georgina. I won't see you again after tonight. I want to be the first man that's ever been inside you."

"No," Geo said. "I don't want to, okay? Please —"

He was on top of her before she could continue, and the weight of him felt heavier and more forceful now. One hand pinned her arms down over her head, the other spread her legs open wider, pulling down her panties. She was wet from his earlier touch, but she didn't want to be touched anymore. She didn't want this to go any further. She wanted this to stop.

She wrangled an arm free and thumped him on the back. "Calvin, please, I don't want to —"

"I'm going to be your first, Georgina. So you don't ever forget me."

His penis entered her, suddenly and force-fully. The pain was searing and intense. She cried out, and he put a hand over her mouth, continuing to thrust inside her, go-ing deeper, and it hurt more than she ever imagined it would. She clawed at his back, her short fingernails ineffectual as she tried to scratch him. This was not the Calvin she thought she knew, who'd always been gentle with her sexually, who took pride in pleas-ing her. This wasn't sex at all, was it? This was something else entirely.

This was dominance. This was taking something he wanted that she didn't want to give. This was rape.

"Stop," she whimpered, when the hand covering her mouth slipped a little. "Please. Stop."

He heard her, of course he did, but Calvin was in own world, where the only thing that mattered to him was what he wanted, what he needed. Nothing else existed. Eventually, Geo went limp, letting her arms rest on the mattress. There seemed to be no point in fighting. Fighting made it hurt more. Fight-ing made it worse.

Karma had come for her, and it was ter-rible.

He left the same way he came in, through the window. Geo never saw him again after that night. Not until years later, not until the trial.

Kaiser had asked her the other day if she ever worried about Calvin coming back for her. She'd told him that she wasn't concerned, which was true. Calvin had already taken the best part of her the night she'd watched him rape and murder her best friend. What was left, he took the night he raped her in her own bedroom, with her father sleeping right down the hall.

Geo stares at the empty Mason jar on the nightstand now, the one that used to contain all her innocence, all her goodness. She'd kept it all this time. A therapist might have a field day trying to analyze why she had never thrown it away and, more important, why she'd kept it in a spot in her bedroom where she could clearly see it.

The answer was simple. It was punishment for what she'd done to Angela. And a reminder of her own trauma, her own pain, which she'd brought on herself for being so young and so stupid.

Her phone pings. Geo checks the text message, her heart lifting a little when she sees it's from Kaiser. A small smile crosses her lips. Maybe it can work out between them . . . as long as she never tells him the whole story.

No one, not even Kaiser, could love her if they knew the whole story.

Her face falls when she sees what he's sent her.

Two more bodies found in the woods behind St. Martin's. Adult female and a child, killed same way as the first two.

A second message follows a few seconds later.

Calvin spotted in town. Stay inside. Lock the doors.

■ ■ ■ ■

PART FOUR: DEPRESSION

■ ■ ■ ■

"There is nothing more deceptive than an obvious fact."
~ Arthur Conan Doyle

25

Mo has long blond hair, warm brown eyes, an easy grin, and a drooling problem. That's because Mo is a dog. And not just any dog, but a cadaver dog. The golden retriever's tail thumps on the grass as Kaiser approaches the tree he's resting under, about twenty feet from where he found the bodies, in the woods behind St. Martin's High School. He and Kaiser have met a few times before.

Mo's owner looks up and smiles. In her early sixties, Jane Bowman is dressed in hiking gear — waterproof shell jacket from The North Face, Dri-FIT pants, Merrell boots. No makeup, but Kaiser's never known her to wear any, and her long gray hair is pulled back from her face with a black scrunchy.

"Thought you two were retired," he says to Jane with a smile, and they embrace warmly.

"Thought we were, too," she says, and Mo

stands up. He nudges Kaiser, who kneels and gives the dog a full minute of pats before straightening up again.

"So walk me through what happened."

"Well, you know Mo's an old guy now, like me," Jane says, looking down at the furry yellow face with fondness. The dog is resting on the grass once again, gnawing on a chew toy, unbothered by the activity of the police officers and crime-scene technicians not far away. "Bones are getting creaky, hips are starting to go, and so it was time for us both to retire last year. But working dogs, just like working people, tend to get bored in their retirement. So you can imagine how happy he was to be walking through the woods this morning and suddenly pick up a scent. We were on the east side of the woods, on the trail, when he got all excited, put his nose to the ground, and started running. At first I didn't know whether to restrain him or let him go, but I hadn't seen that zest in him in a long time. So I let him run and followed him, bad hips be damned. He finally zeroes in on the spot and stands there and barks and barks. I caught up to him and saw that the earth had been disturbed. I didn't realize we had made it all the way through the woods to the high school."

"If you were on the path on the east end, you two had to have to come almost a quarter of a mile," Kaiser says, marveling at the old dog. Mo looks up and grins.

"Around that, yeah. Anyway, I know the drill. Called an old friend at Seattle PD to ask if you guys wanted to come see if there's something in the ground. Took a few hours for you guys to show up, but you did." Jane smiles. "And wouldn't you know, there is."

Kaiser reaches down, gives the dog another pat. "Hope he got a cookie."

"Gave him two. He earned it." She pauses, her smile fading. "I caught a glimpse of what they dug up. Pretty bad what happened to the woman. And a child, wow. Hope you catch the bastard, Kai."

They say their good-byes and Kaiser heads back to the crime scene. Two bodies, like the time before. The woman looks to be a few years older than Claire Toliver, the last victim. The child — a girl, this time — is a bit older as well, maybe three or four. Her Elsa doll from the movie *Frozen* was found a few feet away. Other than that, the scene is identical. The woman was dismembered, the child strangled, and on the little girl's chest was the same heart drawn with the same lipstick. Inside the heart were the same words.

SEE ME.

Like Claire Toliver, the woman's eyes are gouged out. Empty sockets where they once were, the edges rough. And like Claire Toliver, Kaiser doesn't feel optimistic they'll find them.

He wonders if the killer keeps them in a jar somewhere, like Ed Gein. Or if he eats them, like Jeffrey Dahmer. Or if he simply throws them away, the act of scraping them out satisfying enough on its own. What's the significance? *See me.* What does the killer want them to see?

Or is it some kind of punishment to the woman — all women? one specific woman? — for *not* seeing?

Kim stands beside him. He can hear the scratching of his partner's pencil against her notepad, and the sound is intrusive and irritating. The act of writing things down gives them significance in her mind, helps her remember things later. Kaiser doesn't work this way, never has. He takes mental pictures, allowing his thoughts to meander unrestricted where they will. He also prefers to do this quietly, and her scratchy note taking is ruining his silence.

They haven't spoken on a personal level in a couple of days, and he notices she's wearing her wedding band. She normally doesn't while she's on the job or when she's alone with him, so he's not sure what makes today special. Perhaps she and Dave had a good weekend away, celebrating their anniversary, rekindling the fire in their marriage. He's curious, but he'll never ask her; it isn't his business and honestly never was. The only thing deader than their affair were the two bodies in the ground, one of them in pieces.

Kim tucks her notebook away. "You think she's Calvin James's daughter, too?"

"I don't think anything right now," he replies. His tone is a bit more hostile than he intended, and he adds, "We'll find out soon enough."

"I don't get it." She shakes her head, blond ponytail swinging, her face twisted into a grimace. Kaiser understands. It's hard seeing victims this way, especially children. And that's fine; it should never be easy; it should never not be horrifying. "Why kill your own child? And, if this is similar to the other case, why kill her mother? Why take her eyes? This is so confusing, I can't even begin to make sense of it."

"Lesson number one when dealing with serial murder is that it never makes sense," Kaiser says. "Calvin James isn't like you or me. He might have been once, but he's morphed into something else. His sociopathy was clear when I was arrested him five years ago. They don't operate in logic. The whys of it are unimportant; he can save that for his prison shrink. All I care about is catching the motherfucker."

"Got the ID on the little girl, Detective," an officer says, coming up behind him and waving a cell phone. "Parents filed a missing-person report this morning. I have it here. I can forward it to you."

A moment later it's on Kaiser's phone. He opens up the document, scrolls through it.

"Who is it?" Kim asks.

He hands her the phone, lets her read it for herself. The child's name is Emily Rudd. Her birthday was two days ago; she just turned four. She went missing from her home in Issaquah, a city about thirty minutes east of Seattle. Same story as with Henry. Parents woke up to find her gone. Didn't panic immediately, as Emily was a sleepwalker and they'd found her in various places inside the house before this. Issaquah police had no reason to suspect foul play.

But it was foul play, of the very foulest kind.

"Jesus," Kim says, handing the phone

back. "Those poor parents."

"Have that officer look into whether she was adopted. I put a rush on the DNA, but if we can confirm that the child is adopted, that will tell us enough to get started. Keep working on the woman's ID in the meantime."

"Will do. But I think we need to talk with Georgina Shaw. She's the only person we know of who had any kind of intimate relationship with Calvin James and is still alive. Have you been in contact with her?"

"A little." He feels his jaw clench, tries to stop it, but she catches it and knows instantly what the facial tic means.

"Kai," Kim says, shocked, and he can hear from her tone in that one syllable that she knows what he's been up to. But he doesn't want to hear about it, not from her. They're both guilty of bad judgment, and she's in no place to lecture him. She does, anyway. "You can't be serious. She's a person of interest in this case."

"She has nothing to do with it."

"It's completely inappropriate."

He turns to her. "Pretty sure I don't need a lecture from you about which relationships are inappropriate," he says softly.

Kim's face reddens. "Okay, I deserved that," she says, admonished. She looks over her shoulder to make sure nobody nearby can hear them. "But still, if you're involved with her because you're upset with me, I really think —"

"Don't flatter yourself," Kaiser says with a small smile. "Seriously. I'm happy you and Dave are back on track. We fucked for a while, it's over now, and it's cool. But it means my personal life is no longer your concern. Got it?"

Kim looks as if she's been slapped. Her cheeks flush deep crimson and her eyes fill with tears. She turns away, wiping her face quickly, pulling herself together.

He knows they'll never speak of it again, and he won't be surprised if she puts in for a transfer once this case is closed. That's the thing with affairs. They are, by definition, a temporary relationship. They always end, one way or another, and they almost always end badly.

"Detective?" A different officer is standing behind Kaiser, cell phone in his hand. He touches Kaiser's shoulder. "The parents just arrived at the precinct."

"That was fast."

"They both work here in Seattle," the officer says. He indicates the phone in his hand, the call from the precinct still connected. "What should I tell them?"

"I'm on my way."

Grief manifests differently in different people, and Kaiser learned a long time ago to stop judging. You can't tell people how they're supposed to feel, when they're supposed to feel it, or how they're supposed to show it. Daniel Rudd and Lara Friedman, Emily Rudd's parents, nearly collapse at the news of their young daughter's death at first, crying and shaking and wanting details Kaiser doesn't have yet. He assures them her death was quick, and that there were no outward signs of abuse.

They demand to see her, but the bodies are being examined in the morgue. Kaiser shows them a picture instead — the kindest one he has, where it appears the little girl might be sleeping — and they confirm it's their daughter. Less than an hour later, they're calm and polite, almost professional in their demeanor. Their eyes are bloodshot, but dry. They sit close to each other, breathing and speaking normally, but not touching. Daniel Rudd is a cardiothoracic surgeon at Harborview Medical Center, and Lara Friedman is a pediatric surgeon at Seattle Children's Hospital. Kaiser can only assume that their professions are the reason they're able to compartmentalize this way.

They have two other children, twin boys conceived via in vitro fertilization. Shawn and Shane are six years old, and Lara Friedman shows Kaiser a picture of her sons sitting on a park bench, with their little sister in between them. Emily bears no physical resemblance to her brothers — they're blond and blue-eyed while she had dark hair and dark eyes — but the bond among the three of them is unmistakable. Their parents confirm Emily was adopted.

"Even after the twins, it didn't quite feel like our family was complete," Lara says, hands in her lap. The coffee Kaiser brought her from the precinct's break room is cooling in its paper cup, untouched. "I couldn't go through IVF again, so we started the adoption process through a Christian agency that specializes in placing babies born to unwed teenage mothers."

"What can you tell me about Emily's biological parents?" Kaiser asks.

"Why is that important?" Daniel Rudd frowns beside his wife. "They're not in the picture. Sasha wouldn't even tell us the father's name. He's not aware she even had a child."

"Sasha's the biological mother?"

"Yes." The man stares at him. "Again, why does it matter? She never had a relationship with Emily after she gave birth."

"It's relevant to the case," Kaiser says gently. "That's all I can say for now. But I would appreciate any details you can give me."

"Her name is Sasha Robinson," Lara says, giving her husband a look that shuts him up. "She was actually a sweet girl. We met about halfway through her pregnancy. We invited her to our house to spend time with us and the boys. She was eighteen then, living with her grandmother in a trailer park. High school dropout, recovering drug addict. She grew up poor, and it was clear that it was extremely important to her to have her baby go to a family with money. She emphasized that she wanted her child to have access to the best education, and she thought it was great we already had twin boys, because the baby would always have big brothers to protect her. . . ." She stops then, her voice choking.

"We saw her twice during the pregnancy, and then once right after she gave birth," Daniel says, sounding defeated. "Then we didn't see or speak to her again for over two years. It was her choice. She was doing drugs again, she was in no shape to see Emily. We told her if she got clean, we'd be okay with limited contact, but she said she didn't want to meet Emily even if she was clean. Deep down, it was a relief. That kind of thing can get complicated."

"But you had contact with Sasha when Emily was two?" Kaiser asks.

"We called her," Lara says. "We were experiencing serious behavioral problems with Emily. Hyperactivity that was well beyond what was normal for a child that age. She was quick to anger, and very aggressive, even violent. Hitting, biting, clawing, shoving — she even tried to choke Shane once when he wouldn't let her play with a toy she wanted. There were actually times when the boys were scared of her."

"The obvious decision was to medicate," Daniel says. "But we opted not to. Those meds for ADHD can turn a kid into a zombie. We put her in therapy instead, changed her diet, hired an extra nanny part-time to take some of the burden off Maria."

"Maria is . . . ?"

"The full-time nanny," Lara says. "She lives with us."

"Did the extra support help?"

"Not even a little bit. She was a really difficult child. It was hard." She bites her lip, looks away, the guilt of having said something negative about her dead daughter etched all over her face.

"And what about the father?" Kaiser asks. "Did you ever learn anything about him?"

"All Sasha would say is that their relationship was very brief," Daniel says. "Sounded like a fling, maybe even a one-time thing. She wouldn't tell us his name."

"Or maybe she never knew it." Lara sighs. "Of course, if you ask her, maybe she'll be more forthcoming. She no longer speaks to us."

And she never will again. "Why's that?" Kaiser asks.

"When we talked to her about Emily a couple of years ago, we told her we needed to take a complete genetic history," Daniel says. "We told Sasha that while we understood she didn't want to tell us anything about Emily's biological father, it was necessary to know more about him in order to help our daughter. We explained about the violence, the aggression, that we were concerned she might hurt her brothers. The conversation upset her. She hung up on us and never returned our calls again."

Emily Rudd's parents seem like practical people. Determined, eager to be helpful, motivated to get to the answer in the most efficient way possible. Kaiser decides it's time to be honest with them.

"I want to be straight with you here," he

says. "When we found Emily, we found another victim as well. A woman."

The parents exchange a look.

"You think it's Sasha," Daniel says flatly. "You must, or else you wouldn't have asked all those questions. Look, like I told you, Sasha had zero relationship with Emily. Any contact we had with her was between us —"

"Is it okay if I show you a picture?" Kaiser asks, pulling out his phone. "It's of the female victim."

Lara shakes her head. Sighing, Daniel holds his hand out for the phone. Kaiser figured out how to use the censor-bar app Kim downloaded for Claire Toliver, and he'd cropped the photo to show only the victim's face. He doesn't plan to tell Emily's parents that the woman was dismembered, and that the head isn't actually attached to a body.

The man looks at the photo. His expression doesn't change. Again, Kaiser figures it must be his surgeon's poker face. "Well, it certainly *resembles* Sasha. Same nose, same chin. What's with the black bar?"

"There's significant damage to the eye area."

Daniel rolls his eyes. "I'm a trauma surgeon, Detective. I had a teenager come in the other week with a detached eyeball due to head trauma. Popped out during a football game and was dangling from his goddamned eye socket. I see things like that, and much worse, every day. If you show me the uncensored version, I can probably verify that it's her."

Kaiser sighs. Swipes to change the photo. The uncensored photo causes Daniel Rudd to blink exactly once, but that's it. The man is unshakeable.

"Yes," he says. "That's Sasha." Short and to the point.

Lara makes no move to look at the phone, so Kaiser slips it back into his pocket.

"How was she killed?" Daniel asks, standing up. He begins to pace. The calm demeanor is beginning to fade.

"Strangulation, we think," Kaiser says, and stops there. "We'll confirm cause of death later today."

"Why did you want to know about Emily's biological father?" From the tone of Daniel's voice, it's clear he's growing agitated. "Do you think he had something to do with this?" When Kaiser doesn't respond right away, he stops pacing. "My god. You do."

"We're looking at him as a suspect, yes."

"But you don't know his name," Daniel

says. He exchanges another look with his wife. "Oh, hell. You do."

"I can't believe this." Lara's voice cracks, and she buries her face in her hands. The grief, pushed away earlier, is beginning to surge back, and her breathing is becoming shallow. "You think Emily's own biological father killed her, and Sasha. What kind of depraved —" She stops, then gasps, as if hearing what she just said. *It was genetic.* Her breathing becomes more rapid, and a light sheen of sweat appears above her brow. "That's where Emily got it from. Oh god. Oh god, I don't understand any of this. Why would he kill his own child?"

"Deep breaths," Daniel says, looking over at his wife with concern, pacing once again.

"I know what to do," Lara snaps. It's the first time she's spoken sharply to her husband. She takes several deep breaths, her chest expanding and contracting in an exaggerated way, and after a half-dozen or so breaths, she calms down. "You should talk to Sasha's grandmother. She mentioned they were close, that her grandmother was the only person who stood by her through the drugs and the drinking. She might be able to confirm whether the person who murdered our daughter is the person you're thinking it is."

"What's his name?" Daniel asks. He's sitting beside his wife, but they're inches apart, not touching, not looking at each other. "The killer?"

"I'd rather not say until I know for sure," Kaiser says.

"Well, I hope you catch the sonofabitch," the man says. "And I hope he tries to attack you, so you can kill him."

"Dan," his wife says, but her voice is weak. She's not disagreeing.

At this point, secretly, Kaiser doesn't disagree, either.

26

The Willows is a pretty name for a group of run-down trailers in a clearing off Highway 99. There are about four dozen of them in various sizes, all white, all dirty, propped up on two-by-fours. In the middle of the trailer park are a handful of wood picnic tables and a run-down play center for kids, complete with a broken swing set and a cracked slide. The place is depressing, and despite the name, there's not a willow tree in sight.

Emily Rudd's biological great-grandmother lives in a trailer at the back of the park, indistinguishable from the rest, save for four rose bushes not currently in bloom. Kaiser imagines they'll look quite beautiful in the spring. Stepping up onto the cracked wood porch, he knocks on the door.

An elderly woman answers. Round and bosomy, she appraises him through the chipped screen. Her fluffy hair is mostly white with a few specks of black, her blue floral-print housedress clean and pressed. Reading glasses hang around her neck, attached to a string of tiny seashells.

"Can I help you?" she says through the screen.

Kaiser holds up his badge. "Sorry to disturb you, ma'am. I'm looking for Caroline Robinson."

"You've found her."

He blinks, surprised. Emily Rudd appeared to be white, as did her biological mother, so Kaiser assumed that Sasha's grandmother would be white, too. But the woman standing in front of him is black, her skin the color of coffee with a few drops of cream. Serves him right for making assumptions.

"I'm Detective Kaiser Brody, Seattle PD. I'm here to talk to you about Sasha."

The woman's eyes narrow. She has to be in her mid-eighties, but he has the feeling that she's sharp as a tack. "What are you accusing her of now?"

It's an interesting way to phrase the question. As the grandmother of a drug addict, Kaiser might have expected a more weary response. But the woman is on already on Sasha's side. Which will make the death notification even harder.

"Not a thing, ma'am," he says. "Can I come in?"

"Then she's dead?" Caroline Robinson's voice is steady, but the screen door jiggles a bit.

He would have preferred to tell her inside, but she's not giving him a choice. "Yes, ma'am, she is. I'm so sorry."

"Come in." She opens the screen door.

Kaiser steps into the trailer, which turns out to be larger than it looks from the outside. The entryway is between the kitchen and the living room, marked by a colorful doormat that reads WELCOME in bold letters. The kitchen is light blue, the cabinets painted white with clear plastic knobs. Floral curtains hang at the window, and potted wildflowers brighten up the small round table, which could comfortably seat three; four if you squished. Appliances are circa the early 1980s, but pristine. The living room is pale yellow, the brown carpet frayed but spotless. It's sparsely decorated with a plaid sofa bed and wooden coffee table, a thirty-two-inch flat-screen TV on the console. *Ellen* is on, but the volume's been muted. At the back of the trailer are two bedrooms.

It's as nice a trailer as Kaiser has ever seen. The smell of fresh coffee permeates the space, and he spies a fresh pot on the counter.

"Would you like a cup?" Mrs. Robinson asks, following his gaze. "I know it's the afternoon, but it's my one vice."

"We have that in common," Kaiser says. "And I would love one, thank you."

She pours for them both, then gestures to the counter where she's laid out cream and sugar. He declines both, and waits while she fixes her coffee and then settles herself at the small table.

"What happened to my granddaughter?" she asks after they've both taken a sip.

Kaiser senses Caroline Robinson is the kind of woman who's been through a lot, and can handle a lot, and would prefer no sugarcoating, only the truth. He won't insult her by giving her anything less.

"Sasha's body was found early this morning, buried in a shallow grave in the woods behind St. Martin's High School."

"Buried?" She frowns. "I don't understand. I assumed it was an overdose. She's been clean for over six months, but drug addiction is a wicked thing, Detective."

Kaiser nods. "We'll be checking for drugs in her system, but for now, it looks like she was murdered."

A sharp intake of breath. "How?"

"Strangled." He pauses, then says, "Her biological daughter was found with her. Also strangled."

Caroline Robinson's head snaps up. "Emily's dead?"

"Yes, ma'am. I'm deeply sorry."

"Lord help me," the woman whispers. Her lip quivers, and for a moment Kaiser thinks she's going to cry. But she doesn't. The quiver passes, and she straightens up again, fixing him with those sharp eyes. "Do Emily's parents know?"

"I was just with them."

"Sasha didn't have a relationship with Emily," Mrs. Robinson says, her forehead creasing. "I wanted her to when Emily was older, but Sasha thought it was a bad idea. She didn't want her baby to know who she was. She wanted a better life for her. What were they even doing together?"

"I don't know. I'm still trying to figure it out."

The woman looks at him closely. "I can spot a liar from a hundred feet, Detective. Comes with living with drug addicts my whole life. What aren't you telling me? You're deliberately leaving something out, and I would very much like to know what it is."

If it were appropriate, Kaiser would smile,

but it isn't. "Sasha was . . . we found her body dismembered, ma'am. It likely happened after her death," he adds, as if that makes it better. "There was a similar murder not long ago. A woman and her biological child were killed and buried the same way."

"Lord help me," the old woman says again. Her coffee cup shakes, and she sets it down on top of a coaster made of cork. She cries for a few moments, and Kaiser looks away in an effort to give her some privacy. Then she pulls a handkerchief from her dress pocket and dabs her eyes, calming herself. "I've been through a lot, but this takes the cake. Someone cut my baby girl up? Why?"

"I don't know, ma'am," he says, and it's the truth. "I'm so sorry."

It's the one piece he hasn't figured out yet. Other than Angela, none of Calvin James's other victims were dismembered, and Kaiser's best guess is that the Sweetbay Strangler is somehow trying to recapture how it felt that first time with Angela Wong.

"You said this is similar to another crime. Is it a serial killer?"

"We have a theory that it might be, yes," he says.

Caroline Robinson lets out a long breath. "I've expected someone like you to show up for years now to tell me Sasha was dead, but not quite like this." She speaks plainly. "My granddaughter's been an addict since she was fourteen, treated her body like a garbage can. Started by smoking weed in the woods behind the trailer park with the other kids. Almost an impossible thing to prevent, when it's the parents' stashes they're helping themselves to. Eventually she graduated to painkillers — mine, mostly — and when she ran out of those, she started on heroin. That was the beginning of the end. In and out of drug treatment for three years. She was living here when she got pregnant, and I actually thought it might have been the best thing that happened to her, because it forced her to get clean. I didn't even have to ask her. When she got the positive pregnancy test, she just stopped, cold turkey. And I said to myself, thank the lord. Maybe the dark days are over. I assumed she was keeping the baby, and that we'd raise the child together."

Kaiser nods.

"Three months into her pregnancy, it hit her what she was in for. She asked me what I thought about adoption, and I told her I'd support whatever she wanted to do. She went back and forth for a bit." The crease between the woman's brows deepens, and she looks away, remembering. "One day she wanted it, the next day she didn't. She was terrified the baby would grow up to be like her. Despite my best efforts, Sasha had very little self-esteem. Her mother — my daughter — was a junkie, too, got stabbed in the neck fighting with another junkie when Sasha was only two. She never knew her father. He died of an overdose the year she was born. Sasha never finished high school, but she was far from stupid. She recognized the pattern, knew that if she raised her baby here, the chances that the same thing that happened to her parents and to her would happen to her little girl. She wanted better for her baby."

Kaiser offered a small smile. "You seem to be doing well."

"I don't have the gene," Mrs. Robinson said flatly. "Whatever thing it is that makes a person an addict, I don't have it. My father was a raging alcoholic, but my mother never touched a drop. Oh, I tried it once. Took a shot of my father's whiskey when he wasn't looking, found it disgusting. Smoked once, too, and felt physically ill for a whole day after. They say addiction's genetic, and I believe it. I grew up surrounded by it my whole life and was never tempted."

Kaiser nods again, and they sip their coffee in silence for a moment. Then, "Did Sasha tell you anything about Emily's father?"

"Not much. It didn't last long, and she mentioned he was a bit transient, always moving from place to place. I met him once. I didn't like that he was older, but he seemed nice enough."

"You met him?" Kaiser says, surprised.

"He dropped her off one evening while I was taking the garbage out. Forced him to talk to me." A small smile. "He got out of the car. Handsome."

"Can I show you a photo?" When she nods, Kaiser pulls out his phone. "Is this the father?"

Caroline Robinson puts her glasses on, the seashells around her neck dangling. "Yes," she says after a few seconds, peering at the screen. The photo was Calvin James's mug shot. "He looked a lot different when we met, but that's him. I think his name was Kevin. Wait, no, that's not right. It was *Calvin*. Like the comic strip *Calvin and Hobbes*."

Kaiser lets out a breath. "I know this was four years ago, but do you remember anything distinctive about him? Was his hair dark like in this picture?"

"No, it was a lighter brown, longer, a bit

shaggy. He had a scruffy beard and glasses. I also remember he had a tattoo on his wrist. Here, on the inside," she says, tapping the spot two inches below her palm.

Calvin James had not had a single tattoo when Kaiser arrested him, so he'd have to have gotten inked in prison, or soon after he escaped. "What did it look like?"

"It was a heart," Mrs. Robinson says. "Red. But just the outline. I think there were initials inside, but I don't remember what they were. I only caught a glimpse of it when he shook my hand."

Kaiser has a pretty good guess what the initials are. He thinks back to the sheet of paper Calvin doodled on during the trial. He'd drawn a heart. And inside it, *GS.* For Georgina Shaw.

"Do you remember the car he was driving?"

She shakes her head. "Oh, lord, I don't know much about cars. It was nice, though, like a muscle car. American."

"Washington plates?"

"I didn't look."

"Color?" Kaiser couldn't imagine Calvin would still be driving the red Trans Am he'd had back in the day.

"Black," she says. "I think."

Not the same car, then. But Calvin James

did like his American muscle cars. He'd been driving a blue Mustang the day Kaiser had arrested him near the Canadian border.

Caroline Robinson stands, heading into the living room. She motions for Kaiser to follow her, and he does. On the living room end table is a framed photo, and she hands it to him.

"I know you saw Sasha dead," she says. "This is what she looked like in life. She was only eighteen here, in her second trimester, and completely clean. She was beautiful." There are tears in the woman's eyes, and her hands shake. "Unfortunately, I don't have any recent photos of her."

She isn't exaggerating; if anything, she's understating. Sasha Robinson was gorgeous. Tall, maddeningly curvy, her tawny skin tone the only hint of her black ancestry. Her eyes were dark, her hair long and brown. She appears to be sitting on one of the picnic tables in the courtyard outside the trailer, long legs crossed, her flowy dress disguising whatever pregnancy bump she might have had. Kaiser stares at the photo, his breath catching in his throat.

Sasha Robinson is a dead ringer for Georgina as a teenager. The resemblance is not only striking, it's . . . uncanny.

Come to think of it, Claire Toliver resembled Sasha, too. Long dark hair, golden complexion, voluptuous. *Lush* was the word Kaiser remembered thinking to himself. Like Sasha Robinson.

Like Georgina Shaw.

"She was beautiful," Kaiser finally says, and he means it. "Again, I'm so sorry for your loss. I won't keep you any longer, Mrs. Robinson. Thanks for your time."

He heads back to the kitchen, finishes his coffee in one gulp, then quickly washes his mug in the sink, placing it on the dish rack to dry. When he turns back toward Mrs. Robinson, she's smiling.

"Your mama raised you right."

"Yes, ma'am." He smiles back.

"You're a lot more polite than the other person who came around the other day, asking questions about Sasha. Actually, when you knocked on the door, at first I thought you were him."

Kaiser frowns. "What other person?"

"Oh, it was a week ago, maybe a little longer," she says. "Some young man knocked on the door, said he worked for social services and was doing a follow-up on Sasha and how she was doing. She'd been to state-sponsored rehab twice and had recently reapplied for welfare, so I wasn't overly surprised at the visit. He got a bit rude when I told him she wasn't home, and when I refused to tell him where she was, he acted like I was personally trying to inconvenience him. I didn't like his attitude and told him so. These millennials, I tell you. They don't know how to move in the world, if that makes any sense."

"Had you seen him before?" Kaiser asks, his mind churning. It couldn't be Calvin, the woman would have said so. Plus, she just said he was younger. "What did he want to know specifically?"

"He asked a little about her drug use, and I said she was clean. Mainly he wanted to know about the baby. He wanted to know where it ended up, whether it was a boy or girl, said that the records didn't show those things. I asked him why any of it mattered if Sasha was no longer the parent. After all, she'd been claiming welfare as a single person, not as a single mother. It surprised him; he didn't know Sasha had given the baby up for adoption. He asked for the name of the agency, and I gave it to him, hoping he'd leave. In hindsight, maybe I shouldn't have. Sasha had no legal claim to her child, so the adoption wouldn't be any of his business."

"Did he leave a card?"

Mrs. Robinson shakes her head. "No, and

I forgot to ask for one. I don't know, maybe I'm reading too much into it. He was strange, and I didn't like him, and it made me defensive."

The whole thing sounds weird to Kaiser. The woman was right to be suspicious.

While it was common practice for the state to check up on a woman who'd had a baby applying for welfare, Sasha had given her child up. And according to her grandmother, she hadn't lied about that on her application.

"Did he tell you his name at least?"

She shakes her head again. "I'm sure he did at the beginning when he introduced himself, but I couldn't remember it by the end of the visit. You think this is related to Sasha's and Emily's deaths somehow?"

"I'm considering every angle." It's all Kaiser can tell her. He opens the screen door and takes a step out into the cool afternoon air.

"By the way, Detective," Mrs. Robinson says, her voice soft. "How are Emily's parents doing?"

"They're coping," he says.

"I imagine in their line of work, being surgeons and all, they deal with death every day. But not like this. Not so close to home." She sighs. "When can I see Sasha?"

"Ma'am, I —"

"Oh. Right." Caroline Robinson's whole body sags. "Oh, lord, I forgot. She's . . . . she's not . . ." Her knees buckle, and Kaiser catches her before she can fall.

"I'm sorry," she says, gasping. "On some level I braced myself for this day. Losing my daughter, losing my father, I thought I was prepared. But not for this. She was really trying to put her life back together. . . ." A sob escapes her lips, and she quashes it before it can grow. "I guess I have something to talk about in grief group this week."

"Grief group?"

She straightens herself, shaking Kaiser off gently, and takes several deep breaths. Her glasses dangle on her heaving bosom. After a moment, she attempts a smile. It isn't for him; the smile is for herself, self-reassurance that she's got this, that she'll be fine. He's seen it before on other mothers, grandmothers, and sisters who've just been told the worst possible news.

"I've been going for twenty years," she says. "I lead the weekly meeting at St. Andrews, the church three blocks away. It's how I push through all this, Detective. It's been one grief after another."

"How do you do it?" It's none of Kaiser's business, but he honestly wants to know.

He could kill Calvin James for a lot of reasons, and causing this admirable woman more heartache after everything she's already been through is one of them. "How do you handle it?"

"I just do," Caroline Robinson says. "Someone has to be alive to remember them. If they're not remembered, then it's like they never existed in the first place. And so, if not me, then who?"

She looks away for a moment, and then back at him. "Who?"

27

Kaiser was present in the courtroom the day the judge sentenced Calvin James to four consecutive life sentences, one for each of the murders he committed, including Angela Wong. Georgina was not there. She was already in prison, so she missed the big show.

After hearing several statements from bereaved family members of the victims, the sentence was read. The families cried. Justice was served, but in criminal cases it doesn't feel like other victories. There's no reward. At most, there's a sense of relief, the closing of a chapter that never should have been written in the first place. But it doesn't fix the wounds of the injured. And it doesn't bring back the dead.

Kaiser comforted Angela's parents that day in the courtroom. Candace Wong Platten hugged him tightly, whispered her thanks, and kissed his cheek, leaving a lipstick smear that would be rude to wipe away until after she left. Victor Wong had gripped Kaiser's hand with two hands, pumping his arms.

"Our girl can rest in peace," he said, tears in his eyes.

Kaiser could only nod. He believed that the dead were already at peace. It was the living who suffered.

Calvin James, clad in a suit and tie, looked over at Kaiser as the bailiff handcuffed him. In a few minutes he'd be back in an orange jumpsuit. His attorney was packing up his briefcase. Calvin opened his mouth and appeared to say something, but Kaiser couldn't hear him above the din. He walked over.

"Are you trying to say something to me?" he said.

The two men weighed about the same and had similar builds, but Kaiser was an inch or two taller. Funny to think that when he was sixteen and Calvin was twenty-one, Georgina's boyfriend had seemed so much bigger, so much stronger, so much more intimidating. Now he was just a man. A murderer, yes, but a man growing older like the rest of them, with no special skills or training, just a lust for hurting women in the worst way possible.

In a fair fight, Kaiser was 98 percent sure he could rip Calvin's throat out.

"I said I was surprised they didn't give me the death penalty," Calvin said.

"That's a conversation for your lawyer." Kaiser glanced over at the defense attorney, who was already talking on his cell phone, then back at Calvin. "Would you have preferred that? I know I would have."

The bailiff had Calvin by the arm and was beginning to move him toward the side door that led to the holding cells below. From there, he would be transported to Walla Walla, Washington, where he would spend the rest of his life in prison.

"People like me shouldn't exist," the Sweetbay Strangler said, looking over his shoulder. "You hear me, Kaiser? People like me should not exist."

Kaiser's phone pings, bringing him back to the present. There's an email about the DNA results on Emily Rudd. Confirmed: She's Calvin's biological daughter. It's the least surprised he's felt since this all began. And it also confirms another important fact: Despite the few dubious sightings of the Sweetbay Strangler across the globe over the years, Calvin James has been in the Seattle area at least twice since his escape from prison, long enough to have fathered two children.

That's two times the serial killer has been close enough to catch, and two times that Kaiser didn't catch him. He heaves a long sigh and rubs his temples, feeling the onset of a headache.

Kim is at her desk across from his in the precinct, working on something unrelated to the murders. TV shows make it look like cops work one case at a time until it's solved and the bad guy — or girl — is arrested, tried, and convicted. In real life, it doesn't work like that. Kaiser juggles multiple cases. So does Kim. Sometimes they work cases together. Sometimes they don't. She senses his eyes on her and looks up. He looks away. When he glances back again, she's up from her desk and heading toward the break room, presumably to get away from him.

He's not angry she's back with her husband, especially considering she and Dave were never really apart. He's not even upset that she didn't talk to him about it first. Kim doesn't owe him anything; Kaiser knew the drill when they first hooked up, when things morphed from work to friendship to sex.

But still, the sense of loss is there. He understands now how you can feel loss at the absence of something you never even really wanted in the first place. Kaiser was never fully invested in his personal relationship with Kim, and therein lies the problem. That space — that in-the-middle place somewhere in between being fully invested and not caring — simply isn't worth it. When you're in a relationship like that, it's rarely fulfilling, and all you can see is everything wrong with it. But when it's over, it stings, and you still somehow feel like you've lost.

His relationship with Georgina, however, is the exact opposite. There's no in-between with her, no gray area. There's no way to be with her just a little bit — he's either all in, or all out. And after yesterday, he knows he's all in. He has no choice, really. Georgina is the woman he's loved since he was fourteen, and nothing — no amount of years, distance, or criminal activity — can make that disappear. And it's fitting, really. Kaiser has a history of picking the wrong women. Georgina fucks with his head and his heart, she diminishes his capacity for good judgment, she brings out all his protective instincts. The fact that she's an ex-convict is the least of his issues with her.

As a cop, he can't afford to love someone like that. But he does. And so be it.

He can still remember how her hair smelled that night at Chad Fenton's party all those years ago, when she pressed against him in the laundry room, the length of her body touching the length of his. There was no place else he wanted to be; for a moment, the whole world disappeared. He can remember the softness of her lips and the scent of vodka-infused fruit on her breath. He remembers his physical arousal, and the conflicting feelings of wanting her to know how he felt and not wanting to scare her. Nothing feels as powerful as longing for someone you can't have when you're sixteen. Georgina occupied all the places in his heart.

The same way Calvin James occupied all the places in hers.

"I got a call from the lab," Kim says, and he looks up. She's back from the break room, two cups of coffee in hand. She places one on his desk and pulls her chair over. "They confirmed there's no foreign DNA on Emily Rudd and Sasha Robinson, same as the other two."

Kaiser nods, wishing she'd roll back to her own desk, although this is how they typically work. "Thanks," he says, taking a sip of the coffee.

"The thing that bothers me, and I'm sure

you've thought of this," Kim says, "is that a lot of this doesn't fit with Calvin James's old MO. I get that people can change, but serial killers tend not to. Their patterns are fixed. Most killers don't deviate from their way of doing things."

Kaiser has thought about it, of course. But in the absence of other leads, he hasn't dwelled on it. Calvin James is still the best suspect they have.

"He dismembered Angela Wong, his first victim, but not the three he killed after that, years later." Kim sips her coffee. "But these last two females, he dismembered again. And now he's killing children. And not just any children — his own. And not the way most parents who murder their children do — in a rage, after a psychotic break of some kind — but deliberately. He's tracking them down. Hunting them."

"He's escalating."

"Is he, though?" Kim says. She's not being argumentative, but he can see she's trying to make a point. "If not for Georgina, and where the bodies were buried, and the lipstick used on the kids, would we even think it was Calvin? He never used condoms before. His semen was found on the three earlier victims. But in these new murders, condom lube and spermicide were found

418

both times. Not a speck of DNA anywhere."

"He's getting smarter. He knows we have his DNA."

She shrugs. "Why would he care? He's leaving the bodies in places that lead back to Georgina Shaw. He's using the lipstick that her old company now manufactures, which isn't widely available. He's drawing hearts on the children. He would know all of those things suggest it's him, so if he wants us to know, why not skip the condom so that we're certain? The last two victims got pregnant with his children, after all. Which suggests that when they were together, they didn't always use birth control. And why track them down now? The kids were two and four years old. What's the motivation for tracking down their mothers and killing them? And tracking down his biological children — both of whom were adopted into other families — and killing them, too? That takes work, planning, research, things he never did with Angela Wong or the three women he killed after her."

Kaiser doesn't answer. He's considered all of these things, of course, but he's never laid it out as methodically and linearly as Kim just has.

"I think we're dealing with two different

killers, Kai," she says. "We still have to find Calvin, of course. But I feel strongly that we're looking in the wrong direction for the other one."

His instinct is to argue with her and point out all the ways that she's wrong. But the problem is, she's not wrong.

"Play along," Kim coaxes, as if she's reading his mind. "Let's at least talk it out. Let's try and discuss these last two double homicides as if they're not related to Calvin James at all."

"Okay," Kaiser says with a resigned sigh. "The mother and child thing *is* different. All by itself, usually the prime suspect would be the husband and father of the child, and we'd be looking at this as some kind of family annihilation. But we now have two mothers and two children, killed in the same way. What ties them together further is that the women weren't raising their children. Both kids were given up for adoption."

"Right. So what kind of killer is attracted to a mother and child?"

"Someone who wants to destroy that bond. Someone —" Kaiser frowns and shakes his head. He's not enjoying this exercise. He's not an FBI profiler, he doesn't believe in digging too deeply into the psychosis of a crime. It's not his job, and it's risky because the chances he's wrong in whatever he comes up with are extremely high. "Someone who wants to desecrate the mother. The rape tells us he wants to dominate her, cause her pain. Assuming she *was* raped, which we can't confirm. The dismemberment tells us he wants to humiliate her, to belittle her life and her very existence."

"But the children were unharmed before they were killed. Why?"

"He doesn't want to cause them pain. But neither does he want them to live."

"And what does *see me* mean?"

Kaiser mulls it over, allowing the theories to swirl in his brain. "He wants the child to see . . . no. He wants to be seen by the child. No. He wants someone else to see him and the child is the messenger." A cold feeling washes over Kaiser as something occurs to him, something that stabs at him. His head snaps up. "Jesus."

Kim's nodding. "Talk it out."

"The child is the messenger," he says, the words coming out slowly. "*He* is someone's child. That's what the killer is trying to tell us. *He* is someone's child."

"Technically, we're all someone's child," Kim says, but there's a small smile on her face. She understands where he's going with this and is pushing him to get there quicker.

"That's the missing piece," Kaiser says, the chill washing over him. "Whoever's child he is, wherever he came from, that's the key to this whole thing."

"Now let's try and tie the rest of it in." Kim leans forward. "The bodies were found in two significant locations. The first is the woods near Georgina's house."

"Not just near it. Right beside it." Kaiser is mentally kicking himself. He'd been so focused on the locations and the parts that tied into Georgina that he hasn't been properly thinking about the rest of it. "Same place Angela Wong was buried. And the body was dismembered in the same way Angela's was — head, upper arms, elbows, wrists, thighs, knees, ankles. Multiple shallow graves. The second site is the woods behind Georgina's high school. Victim was also dismembered."

"I know you don't believe in coincidences, but I need to point out that the locations could have been a coincidence," Kim says. "There are only so many wooded areas in Sweetbay. The killer might have chosen those locations simply because they worked."

"And he dismembered the bodies the

same way as Angela?" He shakes his head. "Even if I could accept the burial sites as coincidences, the dismemberments can't be."

"But why do you think Angela was dismembered in the first place? Think about that for a minute," Kim says. "We know she was cut up because her bones were found in multiple places, consistent with dismemberment. But there might not have been a psychosis behind it. The woods are dense, filled with rocks and tree roots. You can only dig so big and so deep a hole. Her dismemberment might not have been done for any other reason than practical. And if a new killer wanted to bury an adult body in those same woods, he'd probably be forced to do the same thing."

It seemed odd to use the word *practical* to describe the reason for chopping up a body, but Kaiser understood her point. "Okay . . ."

"So the only real thing that ties Georgina to the new murders is the fact that the lipstick is from the company she worked for," Kim says. "She was VP of lifestyle brands or something. I did a little googling, found a five-year-old article in *Pacific Northwest* magazine that profiled Shipp Pharmaceuticals and Georgina. She was quoted as saying that she was hoping to take the company in a new direction, and her plan was to build a cosmetics brand. She has an undergraduate degree in chemical engineering, and an MBA, *and* she went to beauty school for a year. She had a valid cosmetology license, for Christ's sake. Creating a cosmetics line one day was her dream. The killer had to know — *had to* — that using a Shipp lipstick on the children, out of all the thousands of lipsticks to choose from, would get her attention."

"Well, we've known from the beginning that the new murders tie back to Georgina," he points out.

"Georgina, yes, but they don't necessarily tie back to *Calvin,*" Kim says, pounding her fist on his desk for emphasis, causing him to jolt. "We need proof — DNA, a witness, *something* — that Calvin James killed his own children. And we don't have it yet."

Kim's right. Jesus Christ, she's so fucking right. Despite his best efforts to stay objective, Kaiser fell down the rabbit hole that no detective worth his badge should ever fall into — he was looking to make the evidence fit his theory, instead of creating a theory based on the evidence. He assumed that because everything tied to Georgina, Calvin *had* to be the killer.

A potentially grievous assumption.

"He's someone's child," Kaiser says again softly, more to himself than to his partner. "But whose?"

Kim stands up, rolls her chair back to her own desk. "You should go talk to Georgina. You always said there were things she never told you. If there's anything left to know, you're probably the only person she'll tell. You guys have history. She trusts you."

She says it lightly, but he sees it then. The stiffness of her body language, her lack of eye contact, the downturn of her lips.

Married or not, the end of their affair is Kim's loss, too.

28

Kaiser met Georgina in science class. They were freshmen, it was the first day of school, and the first thing he thought was that she smelled amazing. The second thing he thought was that she was beautiful. Not in an obvious way, like Angela, whose presence could never be ignored, even on her worst day. But in a subtle, underappreciated way; the kind of beauty that isn't trendy or obvious, the kind of beauty that seems plain at first glance until you get to know her better, the kind of beauty that doesn't blossom until well after high school.

You can't tell girls like this they're beautiful. They won't believe you. But that's part of what makes them beautiful. Because it doesn't matter.

Georgina took a seat right in front of Kaiser, her long dark hair brushing the edge of his desk as she opened her binder to a fresh sheet of three-hole lined paper. The classroom was only half-full, and she had her choice of desks. She clicked a pen filled with purple ink and wrote the date on the paper. September 3rd.

She turned around. "I'm Geo," she said.

"Geode?" he said, misunderstanding her. What kind of messed-up name was that? "Like a rock?"

"Geo," she said, spelling it out. "Short for Georgina, but I hate that name, so please don't call me that."

"Why not? It's pretty. You might like it someday."

"Doubt it."

"Her name is Geo and she dances on the sand . . . ," he sang. He couldn't help it.

"Like I haven't heard that one before." She rolled her eyes at his terrible rendition of the Duran Duran song "Rio." "That song came out when I was, like, in kindergarten. You're just like my dad. A big fan of eighties music."

Well, that killed it. No teenage boy wants to be compared to a girl's father. It shut him up, and she turned back around. For the rest of the class, all he could see was the back of her perfect head. Sometimes he'd kick her chair accidentally-on-purpose so she'd turn around to tell him to stop it. It was stupid, he knew. But he was smitten.

The friendship that followed was instant and easy, built on their shared struggle with science and desire to annoy the shit out of each other. He didn't like Angela when Georgina first introduced them — her best friend bossed her around a lot, and would pull her away often to talk about "girl stuff," which made him feel like the third wheel he was. But he and Angela grew on each other over time, and by homecoming freshman year, the three of them were inseparable. Oh, he had guy buddies, too, but his closest friends — his *best* friends — were two girls. And they trusted him, told him things about teenage girlhood most boys would never be privileged to know. He was often the voice of reason when they couldn't make a decision on what to wear or eat, the one who could tell them which boys they liked were douchebags and which were okay, the one who played referee when they squabbled with each other (which wasn't often, but when it happened, it was World War III for all of them).

He never told Georgina he was in love with her. But Angela knew, and they talked about it a few times. One of Angela Wong's best traits was that she was honest. Unfortunately, it was also one of her worst. She had no problem telling you if your outfit looked like shit, if your taste in music was abhorrent, if you had something stuck in your teeth.

"She doesn't think of you like that," Angela said to Kaiser one August afternoon, the summer before junior year started. They were at the mall, and he was "helping" her shop for some new party outfits. Which basically meant heaping effusive praise on everything she tried on. Geo and her dad had gone to visit her grandmother in Toronto for the week, and he'd been forced to step in.

"Like what?"

"As more than a friend. You've been in the friend box for two years. Telling her how you really feel isn't going to change that. All it will do is make her feel bad because then she'll be forced to tell you she doesn't feel the same way. Which, even though you knew it was coming, will feel like she lit a match and set you on fire. And then guess what?" Angela turned to him, looking pissed off, although none of this had even remotely happened yet. "At the end of the day, nothing will change. You'll stay friends, but now it's awkward. And by awkward, I mean awkward for *me*."

"But I really think —"

"Start talking to other girls," she said,

pivoting in front of a three-way mirror, her glossy black hair swinging as she turned this way and that. She was wearing a pink dress that looked great on her, but judging by the displeasure on her face, great wasn't good enough. "You're a junior now. You're not my type, but you're cute. You'll have girls lining up this year. Start asking some of them out. See how it feels."

Angela disappeared a couple of months later. It was hard to believe at first. There was a rumor that she ran away, but that didn't make sense to Kaiser, because his friend had zero reason to leave her life. The only theory that did make sense was that something bad had happened to her, but nobody wanted to accept that. It was incomprehensible.

The sudden absence of Angela Wong created a huge hole where she had once been, and the only person in the world who could understand the unique sense of loss that Kaiser felt was Georgina. They should have freaked out about it together, supported each other, held each other up. Instead, Georgina pulled away. It started the Monday after Chad Fenton's party, which was the last time anyone could remember seeing Angela, and the night Kaiser decided to ignore their best friend's advice and take his shot.

After that weekend, Geo started avoiding him. It was subtle at first — not returning his calls, sitting in the library instead of eating lunch in the cafeteria, going straight home after school instead of finding him so they could go to the 7-Eleven. He chalked it up to her being upset about Angela and feeling awkward because of their kiss. But a couple of weeks later, it grew worse. She'd change directions if she saw him coming down the hallway. The few times they did speak, her responses were curt.

"Is it because of the kiss?" he finally asked her a couple of weeks later. He hadn't wanted to bring it up, but not talking to her was like not breathing. He cornered her outside the front entrance of the school. He didn't understand any of it. Their best friend had disappeared. Who better to help each other through it than each other?

She had laughed at him. *Laughed.* "As if," she answered, and walked away.

Over the next month, Kaiser watched, helpless, as she spiraled. In the first few weeks after their friend went missing, Georgina was edgy, skittish, constantly looking over her shoulder, as if she half-expected that whatever had snatched Angela out of their lives might come for her, too. She was bothered by the rumors, defending her best friend vigorously against stories that Angela left of her own accord, that Angela had a secret boyfriend, that Angela wanted to be famous. By mid-December, Kaiser barely recognized Geo. Her hair was greasy, her skin was broken out. Once, she even ran out of the cafeteria because she had to throw up.

She didn't return after Christmas break. When he tried calling her house, her father told him that she was being treated for depression, and that he'd arranged for her to finish her junior year at home via tutor. They spoke for ten minutes, Walter Shaw telling Kaiser that Angela's disappearance seemed to have triggered feelings of abandonment, loss, and grief from her childhood, as her mother died of cancer when she was five.

Kaiser continued to call every few weeks to see how she was doing, but if her father wasn't home, the phone was never answered. On two occasions, he stopped by her house on the way home from school. The first time, Walter told him that his daughter wasn't up for company. The second and last time, nobody answered the door. But as he was walking away, he looked up and saw Georgina's face in the window, peeking out from behind her pink lace curtains. Pale. Exhausted. And terrified.

Whatever she was going through, it was hell; that much was certain.

The following September, Geo was back at St. Martin's for her senior year. It was like the previous year had never happened. She seemed quieter and more contemplative, but she was smiling again, looking more or less like her old self, even though she'd gained a little weight. She didn't try out for cheer or volleyball, opting instead to take extra classes to make up for the ones she'd failed in the first semester of the year before. She skipped all of the parties, and could be found in the library most lunch periods, doing homework. With no extracurricular activities, she was able to work a part-time job after school at Jamba Juice, where she was nice to the customers.

He stopped into the store one Saturday midway through the year, forgetting that she worked there. She took his order.

"How's it going?" he asked her.

"Good," she said, handing him his change, and it was like they were strangers. She turned to make his smoothie. There was no one else in the place.

"Hey," he said. *"Hey."*

She stopped, turned to him, her visor

shading her face just enough that he couldn't read her gaze.

"I'm okay, Kai," she said. "That's what you want to know, right? I'm okay. But I'm sorry, I don't want to talk. I don't want to hang out. I have to keep moving forward, okay? That's what's best for me."

"I understand," he said, his hands on the counter, leaning forward. "But that doesn't mean we can't still be friends. I lost her, too, you know. Or did you forget that part?"

She walked back to the counter. Touched his hand gently, offered him a smile. "I know you did. And I am so sorry for your loss. But you remind me of her, okay? You remind me of who we used to be. And I can't be reminded of that. It nearly killed me. So, please. If I ever meant anything to you, you'll leave me alone."

He left without taking his smoothie, hurt in a way that went much deeper than a broken heart. He didn't know her anymore; that much was obvious.

He never tried to talk to her again. He didn't wave to her or even attempt eye contact if he saw her in the hallway at school. Once, when he was with the girl he dated briefly at the end of senior year, she was craving a smoothie and they stopped in at Jamba Juice. Georgina took their order, the both of them pretending they didn't know each other.

"Whatever happened to you guys? Weren't you good friends last year?" the girl said as they walked away with their drinks.

"Yeah," he said. "We were best friends. At least, I thought we were."

"We see what we want to see," the girl said, sipping her smoothie. "Not what's there."

Kaiser can't even recall that girl's name now. Rachel something, or maybe it was Renée. They'd only gone on three or four dates before it ended over something stupid, the details of which he also can't remember now. But he'll never forget her words that day, which, cheesy and cliché as they were, sounded so profound to his not-quite-eighteen-year-old ears.

He knows now what happened to Georgina. He knows why she stayed away from St. Martin's junior year, why she hid at home, why she refused to see him. Nineteen years later, it all makes complete sense, and Kaiser wants to punch himself for not figuring it out sooner, when it should have been so goddamned obvious.

You see what you want to see, not what's there.

■ ■ ■ ■

PART FIVE:
ACCEPTANCE

■ ■ ■ ■

"I know I can't take one more step towards
   you
'Cause all that's waiting is regret
Don't you know I'm not your ghost anymore
You lost the love I love the most
I learned to live half alive
And now you want me one more time."
            ∼ Christina Perri, "Jar of Hearts"

29

The positive pregnancy test only confirmed what Geo already suspected.

Her cycles had always been predictable, every twenty-nine or thirty days. When she missed two in a row, she bought a pregnancy test at Rite Aid, cutting her last class so she wouldn't run into anybody she knew. The directions were pretty clear, and she peed on the stick as soon as she got home, bathroom door locked tight in case she had mixed up her dad's schedule and he came home earlier than she expected. The results were fast, less than thirty seconds. The instructions said it would be either a plus or minus sign, and that any hint of blue in the plus sign meant she was pregnant.

The stick was so fucking blue it was almost purple. She wrapped it in paper towels and stuck it at the bottom of the wastebin, then sat on the toilet seat lid and cried.

She was pregnant with Calvin's baby. And it wasn't a love child. How could it be, when it was rape?

She made an appointment at Planned Parenthood for the following week, and then spent the days in between genuinely questioning whether it would be better to run out onto the street and let herself get hit by a bus. When she arrived at Planned Parenthood on a Wednesday morning (having faked sick to her dad, so he'd write her a note to get out of school for the day), her appointment had been delayed for about twenty minutes while they dealt with an emergency. It was long enough for Geo to completely freak out.

She called her father from a pay phone in the parking lot, sobbing, and he came to pick her up. She told him about the pregnancy, how she didn't want the baby, but neither could she bring herself to abort it. She refused to tell him who the father was other than that he was someone who didn't go to St. Martin's (true) and that she never wanted to see him again (also true). Walter Shaw listened, growing more upset with every word. He told her to go to bed. She did.

When she woke up the next morning, her dad was waiting for her at the kitchen table, a cup of coffee in front of him, a cup of herbal tea for her.

"Whatever you want to do, we'll do," he said, and she burst into tears again.

Walter's normally stoic face was filled with anguish. "It's because I work all the time and you don't have a mother, right? You wanted something of your own to love?"

"God, Dad, no." Despite her emotional state, Geo managed to roll her eyes. "It just . . . it just happened. Trust me, this wasn't anything I wanted, even on a subconscious level."

"If you were sexually active, I could have made you an appointment at the —"

"Dad, *please.*" Geo knew her face was red. She felt the heat creep up her neck and stop at her eyes. "I wasn't . . . sexually active. It only happened one time."

She closed her eyes, remembering the weight of Calvin on top of her, her inability to move or draw anything deeper than a shallow breath. No, she hadn't wanted it. Yes, it was rape. No, she couldn't tell anybody. If she told someone, and they arrested him, who knew what Calvin would say? About Angela? About her?

Sometimes karma came for you later. Sometimes karma came for you right away.

"So what do you want to do?" Walt asked

her gently.

"I think adoption makes the most sense. Not that I can imagine giving birth, oh god. . . ." She shuddered. She couldn't let herself think about that now. "But I can't imagine getting rid of it. And I can't imagine being a mom."

Her father nodded. It was hard to tell how he felt about what she had said. It would certainly make both their lives easier if she had an abortion. An abortion meant she could finish out her junior year with nobody the wiser. Her body wouldn't have to change; no weight gain, no stretch marks. There would be no painful delivery, no watching someone take the baby, no having to live with wondering what kind of person he or she would grow up to be.

She was nine weeks along. It wasn't even a real person, right?

But it was. To her, it was.

"But I can't . . . I can't go to school pregnant, Dad," she said. "I don't want anyone to know."

Walt's face was set, but grim. "I'll speak to your guidance counselor. We'll figure it out." He cupped her chin with a warm hand. "Are you sure about this? If you don't want to have it at all, that's okay. It's your decision. And there's still time."

"I can't," she said. "I . . . I can't deal with any more death. Of any kind."

Walt assumed she was talking about her mother. Which she was, but only to a degree.

They agreed she would finish out the first semester, but Geo was so nauseated she was missing school, anyway. After Christmas break, she didn't go back. She wrote her exams by proxy, then did the rest of her courses via correspondence and tutor. It wasn't too difficult to conceal her changing body; she carried small, and spent most of her days in her dad's old shirts and a pair of sweatpants that she rolled below her belly. If she did need to go out — to a doctor's appointment, or to the library — she wore a bulky jacket or sweater.

It was ironic to her how she could spend those days with someone else all the time — her baby, growing inside her — and still feel utterly alone. It was almost like her pregnancy was the culmination of all her secrets, in physical form.

By her fifth month, she was working with an adoption agency, which passed along several "family profiles" so she could select the adoptive parents. She interviewed several couples, and while they were all very nice with different degrees of desperation, the couple she liked the most was Nori and

Mark Kent.

They were twenty-eight and thirty, respectively, around five to ten years younger than most of the couples who were hoping to adopt. Nori Kent had something called polycystic ovarian syndrome, which Geo had only heard of because two other hopeful women she'd met with had it, too. She liked the couple instantly. They had been together since their freshman year of college, had been married for three years, and had been on the adoption list since then.

"We know we're young," Nori Kent said. She was Japanese, born in Tokyo, but had grown up in Oregon. Her skin was porcelain and unblemished, her hair long and straight and jet-black, falling over her shoulder in one silky sheath. Her eyes were almond shaped and hazel. "But I was diagnosed with PCOS at twenty-one, after I stopped menstruating. Went to several doctors who said it would be very difficult for me to get pregnant. Adoption has always felt right to us."

"We got on the list because we were told it could be a while before someone picked us," Mark Kent added. He was tall, with sandy curls that were beginning to thin a little at the front. He had a classic white Anglo-Saxon complexion, pale with rosy cheeks, and large hands that gestured when he spoke. "We understand there's a lot of competition, that a lot of other couples are older, have bigger houses, have better jobs."

Mark taught math at Puget Sound State, and Nori was a buyer for Nordstrom. Normal jobs for normal people. They had recently bought their first house, a small starter home a little north of Seattle. They had an English bulldog named Pepper and a Siamese cat named Kit Kat who bossed the dog around. They showed Geo pictures of the room that would be the nursery. It was at the back of the house, with a large window that looked out at the rose bushes in the yard. Nori drove a four-year-old Toyota Highlander, and Mark took the bus to work. They weren't rich, but they were in love. There was a deep friendship and a fierce commitment between them. It was in the way he looked at her, the way he touched her hand when she was nervous and speaking too fast. It was in the way she rested her head on his shoulder when she leaned against him, and the way she rolled her eyes at his cheesy jokes.

Being with them made Geo feel sad and happy at the same time.

"I pick you," she said at the end of the two-hour meeting. They were sitting across from each other on matching red love seats in a comfortable room at the agency office. Between them was a coffee table and their family profile book. "I'm not supposed to tell you directly, I'm supposed to tell the lawyer who'll then tell you, but I've made up my mind and I don't want to make you guys wait."

"I —" Nori began, and then she burst into tears.

"Are you sure?" Mark Kent said. He was staring at Geo in disbelief. "Because we understand if you need a couple of days —"

"I pick you," Geo repeated. She stood up, struggling a little to get up out of the deep sofa. Mark reached out a hand, but she waved him off with a smile.

"Why?" Mark Kent asked, his eyes shocked and huge, and his wife turned to him with a look that said, *Oh god, don't ask her that; what if she changes her mind?*

"Because you remind me of my parents when my mom was still alive," Geo said. It was the best way she could explain it — to herself, anyway. She could see that it didn't make a lot of sense to them. "Do you promise to love the baby?"

"Yes," they said in unison.

"Do you promise to love each other?"

"Yes," Mark said, squeezing his wife's hand.

Nori nodded, her eyes and cheeks wet. "Yes," she said.

"Okay," Geo said, and she allowed them to step around the coffee table and embrace her. She could feel Nori shaking, the bones in her slender frame vibrating from her legs to her torso, and she squeezed the woman tighter.

She gave birth three months later, two weeks early, in a private room at her dad's hospital. The contractions started early Saturday morning and grew increasingly painful until the point where she didn't know if she could get through one more. Then the epidural kicked in and she was able to sleep for a few hours until she was dilated enough to push. Her father stayed by her bedside, although it was Nori she wanted in the room with her in the middle of the night when she started pushing.

The spinal block killed all the pain up until the first push, and from there Geo could feel everything. It was the most unbearable agony, and even though the nurse kept telling her to push anyway, it seemed like an impossible thing to do when it felt like pushing meant splitting wide open. Nori squeezed one hand, her father the other, and Geo pushed and pushed, her hair sticking to her sweaty face in greasy strands, her teeth clenching so hard she thought her molars would crack. Two hours later, she heard the OB say, "One more big one," and she bore down as hard as she could, screaming because the burning and pressure was unlike any other kind of pain she'd felt before. She heard Nori say, "I see the head!" and a few seconds later, after a rush of activity, the baby cried.

"It's a boy," she heard one of nurses say. "Six pounds, thirteen ounces."

The nurse had the baby wrapped in a white blanket with a blue-and-pink stripe, and a pink-and-blue hospital hat. It was noted in Geo's file that the baby was going to the Kents, but the nurse still looked at Geo to see if she wanted to hold him. Geo shook her head, lying back on her pillow as Mark came into the room and Nori took the baby in her arms for the first time. Her face crumpled with joy, and she looked over at Geo and mouthed, "Thank you."

Exhausted, Geo fell into a deep sleep. When she awoke, it was late the next morning. Her father was drinking coffee and reading the newspaper in the small chair in the corner of the room. She was incredibly sore. The epidural had worn off and she felt like she had been run over by a truck. Everything hurt. Her vagina felt like someone had punched it a thousand times. There was a glass vase filled with pink and white flowers near the bed, and a letter with her name on it.

"It's a letter from the Kents," her dad said. "Do you want to read it now, or later?"

"Later," Geo said, looking down at herself.

She was surprised to see she still looked pregnant. She had naively assumed that once she gave birth, everything would snap back to normal, but apparently that wasn't the way it worked. Her belly was still large, but it was deflated, empty. The baby she had carried inside her was gone. She had never seen his tiny face, never held his tiny hand, never got to say hello or good-bye, which was how she planned it, but the ache in her heart was deeper and more painful than the ache in her body. She touched her stomach, feeling the flesh — which only the day before had been stretched firm — yield to her touch.

She had a son, and he was gone. She had never known him, never seen him, never cradled him, but the loss of him was as great as if she had loved him and held him and breathed him in her whole life.

"Daddy," she said, not recognizing her

own voice. It was small and fearful, the voice of a child, the voice of a lost soul drifting away who could never be brought back. "Daddy, he's gone. . . ."

The sobs started in her stomach, and her abdominal muscles, already bruised and tender, screamed out in pain as she cried, for the loss of her child, the loss of her mother, the loss of Angela, the loss of the person she thought she was, and the person she thought she would be. She had taken a life and had now given a life, but neither act made up for the other. It was a loss multiplied by infinity, the grief of it all feeling like a giant hole that would never, ever be filled.

"My brave girl," her father said, his own voice cracking and choking as he stroked her hair. "My brave, brave girl."

In that moment, with her father holding her as tightly as he could, the sobs stabbing and unrelenting, Geo wanted to die.

The adoption was finalized thirty days later, during which time the Kents were careful to stay away. Geo understood why. At any point in those thirty days she could have asked to see the baby, changed her mind, and even taken the baby back. But as the days passed and her body began to heal, so did her spirit. The hole that had ripped open in her soul was beginning to close up, still crazy tender, but no longer a gaping, gushing wound. On day thirty, she read the letter Nori wrote to her. It was filled with gratitude and love.

What you have given Mark and me is a joy unlike any other, and we promise to love him as completely and unconditionally as we know you would have. Thank you from the bottom of our hearts. We named him Dominic John, after our grandfathers. . . .

She wrote them a letter back on day thirty-one, when the adoption was official.

Congratulations to you both. I know you will be wonderful parents to your beautiful baby boy. . . .

They did not keep in touch, although they had all agreed to a semi-open adoption, which meant that if at any point Dominic John Kent wanted to speak to her or meet her, she was willing. But it had to be his call, on his terms, and she was allowed to decide if she was okay with it.

Geo strokes the pile of letters beside her. The ones written on blue stationery, the ones that kept coming in prison that she couldn't bear to read, but couldn't bear to throw away. She's read them all several times by now, letters from the son whom almost nobody knew she had. Dominic is now eighteen, older than she was when she had him.

Dear Ms. Shaw, I am your biological son Dominic. . . .

He wants to know her, to talk to her, to fill the gaps in his life that are there despite Geo's best efforts to pick good parents for him. His letters are well-written, full of details that break her heart. How could she have known that when Dominic was five years old, his adoptive parents would divorce? And that Mark Kent would marry the woman he cheated on Nori with, and go on to have two biological children of his own with her? And that Mark would eventually give up full custody of his adopted son — whom he hardly saw anymore anyway — to Nori, who would never remarry and instead bring home boyfriend after boyfriend in an attempt to heal the anger and bitterness she felt over Mark's betrayal? And that one of those boyfriends, the last one, would touch Dominic in a way that no little boy should ever be touched?

Or that one day, Nori would die in a car crash because her pedophile boyfriend was driving drunk, leaving Dominic in the care of one disinterested extended family member after another, before he finally, inevitably, ended up in the foster care system?

How could Geo have known that choosing her baby's parents based on what she thought she saw, and on what she thought she felt, would all turn out to be lies and bullshit, because in the end, people are only out to protect themselves? How could she have known that her son was going to have a terrible life? And that in hindsight, she, a single teenage mother, might have done a better job of raising, loving, and protecting him?

How could she possibly apologize to her child for his *life*?

And how could she possibly tell him that his biological father was Calvin James, and that not only does she have his life to apologize for, but his genetics, too?

How does she then tell him that his father is killing his children, because people like him "should not exist"? Yes, she knows that Calvin said that, had said it out loud at the sentencing hearing for everyone to hear. She'd read about it in the newspaper while she was in prison. How does she tell Dominic he's in danger? From his *father*?

But she has to. Because there's no one left to protect him now other than Geo.

And after everything, after every terrible

453

thing she's both done and let happen, it's the very fucking least she can do.

454

30

There are people to get in touch with, preparations to be made. But her phone is ringing, and when Geo checks the call display, she doesn't recognize the number.

"G," the familiar voice says when they're connected. "How've you been? How's life outside Hellwood?"

"Ella," she says, surprised. The inmate must be calling from a contraband cell phone, and Geo's mind begins combing through the possibilities of what the call might be about. Hazelwood's premier drug dealer has a new accountant now, and the transition should have been smooth. Geo made it pretty clear that once she was out of Hazelwood, she was out for good, and she hopes Ella Frank isn't calling to ask her to change her mind. She's not the kind of woman you say no to, twice. "I'm fine. It's good to be home. What's going on?"

"I can't talk long because I'm calling from

the library," Ella says. "CO'll be back in a few minutes. This isn't a business call."

Geo exhales, not realizing until she does that she was holding her breath. "Oh, okay. I saw your brother when I got out, gave him all the information. Everything's working out, I hope."

"He told me you stopped by, and we're all good there." Ella hesitates, and when she speaks again, her voice is softer. "Listen, G. I wanted to be the one to tell you. Cat died last night."

No. She can't have heard that right. Geo opens her mouth to speak, but nothing comes out.

"She was found in her cell this morning when she didn't get up for roll call."

"That can't be. I don't understand. She was supposed to get out tomorrow," Geo says, her mind stubbornly refusing to believe what Ella just told her. "I talked to her the other day and she was in good spirits. I was going to pick her up at the bus stop."

"She wasn't feeling well the last couple of days. One of the girls found her in the bathroom, half passed out, tried to make her go to the infirmary, but she insisted she was fine, that she was just dehydrated and a little dizzy. She died sometime in the night." Ella's voice is filled with sympathy. "They think maybe her heart gave out, or she had a stroke in her sleep. You know how sick she was, G. Her body was failing."

"Yeah, but she wasn't supposed to die in there!" The words come out sharper and snappier than she intends, and Geo takes a deep breath, trying to calm herself. "I'm sorry. I didn't mean to yell. It's just . . . she was supposed to live here, with me. I promised her I wouldn't let her die in there. I *promised* her."

"I'm sorry, G. She was a good woman and a good friend. I wanted to make sure you knew. I know they only notify immediate family."

"She didn't have any immediate family. She had me." Ella doesn't respond to that, because they both knew there's nothing she can say. A few seconds pass. Finally, Geo says, "What will they do with her body?"

"They've already moved it. From what I heard, her husband is going to have her cremated. Apparently she left instructions with him some time ago."

The philandering husband who was divorcing her. The cheating, disloyal husband who was already with someone else. Geo closes her eyes. "Thank you for telling me."

"Of course. You take care of yourself, okay? And if you need anything, you have

Samuel's number." The woman drops her voice. "I know he got you a piece, but if you need more than that — if you need protection — he'll hook you up. I told him to watch out for you. I know you got stuff going on, I've been watching the news."

"Thanks," Geo says again, but her voice is hollow.

They disconnect, and the tears come then, hot and fast and furious. Her body racks with sobs. She's only loved three women her entire life — her mother, Angela, and Cat, in that order.

And now all three are dead.

Enough. *Enough* already. She can't bring back the dead, but she can protect the people she loves who are still alive.

Her son, for instance.

The doorbell rings as she's walking into her father's home office, and she peeks out the window to see who it is. It's a police car, and the man standing at her front door is in uniform. Not Kaiser, then.

She ignores the doorbell when it rings a second time, and seats herself at Walter's desk. Her father has a laptop that he uses to catch up on work at home, and it's not password protected. As she boots it up, she glances out the window again and sees the police car is still there. The engine is shut off, and the officer inside appears to be talking on the phone.

Geo's iPhone rings. It's Kaiser, but she doesn't answer. A few seconds later, a text message appears on the screen.

Where are you? Have placed police detail outside your house. Don't be alarmed, taking precautions. Will stop by later to explain. When you get home, stay home.

She doesn't reply. She's already home, and there's business to take care of. Family business.

She finds Facebook and logs in, activating her old account for the first time in more than five years. She could have accessed Facebook through her illegal smartphone in Hazelwood, but it doesn't exactly add to the prison experience to scroll through pictures of weddings, new babies, new houses, new puppies. She couldn't give a shit about politics and who was blue and who was red. She didn't care about who had found spiritual enlightenment, who was checked into the gym, or what someone's fancy meal looked like at the fancy restaurant they'd eaten at the night before. She was eating cafeteria food twenty-one times a week, served on metal plates that were divided into sections. She didn't need to know how the filet mignon tasted at John

Howie's, fuck you very much. (For the record, she'd had it before, and it was pretty fucking phenomenal.)

Now it's different. Geo has someone she wants to find. She types in the name *Dominic Kent* and at least fifty names from all over the world pop up. Frustrated, she tries *Dominic Kent Spokane,* based on the address on the letter, and there's nothing. She then tries *Dominic Kent Seattle.* There are exactly two.

The first one can't be him. The man in the profile picture is in his fifties and carrying a hunting rifle. The second one, however, might be. The profile shows a picture of a children's book cartoon character with a long knife through its skull, and the tagline, "Everything is awesome!"

She clicks on the profile. It's private, no information shared publicly, but it's got to be him. She sends a friend request, and then decides maybe it would help to add a personal message as well. Before she can finish thinking of what to say, a notification pops up.

You are now friends with Dominic Kent.

And a second later, she gets a message in her in-box.

Hi! Wow. U found me. So cool.

Geo writes back.

Hello, Dominic. I've read your letters. Thank you for writing to me. I'm sorry it's taken so long to get in touch.

Dominic: *That's OK, I totally get it. So ur out of Hazelwood?*

Geo: *Yes. Finally.*

Dominic: *How was it? Prison, I mean? Sorry, so many questions, LOL.*

Geo smiles. *That's okay. Happy to tell you whatever you want to know. Are you in Seattle? I would like to speak to you, and it's rather urgent. I'm happy to come to you, or we can meet any place you like.*

A full minute passes. Geo's heart is beating wildly. Just because he wrote her letters while she was incarcerated doesn't mean he's ready to meet in person. The agreement she made with the Kents eighteen years ago was that it would be up to Dominic to decide when he was ready, and that any invitation to meet would have to come from him.

Then again, the agreement they had was that they would love and take care of him. So fuck them.

Of course the easiest path would have been to tell Kaiser about Dominic and have him track down her son to warn him about Calvin. But that wouldn't be right. It has to come from her.

Dominic finally responds. *Is today too soon? I can come there, I have a truck. Do u have family pictures? Is ur father around? Would be good to meet him, too.*

Of course he would want to meet Walt. The adoption agency — or maybe it was the Kents, when he was little — must have told him about Geo's family, that her mother had passed away, because Dominic wasn't asking to meet his grandmother.

Geo: *He's at work until 6, but you're welcome to stay for dinner and meet him when he gets home. I'm at 425 Briar Crescent. It's the house I grew up in, so there are plenty of family photos to look at.*

Dominic: *I can be there in an hour. Can't wait to meet u.*

Geo: *Perfect. See you soon.*

She prepares as if she's getting ready for a first date with a man she's really excited to spend time with, which is, after all, what this is. She takes a fast shower, blow dries her hair, puts on a little makeup in an effort to look polished but not overdone. She throws on a pair of leggings and a cute sweater she forgot she had. She bustles around the kitchen, applying dry rub to the pork roast she had originally planned to make for Cat. It takes about four hours to cook, so best to start now if they want to eat at a reasonable hour. There's a bottle of mid-priced red wine in the pantry, and she starts to reach for it, only to catch herself and shake her head at her silliness. He's only eighteen, for Christ's sake. He can't drink, and even if he does, she's his mother. She can't offer him alcohol.

Oh god, she's his *mother.* The nervousness hits her then, and she goes to the living room to sit down, trying to quell her anxiety.

Will he like her? Will he hate her? He sounded friendly enough over Facebook. Articulate, too, from their short conversation.

An old white Isuzu pickup truck drives down the street, pulling to a complete stop at the curb outside the house. *He's here.* The police officer assigned to protect Geo immediately steps out of his vehicle, and Geo opens the front door.

"It's fine," she calls out to the officer, heart pounding. "I'm expecting him. He's family."

The officer nods, lifting a hand to acknowledge her, and gets back into the car.

She's about to meet her son.

She waits on the porch with the door open behind her as the driver of the Isuzu slowly gets out of his truck. Hesitant at first, he starts up the driveway toward her, and Geo's hand flies up to her mouth when she sees him up close. She takes a giant step backward, almost tripping over the threshold, unprepared.

The man walking toward her is Calvin James.

31

It's not Calvin. Of course it isn't. But there's no mistaking the physical similarities, the six-foot height, the same dark hair combed up and off the face, James Dean style. He's even lean and muscled like Calvin was, and the contours of his arms are visible under the thin hoodie he's wearing.

The only thing missing is Calvin's swagger, the ability to own a room the minute he steps into it. Dominic doesn't have it — his smile is shy, and he seems nervous, too. But he's still a teenager; the confidence may come in time.

"Hi," Geo says, and the word comes out in one long, breathy syllable, making her sound like a Valley girl. *Hiiiiii.*

"Hello. Thanks for inviting me over." Dominic's voice is deep, identical in tone to Calvin's, which also catches her off guard. But Calvin had a lazy way of speaking, and in contrast his son speaks a bit faster, with more precision. More like Walt. "There's a police car outside. Everything okay?"

She's flustered, but he seems to be as well, and they exchange awkward smiles. "Everything's fine," she says. "Don't worry about it, he won't bother us. Please, come in."

The fall day is crisp and a gust of chilled wind follows him through the door as he steps inside. Dominic looks around, notes her socked feet, and removes his shoes, placing them neatly off to the side. He catches her staring again, but he seems okay with it.

"We have the same eyes," he says.

He's right. They do. Dark, slightly almond shaped. She smiles. "Can I get you something?"

He shakes his head. "I'm good. I was early so I stopped at the 7-Eleven down the street and downed a Big Gulp."

"That was the 7-Eleven where I —" She swallows, stopping in time. She was about to say *where I met your dad,* but he doesn't know who his father is yet. It's not right to spring details like that on him before he's ready.

He waits politely for her to finish what she was going to say, and when she doesn't, he looks around again. She's wringing her hands, and forces herself to stop, gesturing instead toward the living room.

"There are pictures on the mantel," she says. "Go and look."

He nods and walks into the living room. She trails behind, noting that he really does move like his father. It's interesting to see how some things are truly genetic — things like posture and gait. He's all Calvin, head-to-toe, with maybe a tiny sprinkle of Walt.

Dominic picks up the photo of her mother and father on their wedding day, and a small smile passes his lips. Geo sees it, and something happens to her heart. A melting and swelling, at exactly the same time. That's her smile. Her thoughtful one.

After all this time, she thinks, *I've never not loved you.*

"Your parents?" he asks. If he notices the look on her face, he doesn't say anything.

"Yes, your grandparents. Walter and Grace Shaw."

"I know a little bit about them from the file," he says, setting the picture back in its place. He sits down on the chair closest to the fireplace and stretches his legs. "When I turned eighteen, I wrote to the adoption agency, asked them for whatever information they could give me. They said I had access to everything and sent me a file. It didn't say much more than what I already knew about you, except it had yours and your parents' names in it. I googled, didn't find much on them, but the local library had an archive of the newspaper obituary from when your mother passed away. It had her picture. She was thirty-three when she died, right? You look so much like her."

Geo smiles. "I know. As I got older, I used to freak my father out. My voice started sounding like hers. He came home from work one day when I was visiting from college — I hadn't told him I was coming home. I was in the kitchen making dinner and I turned around and he was standing there, white as a ghost. He thought I was her. I now know how he feels —" She catches herself again, stops.

"Can we talk about him?" Dominic says. "My father, I mean. I feel like he's the elephant in the room."

Geo takes a breath. How will she find the words? But she has to. Somehow, she has to. "Of course we can."

"I know who he is," he says.

Geo never named Calvin on the birth certificate. She certainly didn't tell the Kents. And while she never specifically told her father about Calvin, he finally put it together during the trial, as the timing fit.

"I did a little investigating," Dominic says.

"My mother told me when I was maybe eleven or twelve what your name was. Dad was long gone by then, had remarried, and his wife had given birth to their second kid. And my mom was drinking. She drank a lot. Not in the early days, but after they got divorced."

"I'm sorry," Geo whispers.

"We were living in Vancouver at the time, had been there for a couple years already. Mom got a job at one of the universities, and her parents were there. She wanted to live closer to them after the divorce. It was why my dad agreed to sign over custody of me. She couldn't move me to Canada without his consent, but apparently he didn't feel too bad about it. Was kind of relieved to be done with me, from what I hear. I barely saw him, anyway."

"I'm sorry," Geo says again. The matter-of-fact way that her son was speaking about all this also reminded her of herself, and it hurt her. She knew that the more unemotional he sounded, the more painful it actually was.

"I'm not," he says. "People change. They say you don't love adopted children any differently than biological children, but I know for a fact that's not true. I remember visiting Dad and Lindsay, his new wife, right after they had their first baby. A boy. I overheard Dad in the nursery, through the baby monitor. He was trying to get Holden to go to sleep, and when he finally did, Lindsay said, 'Is this like when Dominic was born?' and Dad said, 'No, this is better.' "

Geo winces. "Oh god. He should never have said that. And you should never have heard it. Not every adoptive parent feels that way." *Just the ones I picked for you, apparently.*

Dominic shrugs. "Anyway, when my mom told me your name a couple years later, I looked you up, found your mother's obituary from way back. And later, I found a bunch of other stuff. By that time, you were testifying at a murder trial."

Geo closes her eyes. "Yes, that's right."

"The article I read said that you and the accused used to be boyfriend and girlfriend. When you were in high school, when you were sixteen. I did the math. And then I saw his picture. We look a lot alike."

The understatement of the century. "Yes. You do."

"So he is, right?" Dominic says. "The Sweetbay Strangler is my father?"

She wishes to god that he hadn't used the nickname. She's horrified he even knows it. And though her son already knows the answer, it's clear from the way he's looking at her that he needs her to confirm it. Because she's the only person in the world who can. "Yes. Calvin James is your father."

Dominic doesn't move, doesn't react. His eyes grow distant, and for a moment he's somewhere else, thinking about something else. The life he might have had, perhaps?

"Did you kill her?" he asks.

"What?" Geo blinks.

"Angela Wong," Dominic says. "I followed the trial. You signed a plea deal. But did you kill her? A lot of people think you did, and that you got off easy."

Again, he says it with no trace of emotion, no judgment. There's only one way to answer, which is truthfully. After everything he's been through, the life he's led, *and his goddamn genetics,* the least she can do is answer his questions as honestly as she can.

"I didn't kill her," she said. "But I helped Calvin cover it up. And then I lied. To the cops, to her parents, to my father, to our friends, to everyone."

"And you got away with it for a long time."

"I . . ." Geo wants him to understand. "I honestly expected to be caught. I thought they'd figure it out. But somehow, nobody did. Year after year, nobody did, until fourteen years passed."

"Why didn't you turn yourself in? If you didn't kill her, and you were only sixteen, why not come clean? You were practically a kid. I bet nothing would have happened to you."

Geo slumps. Obviously she expected they were going to talk about this, but she didn't expect the conversation to be so hard, for Dominic to be so purposeful in his quest for information. She desperately wants to give him an answer that makes sense to him, but she isn't sure that it's possible, since she's not sure it makes sense to her.

"I think I justified it by telling myself it wouldn't bring Angela back," she finally says. "That she knew I loved her, and I was sorry and never meant for any of it to happen. I was very, very drunk that night, which I know doesn't excuse anything, but I was, and if I hadn't been, I might have been able to save her. But I didn't, and she died. And her family . . ." Closing her eyes, Geo takes a deep breath. "They suffered because of me. They spent years wondering what happened to her, making themselves sick over it, and all that time I could have given them answers. I didn't, and then fourteen years later, when the truth came out, they had new, fresh grief to deal with."

"Covering up her death was a mistake,"

Dominic says. "Even if you killed her, that might have been forgivable. But lying about it for so long? Moving on with your life, while her parents suffered, wondering what happened to their kid? I mean, that's a character issue. That's really the part that makes you a terrible person."

He says it with no trace of humor or irony or bullshit. They are simply words, strung together in a specific way, and they cut deeper than any knife or blade could have. And there is no way to defend herself. He is absolutely right. Her son, only eighteen, has pegged her in one breath. Because she is a terrible person.

"Yes," she whispers.

"I know now where I get it from." Dominic cracks his knuckles, glancing over at the mantel where the family pictures are once again. "Between my biological parents and my adoptive parents, there was really no hope for me, was there? Nori and Mark never really loved me, I don't think."

"But they did," Geo says. She knows she sounds desperate, but she wants him to have something good, something positive, to hold on to. "I saw their faces the day you were born. They were over the moon with joy."

"No, you saw *her* face," Dominic spat. "My mother told me all about that day. She

473

was thrilled, but *he* looked like he was going to throw up."

Shit. That was true. Geo's mind flashes back to Mark Kent's face, how pale he looked, as if he couldn't believe this had actually happened, his eyes roving from side to side as if seeking an escape route. She hadn't really noticed at the time. Or had she?

"My mother was always honest with me," he continues. "Maybe too honest, you know? Like maybe she should have filtered some things, because as a kid there were certain things that I probably didn't need to know. She told me the real reason they adopted me. They had been together since college, and Dad was getting bored. He'd already cheated on her a bunch of times. She thought a baby would fix things, that if they had a family, he wouldn't go anywhere, but she couldn't get pregnant. She had *ovarian issues.*" He said the last two words in a voice dripping with condescension. "So they started the adoption process. She didn't really expect to get a baby out of it — they were young, not much money, had bought their first house. She thought maybe the experience would bring them closer together, prove to Mark how bad she felt that she couldn't give him kids of his own."

"I didn't know all of that," Geo says, blinking away hot tears. It's getting worse and worse, and she hadn't even told him the worst thing of all yet. "I really didn't. They looked so in love. Totally committed."

"I guess you saw what you wanted to see."

She hangs her head. Again, he was right. She had interviewed several couples before the Kents, couples who were older, had been together longer, had tried for a baby much harder. Why hadn't she picked one of them?

Because she has terrible fucking judgment. About everything. All the time. That's why.

"Anyway, she died," Dominic says, the matter-of-fact tone back in his voice. "The last boyfriend, the one who was abusing me, was an alcoholic. They were coming back from dinner, he'd had too much to drink as usual, and he crashed the car into the side of a building. Do you know that fucker is still alive? She died instantly, the airbags didn't deploy properly on her side. But he's alive and living somewhere in Idaho. He's a paraplegic, but whatever."

"I'm so sorry." Geo can't seem to stop saying it. She's full-out crying now, and she wipes the tears away furiously. "Dominic, I'm sorry. I never wanted this for you —"

"Then what did you want?" her son asks her. His gaze doesn't waver. His face is open, his dark eyes alight with what appears to be genuine curiosity. "I'd really like to know that, Georgina. What did you want? What did you think, getting pregnant at sixteen by a murderer —"

"I didn't want —"

"There had to have been signs," Dominic says, oblivious to her reaction. "Warning signs, red flags, whatever you call it. Early on. Was my father — Calvin, not the other deadbeat — controlling? Was he violent? Did he ever hit you?"

Geo is shaking. She can't answer, because she can't speak. But of course she has to answer these questions, because she has to tell him about Calvin. About the monster Dominic's father truly is.

"He did, didn't he?" Dominic says this with wonder. "He hurt you. And you stayed anyway. You had sex with him, anyway. That shit turn you on?"

"It wasn't sex, it was —" For the third and final time, Geo catches herself, stops. But it's too late.

"It was rape." Dominic finishes the sentence for her. The words hang in the air for a moment, and he then throws his head back and laughs. It's a deep, guttural sound, from a place of pain, not amusement. "Holy fuck. This shit keeps getting better and better."

"Dominic —"

"All right," he says. "Deep breath. You were sixteen. That's two years younger than me now, and I remember what a basket case I was two years ago. I get it, Georgina, I really do." He pauses. "Wait. That sounds weird. Should I be calling you Georgina?"

"You can call me whatever you want," she says, stifling her sobs. "Geo is fine."

"Geo," he says. "I like that. Do you have any more pictures? Of my grandparents? Do I have aunts or uncles? Cousins? Tell me more about the family."

"There are a few photo albums upstairs in my dad's room," Geo says. She stands up, grateful for the opportunity to take a couple of minutes to compose herself. "But when I get back, there's still something I need to tell you."

She heads up the stairs and straight for the bathroom. She locks the door, then turns the cold water faucet on full blast. She cries hard for exactly two minutes, sobbing like a child, then forces herself to stop, splashing water on her face until the spasms subside. She stares at herself in the mirror, her skin blotchy, her eyeliner smudged. She wipes it away with a tissue.

Yes, it's all a disaster. But what the hell did she think would happen?

She didn't think, that was what. Years of her baby's childhood, spent with parents who didn't truly love him, or each other, as it turned out. A father who abandoned him. A mother with an alcoholic boyfriend who abused him. Indifferent relatives. Foster care. A biological mother who goes to prison for covering up a murder. A biological father who's a serial killer.

And the best part is — the cherry on the sundae as Walter Shaw would say — that she hasn't even had a chance yet to tell her son that his life is in grave danger.

Before exiting the bathroom, she glances out the small window to check if the police car is still parked at the curb. It is, and from the awkward angle of his neck, the officer appears to be sleeping. Nice. Way to protect and serve. She makes a mental note to complain to Kaiser.

On her way back to the staircase, she sees a figure in her bedroom. Dominic has ventured upstairs, and he's sitting on the foot of her bed, looking through one of her old high school yearbooks. She pauses at the doorway, and at the sight of him, a wave of vertigo hits her.

Sitting there casually, not a care in the world, when her father's not home. Just like Calvin.

He glances up, smiles, and it's as if the horrible conversation they'd had downstairs three minutes earlier never happened. He pats the place beside him.

"Sit," he says, as if he's the parent and she's the child. "This is cool. Your sophomore yearbook, I think. I couldn't find your junior yearbook . . . which I suppose makes sense because you would have been pregnant with me."

She takes a seat beside him on the bed. "Yes, I finished my year here at home."

"This was her?" he says, pointing to a grainy black-and-white photo of Geo with Angela. It was taken after one of the Friday night football games, a candid shot of the two them laughing, ponytails swinging, white pompoms in hand, dressed in matching long-sleeved sweaters and tiny skirts with the Bulldogs emblem. "This was Angela?"

"Yes," Geo says. She hasn't seen that picture in decades, and it hurts to see it now.

"She was beautiful," he says, and again, his voice contains no trace of judgment. "But so were you."

"I didn't think so back then."

"I can see why," he says, and she looks up at him. "And not because there was anything wrong with you. I counted at least ten pictures of her in this yearbook. Her star burned really bright, am I right? I can imagine it would make anything else — even another star — look pale in comparison."

"That's sweet of you to say." She smiles. "And rather poetic."

"How did you meet my father?"

Geo tells him the story of the 7-Eleven, how she was smitten from the moment she laid eyes on him.

"We spent a lot of time together," she says. "My grades were slipping. I was staying out late. Sometimes he'd sneak in here, if my dad was home early and I couldn't go out. But we never . . . he was a gentleman."

"Up until he wasn't."

She nods.

"It's the little things that have me curious," Dominic says, closing the yearbook. "I've read a lot about the two of you. The case was reported pretty thoroughly in all the major newspapers here in the Northwest. It was easy to access that stuff from the Vancouver library, and when we moved back to Seattle, it got even easier. But there's a lot the papers don't say."

"What do you want to know?"

He shrugs. "Like I said, little things. I remember reading a profile about him once, and it mentioned that he loved cinnamon hearts. Me, too." He reaches into his pocket, and pulls out a small pack. It's already open, and half are gone. He offers her one, and once again, a wave of déjà vu hits her.

"No, thanks, I can't stand them," Geo whispers, and though it wasn't intended as a joke, Dominic laughs. "Little things, let's see . . . he always smelled good. He was good with cars. He loved live music, we went to a few concerts together. Soundgarden. Pearl Jam."

"So he had good taste in bands, then." Dominic nods his approval and pops a candy into his mouth. He puts the pack away. "So. Where do you think he is now?"

"I honestly don't know," Geo says, and just like that, it's time to tell him. This is the moment. She takes a deep breath and turns so she's facing him directly. "Dominic, obviously you know that Calvin escaped from prison five years ago, shortly after I went away. So the police have been looking for him."

"I know."

"But they're not looking for him just because of the prison escape. He's done some things. . . ." Geo takes another breath.

"Calvin has committed four more murders. Two women . . . and their children."

Dominic freezes.

"*His* children," Geo says, her voice cracking. "His flesh and blood. He's hunting them down, and he's killing them. And I'm afraid . . . I'm afraid he's going to come after you. That's why there's a police car outside. It's for my protection. And yours."

Dominic's expression is hard to read. She can't tell if he's shocked or not. Her son has Walter's stoicism, that's for damned sure.

"So those bodies I've been reading about in the paper, Calvin killed them?" Dominic leans back a little, the yearbook slipping off his lap and falling onto the floor. Neither of them make a move to pick it up. "He's the one who cut up those women, and strangled the children, and then drew hearts on the kids with lipstick? It all makes total sense now. Sick fucker. Wow."

"Yes," Geo says, her heart aching. He's only eighteen, for Christ's sake. It's too much for him. It's too much for anyone. "At least that's what the police think. I know it's what I think."

He nods, his face expressionless. "Do the cops know I'm here? Your high school friend, the one who arrested you — does he know I'm here?"

"No," she says, surprised again. He really has done his research if he knew that she and Kaiser were friends in high school. "I wanted to tell you first, alone. But I do think I should call him now. He's going to want to put you somewhere safe. I need to go downstairs and get my phone."

She moves to leave, but Dominic puts a hand on her arm. "Don't call."

"I have to." She meets his gaze. "You're not safe. We're not safe. You read about what he did to his other children —"

It hits her then. The thing her son just said, about the lipstick, about the hearts on the chest. That detail wasn't reported anywhere, not in any newspaper or TV broadcast. Kaiser was the one who'd told her about it. Nobody outside the investigation knew.

Dominic's eyes are fixed on her face, and she sees it change as the realization of what he said dawns on him, too. He wasn't supposed to say anything about the lipstick. He isn't supposed to know anything about it.

But he knows. And now he knows that *she* knows.

She springs off the bed, but before she can take a step, she's yanked back down onto the mattress in one forceful swoop. She feels strands of hair rip out of her head. He's strong, stronger than maybe even Calvin was back in the day, and he's on top of her, pinning her down with his body weight as she kicks and squirms. His hands are around her throat, squeezing so hard it feels like her trachea might break in half.

He licks the side of her face languorously, the tip of his tongue moving from her chin to her cheekbone, his hot sweet breath smelling of cinnamon fire.

"Mother," he breathes, looking directly into her eyes. "Do you see me?"

He keeps one hand at her throat while the other yanks her leggings down, and then his jeans, never looking away.

Calvin's eyes were green. Dominic's eyes are brown. Like her own. It's like she's staring into herself.

She fights hard, harder than she's ever fought before, struggling with every inch of her body, understanding on some level that it has come full circle. That this will end where it started, and that this was always her destiny, to be destroyed by the beast of her own creation.

Every decision she's made, everything she's done, has led to this. Her son is a monster, yes. But he didn't get it all from his father.

Some of it, he got from her.

When the new bodies turned up, cut into pieces, she should have known it wasn't Calvin.

32

It was almost two A.M. by the time they got Angela's body rolled up into the plaid comforter and out the door. The street was quiet, the neighbors asleep. Calvin hoisted the body over his shoulder and made his way down the stairs of his studio to the driveway, the wood creaking beneath his feet. Geo followed behind him, wearing one of his sweatshirts over her thin cotton dress. When they got to the driveway, he handed her the keys. She opened the trunk, standing aside as he stuffed the most popular girl in school inside it.

It took him a while to arrange Angela's body so that the trunk would close. Geo stood away from the car, closer to the curb, taking deep breaths. A heavy fog had descended, not unusual for this time of year, and it felt both protective and suffocating even with the light of the full moon. The streetlamps were on, and hazy domes of

486

light emanated from each one, dotting the sidewalk in either direction. Her house was a twenty-minute walk away, about sixteen blocks. She could start walking. She could go home, call 911, report a death.

Report a murder.

It was easy to picture what would happen if she did. She'd seen enough movies to understand the basic timeline of how things would go. Cop cars with flashing lights would descend on her house, and then Calvin's, and then the whole neighborhood as the police officers drove around, hunting him down. Arrests would be made. Hers, Calvin's. The interrogation. Questions and more questions, all night long. Her father sitting beside her, still wearing his hospital scrubs, his face a mask of horror and disappointment, unable to understand or process what happened. The newspaper headlines, shouting in black capital letters what Calvin and Geo had done, their grainy pictures printed beneath them, the two of them looking like fresh-faced criminals, Angela looking impossibly gorgeous. The gossip at school would flourish, everybody knowing what she did, the whispers, the rumors, Tess DeMarco insisting that Geo was always jealous of her supposed best friend and that she's not a bit surprised that Angela was dead. The sobbing faces of Mr. and Mrs. Wong, turning angry and accusing when they ask Geo why she didn't stop him, why their little girl was gone. A trial. More newspaper headlines. Jail time, certainly. She was sixteen, not fourteen, and surely she'd go to jail.

"Get in," Calvin said, his breath coming out in one long, white stream. He was dressed in jeans and a T-shirt, but if he was cold, he didn't look it. His color was high, his cheeks flushed from the exertion of moving a dead body from the top floor of the house to his car. The trunk of the Trans Am was closed, and it was hard to picture that inside it was the body of a girl she'd loved almost her whole life. "Hurry up."

Geo took one last look down the street. It was so quiet, so still. Everybody was asleep, warm in their beds, oblivious to the horror that had already taken place, and unaware of the horror that was still to come. The fog, heavy and white in the soft light of the streetlamps, obscured her long view; she couldn't see beyond the fifth or sixth house. She turned and looked in the other direction. Foggy there, too.

Visibility greatly reduced.

There was no clear path.

She got into the car.

Geo knew the area better than Calvin did; she grew up here, he didn't. She directed to him to her street, and as he turned onto Briar Crescent, she said, "Cut the lights."

He did, and they were cast into darkness. Briar Crescent had no streetlamps. The fog surrounded them like a cocoon.

"I can't see anything," he said.

She could smell the sweat coming off him. Like ripe onions and salt. "Keep driving straight. Go slow."

He drove down the street until they reached the end of the cul-de-sac. Only then did he seem to realize where they were.

"This is your house," he said. "You're going home?"

She glanced through the window in the direction of the house, the one she'd lived in since she was born. Nobody was home. The porch light was on, and through the fog she could see the faint blue of the front door.

"Not yet," she said.

They got out of the car and Calvin popped the trunk. Every noise seemed loud in the stillness of the night. They took Angela's body out of the trunk, and Calvin once again hoisted it over his shoulder. He handed her the penlight on his keychain, but Geo didn't need it. She knew where the path was, and it was nothing formal, just worn-out grass leading deep into the woods she used to play in when she was a small child. The light of the moon was just enough.

Geo knew that at any point, a neighbor coming home late from a party could have seen them pulling something long and heavy and wrapped in a blanket out of the trunk of Calvin's car. At any point, a neighbor with a full bladder could wake up to use the bathroom, glance out the window, notice the Trans Am parked at the edge of the cul-de-sac, and feel compelled to come outside to investigate. At any point, a neighbor who couldn't sleep might put her book down to go look out the window at the thick fog that had descended, to contemplate its secrets and wonder what it was hiding. At any point, any of the people living anywhere on Briar Crescent might catch a glimpse of shapes moving through the fog, at the end of the street, near the mouth of the woods, and decide to call 911 just to be on the safe side.

But nobody did.

Nobody saw or did a goddamned thing.

They stopped when they reached a small clearing about a hundred yards deep into the woods, the length of a football field. Geo hadn't realized how much she was sweating until she swiped an errant hair out of her face, only to realize it was soaked with perspiration. She finally clicked on the penlight, the beam bright but small, using it to look around.

"This is the only place we can put her," she said. "Everywhere else, there's too many trees."

He nodded his agreement. The shift was so subtle almost neither of them noticed it had happened. Geo was in control now. Though unspoken, it was clear.

"Go back to my house and go into the shed in the backyard. It's not locked. Get both shovels and grab two pairs of gloves. My father isn't home, but be quiet and be quick because the shed door rattles when you open and close it. Go."

She handed him the penlight and stood with the body in the dark fog, feeling the cold air bounce off her hot sweat. She felt like she was steaming. The ground felt springy beneath her feet, and the smell was earthy, moist. The air tasted much the same, and she inhaled deeply. Somewhere beyond, there was a scuffle, a rustling of leaves, but the smallness of the sound told her it was a squirrel or a chipmunk. She didn't panic. She didn't move. It was almost like she was deep inside herself, away from the chaos, all the way into that place everyone has inside them but hardly ever taps into.

The place where you feel nothing.

Calvin was back with the shovels a few moments later, and they put the gloves on. They started digging. At first it was easy — the soil on the surface was dense, but soft. About a foot down, though, the earth felt hard. Rocky. It wasn't long before Geo's arms and hands were aching from the exertion. She paused to rest, letting Calvin continue for another few minutes until finally he had to stop, too. They had started digging two holes next to each other, separated by a foot of what felt like pure stone. There seemed to be no way to connect them to create the grave they were intending to dig.

"I'm three feet down, but I can't seem to go any deeper or wider," he said. "There's too many rocks."

"We have to keep digging," Geo said calmly, and though she said *we*, they both knew she meant *you*.

"I can't. I'd need a bulldozer."

"Go back to my house and go back to the

492

shed. Get a saw. There are three hanging on the wall at the back. Bring back the big one. You'll know it when you see it." Even though Geo recognized her own voice, it felt like someone else was speaking. With the detached but direct tone of her voice, she could have been reading the news.

He was back again in a few moments, saw in hand, his T-shirt sticking to his skin. He'd been back and forth and back again. With every passing minute their risk of being found out grew.

But again, somehow, nobody saw.

He looked at her, awaiting instruction. It didn't matter in that moment that he was the one who raped and killed Angela, that he was twenty-one and she was only sixteen. She was in charge. He needed her to tell him what to do.

"Cut her up," Geo said.

"What?" Calvin said, staring at her. "I —"

"I'll start digging another hole. If we can't dig one big hole, we'll have to dig a few. Cut her up."

"No. Fuck that. No fucking way." His face was a mask of disgust. "Are you out of your fucking mind? There's no way I can do that."

"We've come this far," Geo said. "Do you want to finish it, or not?"

He unwrapped the body, rolling it out of the comforter, grunting with the effort. They were both startled when they saw Angela's skin. Though she hadn't been dead long, her color had paled, with a grayish cast that hadn't been there before. There was a slackness to her face, a heaviness in the way her arms and legs flopped, and a dullness in her eyes, which were still open.

She didn't look like she was sleeping. She didn't look unconscious. She looked dead.

Calvin bent over her with the saw, his face contorted in a grimace. He looked up at Geo one last time. She nodded, then began to dig, starting a fresh hole about two feet away from the others.

"I can't," he said, his voice weak.

She ignored him. Continued to dig, ramming her shovel into the dirt. Push, scoop, toss. Push, scoop, toss.

A few seconds later, he said again, "I don't know where to start."

She looked up, annoyed. He was soaked in his own sweat, his damp hair plastered to his forehead, his face still knotted in disgust and revulsion. It was a version of him she'd never seen before. He looked ugly. Weak. In that moment, she couldn't remember why she'd fallen in love with him at all.

"Start in the middle," she said, resuming

her digging.

The sound of flesh tearing isn't like other sounds. It's not staccato, like cutting into wood. It's not silent, like slicing into dough. It's deeper somehow, wetter, slightly resistant, but ultimately yielding. Back and forth and back again, the saw tore her best friend open. She heard the moment when the saw hit bone. It made a scraping sound.

She looked up when he gagged, just in time to see him vomit all over himself. Tears streamed down his face. Angela lay in the dirt, her leg almost detached from her hip, but not all the way.

"I can't . . . ," he said, choking.

Geo gripped the shovel tighter. She could smell his vomit, a curdling blend of pizza and beer and gastric juices, almost identical to what hers had smelled like when she'd vomited inside his house earlier. She had never seen Calvin vulnerable before, and in that moment she had no doubt she could walk over, hit him over the head with the shovel as hard as she could, as many times as it took, until he was dead, too. Maybe the fog would stick around long enough for her to dig holes for both of them.

But she wasn't a killer. She didn't know who the hell she was, but she wasn't that.

"Come here and take the shovel," she said.

They changed places.

Geo took the saw in her hands, the wood handle feeling warm from Calvin's grasp even through the gloves she was wearing. Her dad was an emergency-room doctor, had discussed his work with her many times, had even given her details about the surgical rotation he'd done during medical school. She had some knowledge of how to cut at the joint for minimal resistance. Hadn't she done this with chicken wings for dinner the other night? She couldn't remember now. Maybe it was last week. Or last month.

She kneeled over Angela, whose eyes were still open. Brushed a hand over her best friend's face. Now they were closed.

Don't look, my love. Don't look.

She lifted the saw, gritted her teeth, and finished what Calvin started, the teeth of the blade ripping into her best friend, desecrating Angela's human body.

Desecrating Geo's soul.

When she was finished, they both placed Angela's body parts in the graves wherever they would fit, packing the dirt on top of them and pressing it down firmly. They left the woods covered in blood and vomit sometime after four A.M. By then, the fog had lifted a little.

And still, nobody saw.

Calvin rinsed the shovels and the saw in the backyard with the hose, the water rinsing red into the grass and then disappearing altogether. They walked back to the front of the house. Calvin tried to speak to Geo before getting into his car, but she did not reply. He drove away. It would be days before she would see him again, before he would show up at her bedroom window in the middle of the night, duffel bag in hand, to say good-bye and take what little was left of her, by force.

Assuming they weren't caught by then, of course. In the movies, it seemed the bad guys never got away.

For now, though, it was finished. Geo did the only thing left to do.

She went home.

33

Dominic is still on top of her, the weight of him becoming unbearable. He's fumbling, and he's furious, because what he came here to do isn't working. And if he can't do it, he'll simply kill her.

Which would be Geo's preference. Though the legal system may disagree, there are worse things than murder. She knows that now. Rape isn't about sex. It's about dominance and control. It's about taking the best parts of a person and leaving the empty shell behind.

Unconsciousness threatens to overtake her. Dominic's hand is still at her throat, and he's impossibly strong. She can't scream, she can barely move, and little by little, she feels the fight going out of her.

Then, a second later, he's ripped away from her. In the sudden absence of pain, there is relief, and she wilts under it, gasping for breath. Her vision is hazy, and all she can see is a shape looming over Dominic, who's now on the floor.

The shape through the haze reminds Geo of the fog the night of Angela's murder. When her vision finally clears, she sees why.

Calvin.

He's standing over Dominic, who's stunned, a dark-red welt forming on his cheekbone where he was punched. His lip is split open, and he's lying on his side, hurt and vulnerable. In this moment Geo can finally see a glimpse of the boy she might have known had she chosen to keep him.

"Are you all right, Georgina?" Calvin asks her.

He doesn't look anything like the last time she saw him. His hair is longer, lighter, and a full beard specked with gray covers half his face. He's dressed in old clothes. She nods, sitting up on the bed, and his eyes move down to her stomach and her thighs, which are bare. She's aware suddenly that she's exposed, and hot tears fill her eyes as she frantically pulls her leggings and underwear back up.

Because someone has seen. Someone has borne witness to what her son just tried to do to her. Even if that someone is Calvin, it's still the worst thing for anyone to know.

On the floor, coming to, Dominic lets out

a small laugh. Calvin looks down and kicks him in the head.

"Wait," Geo gasps, struggling to speak. She's still on the bed, and she scooches as far back as she can until her back is resting against the headboard. "Calvin, wait. Just . . . just back away from him." She forces herself to focus. "How did you get in here? There's a police officer out front."

"I took care of the cop," her old boyfriend says, his brow furrowing. His gaze moves from her to the young man on the floor, and then back to Geo. "I've been keeping an eye on you. These new murders, they're not me. I would never hurt a kid."

"I know." She closes her eyes briefly. The police officer assigned to guard her couldn't have been more than thirty. His poor family. His poor mother.

Another laugh from Dominic.

"Can I pull my pants up?" the younger man asks, and though his words are a little thick because his lips are beginning to swell, he sounds almost pleasant. "I'm feeling a little chilly down here."

The gun she got from Ella Frank's brother is still where she hid it, and Geo's hand snakes under the pillow as the two men talk to each other. The small grip fits comfortably in her palm, and once it's firmly in her grasp, she clicks off the safety. The sound is muffled by the pillow.

"No, asshole," Calvin says, sounding equally pleasant, the arrogant drawl unchanged in almost twenty years. "You seemed to have no problem pulling them down, so why don't we leave them that way?"

"Mother," Dominic says, not moving. Geo glances down to the floor to find him smiling. It's a terrible smile. "Maybe you should tell Dad that it's not nice to refer to his kid as an asshole. It isn't good for my self-esteem."

Calvin's eyes widen and cut immediately to Geo, reflexively seeking confirmation that this can't possibly be true.

"Surprise," Dominic says, his voice dripping with sarcasm. "It's a boy."

"How?" Calvin asks, locking with eyes with her. "How is that possible?"

"So the man's erect penis enters the woman's vagina —" Dominic begins in a monotone voice, parodying what one might hear in a middle school sex-education lecture.

"Shut up," Calvin says, but he doesn't kick him again. His eyes are still fixed on Geo. "How?" he asks, more urgently.

"You know how," she says, her voice small.

Her gaze shifts to the heart tattoo on Calvin's inner wrist. She hasn't seen it before, but it has to have been there awhile, because the red ink is a bit faded. She can see the initials inside it. *GS.* He immortalized her on his goddamned arm.

"Why didn't you tell me?" His voice is soft. "I would have wanted to know."

"You were gone," she answers. "And I was glad. I never wanted to see you again."

Calvin stares at her a second longer, then looks down at the young man on the floor, who is still lying on his side, but watching the exchange with bright eyes. "Stand up. Pull your pants up. And don't make any sudden moves or I'll rip your throat out."

Dominic does as he's told, slowly bringing himself to a standing position. Side by side, there's no question that he's Calvin's son. They're the same height, with the same features. But where Calvin has confidence, his son has bravado, and they're not the same thing at all.

"Jesus," Dominic says with a mocking roll of his eyes. "Now I know where I get my violent tendencies from."

"Shut *up,*" Calvin says again.

Geo pulls out the gun. The two men look over, their faces making identical expressions of surprise. Dominic takes a step toward her, but Calvin grabs his arm. He nods to Geo, who gets up off the bed and stands, facing them. Calvin pulls Dominic back toward the wall, putting about five feet of distance between the two of them and Geo. It might as well be five inches. The bedroom feels tiny and stiflingly hot.

She focuses her gaze on her son. "How do you want this to end, Dominic?"

"Oh, so now I have a choice?" he says with another terrible smile. "You're letting me decide what happens to me? That's rich. You should have aborted me, by the way. Why didn't you?"

"Because I loved you," she says, and it's true.

He doesn't believe her, and she doesn't blame him. He doesn't know what love looks like. He doesn't know what love feels like. Love — healthy love, the kind that doesn't hurt or bruise or take away someone's sense of self-worth — is like anything else that's important in life. It has to be taught.

"I hate you," Dominic says, and his voice chokes. But not from sadness. From fury. It colors his words, punctuating each syllable. "I fucking hate you so much."

"I'm sorry," she says.

Calvin watches them both, saying nothing.

They're at a standstill. She doesn't know what to do. She doesn't know if she can shoot either of them, but neither can she let them get away. Especially her son. Hurt people will always hurt people, and the wounds gouged into Dominic over the years can never heal. They're too deep.

"Well, this shit is hilarious. After eighteen years, I finally have both my parents," Dominic says, and he's laughing. It's hysterical laughter, the laughter of someone who's laughing even though nothing is funny, an expression of pent-up, toxic emotion. "You assholes. Look what you've done."

He laughs even harder, his whole body shaking. In the distance, there are sirens. They grow louder, their wails filling up the normally quiet neighborhood. The police are getting closer.

Dominic throws his head back, almost convulsing. "LOOK WHAT YOU'VE DONE!"

It's not quite a howl, not quite a roar; it's something in between, animalistic and predatory and insane, and it fills Geo with a sadness that goes way beyond grief and guilt.

"How did you know?" she says, directing

her question to Calvin. "How did you know to come here?"

"I came back when I read about the first pair of murders," Calvin says. "I knew then. Buried in the woods, their bodies cut up the same way . . . of course I came back. It felt like someone was trying to call me home."

Their eyes meet. It's the one secret they still share, after all these years. He never told the cops the whole story of that fateful night — about the saw, the vomit, how Geo took over and finished it — none of it ever came out at trial. And Calvin could have revealed it, could have told the whole truth, not only about himself, but about her. But he never did. He never said a word. Instead, here he is, a silly heart tattoo on his wrist with her initials inside it, even though they will never, ever end up together. It was classic Calvin, just like the jar of hearts, full of candy he'd given her that only he ended up eating.

She stares at the two of them. Her first love and her last love. Was this what love was? Was *this* what it looked like, demented and malformed and diseased and monstrous?

"I understand it now," Calvin says, looking at Dominic. "Why you killed the children, too. *My* children. You did it to hurt me."

"No, you fucking idiot." Dominic lets out a mirthless laugh. "I did it to hurt *her*. Why did your other kids get to have good mothers? Why weren't they fucked with? Why me? I want to finish what I started, *Father*. Want to help? I'll let you go first." He laughs again, and the sound is as humorless as the first. "Oh wait. You already did."

"Georgina, go," Calvin says, not taking his eyes off his son. "Leave right now. I won't let him hurt you. Go out the window."

"I can't leave it like this," she says. She's shaking now, the weight of nineteen years of secrets and lies threatening to crush her from the inside out. "He's our son."

"Yes, he is. And people like him — like *me* — shouldn't exist."

He's right, of course. And if she leaves, Geo has no doubt they'll kill each other. The looks on their faces are identical. They're beyond reach, beyond hope. And for the first time, she makes the decision she never made all those years ago.

"I love you," she says, the words choking in her throat. "And I'm sorry. I am so fucking sorry."

She aims the gun, and fires.

Then aims it again, and fires once more.

Her fingers go numb. The gun falls to the floor, landing soundlessly on the bedroom carpet. She collapses beside it, sobbing so hard she feels her insides might break, crying even harder than she did the morning after she gave birth.

She crawls toward Dominic, reaching for him, and cradles his head in her lap. Her chest heaving, she strokes his sweaty mat of hair, moving the loose strands away from his face. Caresses his cheeks, his chin, the bridge of his nose, the arch of his brow. Puts her nose to his forehead and breathes him in. His eyes are open. Through the blur of her tears, she can see her son looking up at her.

They're her eyes. Her mother's eyes. Brown. Soft. And dull now, from the absence of life behind them.

Her son. Her beautiful boy.

She opens her mouth and wails. The shriek is guttural, unlike any sound she's ever produced before, and at first she doesn't realize it's coming from her. Beside them on the floor, Calvin twitches. His leg moves, then his arm. He's down, but he's not dead, despite the hole the bullet punched in his chest.

Continuing to stroke her son's hair with one hand, Geo reaches for the gun again, and shoots Calvin in the head.

Maybe this is how it's supposed to end, after all.

EPILOGUE

Angela Wong's grave sits in an open area at Rose Hill Cemetery, on the side that gets the most light. Her parents chose a rose quartz headstone for her, and the flecks of silver and gold sparkle brilliantly when the sun is out, as it is right now.

Geo stands in front of it, her cardigan stuffed into her oversized purse, enjoying the soft spring breeze on her bare arms. She's brought roses this time, pink. But instead of placing the entire bouquet at the base of the tombstone like she has the last half-dozen times she's visited, she tears off the petals one by one, scattering them all around. The pink petals look pretty against the green grass, and she thinks Angela would have liked it. Leaning forward, she touches the headstone, tracing the engraved letters on the quartz that spell out her best friend's name, date of birth, and date of death.

Angela Wong had lived sixteen years, two months, and twenty-four days. A fraction of time in what should have been a long, full life.

"I love you," Geo says out loud. There's a groundskeeper about forty feet away, trimming the shrubs that border this section of the cemetery. He can't hear her, and even if he could, he's seen and heard this kind of thing before. "I brought you a Slurpee — grape, of course — but I ended up drinking it on the way over here. You should see me right now. I've gained twenty pounds. I wish you were here to tell me my thighs are getting fat."

She smiles. For the first time since before Angela died, she can think of her best friend and feel more happiness than grief, though both emotions still exist, sitting side by side like old friends. The difference is, they no longer interfere with one another.

"I miss you, Ang."

She stands for a moment longer. The groundskeeper looks over, gives her a little wave. They've become familiar with each other, though they don't know each other's names and have never spoken. She waves back, and starts heading for the paved path that winds around the hill to the other side of the cemetery.

Her mother's grave is in the shade, underneath a giant oak tree. Geo only recently learned that her parents had family plots, purchased decades ago by Walt's parents when they first moved into the area. There'll be space for Geo one day, if she wants it, but hopefully that's a decision she doesn't have to think about anytime soon. It's chilly under the tree, and she digs her sweater out of her bag and slips it on. Her mother's headstone is simpler and smaller than Angela's, made of white marble. Grace Maria Gallardo Shaw had lived thirty-three years, seven months, and five days. It's hard for Geo to comprehend that's she older now than her mother was when she died. Not by much, but it feels strange. She remembers her mother as being the wisest, most beautiful person in the world.

With some effort, she sits in between her mom's grave and the one nearest it, which is newer. The grass has grown in completely, and the headstone Geo ordered months ago has finally been finished. It's similar in shape to her mother's, but the marble is a deep gray. It causes her pain to look at it, because unlike the others, this loss is fresh.

Her phone rings, and she pulls it out of her purse to check who it is. She smiles and answers the call.

"Hey," she says.

"Hey," Kaiser says. The background noise tells her he's driving and she's on speakerphone. "How are you feeling?"

"Not too bad. I'm at Rose Hill, visiting. The headstone is done, finally. I came to see how it looks."

There's a slight pause, and she knows Kaiser is trying to think of the right words. All he comes up with is, "And?"

"It's beautiful. I'm glad we did it."

Another pause. She can hear a horn honking in the background.

"I'm okay," she finally offers, even though he hasn't asked.

"I know you are." She can hear Kaiser's smile over the phone. "I'm on my way home. I'll pick up some fried chicken. You said you had a craving, and now every time you do, I do. Your dad still coming over? If so, I'll get that beer he likes."

Geo manages a chuckle. "Way to kiss ass."

They disconnect, and she sits for a bit in the shade, looking at the headstone that now sits near her mother's. Dominic Kent had lived eighteen years, six months, and two days, until he was killed by his biological mother at his biological grandfather's house. Mark Kent had been notified by the police of his son's death, and they invited him to

512

come and claim the body once the autopsy was completed. Mark had declined, and didn't object when Geo said she wanted him. It had taken some maneuvering to get Dominic's body moved from the morgue to the cemetery, but she was able to make it happen, bringing him here to Rose Hill to be laid to rest in the family plot.

Yes, it had raised a lot of eyebrows, particularly among those in the neighborhood. But the ugly graffiti messages on her father's garage had finally stopped. They never did find out who was behind them, and people seemed to be moving on. In any case, Geo didn't expect anyone to understand. The best way she could explain it to herself is that she wanted to give her son the peace and safety in death that she should have given him in life.

She never did ask Kaiser what the police had done with Calvin's body.

Walter hadn't protested. Instead, her father had offered to pay for the burial, and later, the headstone. Because he loves his daughter. And had different choices been made, he might have loved his grandson, too. In any case, he'll get a second chance. Geo rubs her belly, feeling the baby move.

Before she leaves, she reaches into her purse and pulls out the package of cinnamon hearts she bought at the 7-Eleven on the way over. She rests them on Dominic's headstone. The groundskeeper will probably eat them, but that's okay. The thought makes her smile.

Geo turns and heads for home, stepping out of the shade, and into the sun.

AUTHOR'S NOTE

Though my books are all stand-alones, they're set in the same semi-fictional Pacific Northwest "world" I've been writing about since my first novel, which is why characters from older stories will often pop up in a new book to say "hello" (Kim Kellogg and Mike Torrance, anyone?). If you've read any of my earlier novels, you'll recognize places like the Sweetbay neighborhood, Puget Sound State University, and the Green Bean coffee shop, which are all invented (and hooray for that, because people get murdered in Sweetbay).

Hazelwood Correctional Institute, which is where the first part of this novel is set, is a completely fictional women's prison. Writers invent places for lots of reasons, but the main reason is always because it best serves the story. In this case, Geo's experiences inside "Hellwood" stem from a blend of several real-life prisons I've researched (including the Washington Corrections Center for Women in Washington state), plus my own twisted imagination. But I do understand that some readers prefer to read only about real places in contemporary fiction, and as always, I hope you forgive me.

ACKNOWLEDGMENTS

Writers write alone, but we edit and publish with the help of others who are usually much smarter than we are. I am incredibly fortunate to have a great team of people, in both my professional and personal life, supporting me every step of the way.

To my editor Keith Kahla, thank you for connecting with this book from the beginning and for understanding my vision. You pushed me to make the novel the best it could be, and it's been a pleasure working with you and the rest of the fantastic team at St. Martin's Press and Minotaur Books. Alice Pfeifer, you solve all my weird problems quickly and without breaking a sweat. Andrew Martin, Sally Richardson, Jennifer Enderlin, and Kelley Ragland, I'm so grateful for your support. I hope we all work together on many more books.

To my husband, Darren Blohowiak, thank you for never allowing me to doubt that this crazy creative pursuit is the right one. Thank you for listening to me obsess and stress, and for being cool with me fictionally murdering people for a living (which requires a lot of "research" — if I ever get arrested, promise me you'll burn my computer). It takes a special guy to love me just as I am, and you are that guy. I love you.

To my son Maddox John Blohowiak, you weren't even two years old when I wrote this book, and I loved hearing you in the next room, singing and laughing. Parenting can make doing most things harder, but I'm a better writer since having you. I know what I'm missing when I'm holed up in the office each day, and I know that the sooner I finish, the sooner I can come out and play with you. Thank you for keeping me focused. You are the light of my life. Mommy loves you, Mox.

To my friends Dawn Robertson, Annabella Wong, Lori Cossetto, Shellon Baptiste, Ed Aymar, Micheleen Beaudreau, Teri Orrell, Jennifer Baum, Jennifer Bailey, Scott Kubacki, and Maki Breen, I'd be lucky to have just one of you in my life. To have all of you means I must be doing something right. Thank you for a thousand conversations, and I'm looking forward to ten thousand more. Love you guys.

To my big brother John Perez, moving back to Canada might not have been possible without you. Thank you for giving us a place to live so I could bring my little family home. Special thanks to Nida Allan and Roberto Pestaño (a.k.a. Mom and Dad) for passing on your love of stories and storytelling. Erika Perez, you're more like my little sister than my cousin, and you inspire me every day with your hard work and determination.

To all the Pestaños and all the Perezes all over the world, you're the greatest cheerleaders a writer could ask for. To the Blohowiaks of Green Bay, Wisconsin, I'm blessed to have such warm, kind-hearted in-laws. Sorry for being a Seahawks fan (except not really). Love you all.

To Minty LongEarth, one chance meeting in the New Orleans airport security line led to a two-hour conversation over cocktails. Your perspective on prisons, foster care, serial killers, and psychopaths was fascinating, and you confirmed that real life is worse than anything I could ever make up. Thank you for sharing your experiences with me.

To my readers, thank you a million times over for sticking with me. Your emails, Facebook messages, Tweets, and Instagram posts light me up every day. Thank you for caring about my stories, and for being on this journey with me.

The writing community is an extremely supportive one, and I know how lucky I am to be a part of it. Writing friends are worth their weight in gold, and I owe a mountain of thanks to Mark Edwards for talking me off the ledge more times than I'd like to admit. Also, big thanks to the Thrill Begins gang, who provide an almost daily source of bad gifs and inappropriate jokes to help me get through the day. Over the years, I've been fortunate to have made so many connections with fellow writers and publishing professionals. Thank you all for your kindness, humor, and support. See you at the next conference, and save me a seat at the bar.

Somewhere out there is a man named Mr. Rogers, who was my Enriched English teacher in tenth grade. He was the first person to ever read one of my short stories, assign me a grade, and suggest ways to make the story stronger. When I showed him the revised version, he upped my grade and published it in the high school anthology. That was the first time I ever worked with an editor, and the first time I ever saw my name in print. Wherever you are, Mr. Rogers, your editorial advice has stayed with me to this day. Thank you.

Last, but most certainly not least, to my agent. Working with you is still the best and smartest decision I ever made. Thank you for believing in me and for fighting for me, and for your optimism and encouragement when the time came to make a crucial decision. There aren't enough words to tell you what you mean to me. Victoria Skurnick, you are my ambassador of quan.

ABOUT THE AUTHOR

Jennifer Hillier was born and raised in Toronto, Canada, where she lives with her husband and son.

The employees of Thorndike Press hope you have enjoyed this Large Print book. All our Thorndike, Wheeler, and Kennebec Large Print titles are designed for easy reading, and all our books are made to last. Other Thorndike Press Large Print books are available at your library, through selected bookstores, or directly from us.

For information about titles, please call:
(800) 223-1244

or visit our website at:
gale.com/thorndike

To share your comments, please write:
Publisher
Thorndike Press
10 Water St., Suite 310
Waterville, ME 04901